Rites & Wrongs

Rites & Wrongs

A Novel by Holly Harrison

Golden Word Books
Santa Fe, NM

Library of Congress Control Number 2020945962

Published by Golden Word Books, Santa Fe, New Mexico.

ISBN 978-1-948749-73-2

At the beginning of the nineteenth century, a young boy was sent to look for a sheep that had strayed from the herd near the foothills of the Sangre de Cristo Mountains. As he rounded a bend, he saw a group of men. One of them, dressed in a white robe, struggled as he carried a huge cross on his back. The other men marched behind, lashing their backs with yucca stalks and cactus whips. They stopped periodically, murmuring prayers. The boy watched the ceremony, mesmerized. The group came to a stop, secured the robed man's hands and feet to the cross, and hoisted him up just as the clouds parted.

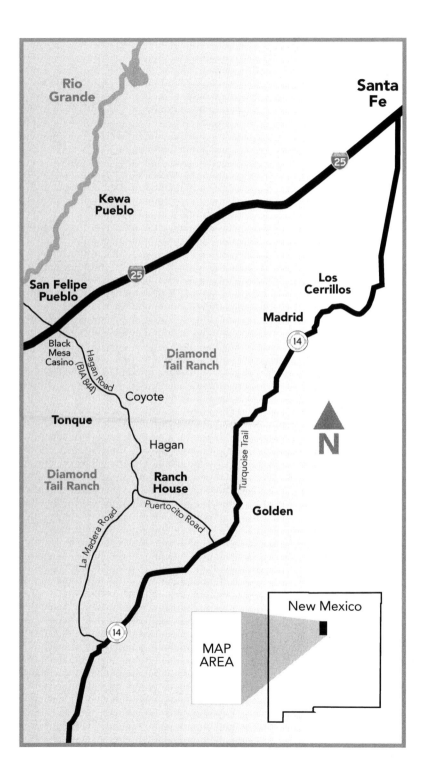

~1~
Palm Sunday

PASCAL RUIZ WAS AWAKENED FROM A DEEP SLEEP A LITTLE AFTER six Sunday morning. With his eyes still closed, he reached for the phone on his bedside table. He brought it to his ear without looking at the screen and stifled a groan when he heard his father's gruff voice. "Truck won't start." Pascal tried to placate his father, assuring him he would drive over later with jumper cables. But it turned out his father wasn't at home. Ten days ago, he had taken off without telling anyone to camp and fish out at Ghost Ranch, eighteen miles north of Abiquiú. He hadn't caught any fish and was now ready to come home.

The last thing Pascal wanted to do on his day off was spend time with his father. It was Sunday, and nothing would be open out there. His relationship with his father had been tenuous over the years, but after his mother died, leaving no one to mediate, it had dissipated. His father, a wrestling coach at Española Community College, had tried to instill in Pascal the importance of being on the offensive. Pascal's stomach still clenched when he thought of his father's sucker punch coming at him as he tried to duck away. "Always make the first move, son."

He could hear the branches of the lilac bush outside his window scratching the screen, and knew the wind was still blowing. It would be the second day of 40-mph winds. The wind made him cranky, but he wasn't alone. Santa Fe seemed to be on edge. Basic courtesies seemed nonexistent. When possible, people stayed indoors, and if they had to venture out, they kept their heads down. His friend Gillian seemed oblivious to the wind, but this was her first New Mexico spring and she was from the East Coast where hurricanes blew off the Atlantic. When Pascal had first griped about the wind, Gillian had ruffled his hair and laughed. Now when he mentioned anything about the weather, she would burst into the old Kingston Trio song, "They Call the Wind Maria."

Away out here they've got a name
For rain and wind and fire
The rain is Tess,
The fire's Joe
And they call the wind Ma–ri–a

Pascal hated the winds. He had suffered them most of his life, but each spring, he swore it would be his last. The winds clogged his head and dried his nose until it bled. His lips cracked painfully no matter how much balm he used. His eyes stung as if packed with tiny particles of glass.

As Pascal sat on the edge of his bed, the wind continued to threaten his window screen. He ran his hands through his pitch-black hair. It had started to curl over his ears, and he knew he was in danger of eliciting a reprimand from the captain. He needed a haircut. But the wind paralyzed him.

He remembered how exasperated his mother became when he complained about the wind, throwing her arms up: "It's only air blowing around." Her family had come to northern New Mexico from Italy to work in the mines. It wasn't an easy life. She had learned early on about things you couldn't do anything about. She resigned herself to the whims of the weather. She couldn't stop the wind, so it never bothered her.

He wished he could be more like his mother, always finding the possibilities in things, even the wind. One spring when he was in his early teens, he had whined about the wind all day long until his mother took hold of his arm and dragged him out in the yard. The wind blinded him. He gripped his mother's arm and stumbled alongside her. At the back of their property, a steep hill descended into a ravine. As they made their way down the rocky slope, they dodged rabbitbrush and kicked aside tumbleweeds that would spin in the air. At the bottom of the gulch, a huge boulder was wedged up against the hill. The boulder had served as Pascal's playground as a youngster, a stage for his plastic dinosaurs' endless scenarios.

His mother pulled him gently down, and they scooted their butts up against the boulder. Immediately, the wind seemed to quiet. It was such a relief. She told him to close his eyes.

"Listen, the wave is coming, hear it? Getting closer, closer, it's lapping at the shore. Now it's retreating, going back out to sea, tugging at our feet."

Pascal had never been to the ocean, but as the next wave of wind approached, he imagined sitting on the shore sunk in warm sand at the edge of the sea. He sat with his mother and leaned against the rocks with his eyes closed for a long time. Pascal sighed, at peace with the wind. Afterward, he saw things differently, at least for a time.

Thoughts of his mother always made him melancholy. Another gust of wind rapped against the glass. He wished he could hunker down in the ravine, eyes closed, and imagine the sound of waves. He stood up and unsettled the memory.

As he headed north through the stunning red rock landscape of Georgia O'Keeffe, the drive under different circumstances would have buoyed his mood. But today he battled the wind, held tight to the steering wheel, and tried to ignore the flying debris. Pascal sulked at the thought of what was in store for him. He had a tendency to self-pity, and this wasn't the day he had mapped out.

He found his father's truck wedged between two trees, which made it difficult to maneuver his car into place. The truck was thirty years old and rarely serviced. It wouldn't take a charge. If the problem wasn't the battery, the ignition or generator would be more serious. Pascal didn't want to guess—he didn't know much about cars. And sure enough, services were nonexistent at Ghost Ranch, and the one gas station in Abiquiú, the nearest town, was closed Sundays. It took the rest of the day to arrange for the truck to be towed to Española.

His father, not a patient man, griped about everything from the price of coffee to the lack of fish in Abiquiú Lake. Pascal did his best to tune him out, humming under his breath. But as the wind relentlessly blew dust around them, his patience waned: "Got to see a man about a horse." His father stared at him with a bewildered look. Pascal almost laughed but turned and trudged off across the dried field toward the main building. A pang of guilt struck him, and he looked back at his father, shrunken, head hanging down, leaning against the truck, an old man, widowed, alone, few if any friends. The one thing he loved, wrestling, had been snatched away. There had been rumors of circumstances and charges, but nothing came of it except the loss of his position.

Once the tow truck pulled away, Pascal drove his father home. He heated a frozen dinner in the microwave. It took all his resolve to stay there, sitting in silence at the small Formica table as his father chewed each bite carefully and Pascal nursed a Bud Light.

When he climbed out of his car at home, Pascal's shoulders sagged, and for a moment, he worried his neck wouldn't hold the weight of his head. He was drained. His father had that effect on him, sucked out all his energy. Pascal looked in the refrigerator— empty except for a half carton of milk and a six-pack of beer, and was sorry he hadn't eaten one of his father's frozen dinners. He filled his cat's dish and topped off her water bowl. She jumped off the counter and rubbed her head on his legs before turning up her nose at the dry kibble. He turned his head to the side and shrugged as he popped open a beer, then stretched out on the couch and turned on the television, glad he didn't have to go to the station today.

~2~

ALTHOUGH WINTER HAD FINALLY CALLED IT QUITS, NOW IN place of the ice and snow there were the spring winds. The latest round had begun in earnest yesterday. They whipped off the west mesa and through Santa Fe. Every surface was suffocated in layers of dust. The swirls of debris enveloped the mountains and left only a ghostly image of the verdant Sangre de Cristos.

Louise Sanchez had been a patrol officer for the past twenty-four years. It wasn't the career she had imagined, but it suited her. She had finished her shift and was heading back to the station. The day had been uneventful until now. Most people stayed indoors, out of the wind. It was Palm Sunday, when Catholics attended early mass and now were home for a family dinner.

As Louise drove up Cerrillos Road, gusts of wind did their best to obstruct her vision. The air was filled with dust, and occasionally a tumbleweed would bounce off her patrol car bumper, startling her. Several blocks from the intersection at St. Francis Drive, the traffic came to an abrupt halt. She was in the middle lane, and when she turned on her siren to inspect the holdup, havoc ensued. Cars attempted to inch out of her way, but with three lanes of stalled traffic bumper-to-bumper, there was nowhere to go.

Louise turned on the flashers and opened her car door. She lowered her head against the wind. It tugged at her ponytail, pulling wisps of hair out and propelling them across her face. She brushed the hair out of her eyes and again regretted her last haircut. Melinda at Supercuts had talked her into wispy layers, saying they would soften her look. Now the short strands' refusal to be contained was another annoyance in her life. She weaved in and out of the vehicles toward the obstruction. Two cars blocked traffic at the busiest intersection in Santa Fe. The accident was a minor fender-bender, but two bull-headed men faced each other and looked as if they intended to duke it out. Either they imagined they still lived in the Wild West, or the wind had inflamed their tempers. It took an hour and half to settle them down, send them on their way, and untangle the traffic jam.

As she was on her way back to the station, a lone palm frond, discarded after the Palm Sunday Procession, crumpled under the tire of Louise's cruiser. She bit her lip as a twinge of guilt radiated through her body. She glanced up at the cathedral, darkened after the morning Mass, and had an urge to cross herself. St. Francis Cathedral had been built in the French Romanesque Revival style, and although it was a celebrated landmark, she found the architecture incongruous alongside the adobe buildings.

Today was the last Sunday in Lent, the beginning of Holy Week, the big enchilada for Catholics and other Christians. Louise's parents, devout Catholics, dutifully had her baptized as an infant, and she was confirmed at age fifteen. For years, she attended Mass regularly but never believed. The memory that remained for her was of the Palm Sunday services, grasping the frond with both hands, holding it up toward the cloudless cobalt sky, marching around the cathedral with her fellow parishioners. It was as if they were going into battle. But now the church, like everything special in her life, was a distant memory.

Louise swung open the station house door and caught the look in Susie's eye.

"Oh no." Louise glared at the woman as she shook her head defiantly.

"Sorry." Susie held out a paper.

"You got to be kidding?" Louise groaned like a bull elephant. She was usually amiable, eager for extra shifts, but last night she hadn't slept well. A steamy bath and glass of chilled Chardonnay were in order this evening.

Susie shrugged. "Break-in on the opera grounds. The costume storage building."

"Where's Ruiz?"

"No lo sé, senorita. Left him a message. No communicado."

"It's not my pay grade."

"Again, sorry. Take it up with the captain."

Louise snatched the paper out of Susie's hand and glanced at the assignment.

"It shouldn't take long," said Susie. "I already called forensics. Tape the area, secure the shed, and have a chat with the security guard. As soon as Ruiz calls in, he can take over. I promise."

~3~

BOBBY PILOT HUNKERED DOWN ON THE FOLDOUT BED OF HIS cousin's Chevy conversion van parked behind Diamond Tail Ranch. The old van was dreary with its worn plaid decor but better than the tedious commute back and forth from Santa Fe. He had endured the drive for three weeks so his girlfriend, Jessie, could act in a western TV pilot that was being filmed at the ranch. Even though it was Jessie's dream to be an actress, take after take of the same mind-numbing scene, not to mention the cramped living arrangements, had worn on her over the weeks. She either snapped or sighed dramatically when Bobby opened his mouth. By the end of the day, both were worn out.

The bed was piled with unread books, discarded clothes, and various dishes stained with dried food. Bobby looked out the grimy window at the gray winter sky and knew that although it was near the end of March, spring wasn't in sight. His recent college degree had only resulted in debt with no job prospects. In a burst of frustration, he shoved everything onto the floor of the van. He reached down and picked up the Atlantic magazine he had taken from the dentist's office last month when he had his last teeth cleaning. Now that he'd finished college, his father could no longer keep Bobby on his insurance.

He reread the same article he had over the last month. It was short, only two pages, mostly taken up with photographs, and featured the annual Easter pilgrimage to El Santuario de Chimayó. When Bobby had first read the article, he realized he hadn't given Chimayó a thought for a long time. It brought back distant memories of family outings to see the fall leaves and eat combination plates of enchiladas, tamales, and chili rellenos at Rancho de Chimayó. But it also brought back the memory of his father's desperate stab at fate when Bobby's mother fell sick.

It had been his fifteenth birthday, but he knew this year, there would be no cake. His father had awakened him before dawn to go to Chimayó to collect healing dirt from the chapel. He had found the idea ludicrous. They weren't Catholic or even very religious.

On the drive, his father, silent and morose, gripped the wheel so tightly his fingers turned dead white, the blood squeezed from his knuckles. It soured Bobby's stomach.

He had to look away, tried to concentrate on what his father said: Go to the altar . . . say a prayer for your mother . . . light a candle . . . give a small donation. The mention of a donation unnerved him. Bobby wondered what qualified as a small donation. He dug his hand in his pocket and was relieved as his fingers closed on a quarter.

When they arrived at the chapel, his father turned the car off but didn't get out. He was slumped forward, and for a moment Bobby worried his father had passed out. Again, an uneasy feeling settled over him. He could feel his heart pound faster in his chest as he stared out the windshield, unsure what to do.

After a few minutes, his father opened the car door and grasped Bobby's arm for support. His father seemed to have shrunk, no longer the formidable man of Bobby's childhood.

Once they were inside the chapel, his father pushed him toward the altar and took refuge in the last pew. Bobby was relieved that they were alone. After he lit a candle, he mumbled, "get well" under his breath, took out the quarter, and dropped it in the offering box. It clinked as it hit the bottom of the container.

His father rose and steered him toward the back room. The entryway was low, supported by a heavy beam. They had to duck their heads. El pocito, the pit, took up most of the room, so they had to skirt their way around the periphery. Bobby stared down at the pit filled with the holy dirt allegedly capable of both spiritual and physical healing. He was a realist and had his doubts about the dirt's power. And how did the pit magically replenish itself? It was always full, never ran out of dirt. He was sure that someone, probably the janitor, brought the dirt in from the surrounding hillsides each night when no one was around. He was surprised that his father, usually a pragmatic man, insisted that the dirt was blessed and possessed special powers.

Gently his father pushed him toward the pit. The room was air-less and oppressive, and smelled of sickness. A wave of claustropho-bia enveloped him, and he had to use his sleeve to wipe the perspiration that dripped off his brow. Bobby starred at the thick adobe walls, covered floor to ceiling with discarded implements: crutches, canes, braces, walkers. A wheelchair was shoved into a cor-ner, abandoned. The entire wall was plastered with messages of thanks from the "cured," taped haphazardly among the assistive de-vices. The room was intended to project a sense of the miraculous, the discarded equipment no longer needed and left behind. As he scanned the walls, his stomach flip-flopped and left an acrid taste in his mouth. For a moment, he thought he would be sick.

His father, impatient, shook his shoulder, placed a small felt sack in his hand, and motioned for Bobby to fill it with the holy dirt. Bobby had little faith that this would save his mother but wasn't about to pass up any chance.

Seven years had passed since that trip to Chimayó, although, like most New Mexicans, Bobby was aware of the annual pilgrimage during Easter week. The highways would be glutted with hundreds of pilgrims making their way north. But when Bobby first read the article, he was surprised to discover that the procession had gone on for over two hundred years and involved so many people: thirty thousand. Who were these people? he wondered. At that moment, he decided to write about the Chimayó pilgrimage.

Bobby had done an internet search for the sanctuary and found that the shrine was a National Historic Landmark built on the site of what many believe to be a miracle associated with the crucifix of Nuestro Señor de Esquipulas (Our Lord of Esquipulas). The web-site described the pit of holy dirt and acknowledged that some people believed it had remarkable curative powers, but Bobby now knew differently. It hadn't saved his mother.

Bobby thought about the trip to the university's Zimmerman Library, where an elderly man had taken him up to the stacks. The man's hair was white as snow, and his patchy skin so pale you could see the blue veins under the surface. Bobby had figured the man had spent his entire life cloistered in the library away from the sun. Bobby remembered the conversation when he asked for information on the Penitentes.

The man had tilted his head: "The Brotherhood?"

"Yes."

"Well young man, my advice is don't believe everything you hear or read."

"Oh, I never do, sir."

The man smiled and started to rise but had to use his hands to steady himself; it was a slow process. He looked stiff, probably from hours of sitting.

"Are you writing a paper?"

Bobby hesitated. He didn't want to lie but never had said out loud that he was a writer. But maybe it was time. "I'm a writer, working on an article."

The man had nodded as he reached for his cane leaning against the desk. The wood looked exotic and appeared to be hand-carved. A useless gold tip on the bottom slipped on the tile floor and made a clicking sound each time the man set it down. But what caught Bobby's attention was the top of the cane, where the head of a gargoyle with toothy fangs, bugged eyes, and floppy elfin ears rested.

The man told him that architects had incorporated gargoyles as devices to avert evil and protect the buildings from harmful influences, but then winked at Bobby. He added that some claim gargoyles have the power to deflect misfortune—avert the evil eye.

Bobby remembered thinking it might be a good idea to find a cane with a gargoyle—you never know.

The man had led him to an ancient elevator. Thinking about it made Bobby's chest tighten. Ever since he had collected the dirt from El Pocito at the Chimayó chapel, he had suffered from claustrophobia. But he had steeled himself and followed the man as the car sluggishly ascended up into the stacks and the old man continued his lecture.

"Not everyone took a favorable stance on these creatures, especially on religious buildings." The old man chuckled until his eyes watered. He pulled out a white handkerchief from his coat pocket and dabbed away the tears. "In the twelfth century, St. Bernard of Clairvaux spoke out against gargoyles. He was particularly incensed about the ones that decorated the walls of his monastery's cloister. He ranted about the figures' absurdities. He disparaged them as monsters, creatures like unclean monkeys, strange savage lions, half beast, half man, spotted tigers, several bodies with one head and several heads with one body. St. Bernard believed his clergy should at the least regret the money they spent on the gargoyles."

When they reached their destination, the elevator came to a jarring halt and Bobby remembered sucking in his breath. He stumbled out of the elevator and was confronted with a series of narrow stacks packed floor to ceiling with books.

"Later, the gargoyles were merely used as rainspouts," the man said. The floor's low ceiling, barely six feet high, narrow aisles, and overflowing shelves packed with books momentarily paralyzed him. Bobby closed his eyes and forced his body to move. As they worked their way toward the end of an aisle, the gold tip of the man's cane continued to slip on the tiles and caused him to stop to regain his balance.

Bobby had been thankful he was not alone. The air was thick, stale, and suffocating. Dehumidifiers hummed at the end of every stack and created the sensation of being in a spaceship, a sensation that Bobby couldn't imagine bearing.

The old man came to a halt at the end of a row, reached up, and took down a small book. "Keep in mind, son, in the early days, the Penitentes served an important role in their community. The Catholic Church didn't have enough clergymen to send to all the small rural towns in New Mexico. The Penitentes filled the gap. They served as community liaisons. They took care of members of their community both financially and spiritually. So don't believe everything you read."

"Yes, sir."

The man handed Bobby the book and waved his hand around the shelves. "This section has several reference books about the Penitentes. The books can't be checked out, but there are a few vacant carrels along the windows. You're welcome to use one. When you finish, leave the books in the carrel for the library staff to shelve."

The old man had left him with a cautionary tale. "You may come across depictions of brutality, even flagellation. But that's the exception. Most practice penitence through reflection and sacrifice."

Bobby had scanned the shelves, randomly pulled out several books, then chose one of the carrels next to a small window overlooking a courtyard. The view helped lessen his uneasiness. After a few hours of working in the dim light, his eyes itched and watered and his hand cramped. He wished he had brought his laptop.

Bobby forced himself to get back in the elevator, and let out an audible breath he hadn't realized he had been holding when the doors opened on the first floor. The Penitentes swarmed in his head and engulfed him. He had found, like the old man had said, that most Penitentes paid penitence through service to mankind. Although the Catholic Church did not sanction them, they served an important religious role in their communities.

But the depiction of the few tormented ones had captured his imagination. One account had afforded an indelible graphic burned into his mind: masochistic self-flagellation as the Penitentes walked the Stations of the Cross to recreate Jesus's last days on earth. A slight twinge of guilt nudged Bobby as he remembered the old man's admonishment about these practices. But he quickly brushed them away. Who wants to read about reflection and sacrifice when you can witness people writhe as they whip themselves?

But he did not want to write about the thirty thousand penitents depicted in the Atlantic article. He wanted to describe someone's personal story: someone who had suffered poverty, sickness, or tragedy, and through penitence had survived. That would be his story. That would be his hook. But so far, he hadn't been able to find anyone.

~4~

R AYMOND ALMOND, BOBBY'S FRIEND FROM HIS COMMUNITY college days, had secured a gig with the Film Industries Crafts Services. Basically, the job consisted of cooking food for the film crew: the grips, makeup artists, camera and lighting, and costume department people. It was a stepping stone, paid well, and provided the promise of steady work with New Mexico's growing film industry. Raymond was holding court in front of the Brew Pub when he spotted Bobby getting out of his car.

After Bobby's visit to the library, he had wanted a beer before meeting Jessie for dinner. He needed to wash away the stale air from the library stacks, soothe his lungs, and clear his mind of the images.

Raymond, gregarious as usual, had captivated a small group of people with some wild tale that had everyone in hysterics. As Bobby approached, Raymond turned and grinned warmly, spreading his arms. "Bobby, my Pilot."

"Hey, Ray Man." The greeting was left over from their college days.

Raymond disentangled himself from the group, put his arm on Bobby's shoulder, and guided him up to the bar. They climbed onto stools and ordered draft beer.

"What's up with you? Still trying to be a foreign correspondent?" Raymond asked.

"I'm setting my sights a little lower these days. Nothing has panned out in the newspaper world."

"Yeah?"

"You know, because you want something doesn't mean it's going to happen. Never was going to land a job at the New York Times."

"Yeah, I hear you. I haven't heard from Hollywood."

"I polished my resumé, sent out queries to the major New Mexico newspapers. Nada nada. Lowered my sights, cast a wider net. I sent my resumé to each small town newspaper in the state's thirty-three counties."

Raymond shook his head, chuckling.

"Got one interview."

"Don't want to ask where that was."

"Quay County Sun, Tucumcari."

Raymond burst into laughter and flagged the bartender for another round of beers. "Tucumcari? Tucumcari tonight?"

"Yeah. Hundreds of motels, so the billboards say."

"Did you take the interview?"

"Did my research first. Disheartening: small enclave, five thousand residents, and worse yet, it's near the Texas panhandle. But what the hell." Bobby took a sip of beer. "Did the interview, didn't go well—surprise—didn't get the job."

"That was your lucky day, Pilot." Raymond said as he held up his hand for Bobby to slap.

Bobby decided to change the subject. "Hey, remember Jessie?"

"Yeah, how could I forget?"

"You know of any open auditions? She still has her heart set on being an actress but is getting discouraged with the movie biz. Been talking about grad school. You know what that means? Bye bye, Jessie."

"Can't believe you are still hang-dogging around that chick. She always had a tight grip on your balls."

Bobby felt he should defend Jessie but knew Raymond was right. He stared down at his beer.

Raymond leaned over and clinked Bobby's beer glass. "Come on, Pilot—only kidding. I have a gig out at Diamond Tail Ranch. They're getting ready to shoot a TV pilot, a low-budget western. Tell your little lady they're looking for extras willing to work for cheap, and who knows, maybe an audition."

"Thanks, Ray Man. I'll let her know."

When Raymond left the Pub, Bobby moved to a booth along the wall. As he waited for Jessie, he ordered his third beer. He needed to sell her on the idea. She wasn't going to like the idea of being an extra, especially in a Western. He would need to stretch the truth about the audition. Diamond Tail Ranch would be the perfect place to work on his Penitente story.

~5~
Holy Monday

MOST OF THE TOURISTS WHO CAME TO SKI HAD GONE HOME, and the next influx wasn't expected for a month or two, after the weather warmed. Crime was down, almost nonexistent. Pascal Ruiz assumed it was the spring winds that kept people sequestered in their homes. After the thrill of locating the stolen Stradivarius violin, he found his job tedious: petty crimes and paperwork. The wind added to his ennui, and he wondered whether solving crimes would be enough to satisfy him.

As Pascal came into the police station, Susie, the receptionist, popped up from behind the counter. She arched her eyebrows, hands on her hips. "Where have you been, handsome? Tried calling you yesterday. The captain wants to see you ASAP."

The hair on the back of Pascal's neck prickled with anticipation. He envisioned the possibility of another high-profile incident. His handling of his last case, the stolen violin, had secured him both recognition and security in the department. Pascal had hoped the new crime would be something he could sink his teeth into. But as the captain shared the details of the crime, Pascal's hopes withered: a break-in at an outbuilding on the Santa Fe Opera grounds. That wouldn't be any more exciting than his last case: stolen koi from the Francisco's Landscaping nursery pond.

The captain had been on his way out the door to attend Palm Sunday mass when he received an irate call from the commissioner, who complained that another crime had targeted the arts. He had whined that Santa Fe's tourist reputation was in danger. The break-in would be more bad publicity. It had occurred only a few months after the violin robbery in January. The captain was incensed that

the commissioner had suggested the police department's ineffective-
ness was responsible and ranted that crimes against the arts were becoming an epidemic. The captain shook his head and mumbled
under his breath, "Mary, Mother of Jesus."

The building stored the previous season's opera costumes and
props for the annual sale in April. After each season, the opera offered the used goods to the public during a one-day event. Catherine
Aubusson, a wealthy patron of Santa Fe's opera, had volunteered to
organize this year's sale. She had spent the last six months cataloging
the costumes and props and promoting the sale.

Early Sunday morning, a security guard during his rounds had
noticed the broken lock on the door of the building. He notified
Donald Leather, the opera's costume manager, who in turn notified
Aubusson. Then Leather telephoned the police to report the crime,
and for some reason complained to the commissioner.

"Louise Sanchez saved your butt yesterday." The captain shoved
a one-page summary of Sanchez's interview with the guard across
the table. "She secured the scene and interviewed the security guard
after her regular shift, which had entailed untangling a big mess at
St. Francis and Cerrillos."

Pascal considered offering an excuse. It had been his day off and
he had to go out of town to help his father. He wanted to say he
couldn't be available 24/7 but thought better of it.

"Get the brass off my back," the captain snapped. "It's Holy Week."

Pascal stifled a laugh at the captain's non sequitur but nodded.

Sanchez had summarized the interview with the security guard.
Every six hours, the guard made rounds of the opera property.
His last check of the storage building had been around midnight.
At 6 a.m., he discovered the broken lock on the door. The place
had been ransacked. Between the physical rounds of the property,
the guards monitor the grounds with a video feed. Pascal groaned
audibly at the thought of watching six hours of video footage.
Maybe he could delegate the task but to whom? His unit was
down to only him. His partner, Matt Padilla, was recovering from
surgery.

He arranged to meet Aubusson at the opera grounds after lunch, but when he arrived, she wasn't there. The guard unlocked the building. As Pascal pushed open the door, the room reeked of stale marijuana, causing his eyes to water and his throat to constrict. He figured the vandals were teenagers, as his irritation escalated into a coughing fit. Finally, he suppressed his hacking, reached in, and turned on the lights. Whoever broke into the building had sure smoked a lot of pot.

He looked around, shook his head, and almost laughed at the scene. In their drugged haze, probably enraptured with the ornate costumes, the vandals had arranged furniture and props into theatrical scenes. It was apparent they had rummaged through all the costumes, tried them on, then discarded them in scattered heaps around the room. As he scanned the mess, Aubusson burst through the door, took one look around the room, and sucked in her breath.

"Oh . . . my . . . God!" She turned and stared accusingly at Pascal.

Pascal pulled out his card and handed it to her. "Detective Ruiz."

She hesitated for a moment, then snatched the card out of his hand and stuffed it in her purse. Pascal figured Aubusson to be in her 50s, but she could have been older. Seemed like the type to undergo face work. She was dressed in that way you never see people dressed in Santa Fe, with a black wool pencil skirt tight around her butt, robin's egg blue cashmere sweater smoothed over her ample bust, and spiked heels that probably cost more than his monthly rent. Her outfit didn't do much to soften her demeanor. He was amazed that she could lift her hand with the mammoth diamond on her ring finger.

"What is that ghastly smell?" she asked, wrinkling her nose.

"Marijuana."

She looked at Pascal with pursed lips, and for a moment, he thought she might slap him.

"Do you think anything is missing?" Pascal asked.

Aubusson put her hands on her hips, pursed her lips again, and stared at him, exasperated.

"I couldn't say, detective. I will need to catalogue everything." She looked around the room, dismayed. "Somehow before the sale next weekend, these costumes have to be cleaned and repaired if necessary."

Pascal couldn't conjure up any sympathy for the woman or her task at hand. She represented what he found wrong with Santa Fe. "Send me a costume list and note if anything is damaged or missing," he said. "We will provide the necessary documents for insurance purposes."

"And that's it?"

Pascal knew she wanted more. He also knew that if she didn't get what she wanted, she would lodge a complaint with the captain and possibly the commissioner. He wished Matt Padilla were there. Although they had been thrown together on the Stradivarius case at the captain's insistence, Pascal had begun to rely on his partner. Matt was good at voicing the necessary platitudes to crime victims; instinctively, he knew how to deal with people in the aftermath of a crime. On the other hand, Pascal, without meaning to, often rubbed people the wrong way.

"I'll check the security video feed," he said. As soon as the words were out of his mouth, he could have kicked himself. That was the last thing he wanted to do. Maybe he could get the guard to go through the tapes. After all, it was his job to secure the grounds. But who was going to pay him overtime to do it?

"And?" Aubusson demanded.

"I'll look into it." It was the best he could offer her.

~6~

Bobby Pilot had been thankful that Jessie secured not only an audition for the TV Western but also a role. The director had spotted her soon after they'd arrived and pulled her out of the line of extras for an audition. It had kept her busy and out of his hair most of the time. But now, he had less than a week to find a Penitente, someone from the Brotherhood willing to share his personal story. Bobby, never athletic, also had to get in shape for the Good Friday procession. He needed to focus, but his attention wavered as his spirits sank.

As he left the ranch and trudged along the dirt road, the air was brisk, but the sun warmed his back. He wound his way up a hill contemplating his fate. What did life have in store for him? He wondered whether he would be able to accept his destiny without question. With each step, he felt something building inside him. His soul or essence started to take hold of him. He remembered a quote written somewhere. "There's nowhere you can be that isn't where you're meant to be." It comforted him. He thought of Los Hermanos, the Brothers, and their rituals of flagellation and crucifixion. He remembered the Etonian students in Brave New World who derided the primitive rituals as "horrible" and "abusive." But now he had a new understanding of the Penitentes.

Destiny.

Bobby had planned to put some more miles on his new boots today, hike to Hagan to take some photos of the ghost town. Never having been athletic, he realized that if he didn't get into shape, at least he could break in his boots. The walk to Chimayó was long but flat. He wasn't going to have to climb mountains.

As he approached Hagan Road, something pulled him east toward Golden. He had never been a spontaneous person, but the tug unbalanced him, caused him to make a spur-of-the moment decision, change course, and veer.

God's will?

His boots, the expensive ones he'd ordered from Australia, fit perfectly and made it easy to hike on the rough surface. The road was covered in gouged tire tracks made after the last rain and then baked hard in the sun. He marched through the town of Golden as if a force, a higher power, was tugging him onward. When he reached the far outskirts, he stopped to catch his breath and bent over, hands on his thighs. When he looked up, he saw a small chapel, not much bigger than a shed, on top of a steep hill. A small plaque told him it had been built of hand-made adobes in the 1800s. Bobby made his way up the hill to where a large wooden cross shadowed the arched doorway.

Fate?

As he stood in the entrance, something drew him in. This would be the first time inside a church since his mother passed. Although it had been seven years, an involuntary shudder crept down his spine as he remembered the trip with his father to Chimayó. His father's rasping instructions still hummed in his head: "Go to the altar . . .Say a prayer for your mother . . . Light a candle . . . Give a small donation."

The chapel was dark and gloomy, with air so dank Bobby had to stifle a coughing fit. The altar, only a few steps from the door, appeared unkempt. Bobby began the ritual as if a spell had been cast over him; he no was longer in control of his body. He mumbled a prayer, lit a candle, and pulled out a handful of change. But as he dropped each coin in the box, its sound against the empty container reverberated like a shock wave through his body. The spell was broken, and he couldn't wait to get out of there.

In his frenzy to escape, he slipped down the steep hill and landed hard on his bottom. Relieved that no one was around, he dusted himself off and walked back into Golden. Like the chapel, the town had seen better days. A general store was the lone business. He took the last sip of water from his canteen. He would need to buy a bottle for his hike back to the ranch.

Kismet (mystical fate).

When Bobby entered the store, the darkness blinded him momentarily. He stood and waited for his vision to adjust to the dim surroundings. The clerestory windows, crusted with years of dirt and mineral deposits, admitted little light. The store, cool and cavernous, resembled a trading post like the ones seen in old TV Westerns. Display cases crammed with handicrafts and Indian jewelry lined the walls. Piles of Indian rugs were stacked around the room. Shelves stretched up to the high ceiling, displaying pottery and other articles. Canned goods and boxes of nonperishables were stacked everywhere.

Near the back of the store was a long counter. The clerk seemed to be engrossed in a conversation with a customer. He looked up and stared at Bobby before turning back to the man. The two leaned over the counter and resumed their conversation in hushed tones. Bobby made his way through the store and tried to pick up bits of their conversation. He heard the clerk raise his voice: "Come on, Alcazar." The men were speaking Spanish, and Bobby could only grasp a word here and there until he heard mention of "Procession de Pascua."

Bobby dug through the cooler for a bottle of water, then took his time choosing a chocolate bar before walking to the back of the store to pay. He nodded at the other customer, who didn't acknowledge Bobby's presence.

When he left, he saw that there was only one truck parked in the dirt lot. Bobby assumed it belonged to the customer, Alcazar. He decided to hang around and wait. When the door of the store opened, the man saw Bobby next to his truck and hesitated. Then he slammed the door shut and kept his head down as he marched across the lot. Alcazar opened the driver's door, ignoring Bobby.

"Hey, you going down Hagan Road?" Bobby asked.

The man fidgeted as he glanced back at the store, then nodded. He couldn't lie—it was a sin.

"Could you give me a lift? I'm going to Diamond Tail Ranch."

"Not going that far." The man started to pull the truck door closed.

"That's okay. Could you take me a ways? Not much traffic on that road. Anything would help."

Bobby could tell the last thing Alcazar wanted to do was give him a ride. But he nodded.

Karma?

Bobby swung open the passenger door before the man could change his mind and pulled himself into the cab. The man sat silently, eyes on the road while Bobby, always good at small talk, chattered about the weather and scenery. As they turned onto Hagan Road, Bobby changed the conversation.

"I'm planning to walk the procession on Good Friday. Looks like good weather."

The man's head whipped around. He stared at Bobby and narrowed his eyes. The stare went right through him like an x-ray, as if he had been splayed open, exposed. The man could see into his core, his essence, his soul. Bobby suspected the man doubted his earnestness, wondering what Bobby wanted and whether he wanted to give it to him.

Bobby's heart sank as the truck started to slow down. The man steered it to the side of the road, careful to keep his tires out of the muddy ditch.

"Far as I'm going, son." The man stared out the windshield and waited for Bobby to get out.

"My mother, she died of cancer, I was fifteen. I wanted to do the walk for her. Need to redeem myself. Atonement."

A twinge of guilt made Bobby's throat tighten. Did he have no shame? His mother's death? But he was desperate. He wanted to understand this man, his commitment, his motivation. If his article was to be genuine, real, it needed to represent actual people who were entrenched in their belief.

"I don't know the route, hoped to find someone to join—help me." Bobby hoped he sounded sincere. Again, he swallowed his deceit, the lump still lodged halfway down his throat. But it wasn't only the article; Bobby realized he needed absolution, freedom to . . . he wanted to experience the spirit of God . . . find peace.

Bobby looked over at the man, who seemed fixated on the windshield. The man was so still and composed, as if frozen. Alcazar turned toward Bobby and frowned. "The procession is for Jesus. His suffering. His death and resurrection. You don't do it for your mother, so you feel better. You don't do it for yourself. You do it for God."

Bobby wanted to say he realized that, that he had done research on the Penitentes. He wanted to say they had gotten a bum rap. But instead he said, "I want to understand the Brotherhood." Bobby knew Penitentes didn't have to be a secret sect any longer. The Church had all but sanctioned community involvement and contribution to religious rituals. But he didn't say that. It would make Alcazar suspicious, and he needed to come across as sincere. So he looked down at his hands.

"Penitentes participate in the Good Friday procession to demonstrate their commitment to acts of charity," Alcazar said. "Others may do so for other reasons."

Bobby was elated. This Alcazar must be a real Penitente.

"Are you going to walk to Chimayó on Good Friday?"

Alcazar wanted this kid out of his truck, out of his life, but something made him reconsider. He thought of Mary Theresa, his ex-wife. She would be thrilled that he had gone beyond his comfort zone—helped someone with not a legal matter but a personal request. He didn't need to be uncharitable, unkind.

"I'm not going to participate." That was as much as Alcazar was willing to say on the subject. He didn't feel a need to explain further but then added, "I know someone who is participating. I can ask them if you could join the walk on Friday. No promises."

Bobby's lips parted, and he forced his mouth not to drop open in surprise. He barely croaked, "Thanks."

Alcazar tilted his head toward a group of houses off to the north. "My house is the adobe on the left with the white porch. Stop by tomorrow morning around nine."

Bobby reached his hand across the truck cab. "Thanks. I really appreciate it, Mr. Alcazar."

Alcazar shook Bobby's hand, then turned away and started his engine.

~7~

MARCOS ALCAZAR WAS RELUCTANT TO GIVE THE KID A RIDE. He'd noticed the boy when he came in the store. The kid had wandered around, taking more time than needed to choose his purchases. Alcazar and Branch, the store manager, were suspicious of him. Seemed like he was eavesdropping on their conversation. Branch had been trying to convince Alcazar to walk with him on Good Friday to Chimayó: "The procession is what you need, Marcos. It would be restorative, cathartic."

Alcazar thought, "whatever that meant." Branch had a habit of interspersing psychological terms into his discourse, and it annoyed Marcos. He knew Branch picked them up from his wife, who provided couples counseling at the community center in Madrid. Alcazar had met Branch's wife and doubted she was a licensed counselor, but supposed she provided a service to the community. There weren't many resources available in small towns like Madrid. The village had once been a historic coal mining town, then a ghost town, but was now a "creative community," which meant a hippie enclave.

Alcazar grimaced as he leaned heavily on the counter toward Branch.

"You okay?" Branch asked.

"The barometric pressure must be sky high today—my left knee is killing me." Alcazar had been told the cartilage was almost gone, bone on bone. But he knew it wasn't just his knee that made him reluctant to walk with Branch. The procession meant having to talk to people, people who suffered from various problems: spiritual, physical, financial, social. As a member of the Brotherhood, he knew it was his duty to help and support his fellow man. He wasn't sure he had it in him anymore. It was the right thing to do but . . . .

"I'll let you know about Friday." Alcazar winced as the pain in his knee made its way up his thigh. "Promise." As he left the store, he saw the kid next to his truck. Pain always made him grouchy. He clenched his teeth and wondered if the kid was a stalker, although he knew Mary Theresa, his ex-wife, would accuse him of paranoia.

Last year, Alcazar had quit his job with Valencia County Legal Aid, where he provided pro bono services to the disadvantaged, which included almost everyone in the county. Mary Theresa had up and left him without so much as an explanation. Over the years, she had compiled a litany of complaints and dished them out periodically: He was moody, uncommunicative, cold, uncaring. She was right, but he hadn't always been that way; it was who he had become.

For years, a cloud had hung over their marriage, and nothing could make it dissipate. The time they'd spent trying to conceive a child had worn on them. Then when they finally gave up, Mary Theresa got pregnant. She miscarried in her fourth month. They tried again, but it wasn't to be.

Marcos moped around for months until one day he announced out of the blue that he was going coyote hunting. He had no intention of killing anything, much less a coyote. But it was the final straw. Mary Theresa went berserk. She ranted and raved about the useless killing of defenseless animals. It was plain mean.

Alcazar hesitated on the mercantile porch, wondering what the kid wanted—hopefully only a ride somewhere. The last thing he needed was for Branch to see some Anglo climb into his truck. Branch had a loose tongue and loved to spread gossip. But Marcos knew he never had been good at saying no, even to a stranger. If the kid needed a ride, he would have to give him a ride.

The kid had told him he was staying out at Diamond Tail Ranch with his girlfriend. That boy was a talker. From the time Alcazar pulled out of the parking lot, the kid never shut up. He was one of those people who drove Marcos crazy, rambling nonstop and, unlike him, seemed comfortable in his skin. The dirt road was clogged with ruts, so Marcos had to concentrate to avoid bottoming out his truck.

The kid droned on about the weather and the landscape until Marcos pulled over and stopped.

Then the kid started in about the procession. He practically begged Marcos to talk to him about the Penitentes. Some sob story about how he was responsible for his mother's death. The kid seemed sincere, although Marcos wasn't always the most accurate judge of character. In his work as an attorney, his inability to distinguish between a bullshitter and a straight shooter had impacted his success rate in court.

Against his better judgment, partly to get rid of the kid and partly because thoughts of Mary Theresa had seeped into his heart, he had agreed to meet the kid the next morning at his house. Now it was almost midnight and he still was wandering around the house, restless and agitated. The wind had cranked up to a good clip. Each gust banged the broken clasp on the screen door, startling him. If only he could drink a few beers, relax, but he had put those days behind him.

Alcazar leaned back in his tattered recliner, one of the few items he had taken after the divorce. He slipped in his favorite Willie Nelson CD, Moment of Forever. The ancient boom box buzzed and whirred, but finally the first song caught. Alcazar floated listlessly on Willie's voice. It was such a comfort, different like him, scratchy and slightly off key. He promised himself he only would listen to one album, then go to bed.

Last week, he had woken in the morning still in the chair fully dressed. It made him feel like a degenerate. The first song on the album, "Over You Again," was his favorite, and he wanted to hear it one more time, so he hit the replay button.

When Marcos Alcazar had moved out near Golden, his sister put her foot down and insisted he have a phone. She'd bought an inexpensive flip phone and added him to her cell plan. She even paid the bill but told him not to expect anything for his birthday or Christmas.

As Willie finished the last line of the song, Alcazar's phone rang. Few people had his number. He rarely got calls, and never late at night. He leaned over and tried to reach the phone from his chair, but he knocked it off the table and it skidded across the floor. Annoyed, he pushed the button on the arm of the recliner. The chair squeaked and slowly came upright. He pushed himself out of the chair, bent down and picked up the phone.

~8~
Holy Tuesday

S USIE BEGAN CHANTING "SPECIAL DELIVERY" IN A SINGSONG voice as Pascal came into the station Tuesday morning. She pushed a manila envelope across the counter and suppressed a laugh.

He groaned as he picked up the hefty package. Susie winked at him, grinned, then turned to answer the phone. He stopped at the break room and poured a cup of coffee, then tilted the cup to his lips and took a sip. Immediately, he was sorry: Not only was the coffee weak but it was also stone cold. Not a good omen. He emptied it into the sink and headed for his office.

Aubusson hadn't wasted any time compiling an elaborate report on the storage shed burglary. Pascal sank into his chair, reluctantly tore open the envelope, and pulled out an enormous bound document. The front, back, and sides of each costume in the shed had been photographed draped over a mannequin. A separate sheet gave a detailed description of the garment and its general condition, as well as any need for repair or cleaning. For some reason, Aubusson had been compelled to supplement the report with the name of the opera in which the costume appeared and a description of character who wore it.

On the last page of the report, an entry caught his attention. It described the one costume that was missing, that of Jesus Christ used in Anton Rubinstein's "sacred opera," Christus. She explained that it hadn't been used in the traditional summer opera season but for a special performance during Christmas holidays two years ago.

Aubusson, apparently feeling an almost-apologetic need to defend presentation of the obscure work, expounded on the composer. Pascal chuckled as he read her description of his "use of polyphonic choruses and a sober, edifying style relying on exalted declamation." He would have to ask his friend Gillian, a violinist, what the hell that meant.

Apparently, the costume had been offered at last spring's sale, but Aubusson said no one had bought it. The costume, depicting the iconic biblical figure of Jesus, consisted of a full-length tie-closure robe with red sash and a loincloth, along with various accessories: Roman sandals, a shepherd's crook, monk's cross, wig, beard, and crown of thorns.

Pascal was amused but perplexed that it was the only costume taken. Although Easter was right around the corner, he couldn't fathom anyone stealing the costume for a church play or nativity re-enactment. That would be blasphemy. And it didn't fit with the merrymaking potheads. Most likely, teenagers were responsible. Probably, in their stoned haze, they took the costume as a joke.

He ran through a list in his mind of the local juvenile delinquents who might be responsible. Michael Cody would have been at the top of his list, but he was on probation. It wasn't likely he would risk jeopardizing the probation and landing in jail for a prank.

Pascal decided to schedule a visit with Marilyn Chavez, the Santa Fe High School guidance counselor. She had been at the job for twenty years and had an in-depth knowledge of the school's students and their families. She had the inside scoop on which kids took drugs and who were likely to get into trouble. Maybe he could get a decent cup of coffee on the way.

~9~

WHEN BOBBY WOKE TUESDAY MORNING, HE WAS ALONE IN the van. He was disappointed and hoped Jessie hadn't left for her shoot. He needed to apologize for last night. Bobby struggled to pull free from the tangle of covers on the bed. When he shifted his weight to the floor, he realized that not only was he groggy but his body also ached all over from weeks of sleeping on the lumpy mattress. He splashed icy water on his face making it numb.

Last night, Jessie had pleaded with him to go to the casino. She hadn't asked much of him since they'd come to Diamond Tail, but the casino was the last thing he wanted to do. He had put his foot down and told her he planned to hang with Raymond. He knew right away that it was a blunder, like rubbing salt in a wound, once the words were out of his mouth. Jessie had stood stock-still with lips pursed but said nothing. As usual, Bobby had no idea what was going on in her head. He wished she would scream, yell, throw something. Her stillness unnerved him, and she knew it. He tried to stand his ground, not to fidget as he clenched his fists. There would be hell to pay later, but the casino was a distraction, and he needed to focus.

Once Jessie had stormed off, he realized that shooting the breeze with Raymond over a few beers wasn't what he needed either. The overheated ranch house made him restless. He needed to be out in the open—alone. Bobby saw the disappointment on Raymond's face when he begged off, but he didn't protest.

The night was pitch black, no moon up yet. The thick air shrouded him like a heavy veil. The cold soothed and calmed him. Visions of the procession and the Penitentes floated around in his mind. Down the road, he took the cutoff to the ghost town of

Hagan. Bobby had explored the ruins once before, but that was during the day. When Hagan came into view, his heart sped up. He could feel it beat in his chest. But then a weariness came over him, and he sank to the ground in a clearing. He stared at the night sky. The stars, millions scattered across the horizon, drew him in. His body relaxed and eased into the ground, and he tried not to think of snakes or ghosts. Bobby wished he knew the names of the constellations, but then the wish passed as he let the endless span of stars encompass him.

While he lay on the ground, the cool earth seeping into his bones, he strained to think about his article, what he wanted to say. When he had read about a secret sect and its bloody rituals at the library, he was certain that would be his hook. But now, after meeting Alcazar, he wasn't sure. Alcazar seemed like a normal guy, even though there was a sadness about him. Bobby could tell he was educated. The image of him thrashing himself with a cactus whip seemed preposterous. As Bobby stared upward, all the ideas for his article seemed to vaporize and disperse into the night. A loss came over him, an emptiness, as if someone had died.

Bobby made it back to the ranch after midnight. Jessie was home and ready for a fight. He tried to explain his dilemma, but it only infuriated her more. She refused to listen to anything he had to say. She didn't want to know any more about the Penitentes, the procession, or his bloody article. They had argued for what seemed like hours, and he didn't get much sleep.

Bobby quickly pulled on his clothes and went from the van to the kitchen. As he came in, Jessie didn't bother to look up. She sat leaning over her cereal, morose and silent. Maybe Raymond was right. But every time Bobby looked at her, he became totally smitten all over again. He opened his mouth to apologize but she pushed her chair back, turned away and left the room. When she left for her shoot, Bobby took off for Alcazar's.

The brisk air helped clear his head. By the time he arrived at the house, he felt invigorated, revitalized, ready to go. But as he approached the house, he sensed that something was wrong. It seemed too quiet. Uneasiness settled in his stomach as he climbed the porch steps. He looked for a doorbell but didn't find one. He knocked.

The front door was painted Taos blue, the color that was supposed to shield the house and its inhabitants from evil spirits. He knocked again, waited, knocked harder, then pounded. Nothing. The stillness made him edgy. The cool air hung stagnant, no breeze. He circled around to the back of the house and found a sliding glass door with a ripped screen. He pulled the screen to the side, cupped his hands around his face, and pressed his eyes close to the glass. The kitchen was dark except for a sliver of light from a tear in the faded curtains that hung above the sink. The room was empty. If anyone had been there that morning, they had left it tidy—no pots, pans, or dishes unwashed—everything in order.

Bobby couldn't believe it. The disappointment hit him like a sucker punch. Alcazar had promised to help him, or at least had agreed to. Although Bobby could tell the man wasn't eager to do so, he had seemed sincere. Now what would he do? Who would he walk with on Good Friday? If Alcazar was a true Penitente, he wouldn't abandon Bobby, would he?

But it was obvious: Alcazar wasn't home. Bobby lashed out with his boot but missed the screen door. He was disgusted with himself, not even able to muster up enough anger to cause some damage. Pitiful.

He looked around at the nearby houses and briefly considered knocking on one of the doors. But he knew the neighbors wouldn't welcome some stranger, especially an Anglo. If they were indeed Penitentes, he knew, they were private, maybe secretive, people. Since he was on foot, he would be even more suspicious. But what now?

His camera swung back and forth around his neck as he jumped off the porch. At least he could take some pictures of Alcazar's house, snap some shots of the neighboring village. Bobby kept his camera around his neck, close to his body, careful not to be too obvious. He bent down pretending to tie his shoe and aimed his camera up at the cluster of houses. They appeared uninhabited, frozen in time and space. He watched for any sign of movement behind the closed curtains.

Bobby didn't want to go back to the ranch empty-handed and admit defeat, that his big meeting hadn't materialized. He couldn't face Jessie, not yet. After last night, he wasn't sure he wanted to face her ever again. Raymond might be right; it seemed to be all about her.

He stomped up the back porch steps and pounded on the glass door in frustration. Nothing. He reached out, grabbed the handle of the sliding door and yanked, expecting it to be locked. But the door slid open easily. Before he could censor himself, he stepped in and pulled the door closed behind him. A shiver ran through his body, but he couldn't tell if it was from lack of heat or his trespass. He had never entered a house uninvited before, but it gave him a sense of adventure. Bobby figured there must be a simple explanation for Alcazar's absence. Any minute, he expected Alcazar to drive up and apologize; maybe he would have a Penitente brother with him who would show Bobby the way on Good Friday. Alcazar wouldn't say anything about Bobby being in his house uninvited so not to embarrass him in front of his Penitente friends.

As Bobby looked around the house, he tried to formulate a picture of Alcazar. The rooms were orderly, tidy, and clean, but the house showed signs of age and neglect. Peeling paint on the windowsills, linoleum floors faded and scratched, sinks stained, faucets dripping.

The small eat-in kitchen had a farm table but only one chair. Alcazar wasn't expecting company. The cabinets, mostly empty, contained only a few essential dishes. The counters were bare. The window over the sink was dappled with hard water stains.

The living room, although a parlor would be more fitting, was cold and uninviting. There were only a few pieces of furniture: a loveseat-sized plaid sofa that sagged in the middle and an old recliner chair covered in drab worn corduroy. Next to the chair was an orange crate with a boom box, like the ones guys in the '70s carried on their shoulders. A shoebox with a dozen CDs sat on the bottom of the upturned crate. Otherwise, the room was unadorned: no pictures, knickknacks, or books. The windows were bare. The decor was nonexistent. The sadness that Bobby had sensed from Alcazar hung heavy in the air. The house felt cloistered, monastic.

Bobby promised himself he wouldn't touch or move anything, only get a sense of the man who lived there. The one bedroom was sparse. There was a neatly made twin bed. Bobby bent down and took in a deep breath; the sheets smelled clean. A Pendleton wool blanket was folded at the end. Bobby opened it up, revealing a design that looked similar to the New Mexico Zia symbol, a circle divided into quadrants of yellow, white, red and black. He read the label: The Circle of Life. The design was attributed to tribal elders, the wisdom keepers who hand down teachings and spiritual direction to future generations. Bobby thought that was a fitting role for Alcazar, a Penitente brother. He folded the blanket and set it on the foot of the bed.

The bedside table held a lamp and a paperback book. It was Tony Hillerman's Listening Woman. Bobby had read a few Hillerman mysteries but wasn't familiar with this one. He read the back cover. Like most Hillerman mysteries, it featured Joe Leaphorn of the Navajo Tribal Police. The story involved a brutal murder of an old man and a teenage girl. The Listening Woman was a blind Navajo who spoke of ghosts and witches. Bobby set the book back on the table and crossed the room to the closet.

The door was weathered, and he had to pull up and yank the handle hard to get it open. He was surprised to find four dark-colored business suits hung on one side of the closet. The only other item was a large cardboard box. Bobby knew he should close the door and leave the house but couldn't resist. He reached down and pulled the box out of the closet. Now he was not only guilty of trespassing but also snooping, prying into someone's personal life, no longer just observing. It seemed like Pandora's box: It could be a source of great and unexpected troubles, or a present that seemed valuable but in reality was a curse.

The box probably contained revealing information about Alcazar. Bobby struggled and tried to rationalize that he was entitled. Alcazar had stood him up, after all. But he didn't need trouble or a curse, so he put the box back in the closet and pushed the door closed.

It was almost noon, and Bobby was getting hungry. He hadn't eaten much breakfast but had taken the time to pack a hearty lunch, expecting maybe to share it with Alcazar. He rummaged through his backpack and laid out the food on the table. After his lunch, he settled in the recliner chair. Like everything else in the house, it had seen better days. He had to work to get the chair to recline and then had trouble getting it back upright. He reached over and turned on the boom box next to the chair. Willie Nelson's melodic voice drifted dreamily through the room. It was a sad song. Bobby wasn't a fan of Willie, but there was no doubt Alcazar was. All the CDs were Nelson's. He reclined the chair once again and closed his eyes. Last night, the little sleep he'd had was fitful. The heavy food settled in his stomach, making him drowsy. He drifted off as the album came to a finish.

Bobby had stopped expecting Alcazar to show up. He didn't think he was coming back. Something must have happened, maybe an accident. Maybe he'd skipped town. Maybe he wasn't who he seemed at all.

~10~
Holy Wednesday

L AST NIGHT, BOBBY HAD FALLEN ASLEEP IN ALCAZAR'S LA-Z-BOY chair, but something woke him in the middle of the night. He had checked his phone, but it was dead because he didn't charge it the night before. Jessie would be pissed at him again. But he had dreamt of witches and ghosts, and there was no way he was going to walk back to the ranch in the dark. He resigned himself to stay the night.

The next morning, Bobby pulled the sliding door closed and stepped off the back porch. Although the sun hadn't made it over the east mountains, it was plenty light out. He stared at the barren landscape and wondered what to do. He dug into his backpack for his water bottle, and his hands closed on the pamphlet Raymond had given him yesterday. It described an abandoned pueblo, Tonque, on the San Felipe reservation just south of the ranch. It would be practically on his way back. Bobby studied the hand-drawn map of the ruins. He didn't have much interest in archaeology, but the hike would give him time to regroup and think of Plan B.

From the look of the brochure, there wasn't much left of the six-teenth-century pueblo, but supposedly, the canyon walls still carried pictographs and petroglyphs. Maybe if the procession didn't pan out, he would find a story at Tonque Pueblo. Always got to have a backup plan, as his father used to say.

The canyon ridge that marked the upper boundary of the pueblo came into sight. He skirted along the rim and looked for a way down to the bottom of the canyon. Finally, he came across a trail. It was little more than a narrow slit covered in scrub brush and loose rocks. As he started down the decline, the stones slipped under his feet, causing him to repeatedly lose his footing. He was disappointed his new boots didn't provide more traction. As he continued to skid out of control the rest of the way down to the bottom, he cursed under his breath. The sound of a car engine grew closer. He looked up, and near the crest was a faded red truck. The engine quit and a door slammed. Bobby knew he was trespassing on Pueblo land. There was nowhere to hide, nothing but cacti, tumbleweeds, small junipers, and a few scraggly mesquites that barely reached four feet. He scrambled to his feet and stepped across the trickle of water that had etched a rivulet through a dry tributary and scrambled up the bank. He ducked down and again heard the slam of a door, and then the engine started up. He breathed a sigh of relief. Probably someone had stopped to take a leak.

Bobby became more and more disenchanted as he continued to explore the area. The Tonque arroyo was a tortuous route with hills and washes littered with desert mountain overgrowth. The pueblo, nothing more than a severely eroded ruin, was difficult to decipher. He took out the pamphlet and searched the map to get his bearings. The remains of the kiva were on a mound to the southwest. It was used for religious rituals, spiritual ceremonies, and sometimes political meetings. The pamphlet explained that the Pueblo had followed the Tanoan custom of one kiva serving a large population of various clans.

Bobby's disappointment deepened. The only remains of the supposedly once-great structure was a section of the kiva wall a couple of feet high that was barely held together with corroded mortar. As he studied the outcroppings of single-layer adobes, he couldn't picture the pueblo. Originally, it had consisted of more than fifteen hundred rooms configured in an expansive E formation.

Bobby snapped random photos as he made his way through the canyon. He searched the ground and found pottery shards, some from polychrome vessels in black and white, and other remnants in shades of faded orange. He left them in place. It was forbidden to remove artifacts, and he didn't need any more bad karma. He searched the canyon walls for pictographs and petroglyphs but found nothing. Another disappointment. It wasn't his lucky day.

Bobby was ready to call it quits and return to the ranch when he heard faint laughter from inside the canyon. He assumed it was teenagers, but all the same, he didn't want to run into anyone out there.

He considered retracing his route back to the road, but that would take at least an hour, and his disappointments had drained him. If he could get a little higher up, he might be able to see who was in the canyon and assess the situation. Twenty yards away sat a huge boulder. The top was above the opening of the canyon. He hoped he could somehow climb to the top. Careful not to attract attention, he made his way as quietly as possible to the boulder. When he reached the outcropping, he looked up and started to have doubts. The boulder was bigger than it had seemed from a distance. He had never rock climbed, unless you counted one lame attempt at REI's rock wall.

Bobby steeled himself and slowly began to pull his body up the rock face. The boulder wasn't at all like the one at REI. It was slippery and offered few hand or toe grips. In addition, the exertion made Bobby realize he wasn't in great physical shape. He wondered if he had the stamina to walk the twenty-eight miles to Chimayó on Good Friday. Would he collapse beside the road, defeated, ashamed, never fulfilling his goal?

He braced himself and continued the climb. He inched up, rested, and inched up some more. When he was almost to top, a sense of elation came over him. He looked up and spotted a small bush at the edge of the boulder. Without thinking, he reached for it. As his hand closed around the plant, a pain shot up his arm and caused him to immediately release his grip. His foot, secured in a narrow crevasse, became dislodged. He began a slide down the rock face, madly grasping at the rock surface, but nothing took hold.

His head scraped against the boulder. Then he hit the ground with a thud that knocked the air out of him. Afraid to move, he lay still as he tried to force air back into his lungs. His right leg sat twisted at an awkward angle. His hands and knees were scraped and bleeding. A fuzziness clogged his mind. He was disoriented. He inched his butt up to the boulder and rested his head against the cool surface.

Finally, his head stopped spinning and he tried to stand. His leg, the one that looked wrong, wobbled under his weight and sent a blast of pain through his body, followed by a wave of nausea. He sank back down against the boulder and tried to suppress his growing panic. The queasiness continued to churn in his stomach; his breath was raspy. Then there was a noise, a snap of a twig, faint laughter. He stared toward the opening of the canyon. As he rested there, he figured his leg either was broken or dislocated, maybe both. When he had tried to stand, the leg had buckled as a sharp pain shot up through his body. His head pounded, bringing back more waves of nausea. He reached up and lightly rubbed his fingers through his matted hair. It was wet and warm. A shudder went through his body. He didn't remember hitting his head when he fell, but the accident had happened so fast, a blur. One minute he had reached up for a branch, the next, he was on the ground.

BOBBY TRIED TO QUELL HIS PANIC AND SLOW HIS BREATH AS Jessie had taught him. On his third exhale, he saw something coming toward him. His eyes watered, blurring his vision. The image resembled a giant triangle, but as it got closer and his vision cleared, he saw that it was three men. The man in the middle dwarfed the companions at his sides. An overwhelming surge of relief came over him. He recognized one of the men, Leonardo Coriz.

Coriz was a formidable figure, with his six-and-a-half-foot frame carrying over two hundred pounds. There was no doubt, even clothed, that he was muscular and fit. His straight black hair swung as he walked, brushing below the waistline of his low-slung jeans. Tattoos of various creatures circled up both his arms from the wrist and disappeared into the sleeves of his T-shirt. When Coriz was fifteen, his mother had remarried and moved him from their pueblo to Santa Fe with his two sisters. He had enrolled in Santa Fe High, where his height and talent earned him hero status on the basketball team. In his junior year, he was almost solely responsible for a state trophy, the first time for the high school in a decade.

Bobby and Coriz had attended the same jewelry class during their junior year at Santa Fe High. Coriz came from a pueblo known for making exquisite jewelry, so the class served as a place for him to talk story. He claimed his mother named him after Leonardo da Vinci, but Bobby suspected it was more likely Leonardo DiCaprio, not that Coriz didn't possess artistic talent.

Bobby hadn't seen Coriz since high school but had heard he attended the Institute of American Indian Arts in Santa Fe. He had dropped out at the end of his second year. The school focused on traditional Indian imagery and media, which didn't interest Coriz. He had set his sights on becoming a filmmaker and started a small film company, YinYangYazzie. The YinYang was meant to represent opposite forces interconnecting and counterbalancing, and the Yazzie was in honor of his Navajo grandfather.

The other two guys, Thomas Eubank and Steg Engle, Bobby recognized also. Last spring, he had taken Jessie to see one of Coriz's films at the university. It was both disturbing and enlightening but too sophisticated for most college students. Jessie had wrinkled her nose and said, "That was weird."

The three men had met at the Sundance Film Festival in Utah a few years ago and began to collaborate on film projects. YinYang Yazzie had earned a respectable reputation as avant garde filmmakers.

The group came to a stop around ten feet away. Bobby, with his vision blurred, found them a striking if not haunting image: Coriz's massive stature framed by Eubank's dark lanky almost-feminine perfection and Engle's small wiry white ghostliness.

"Pilot?" Coriz said.

"Yeah."

"What you doing out here?"

"Sightseeing."

"Always the comedian," Coriz grinned.

"Fell off a boulder."

"Yeah, kind of looks that way, dude."

Eubank and Engle swayed slightly, or at least they looked like they did. Bobby tried to focus on the men. He was sure their eyes were way too dilated for the bright sun. Stoned. He hoped they were on a happy trip.

"What are you guys doing out here?" Bobby said.

"Taking a few mushrooms, getting in touch with our inner psyche, getting our creative juices running." Coriz chuckled as he turned toward his companions. The two men stared back expressionless but nodded slowly.

Mushrooms. An uneasy feeling came over Bobby.

"We're filming, dude." Coriz laughed again. "Ready to wrap but having a little trouble with the last scene." Coriz jutted his chin toward Engle. "Steg can be a little challenged with the abstract. Wants people to get with his redemption obsession." Coriz raised his fingers to his lips and released them with a kissing sound. "It's as if the gods dropped you from the sky."

Both Eubank and Engle had attended film programs. Eubank, the nephew of a second-rate Hollywood producer, had grown up in Pasadena and attended the film program at Cal State at Northridge. Engle, whose father was a German physicist at the Los Alamos lab, attended Yale's world cinema program, but its focus on the "coexistence of globalization and the persistence of national identities" held little interest for him. He had transferred to Yale's partner, FAMU, in the Czech Republic, and finished his degree.

Coriz's phone dinged. He reached in his pocket, stared at the screen, and pursed his lips. "Gotta go, bros."

Steg stammered. "Go?"

Coriz shot him a look that would have made anyone else but the little German prick wither.

"Okay. Sure. No problem," Eubank said.

"Hey, man. I think my leg might be broken," Bobby said.

"Yeah, I can see that, dude. But I got to take care of something at the pueblo. I'll send my nephew back to pick you guys up this afternoon."

"Could you call my girlfriend, Jessie, so she won't worry? My leg's killing me," Bobby pleaded.

"Yeah dude, hold on. I'll get you some help. Cross my heart." Coriz looked at his two companions, who were giggling like teenage girls.

Coriz shook his head. He was reluctant to leave Pilot out there with these knuckleheads. Thomas wouldn't hurt a fly, but Steg had an unpredictable mean streak. But he didn't have a choice. He couldn't take Bobby to the pueblo. It was closed, off-limits right now. He reached in his pocket, pulled out a bottle of pills, and tossed them to Bobby. "Take a few of these, Pilot. Someone will pick you up in a few hours."

Bobby figured these guys would be a challenge to deal with when they were straight and sober, but high on mushrooms—and God knows what else—it was a crapshoot. But what could he do? Although he and Coriz weren't friends, they had a history—he hoped that accounted for something. He was certain these guys wouldn't kill him, at least not on purpose. Worst-case scenario, they would forget and leave him behind.

Coriz turned around and faced the two men, who were still swaying back and forth. "Finish the last scene, pack up, and take care of my buddy. Get him some medical care ASAP." Then he bent down toward Bobby. "Sorry, hang in there, dude."

As Bobby watched Coriz walk away, he thought maybe this would be his atonement, the way to make amends. Helpless, out in the desert like Jesus, his destiny in the hands of others.

The sun, although not warm, beat down mercilessly. His head throbbed, and sweat dripped down his forehead, muddling his vision and making his stomach gurgle with queasiness. He looked at the pill bottle. No label. He was out of options. He twisted open the top and downed several pills. After a while, his body felt weightless and no longer rooted to the earth. The sensation made him wonder if it would be possible to slip away into nothingness—not ever know what lay ahead.

~12~

THE WINDS HAD QUIETED BUT LEFT AN EERIE STILLNESS. PASCAL rocked back and forth in his office chair, bored and restless. He yawned, stretched, then sat up and tried to conjure up some enthusiasm for the stolen Jesus costume. The crime seemed ludicrous, almost laughable. The theft had occurred on Palm Sunday; he wondered if there was any significance. He twirled his chair around toward the window, but only a sliver of blue sky could be seen. The adjacent building blocked his view and made him feel trapped. As he rubbed the back of his neck, he wondered if Gillian had heard about the break-in. He started to dial her number as his phone rang.

"Hey, was just going to call you," Pascal said.

"Well, I saved you the trouble of punching all those numbers."

"Thanks. You're a sweetheart."

Gillian wasn't in a mood to banter. "Robert says my mother's lawyer is bugging him about the will. He wants to schedule a reading—that is, a reading of the will."

"Are you ready for that?"

"No."

Pascal didn't know what to say. He wanted to be supportive, but it would be better if Gillian bit the bullet and got it over with: Fini. "Well, you know what they say about closure."

"No. What do they say?" Gillian snapped.

"It's a bitch."

Gillian changed the subject. "What were you supposedly calling about?"

Pascal let the supposedly slide. "Wanted to share my latest case. Thought you would get a kick out of it."

He could hear Gillian sigh but plunged ahead. "A break-in on the opera grounds, the shed where all the costumes and props are stored. Guess out of all those fancy costumes which one was stolen?"

"Jesus Christ," Gillian said flatly.

"How did you know?"

"It was in the papers. Don't you read the newspaper?"

Pascal's office door swung open and startled him. He whipped around and was surprised to see Captain Vargas. He could count on one hand the times the captain had paid a visit to his office. Pascal usually was summoned to the captain's office, and often the summons involved a reprimand.

Pascal ended the call with Gillian while Vargas cleared his throat noisily. He looked as if he suffered from indigestion. Small beads of sweat spread across his forehead. His cheeks were flushed.

Pascal wondered if the man was ill, and started to rise out of his chair, but Vargas put up his hand, signaling for him to stay put. The captain pulled up a chair across from Pascal's desk. He roughly rubbed his hands together as if he wanted to get rid of something on them.

"I'm not going to beat around the bush, Ruiz. I'm sure you know I had misgivings about hiring you, and if it hadn't been for your uncle's recommendation . . . ." He took in a deep breath, let it out, and unclenched his fists. "But I admit I might have been wrong. Your work on the violin case proved it."

Pascal was speechless. The captain had never said much after he recovered the Stradivarius and arrested the perpetrators. He wondered what this was about.

"I have a favor to ask," the captain said.

Pascal held his breath, trying not to fidget, but heard his chair wheels squeak on the linoleum.

"I'd like you to look into something for me . . . off-the-record."

Pascal thought he must have misheard. The captain was strictly a "by-the-book" man. "Off the record" wasn't part of his modus operandi.

The captain looked down, not meeting Pascal's eyes. "You can say no."

Pascal wasn't sure that was true but nodded for the captain to continue. The beads of sweat on the captain's brow now began to drip down his face. Pascal realized how uncomfortable the situation must be for the man, and almost felt sorry for him. Almost. He couldn't imagine what he was going to ask.

"My niece, Jessie, my sister-in-law's youngest—her boyfriend's missing. She called me this morning, hysterical. She's an actress. So who knows?" The captain raised his eyebrows. "She has a part in a Western being filmed out at the movie ranch east of San Felipe Casino."

"Diamond Tail out on Hagan Road across from the old brick factory?"

"Yeah. So the disappearance isn't exactly our jurisdiction. That's the off-the-record part."

"That's a big off-the-record, sir."

The captain narrowed his eyes. He knew Pascal Ruiz was one to talk. Always pushed the envelope and ignored procedures, but the captain decided not to respond. He sat back in his chair and folded his arms across his chest. "You can say no."

"Go ahead." Pascal was curious, and knew it couldn't hurt to help the captain out of a jam. Pay forward.

"Jessie and her boyfriend went to the ranch a couple weeks ago. Her parents don't know, so I hope that doesn't have to come out. Jessie told me that Bobby left after breakfast yesterday morning. He went for a hike, mentioned the old ghost town, Hagan. He didn't come back last night. Doesn't answer his phone, but the cell service out there is hit or miss."

Pascal considered the proposition. Although the assignment wasn't sanctioned, it definitely would be more interesting than looking for pot-smoking juveniles or a stolen Jesus costume, not to mention the paperwork on his desk. Plus, he would get out of town.

"Let's give it another day. You know how young people are, flying off the handle, going off half-cocked. Anyway, Jessie's busy with rehearsals most of the day. If the boy hasn't returned by tomorrow morning, set up an interview with her. Find out if his disappearance warrants other agencies being involved."

"Okay," Pascal said.

"It's complicated."

Pascal waited for the captain to elaborate, but he didn't. For once, Pascal wasn't the one skirting the line.

"Like I said, it's most likely not our jurisdiction, but then again, it depends, if you do find the kid, where he's found. Let's hope it doesn't get too messy. It could end up involving various agencies; San Felipe Tribal, Bernalillo sheriff, Sandoval County, FBI, maybe even us. As I told you, Ruiz, you can say no. No strings."

"I'll look into it."

"Thanks." The captain leaned heavily on the arms of the chair and pushed himself slowly up. "I won't forget it."

"What about the opera burglary? This Aubusson woman isn't the type who would let us sweep the break-in under the rug. She sent an enormous package yesterday that documented the storage building contents and listed the missing costume."

"Missing costume?"

"Jesus Christ."

"Excuse me?" the captain snapped.

Pascal realized his blunder. He wondered if it was subliminal, maybe he was being passive-aggressive. "It's a Jesus Christ costume from some holiday special the opera put on a few years ago."

The captain took his handkerchief out of his back pocket and wiped his brow. "Have Susie prepare the documentation for the insurance company. Then give Aubusson a call, reassure her that you have some leads and are looking into them. That should unruffle her feathers and buy you some time. Give Jessie a call later and arrange a meeting for Thursday morning. Hopefully, the kid will turn up by then and we can forget it."

Pascal knew he shouldn't hope otherwise but he did. He already had started to plan his trip out of town.

"After you get back, let's wrap up the break-in. With any luck, Matt Padilla will be back next week to pick up some of the slack." The captain looked at the paperwork stacked on Pascal's desk and jutted his chin in that direction. "In the meantime, you might want to process some of that mess."

Pascal looked at the pile of papers. The stack seemed to be ready to slide onto the floor any minute. He thought of his partner, Padilla, and hoped he would be back soon. He always was efficient at processing paperwork on time, while Pascal always got distracted.

He needed to finish the conversation before the stack of papers slid off the desk. "I need a number for your niece."

The captain handed Pascal a piece of paper with Jessie's information and turned to leave. He stopped and grimaced as if he had bitten into something bitter, distasteful. "Thanks, Ruiz. Keep me updated."

As the captain closed the office door, Pascal started to hum under his breath. He was beside himself, almost giddy, like a kid with a day out of school. It would be a welcome reprieve from his daily grind. He could ignore the paperwork as well as put off Aubusson and forget about the Jesus costume for a day. But the best part was that he could revisit a place that held fond memories: Tonque.

Pascal's mother, Francesca, used to take him along on her trips to dig dry clay from an abandoned pre-Columbian pueblo called Tonque. He hadn't been back to the area in years. An artist, she had coveted the rich deposits of dry clay in the arroyo banks, which she used for her abstract ceramic sculptures. He remembered the look of surprise and wonder on his mother's face each time she removed a piece from her kiln. The fired Tonque clay had a range of colors from cream to light orange. Pascal loved to watch her work with the clay, her hands magically shaping huge mounds into forms. She had explained to him that if clay was untempered, it would shrink and crack during drying or firing. The Tonque clay, with its crystal tough temper, alleviated that problem. Sometimes his mother collected broken pottery pieces from the pueblo site to crush and add to the clay to increase its temper. She insisted that those pieces possessed the spirit of the Tonque people.

On their outings, while his mother dug clay and gathered shards, Pascal had searched for etched petroglyphs and painted pictographs scattered on the rock facings. After his mother's death, he had researched the pueblo as a way to stay connected to her. He discovered that archaeologists had determined the pueblo was occupied from the early fourteenth century until the middle of the sixteenth. It provided up to a third of the glaze-decorated pottery used by the middle Rio Grande Valley pueblos. For some reason, possibly a severe drought, the Tonque people eventually abandoned the area.

Pascal also searched for old bricks his mom said came from Tonque Brick and Tile. The company had built a factory in the ruins around the early 1900s and used the same clay deposits. Pascal still had one of the original Tonque bricks sitting on his desk at the station to hold down the ever-expanding piles of paperwork.

Tonque was just south of the Diamond Tail Ranch. He hoped that after the interview with the captain's niece and a cursory look around, he would have time to explore the area again. Pascal almost laughed—"off-the-record secret mission!"

Then he thought of Gillian. Although it was against protocol to take civilians along on missions, this one wasn't sanctioned. It would be the perfect opportunity to show her more of New Mexico and distract her from her mother's will. Gillian, an accomplished violinist, had been hired to write for a music journal in Washington, D.C. But when her estranged mother was hospitalized after a serious car accident, her stepfather enticed her to Santa Fe, promising her concert tickets for a Prague virtuoso, Mischa Zaremba, and an interview with him afterward. Her article on Zaremba had been well received, but when she didn't return to D.C., her position was terminated, although she was still welcome to submit articles as a freelancer.

Pascal had been attracted to Gillian the first time they met. She was tall, thin, and moved like a gazelle, her posture perfect. But what caught his attention that freezing January night in the Lensic Theater's parking lot was her auburn hair which resisted confinement and, up close, her thick black lashes that shaded pale jade eyes. Their meeting wasn't the most romantic. A famous virtuoso lay unconscious on the pavement. Gillian had befriended him and helped as an intermediary in the case. But after the violin was recovered, her mother had died. Gillian only remained in Santa Fe to finalize her mother's estate. She made it clear from the beginning that they would be only friends. She didn't need any additional complications in her life.

Gillian, coming from the East Coast, struggled to acclimate to Santa Fe, with the menacing Sangre de Cristo Mountains to the east and the barren landscape to the west. At seven thousand feet, Santa Fe's thin, dry air was the opposite of her home. The nation's capital, encased in thick humid air, nourished a lush and verdant landscape.

Pascal dialed Gillian's number.

"Hey," Gillian gasped into the phone.

"Are you all right?"

"Just got in from a run. Had to stop and catch my breath twice coming up Canyon Road."

"We are at seven thousand feet."

"Yeah," she said, taking in a long breath and letting it out. "What's up?"

"I'm off on a fishing expedition."

"Fishing?"

"The captain asked me to look into a missing person who was staying out at Diamond Tail Ranch south of Santa Fe."

"Whoopie ti yi yo—a real ranch! With horses?" Gillian sounded more sarcastic then excited, but Pascal couldn't tell for sure.

"No horses. Some cows, but it's a movie ranch now. They're filming a pilot for a Western. If you aren't busy tomorrow, you might want to go with me. See some more of New Mexico."

"Will there be movie stars?" Gillian asked.

Now Pascal knew she was being sarcastic. "Probably not."

"I am feeling a little lonely. My little darlings, my violin students, are on spring break. Hallie left yesterday on a school trip to San Diego."

Pascal was disheartened. Gillian hadn't mentioned that Hallie was going on a trip. "I'll pick you up tomorrow around eight."

"In the morning?" Gillian sounded alarmed.

"Yes, eight in the morning. I have to interview the missing guy's girlfriend at nine."

"The plot thickens."

"The guy probably had one too many beers and is crashing with a friend."

"I have to take Birdie along."

Pascal groaned audibly.

"She's still mourning my mother. I can't leave her alone all day," Gillian pleaded. "I'll pack a picnic."

"See you at eight."

~13~
Maundy Thursday

IT WAS MAUNDY THURSDAY, THE LAST SUPPER OF JESUS WITH his Apostles, the day before he would be crucified on the cross. But Pascal, not being religious, was oblivious. His thoughts were on the day ahead. When he pulled into Gillian's driveway, her front door swung open and the rambunctious terrier, Birdie, burst out and hurtled her compact body into the air. Pascal grimaced. He was a cat person. But as he turned to Gillian, he was relieved to see that she had dressed appropriately for the occasion: jeans, hiking boots, down jacket, and one of those silly hats with flaps over the ears. She held a large shopping bag in one hand and a promising picnic basket in the other. He hoped it contained something for lunch, since the ranch was in the middle of nowhere. Pascal loaded the parcels into the car as Gillian tried to contain the dog.

The morning sun had done its best, but the temperature was still barely above freezing. As Pascal started the car, he handed her a bag with two coffees and some empañadas. Gillian doled out the fare as they headed down St. Francis and then cut over to Cerrillos Road. Pascal usually avoided Cerrillos because of the construction, but it was the most direct way to Route 14, the Turquoise Trail.

Birdie, not content to stay in the back seat, leaped into the front and almost overturned Gillian's coffee. The dog wiggled her way into Gillian's lap and settled down. Gillian sipped her coffee and fed small morsels of turnover to the dog.

As Pascal left the city behind, his body relaxed. He slowed down and took in the scenery. "Near the ranch is an abandoned pueblo where I used to go with my mother to dig clay."

"Dig clay? From the ground? I know I'm a city girl, but are you teasing me?" Gillian asked as she offered another piece of empañada to the dog.

"Dry clay. You add water, then it needs to be cured. My mother used the clay for her sculptures."

"How do you cure it?"

"Sheep urine."

"Now you are making fun of me."

"Seriously, back in the day, Native Americans used sheep urine. Hippies in the '60s used their own."

Gillian made a sour face. "Glad I missed that era."

"Vinegar works also. The clay needs something acidic."

"What did you do out there all day?" Gillian asked.

"Explore. Once, we camped overnight, slept in an arroyo in sleeping bags. I remember being mesmerized by all the stars, forgot about the rattlesnakes and scorpions. My mother knew a few constellations—the Big Dipper, Orion's Belt. But she preferred to make up her own. She would point to an area full of stars. "Oh, look, there's Olympia Magna or Boca Negra." I only saw clusters of random stars scattered across the sky. But as she described the shape of the constellation, embellishing the story, Olympia Magna or Boca Negra magically took shape in the sky. My mother loved stars and could have rattled on for hours even after I fell asleep. The next morning when we opened our eyes, a bunch of cows had circled us, heads down, their enormous watery bovine eyes staring as if transfixed. We burst out laughing and spooked the bunch, sent them running in different directions."

Gillian laughed. "You were lucky they didn't trample you or worse."

"Yeah, I guess. But to spend the night under the stars was worth it." Pascal could still remember how black the sky had been and how bright the stars. There was nothing else.

He became silent, engrossed in thoughts of the ghost towns near Diamond Tail Ranch, Hagan and Coyote. They were mere shells of their previous selves: scarce lumber, crumbling adobes, mud buildings washed away, only outcroppings left.

Pascal turned off the road and drove into the small enclave of Cerrillos. "My mother lived here in the '70s, her hippie days, before she married my father and had me."

As they came to a stop, Gillian looked out at the barren landscape and tried to imagine living in the town.

"These hills once were rich in lead and turquoise. Native Americans were pushed out when the Spanish colonial settlements took over the mines. They even sent turquoise back to Spain for the crown jewels, so the legend goes," Pascal said.

As they drove slowly through the empty streets, Pascal continued: "Cerrillos was once a thriving community, but like most defunct mining towns, there wasn't anything to keep people here. There are only a couple hundred residents left." He pulled up in front of an old adobe house that sat alone near an abandoned railroad track. The rusty tin roof drooped precariously over the front door, the windows boarded up. In barely a whisper, Pascal said, "That's where my mother lived."

Gillian didn't know what to say, so she said nothing. She and Pascal, both raised as only children, were accustomed to silence and didn't always expect responses. As Pascal started the engine, Gillian turned and smiled at him. He smiled back.

They headed back to Highway 14 and continued south. As they drove through the town of Golden, Pascal told Gillian about the Golden Inn which used to be south of town: "It was a popular music venue offering concerts on the weekends until it burnt down under suspicious circumstances in 1983. My mother was a regular. The highlight for her was the night Muddy Waters played there. She had stretched a blank canvas in anticipation of getting his autograph. She told me he was wasted after the concert, but that worked in her favor. She cut him off as he went down the hall, shoved the canvas in his face, and used a line from Oliver. 'Please sir, can I have your autograph?' Waters weaved back and forth, and my mother worried he would crumple to the ground. But he grabbed the Sharpie and scribbled his name across the canvas. It's hanging in my bathroom."

Gillian laughed. "Your mother must have been something."

Pascal nodded. He maneuvered the car onto a dirt road that looked as if it hadn't been graded in years, if ever. They bounced around as Pascal tried to miss the potholes, but it was useless. He slowed to a crawl and raised his chin toward a cluster of modest adobes. "Those houses? The first time I came out here with my mother, she told me that Penitentes lived there."

"Penitentes?"

"Los Hermanos, the Brotherhood. The group is pledged to secrecy. Unfortunately, that's resulted in all kinds of speculations and rumors about their practices. Some people say they practice severe penitential rites, self-flagellation, and even simulated crucifixion. But who knows? I've heard some crazy stories about the Brotherhood."

"Like what?"

"Men bound to wooden crosses as they walk through the Stations of the Cross."

"Jesus," Gillian said in a whisper.

"Exactly," Pascal chuckled. "Some say that in order to enter into the Brotherhood, you must receive three Ave Maria cuts on your back. And if you have wronged your family, community or fellow Penitentes, you are flogged or receive some form of torture like crawling back and forth with bare hands and knees on pebbles and stones."

"Jesus!" Gillian stared at Pascal with her mouth open.

"Well, there are those who defend the Brotherhood, say they stepped in when church officials were unavailable. They provided not only religious services but support in isolated communities. They served as a lay religion, tending to their flock and practical matters as well as worship. Nowadays, the Brotherhood claims that penitence is performed through charity, prayer, and good example, not deviancy."

"Jesus," Gillian said for the third time, then turned in her seat and tried to imagine the people who lived in the small adobes.

The dust swirled under the SUV's tires, suffocating the bushy cedars that dotted each side of the roadway. The high desert terrain was mostly sandy dirt, scrub grasses and cactus. The land could not sustain anything except some cattle and a few wild horses. The rangy animals were somehow able to eke out an existence on the meager offerings.

The dirt road abruptly turned west, then north. A ferruginous hawk circled above and scanned for rabbits. Finally, the ranch house came into view. Pascal noted that not much had changed over the years since he had been there with his mother, except that the rusty tin roof had been replaced with sky blue metal sheeting. On each side of the steps, the same ragged collection of cholla edged the covered porch.

Pascal looked over at Gillian, who seemed oblivious to her surroundings as she continued to bob her head to Truckdriver Gladiator Mule, the Neko Case album she had insisted would be perfect for the trip. Pascal raised his eyebrows but said nothing. He had hoped they could quietly take in the landscape as he traveled down memory lane.

Pascal pulled up to the ranch house and turned off the engine, which thankfully shut off the music. He took in the silence. The air, eerily still and lifeless, seemed to drape over the yard. Gillian leaped out of the car, stretched out her arms toward the cloudless sky, and began to spin in a circle. The terrier, glad to escape the confines of the car, followed suit.

"Ah, the West!" Gillian flung her head back, twirled, and giggled.

A pang of irritation rang through Pascal's body. He couldn't put his finger on why but suspected Gillian's euphoric display bordered on sarcasm. He sometimes had trouble reading people, especially those from the East. It didn't always fit well with his job as a detective. He raised his eyebrows and tried to hide his annoyance as he suggested she leave the dog in the car. Then he turned and stomped up the steps.

Gillian picked up Birdie and put her in the car. She stuck out her tongue at Pascal's back as she followed him through the unlocked front door. The house seemed empty, still and quiet. They saw a faint light from a room down the hall and headed in that direction. As they went in, they saw a young woman sitting mermaid-style on a cushioned window seat. She held a book up to the window as if trying to capture the light. Gillian wondered, who sits like that?

If the woman was startled by their presence, she didn't show it. She acted as if she had been waiting for them, or at least for Pascal.

"Detective," she purred as she slowly untangled her long legs. She pushed herself out of the seat and reached out her hand. "Jessie Archuleta." Her voice was seductive, but her expression neutral, no affect, as if she was waiting for a cue from the director on what emotion to display. Jessie still held the book in her left hand, but Gillian noticed that when she snapped it closed, she had not marked her place. Gillian suspected that Jessie had used the book for effect, like a prop in a movie scene.

As Jessie turned back toward the window seat, her long dark curls, with an occasional streak of auburn, cascaded around her shoulders and down her back. She carelessly tossed the book toward the seat, but it fell on the floor. Gillian picked it up and glanced at the title. It was Justine, the first book in Lawrence Durrell's Alexandria Quartet. Gillian's mother had been a big fan of Durrell. When she moved to Santa Fe, she had not only left Gillian behind but also most of her books. Throughout Gillian's adolescence, she had read her way through her mother's abandoned library. She'd found Durrell's writing dated and his lyrical use of poetic, allusive, and indirect prose a challenge. But she had been fascinated with Justine's escapades of passion and deception in Egypt. Gillian couldn't imagine Jessie reading such a book—or maybe any book.

Pascal took Jessie's outstretched hand. It wasn't so much that she was beautiful, although she was, but more her stunning features that drew you in and kept you engaged. Her elusive almond-shaped eyes were a peculiar shade of dark green. She had an almost-perfect nose, although some would argue that it was little too long, and creamy flawless lightly tinted skin. Gillian could tell Pascal had trouble tearing his eyes away from her. Jessie's overly plump ripe lips were slightly parted and revealed a perfect row of white teeth like little soldiers. Her mounds of curls made him itch to run his fingers through them. Even if she didn't have any talent, Pascal figured she could make a living standing there. Her outfit was an incongruous mixture; sexy tan deerskin leather pants hugged her petite frame, paired with a Victorian high-collared white lace blouse with ruffled collar and sleeves. Her ruby red Jimmy Choo spike heels brought her up to five-foot-three.

Gillian, annoyed with Pascal's obvious infatuation with the woman, cleared her throat and gave Pascal a jab with her elbow.

"Oh, Gillian Jasper," Pascal said.

"Ms. Jasper?" Jessie tilted her head coquettishly. Gillian didn't offer any explanation, so Jessie turned her attention back to Pascal. "Thank you so much for coming, detective. I have been beside myself with worry."

Gillian couldn't detect a trace of worry in the woman. She seemed to be the epitome of calm and serenity. But she was sure Pascal would give her the benefit of the doubt. He was a detective and figured people reacted strangely in stressful situations.

"Where is everyone?" Pascal asked.

"The film crew is over at Hagen. The director wanted to shoot some additional footage of the ghost town before they wrap this afternoon. Most of the actors took off and are either at the casino or in Albuquerque."

Pascal looked over and tilted his head toward a group of chairs on the other side of the room. "Let's take a seat." Once the three of them were seated, he took out his notebook and stubby pencil. "What was Bobby doing out here?"

"Good question." Jessie gave a little laugh. "Bobby had a beer with a buddy, Raymond, a few months ago. He and Raymond had been in an English class together at the community college before Raymond switched to the film technician program. Now Raymond manages craft services for the local movie industry. He told Bobby about a TV pilot that was scheduled to be filmed out here. They needed extras." Jessie closed her almond eyes, raised her chin toward the ceiling, and let out a heavy exasperated sigh. "Let me tell you, an extra in a TV pilot is the last thing I would ever want to do—tedious beyond belief. But Bobby was all hot for me to give it a try.

He sugared the pot, said there might be an audition. So I caved. Thank God the director pulled me out of the extras and offered me a part right off the bat." Jessie turned and smiled, proud of her achievement.

Gillian sighed audibly, and Jessie shot her a cautionary look.

Pascal had to admit that Jessie had a fetching profile. "Why did Bobby want to come to the ranch?"

Jessie pursed her plump lips. "Bobby had his heart set on being a journalist, has always been obsessed with newspapers. When he was twelve, he begged his parents to subscribe to the daily paper, but they said it was a waste of money. They could get their news free from television."

Gillian knew the type of woman Jessie was, one who liked to hear her voice out loud. Pascal would need to rein her in soon, or they would be there all day.

"Growing up, Bobby would ride his bike downtown and shell out part of his allowance for the paper. He claimed the New Mexican was one the West's oldest papers. Most boys spent their weekends on bikes or played ball. Bobby hung out in the public library, reading the papers until his hands turned black from the newsprint. After graduation in May, he sent his resumé out to every county newspaper, landed only one interview, the Quay County Sun in Tucumcari."

Jessie laughed and shook her head again, sending her curls cascading around her shoulders. "Yeah. Hundreds of motels—so say the billboards." She closed her doe-like eyes. "Didn't go well, didn't get the job."

Gillian tried to suppress a yawn and wondered how long the interview was going to last. She wished Pascal would cut to the chase. Who cares that this guy wasn't offered some newspaper job? He was missing, maybe hurt or dead.

Pascal could feel Gillian's impatience. "He must have been disappointed, only one interview, no job offers, no prospects? Then you landed a sweet role in the TV pilot. Do you think he was depressed?"

"No. You kidding? He was relieved. Happy I got the role, but I wouldn't call it sweet. After he didn't get the job, he switched gears.

He was all psyched up about an article he had read about the Easter procession, you know, to Chimayó. People traipsing up I-25 slowing traffic to a crawl, causing congestion. Some of them even carry Jesus crosses. It's like the Dark Ages."

Pascal scribbled "Dark Ages" in his notebook. "He wanted to write about the procession to Chimayó?"

"Yes, but specifically the Penitentes. You know—those crazy guys that whip themselves. Seems a little S&M to me. Supposedly, there's a community near here." Jessie shivered. "Bobby's not a flake. He's a super-smart, talented writer but . . .." She gave her head a shake, again sending her curls bouncing off her shoulders. She reached up and brushed her hair back. "Let's say that in the past, he was lacking in the focus department. But this thing about the procession got hold of him—a little too much. He seemed almost obsessed. It was weird, because, you know, he never was religious. I was the one raised Catholic." She raised her eyes to the ceiling. "I know what's it's like being religious. When I agreed to audition, Bobby was adamant. He wanted to participate in the procession, do penance."

"Why did he feel compelled to make amends?"

"I don't know, maybe something to do with his mother. She died when he was fifteen."

"Had Bobby been to Chimayó?"

"He told me his father took him there before his mother died to get some healing dirt from the chapel. The experience creeped him out. Then his mother died."

"Are you staying out here at the ranch?"

"Yes. Bobby borrowed his cousin's camper van. Raymond let us park in the back next to the kitchen. We can use the facilities inside if we need to. There are showers in the dressing rooms. It's not ideal but . . .." She pressed her lips together and shrugged.

"Is there anything else you can tell us about Bobby?"

"Not really."

"Tell me about the day Bobby disappeared."

"During breakfast Tuesday, he rambled on about some meeting with someone. He was super-excited, told me this was his big break.

I tried to encourage him but . . .." She sighed. "He wouldn't go with me to the casino the night before, wanted to hang with Raymond. But then he went somewhere after I left. He got home late. I was pissed off. I had a shoot that morning, was tired, and it was already late. I didn't pay much attention. He said something about the inside scoop, but it was all hush hush."

"The inside scoop?" Pascal asked.

Jessie shrugged for the umpteenth time. "I guess he meant the Penitentes, I don't know. He mentioned taking pictures out at Hagan—you know, the old ghost town. I told him I needed to get dressed and would see him later. That was the last time I saw him."

"Do you remember what he was wearing?"

"Oh yeah, fashion wasn't his strong point. Always the same thing—jeans, plaid flannel shirt, blue pea coat, you know like hippies wore in the '60s. He loved that coat, but thankfully, it was a contemporary knock-off, not some smelly garment he picked up at the thrift store. Oh, and these expensive leather hiking boots from Australia. He had blown his graduation money on them. I told him his Nikes would be fine, more comfortable. It wasn't like he planned to hike the Appalachian Trail."

Pascal couldn't figure out Jessie. Most of the time, she talked like she was reading a script, playing a part. Smooth, collected. But then she lapsed into juvenile lingo.

"Do you have a current picture of him?"

Jessie reached over for her phone. "I'll text it to you."

Pascal gave her the number, and his phone pinged.

"Is Raymond Almond around?"

She looked at her watch. "No, he's gone to Albuquerque to buy supplies, should be back later this afternoon. I can text when he gets back."

"Thanks. We'll take a look around the area, check out Hagan, then stop back before we head to Santa Fe."

Pascal turned to leave and Gillian followed but then turned and said, "Nice to meet you, Ms. Archuleta."

"Yeah, uh, you too."

~14~

GILLIAN AND PASCAL CLIMBED BACK IN THE CAR WHILE TRYING to fight off Birdie. The dog acted as if she had been left alone for days, whining and leaping from the back to the front of the car until Gillian grabbed and held her tight to her chest.

"What do you think?" Pascal asked.

"The butler did it." Gillian burst out laughing. "Sorry—Jessie, there's something a little off about her. Like she's putting on an act."

Pascal laughed.

"What?" Gillian said.

"That's what I was thinking. A little too smooth and collected."

Gillian was relieved that Pascal wasn't totally smitten with Jessie, or at least he had the sense to pretend. She liked Pascal, and if she was honest, she liked him a lot. From their first encounter, even if it had been in a parking lot at a crime scene in the middle of the night, something inside her had stirred. That night, she had been attracted, amused, and irritated all at the same time. But she knew her stay in New Mexico was temporary. It was senseless to get involved in a relationship.

As they left the ranch house and walked toward the ghost town, Pascal scanned the landscape for any sign of movement, but an eerie stillness seemed to have settled on the terrain. Even the cows had wandered off, most likely down in the gully by the creek, crowded around the few morsels of vegetation. He would like to be down with the cows and not looking for some guy who maybe was missing and maybe not.

He wondered if Bobby Pilot had been depressed and decided to cash it in. He wondered about Pilot's search for penance. Pascal knew a little about regret and contrition, and he had learned that

65

the path was full of pitfalls. More often than not, they led you everywhere but where you wanted to go. Better to close that door, get
on with your life.

Gillian held the terrier in her lap and gritted her teeth as Pascal
tried to maneuver around the deep tire tracks that had been gouged
in the mud during rains and dried to cement when the sun reappeared. Not only had the road not improved over the years, it had
deteriorated. The stretch from Highway 14 to Diamond Tail had
been manageable, but this section, left to the elements, was almost
impassable. Pascal had heard a rumor that San Felipe Pueblo had
recently blocked access to the county road east of the casino. It was
an illegal move but probably would be tangled up in court for years.
He was sure that Diamond Tail would put up a fight if movie crews
were forced to meander up the Turquoise Trail instead of using the
interstate to get to the ranch.

The road was owned by the county, and they had a right to drive
on it, but the land on either side was posted NO TRESPASSING.
To the north was ranch land, and to the south the pueblo. Legally,
he couldn't look for Pilot anywhere except from the road. He hadn't
gotten permission from the ranch to search Hagan, and knew it was
unlikely San Felipe would give consent for Tonque. He had no legal
jurisdiction in the area. If they were caught, it would be embarras-
sing or worse.

Pascal could see the ruins of Hagan in the distance and decided
to take a short cut through the brush. But when he pulled his Jeep
off the road, his tires sank into a gully. As he tried to maneuver the
Jeep out, he hoped the scrapes and thuds were superficial and would-
n't damage the undercarriage. He gave the gas pedal one more push
and the Jeep leaped out of the ditch. He swerved to the right to miss
a good-sized mesquite bush, but his right tire hit a hefty piece of
alabaster that brought the vehicle to a halt.

"I think we better walk from here."

"Yah think?" Gillian said with her best Southern twang.

As Pascal opened his door, he looked over at Gillian. "It's a little
early for the rattlers, but watch your step."

Gillian picked up Birdie, swiveled around toward the door, and carefully set her feet on the ground. "Rattlers?"

"Put the dog down. She'll alert us if one is nearby. Anyway, snakes won't bother you unless you step on them."

"I feel so relieved." Gillian started to think the outing wasn't much fun. She was tired of bumping along on the road. Now she had to trudge through the brush and avoid stickers, burrs, and rattlesnake bites to some ghost town. She was cranky. Where was the picnic she had envisioned in some scenic locale, maybe near a stream with an abundance of wildflowers and soft grass for the blanket she'd brought?

"No worries. There are only two of us. You don't want to be the third on a hike." Gillian detected Pascal's sadistic glee as he continued with the snake lore. "The first person wakes the snake, the second makes it mad (that's you), and the third gets bit."

The last thing Gillian wanted to do was make a snake mad, and there was no one behind her to sacrifice. She lowered Birdie to the ground. Instantly, the terrier lunged forward and the leash slipped out of her hand.

Gillian screamed, but as Pascal started to turn around, the dog shot by him. They both took off running as the dog darted left and right out of reach. Finally, Birdie came to a halt in front of a pile of fresh cow dung. Gillian grabbed the leash and pulled her away but not before the dog had taken a mouthful.

"That's disgusting!"

"That's a dog," Pascal said as he caught his breath. He was a cat person, and although cats ate disgusting things like mice and lizards, at least they were useful.

Gillian glared at him but said nothing. She was a city girl. Towering buildings, congested streets, and crowded sidewalks made her feel secure, oblivious, enveloped in an urban cocoon. She was comfortable alone, and where better to be alone than a big city, where you were anonymous. She thrived on structure and predictability. The West with its wide-open spaces full of unforeseeable danger was anything but secure.

Their little chase had brought them to the edge of Hagan. As they came closer, Gillian could see there wasn't much left of the original town. Pascal had told her that Hagan, now a skeleton, once was an ambitiously planned community for five hundred Italian and Slavic miners. The buildings must have had shed roofs at one time but now, exposed to the elements, the adobes were left to crumble. Gillian looked around and shivered with the thought that this was where the rattlers were hiding out, sunning themselves on the rocks during the day and slipping between them at night.

Birdie was enraptured with the wild smells. Her short legs let her oversized head hang down nose to dirt. She was bred to rout out and kill rodents and small animals. Today, the dog was determined to do it.

Gillian kept her eyes to the ground, careful where she put her feet as she poked around the remaining foundations. Only a few brick walls were left of what was once a power plant, general store, and a few smaller structures.

"Can you believe this place once had electricity? And water. They piped it in two miles away from a spring and stored it in a reservoir above the town," Pascal said.

Gillian raised her eyebrows but said nothing. She had seen enough of the ruins, and was hungry and ready to find somewhere for their picnic before Birdie routed out a rattler.

"They even built a school."

Gillian raised her eyebrows again. She couldn't imagine why people would want to live out there in the middle of nowhere.

"The miners hit a layer of shale in the '30s. The coal production came to a halt and—"

Out of nowhere, a helicopter swooped above them. Gillian and Pascal ducked instinctively, then shielded their eyes with their hands as they looked up. Birdie barked and ran in circles, wrapping her leash around Gillian's legs until she picked up the dog. They watched as the chopper circled lower and lower around the outskirts of Hagan, then gently set down on a barely level patch of ground. Before the blades stopped spinning, a young man in commando fatigues jumped out. Even from a distance, Gillian could tell that he wasn't happy to see them. He radiated the look of a twenty-something with a grudge. She would have chuckled at his fatigues and silver-tipped cowboy boots in another situation, one in which they weren't trespassing on posted land.

The man's blond buzz cut glistened in the sunlight as he trotted over to them. He was the model of a soldier: athletic and clean-shaven, although Gillian found it incongruous that his left ear flaunted a turquoise stud. He stopped about ten feet away and took a stance with his legs slightly spread. He tried to make his soft Southern drawl as threatening as possible, "This is private land." He looked over toward their vehicle a hundred and fifty feet away. "It's clearly posted NO TRESPASSING."

Pascal looked at the nametag Wegman on upper left side of the man's jacket. He decided to play innocent. "Mr. Wegman?"

The man stared at Pascal though his wire-rimmed mirrored aviator glasses with a stoic expression.

"My mom and I used to come up here. She knew Tommy Jones over at Diamond Tail. Tommy gave her the okay to scout around, as long as we didn't bother anything."

The man didn't move an inch. "Well, Mr.?"

"Ruiz."

"Well, Ruiz, Tommy's no longer the manager up at Diamond Tail, and you are trespassing on private land. I'm contracted to patrol this area, keep it secure. If you have a problem with that, we can take a little ride to Bernalillo, talk it over with the sheriff. Otherwise, I suggest you, your lady friend, and that little dog turn around and go back where you came from."

Pascal seethed. He knew the man was within his rights, and that they were trespassing—but still. "How often do you make patrols out here?"

Wegman ignored the question. "As I said, turn around and leave the premises now."

"Wondered if you saw anyone out here over the last couple of days," Pascal continued.

Gillian noticed the man shift his stance and put his hand on his holster. She grabbed Pascal's arm and tugged him toward the Jeep.

Pascal hated to be intimidated, especially by some rent-a-cop. But they were trespassing.

Gillian picked Birdie up and held her in her arms to make better time. As she trudged after Pascal, she kept her eyes to the ground, careful where she put her feet. With each step, she prayed she wouldn't see a snake. She was scared being out there in the middle of nowhere. One person had already disappeared. She was beginning to have a bad feeling about the entire situation. She could feel Wegman's eyes burning into her back. Neither she nor Pascal said a word until they were back in the Jeep and had turned around toward the road.

"Now what?" Gillian asked

"We could try our luck at the casino."

Gillian tilted her head and looked at Pascal, not sure if he was serious.

"I'm kidding," Pascal said with a bemused expression.

"I'm hungry." Gillian didn't mean to whine, but she was hungry. She hadn't eaten much for breakfast and had fed most of her empañada to Birdie.

"We could picnic on the road."

They heard the helicopter revving up. As they looked to the sky, they saw it swing east toward the casino. Pascal found it strange. A helicopter patrol out there was overkill. He wondered who had hired the surveillance and why. Maybe the Hollywood folks imagined they needed security. But in the middle of nowhere? Other than a few rattlers, he couldn't see the justification. He needed to find out. It would help to know the chopper's schedule and route, if for no other reason than to stay out of Wegman's way.

Then his phone pinged with a text from Jessie: Raymond Almond was back from Albuquerque.

When they arrived at the ranch, he was preparing dinner for the crew. He had finished concocting a marinade and was starting to cut meat and vegetables. He said he needed another half-hour to finish preparing for the crew's wrap party that evening, then would be happy to talk to them.

Jessie came down the hall with an expectant look.

"Sorry—we didn't see any sign of Bobby out at Hagan," Pascal said.

"Oh." Jessie seemed a little distracted, but maybe she was just disappointed they hadn't found Bobby.

"We were chased out by some guy in a helicopter. Said we were trespassing."

"That's weird." Jessie wrinkled her perfectly shaped nose. "I know the area is posted, but nobody pays attention to that. Most of the movie people hike all over the place. I haven't heard anything about a helicopter."

Gillian offered, "You're welcome to join us for lunch."

"I already ate, but thanks. You guys are welcome to eat in the lounge." She pointed down the hall to the room where they had met earlier.

"Thanks," Pascal and Gillian said at the same time. They looked at each other, and Gillian wanted to blurt out, "knock, knock dibs you owe me a coke," then start counting until Pascal said stop. It was a silly game she used to play with her friends. But Pascal turned away and headed down the hall.

Gillian pulled a side table over to the cushioned window seat where Jessie had been reading that morning. She moved the book that Jessie had tossed on the seat and set it on another chair, then dug into her picnic basket. She arranged the sandwiches and salads she'd made that morning on plates and poured two glasses of Pellegrino. She looked over at Pascal, who was looking at the floor-to-ceiling shelves stocked with books. Gillian patted the cushion next to her. "Lunch is served, Squire."

Pascal turned and bowed. Then he settled next to her on the bench, and they ate in silence. The sun shone through the window and warmed their backs. Birdie sat motionless at their feet and stared with her beady black eyes. Every so often, Gillian would pull off a piece of sandwich and toss it to the poised terrier who would deftly leap and catch it in midair.

"She's quite the little acrobat," Pascal said.

Gillian smiled affectionately at the dog. Although she had never owned a dog and the last thing she wanted was to care for this one, lately she had become attached to her mother's dog.

"Have you decided on a subject for your next article?" Pascal asked.

Gillian's first article about the virtuoso's attack, his stolen Stradivarius, and recovery of the instrument had been well received. But now, she seemed at a loss for something to write about that would have a wide appeal. Santa Fe wasn't New York City, or even St. Louis. There were classical concerts and performances, but she needed something with teeth. "Not yet."

"Have you thought any more about a piece on the opera, maybe the apprentice program? Or the history of the opera house architecture?"

Gillian had done some preliminary research on the Santa Fe Opera. Its website featured a captivating picture of the facility. The setting atop a mesa with a sunset horizon blazing in multicolor strata beneath an overarching sky was stunning. Rugged mountains jutted to the east, and vistas of rolling hills spanned in all directions. She had to admit the structure was surreal, an architectural wonder. But she needed more for an article.

"But what's the hook?" Gillian asked.

"The opera is world-renowned. It's not the Met. People dress however they want. Some people wear blue jeans and cowboy boots and others evening gowns and tuxedos."

"Still, I don't have a feel for a story."

"Before they renovated the opera house, it was only partly covered, leaving some of the seats exposed to the elements. Umbrellas were frowned on. When it rained, which was often in the monsoon season, patrons covered themselves with black plastic garbage bags."

"Yeah, definitely not the Met." Gillian laughed, shaking her head.

"Now the building, although still open air, has a sweeping roof that protects the stage as well as the audience—no need for garbage bags."

"I could write a decent feature article, but the opera season doesn't start until June. I'll probably be back in D.C. by then."

Although Pascal knew Gillian was leaving after her sister finished the school year, he was disappointed that she stated it so matter-of-factly.

"You could write about my latest case. Opera grounds burglary. Missing Jesus costume. Some great copy."

Gillian laughed and shook her head.

Then she packed up the picnic basket, and they made their way back to the kitchen. Raymond had finished preparing dinner. He sat leaning back in a chair with his feet propped on an oversized farm table and a beer in his hand.

"Care for one?" Raymond asked as he raised the bottle.

Pascal noticed that it was a Marble IPA, one of his favorites. "Love to, but I'm on duty. Gillian?"

"Thanks, it's a little early."

Raymond narrowed his eyes, "Never too early for a brewski." He set his work boots down with a thud and rested his arms on the table. He was tall, over six feet, with a stocky frame. His jeans were faded and ripped, but he hadn't bought them that way. His white T-shirt was splattered with food stains.

Pascal and Gillian took seats across from Raymond.

"What do you make of Bobby's disappearance?" Pascal asked.

Raymond shook his head. "It's weird. I've known Bobby for a while, and up and disappearing is not his usual M.O. But I got to say, he hasn't been himself since he came out here with Miss Jessie."

"Miss Jessie?"

"Yeah, she's a piece of work. Wouldn't touch her with a ten-foot pole. Not that she isn't easy on the eye but still a piece of work—strictly hard labor." Raymond took another swallow of beer and leaned his chair back again.

Pascal let the remark go. "In what way was he not himself?"

"Secretive. Like Monday night before he disappeared, we were going to hang, watch a movie, drink a few beers. We had the place to ourselves 'cause the crew was off. Jessie, being Miss Jessie, wanted to go to the casino. She whined and moped, but Bobby didn't cave for once. She stomped off with two of the extras. But as soon as she left, Bobby begged off, said he needed to do something. He got back late that night. I know 'cause their fight woke me up. Miss Jessie was super pissed."

"Did you see Bobby the next morning?"

"Yeah, he and Jessie were in here having breakfast, but I was busy cooking. He left before I could talk to him."

"Did he mention where he was planning to go that morning?"

"No. You might ask Jessie."

"What do you know about a helicopter surveillance around here?"

"Helicopter surveillance?"

"We went out to Hagan to look for Bobby, and this G.I. Joe swooped down in a chopper. He was dressed all camo and was packing. His nametag said Wegman. The guy had an attitude. Said we were trespassing."

"Well, technically you were. Hagan's ranch property and posted. But hey, if you want to explore the ghost towns, you can hire the New Mexico Jeep Tours. They have a contract with the ranch."

"Raymond, we want to find Pilot."

"Yeah, sorry. His disappearance is sort of weird. Can't believe he hasn't shown up or at least called."

"What about the surveillance?"

"I wouldn't think the ranch would bother to hire a helicopter patrol. This isn't Fort Knox or something. If you want, I could ask around."

"Thanks. That would help. Is there anything else you could tell us about Bobby?"

"Pilot's a thinker, a planner. He's not a spur-of-the-moment kind of guy. If he was going somewhere, meeting someone, it's what you probably refer to in your field as premeditated. He does have a dark side, though. Something unsettled in that boy."

"Thanks again."

"Hey, no problem, always enjoy hanging with Pilot. He's a cool dude."

Pascal took out his card. "If anything comes to mind, give me a call. Also, if you find out anything about the surveillance."

As Pascal and Gillian made their way to the car, Jessie rushed out of the house after them. "Hey, you leaving already?"

"We have to get back to Santa Fe," Pascal said.

She stood on the porch, hands on her hips, puckering her lips into a pout. Gillian suspected it was an act.

"Did Bobby tell you where he'd been the night before he disappeared?" Pascal asked.

"He was so wired when he got back. He was supposed to hang out with Raymond that night but took off after I left for the casino. He was psyched up about the article he was going to write on the procession to Chimayó. Something about making a connection. But I was still pissed and wouldn't listen. And now he's missing. Maybe hurt or . . ." Jessie's doe-like eyes filled with tears. "Do you think it's my fault?"

Pascal shrugged. "We'll be in touch, Jessie."

~15~

THEY LEFT THE RANCH, AND AS PASCAL PULLED ONTO THE county road, he stopped the Jeep. He motioned with his chin. "Tonque Pueblo."

Gillian stared out the window and squinted at the barren landscape but could only discern the same monotonous desert scrub everywhere. Something seemed familiar, though. Then she remembered the painting, the one at the Phillips Gallery in Washington. It was a late Sunday afternoon, and she had drifted away from her father for a private moment with her favorite artist, Paul Klee. The Klee room had become her refuge over the years, the playfulness of his work comforting her. Outside the Klee room, a small landscape caught her eye. Not recognizing it, she looked more closely. She took in the barren topography and glanced at the brass plate: Santa Fe Sunrise. This was where her mother lived.

Pascal looked over at Gillian and wondered what she was thinking. She was staring out the window as if she had seen a ghost. He reached over and touched her arm, and she let out a yelp. "We still have a few hours of daylight. Since we're here, let's check out the pueblo. Cross it off our list. I'm sure GI Joe doesn't have jurisdiction on the reservation. With luck, we won't be apprehended."

"Oh, that's reassuring." All she wanted to do was go home and soak in a hot tub, get the dust off. She had had enough of the boonies for one day. Although Santa Fe wasn't much of a city, at least it didn't have rattlesnakes. At least, she hoped it didn't. Ever since she arrived in New Mexico, she had felt trapped in the Twilight Zone. Any minute, Rod Serling would appear and provide a suitable moral for the story, then her life would snap back to what it had been before.

Pascal turned off the road and steered the Jeep down into a gully where it would be out of sight. Gillian opened the door and held Birdie with a tight grip. The dog started to whine and trembled in her arms, Gillian worried she would drop the dog. As she set Birdie on the ground, the dog tugged at her leash. "Jesus, you think it's a snake?"

"Most likely, she's picked up the scent of a rabbit, maybe a coyote."

"Coyote?"

"Keep hold of her. If she gets loose, it'll be impossible to find her out here."

Gillian picked up the dog again and tried to subdue her. The dog squirmed and dug her claws into Gillian's arms. Gillian gave up and let Birdie tumble to the ground but kept a tight hold on the leash with both hands. She was amazed that a twenty-pound dog could be so strong.

As they made their way along the ridge, Gillian kept her head down, careful where she stepped. Birdie continued to yank at the leash, pulling her off balance. Thoughts of the last couple of months, everything that had happened since she'd arrived in New Mexico, swirled in her head. The events seemed surreal. She had helped recover a stolen violin, rescued her sister from a religious cult, and experienced her mother's death. Now she was in the middle of nowhere helping look for a man who had disappeared. Her life had become a soap opera.

Finally, they came to an opening with a steep slope leading to the bottom of the canyon. Birdie had settled down and stopped whining, but periodically, she caught a scent, darted left and right and yanked Gillian's arms almost out of their sockets.

The trail down into the canyon was worse, covered with loose rocks that made her boots skid and slide. The sticker weeds pulled at her jeans, and the burrs stuck in Birdie's paws. As she tried to pull them out, they pricked her fingers, drawing blood. Once a sticker was removed, the dog would take off. As Birdie's speed increased, the ground below Gillian's feet became a blur, and she had to concentrate to stay upright. At the bottom of the ravine, she tripped and fell, and the leash slipped from her hand. Birdie stopped, looked back at Gillian splayed on the ground, and ran.

"Fuck!" Gillian yelled as she watched the dog get away for the second time that day.

Pascal, twenty yards ahead, turned around as the dog raced past him. "Birdie," he yelled. But the dog was gone.

~16~

PASCAL BENT DOWN AND OFFERED HIS HAND TO GILLIAN, WHO sat in the dirt with her legs spread out in an unlady-like fashion. Although he said nothing as he pulled her up, she detected an irritated squint. She was humiliated, but worse, she was panicked. Her breath was shallow as her heart thumped in her chest. She couldn't imagine how they would ever be able to find Birdie out there. The dog would be lost forever, lost to snake bite, to coyote fodder, or merely withering away from starvation and exposure to the elements. What would she tell her sister, Hallie? Pascal was right: She never should have brought the dog along.

Pascal felt justified in his irritation. After all, Gillian was the one who had insisted on bringing the damn dog, and she was the one who had let the dog get away. Twice. But Pascal took pity on her. He could see she was upset, so he offered a helpful suggestion. "Let's see if we can follow her tracks?"

"Really?" Gillian said.

Pascal knew there wasn't a chance in hell that they could track the terrier out there where its paws would not leave an impression in the hardened dirt.

"We can try."

Gillian scrambled behind Pascal, who marched along with his head down as he pretended to search for signs of tracks in the dirt. On his tenth birthday, his father had given him the book Animal Tracks and Scat. Throughout his childhood on hikes, he had been obsessed with identifying animals that had been there before him. Pascal kept a life list of animal tracks tucked in a book on his bedside table. It had been used so often that the binding was frayed and the pages had become dislodged. His mother had rebound it with a new cardboard cover, and Pascal, when he was about twelve, decorated it with magic marker drawings of animal footprints.

As they walked, Pascal periodically held out his arm and motioned for Gillian to stop. They strained their ears for any whines, barks, or growls, but a stillness blanketed the area. It was as if the dog had vanished into thin air. As they moved deeper into the canyon, Gillian's worry increased with each step. She tried to wipe away the tears rolling down her cheeks. She was glad Pascal was in front so he couldn't see her cry.

As they neared the canyon entrance, Pascal came to an abrupt stop, and Gillian, who had been looking at the ground, bumped into him.

"Maybe you should try and call her," Pascal said.

Gillian tried, but her voice came out in a croak. She cleared her throat and yelled the dog's name. They listened as it echoed off the canyon walls. Nothing. As they continued along the trail, Gillian glanced up at the steep walls on each side of the canyon. Though she suffered from claustrophobia, she tried to suppress the urge to turn around and run. She kept her eyes on the ground.

Pascal stopped for Gillian to catch up. "Look," he said as he lifted his chin to the north side of the weathered sandstone wall. "Petroglyph."

Gillian blocked the sun with a hand. Near the top of the ridge, she saw etched into the stone a faint squiggly vertical line that ended with a triangle shape at the top.

"Snake," Pascal said.

A shiver ran through Gillian, and she could hear her heart pick up the pace in her chest. She was a city girl and had no business out there in the middle of nowhere.

Pascal motioned with his chin toward a spiral carving closer to the canyon opening. "Water, maybe flooding."

Great, that's all they needed, Gillian thought as she nodded.

They took a few more steps and stopped. The faint sound of barking drifted from inside the canyon. It had to be Birdie. Gillian called her name, then screamed at the top of her lungs, "Cookie. Cookie. Cookie."

Pascal looked at Gillian as if she had lost her mind.

"She loves cookies, dog biscuits," Gillian stammered.

Pascal smiled, and they continued through the canyon. The barking became louder. Pascal knew they would soon reach the end of the canyon. Climbing up the ridge somehow was the only way out. He didn't remember any trail at this end of the pueblo. If they couldn't get out, they would have to hike all the way back. He hoped it would be with the dog. Clouds were building in the west, and Pascal knew that rain could turn into a flash flood. But in New Mexico, you took the rain without complaint, even if it was inconvenient. That was life in the high desert.

Gillian had a rock in her shoe and couldn't limp any farther until it was dislodged. She was ready for a break and out of breath as she tried to keep pace over the rough ground. Pascal stopped with his hands on his hips. He wanted to find the dog and get out of there before the rain started. He didn't want to have to negotiate Hagan Road in a storm. The mud would be challenging even with four-wheel drive.

Gillian seemed to take forever to untie her boot.

"Hurry up," Pascal said as he scanned the clouds.

Gillian narrowed her eyes and glared up at him but said nothing. She took off her boot and shook it upside down. A pebble hit the ground. As she shoved her foot back in the boot and started to lace it up, the dog again let out a series of frantic barks. Gillian jumped to her feet and ran toward the sound, praying that Birdie wasn't barking at a snake.

She and Pascal maneuvered around the last bend and almost collided with each other as they came to an abrupt halt. They stared in disbelief, their mouths open, as they sucked in breath and tried to wrap their minds around the scene. Birdie, a sandal clenched in her jaw, emitted muffled growls as she leaped in the air and circled a rudimentary cross. The cross, over twelve feet high, leaned at a low angle against the canyon wall. A man, privates draped in a loincloth, lay on the cross, wrists, ankles, waist secured. His white robe hung open and flapped faintly in the breeze. The man's head, decked with a crown of thorns, hung off to one side, eyes closed. One foot bore a leather sandal laced to the knee, the other was bare.

"Oh, my God," Gillian screamed. "Do you think—"

"Yeah, maybe"

Pascal figured it was Bobby Pilot, and the costume was the one taken from the Santa Fe Opera. But what was Pilot doing out there on a cross?

Pascal bristled. "Grab the dog."

Gillian cornered Birdie, yanked the sandal out of the dog's mouth, and secured her leash to a nearby bush. Pascal walked over to the cross for a closer look and released a breath he hadn't realized he was holding. At least, the man hadn't been nailed to the cross, only tied with twine. Pascal hoped he wasn't dead, but the look of his ashen skin didn't bode well.

The top of the cross lay against the canyon wall about ten feet off the ground. Pascal figured the weight of the cross with the man had to be at least three hundred pounds. He had his doubts but thought they should at least try to get it down to the ground.

Pascal turned to Gillian. "We either have to get the man off the cross or pull the cross down to the ground."

Gillian didn't meet Pascal's gaze. She felt hollowed out. There was no way they could move the cross, but she knew Pascal would want to try. "Okay." She wiped the sweat from her hands on her pants and positioned herself at the bottom of the cross.

Pascal's insides vibrated and his mouth went dry as he walked to the other side of the cross and bent down. "Okay, on three, pull. One, two, three—pull."

The cross didn't budge. Pascal ignored the familiar spasm in his lower back, breathed into it.

They tried three times with the same result. The cross didn't move.

"Why don't I shimmy up and untie his foot?" Gillian blurted out.

Pascal swept his arm around as an invitation for her to go ahead. Gillian noticed the doubt in his eyes, and that was all she needed to secure her resolve.

As a teenager, she had climbed her share of trees. Her favorite was a huge poplar that had grown too quickly with the abundant Maryland rains. The tree dwarfed their entire front yard. She would climb as far as she could and nestle in the uppermost crotch. There, she hunkered down for hours and scanned the neighborhood until her father called her in for the night.

But she realized a cross wasn't a tree. There weren't any branches to grasp and, unlike bark, the bare wood would be slick. But she was athletic and had shimmed her share of poles in gym class. The cross lay at an angle and wasn't upright, but still, it was off the ground. The boards were narrow, not more than eight inches wide. She somehow had to find room on them to climb without jabbing a knee into the man.

Gillian reached up as high as she could and took hold of the cross. Her pulse thumped in her neck as she slowly pulled herself up to the man's feet. The difficulty, she soon realized, was how to suspend herself while she undid the twine. She examined the knot that secured his ankle and saw that the rope was loose, barely tied. She chewed on her inner cheek as she tried to make her fingers work. Once she released his leg, it swung off the cross at an awkward angle. Her stomach curdled as she tried to haul the man's leg back on the cross, but it slipped off.

Gillian steadied herself as her stomach continued to sour. A wave of dizziness came over her. The man might be dead. She had never seen a dead person except her mother. And that had been in a lovely hospice room with muted sunlight that bounced off daisy-colored walls. She studied the man and wondered how long he had been tied up there. What was he doing out there in the middle of nowhere?

"What's wrong?" Pascal asked, crossing his arms.

Gillian scowled at him and wanted to scream that she was hanging on next to the feet of a strange man who'd been crucified on a cross in an abandoned pueblo and was possibly dead. But she turned away and steadied herself. "Catching my breath." She wondered what had made her volunteer for this task. After all, Pascal was the detective. He was used to dead people. How was it that she found herself in these bizarre situations?

Gillian raised her head toward the man's face. She was surprised how young he looked, probably in his early 20s. She noticed that his waist had been secured with thick twine wrapped around the cross, to either keep him from falling or make sure he didn't get away. Gillian steeled herself as she shimmied up farther. There was nothing to hold on to except for the man, who was barely clothed in a ridiculous loincloth.

She tried to distract herself with thoughts of Pascal down below with his phone, making videos of her ascent, posting them on Instagram. She reached up and grabbed the man's robe and used it to pull herself up toward the middle of the cross. She didn't want to touch him. Her stomach continued to gurgle uncomfortably as she took in the man's lifeless skin and its muted greenish un-lifelike tint. Not a good sign, she thought. Once she had pulled herself to the center of the cross, she stopped to rest again.

"See if he has a heartbeat," Pascal said.

It was all Gillian could do not to scream. "Really?"

"Put your head on his chest, left side. If he's dead, we can leave him and contact the police."

Gillian bit her lip as her stomach lurched, but she didn't have the energy to protest. She inched herself up toward the man's chest. Now she would throw up. She tried to choke back the bile that rose up her esophagus. She clamped her eyes close, laid her head on the man's bare chest and was thankful he wasn't the hairy type. His skin was smooth as a baby's, with only a few flaxen wisps. She held her breath and tried to concentrate as she strained to hear a heartbeat. A slight murmur deep in his chest cavity was barely discernable. She wasn't sure if she had imagined it but shouted down. "I think I hear something."

"Good, see if he's breathing."

"Breathing?"

"Wet your finger and put it under his nostril."

"Mary, Mother of Jesus," Gillian whispered under her breath as she pulled herself closer to the man's head. She tried to reposition it and pull it back onto the cross, but each time she released her grip, it flopped over to the side. She licked her finger, reached around and stuck it under his nose. A slight movement of air brushed her finger. Relief spread through her body as she sagged against the cross. The man was alive.

She looked at his tied wrists and realized that if she released them, the twine around his waist wouldn't hold him on the cross. If he fell to the ground, he would take her with him.

"I'm coming down," she said.

She steadied herself on the cross and reached up to move the man's head to the other side. She recognized him from the picture: Jessie's boyfriend, Bobby Pilot.

She looked down at Pascal. "It's Bobby Pilot."

"I figured."

"He's tied at the waist."

"Untie his hands first. Then when you untie his waist, I'll try to break his fall."

"What about me?"

"It's always about you, Gillian," Pascal chuckled.

"It's not funny."

"You'll need to grab onto the cross after you untie one of his hands. He'll probably swing in the other direction, give you more room to maneuver."

"Are you crazy? I'm not doing that. He'll dislocate his arm or worse. There's something wrong with one of his legs. It's at a weird angle."

"Want me to come up?"

"No. I'm coming down. We need to get help. If he falls, it might finish him."

Gillian shimmied down the cross much faster than she had gone up.

"We'll have to backtrack to the car or head toward the ranch. I think the ranch is closer; we might even be able to pick up cell service once we're out of the canyon."

"I think one of us should stay here with Bobby," Gillian said.

Pascal looked at her, surprised. Although he didn't think she could find her way to the ranch, he couldn't believe she would stay out there with an almost-dead man hanging from a cross. "Should we flip a coin?" he said, flashing her a smile, the one he used when he already knew the answer.

"You go, Pascal, you know this area. Birdie and I'll stay here."

Pascal looked over at the terrier, who was splayed out like a squashed lizard, her head resting on her stubby front paws. He didn't think the dog would be much protection but at least, she had a good bark. "Are you sure, Gillian?"

Pascal had left his gun in the SUV's glove compartment. He hadn't considered needing it but now wished he could have left it with Gillian. He reached in his jacket pocket. His hand closed around the wooden handle of the knife Celeste had given him when he graduated from the Sorbonne. The knife wasn't an ordinary knife. It was one of France's best, a Forge de Laguiole. The blade was forged of French steel with a polished finish. Celeste had it engraved for him. He thought about the day she'd given it to him. She had leaned in, enveloped him with her jasmine scent, and whispered in his ear, "Un homme a besoin d'un couteau." Whenever he held the knife, it was always with regret. Their relationship had unraveled soon after that. The knife was the only thing he had brought back from France. He pulled it out and handed it to Gillian.

"What am I supposed to do with that?" Gillian said.

"Protection."

Gillian squinted at Pascal in disbelief.

"It's all I got, babe."

He gave her a quick demonstration of how to open and close it, as well as secure it for use without cutting off a finger.

Gillian tentatively took the knife. "Please go before I change my mind."

As she watched him disappear, the canyon seemed darker, cast in a shadow. She shivered involuntarily. For the second time in less than an hour, she had made a rash decision. She looked up and was relieved that it was only a cloud blocking the sun, muting the light temporarily. Then she glanced up at Bobby Pilot on the cross, and her stomach flip-flopped. She felt she might be sick now that she was alone. She wondered if whoever did that to Bobby would come back before Pascal did.

His knife was still in her outstretched hand. She looked down at the exquisite tool but couldn't imagine it would provide much protection. The smooth wood did comfort her as she ran her fingers over the handle. She could tell the handle was made of some kind of rare wood, not your usual walnut or maple. She pushed the button as Pascal had demonstrated. The knife easily snapped open to reveal a shiny metal blade. When Pascal showed her how the knife worked, she hadn't noticed the engraving on the blade. It was in a tiny decorative font that caused her to squint. "Sois à moi pour toujours."

Gillian knew Pascal had lived in Paris when he attended the Sorbonne. It seemed likely he had a girlfriend, and a pang of jealousy hit her. Then Birdie released a series of barks, and she let out a yelp. The dog stood on her short hind legs and tugged at the leash tied to a bush. Gillian untied her and sank to the ground. She bundled up the dog in her lap and nuzzled the back of her neck. They would have to cope somehow.

Gillian prayed Bobby wouldn't die before Pascal got back with help. How would she ever forgive herself? She worried about how they would get Bobby off the cross. And how could they get him out of the canyon?

Now that she was alone with Bobby, the thought of him hanging from the cross became unbearable. She wanted somehow to make him more comfortable, but how?

~17~

P ASCAL MADE SLOW PROGRESS THROUGH THE CANYON AS HE stumbled over the rough ground. He wished he was in better shape—too much time at a desk. He vowed to start an exercise program. Gillian, a runner, was far more fit. She could easily have made it to the ranch in half the time. That is, if she knew the way. Although it had been years since he had visited Tonque, the way out of the canyon was like second nature. He could find the way to the ranch with his eyes closed.

As he climbed the canyon wall, Pascal stopped periodically and held his cell phone as high as possible, hoping to pick up reception. But each time he looked at the screen, there wasn't a single bar. When he had almost reached the top and could see the road, he heard the sound of a helicopter in the distance. Pascal scrambled up on his hands and knees as fast as he could. The chopper headed toward him, but as it came closer, it swooped north toward the ranch. He ran, waved his hands frantically, and screamed at the fading image.

Pascal bent over, hands on his thighs, trying to catch his breath. He held his phone in the air. One bar. He punched 911, but before it rang, the bar disappeared and the "no service" message flashed across the screen. He tried again with the same result. He ran full out down the road for about fifty yards, stopped, raised the phone and saw two bars. He dialed the number again. This time he was connected. He identified himself and his location, but as he started to explain that a man was injured, the line went dead.

Maybe the operator had received the information, but unless an emergency medical helicopter was sent, it would take hours before help arrived. He sprinted ahead toward the ranch but stopped every fifty feet to check for cell service. The next time he raised his phone, two bars lit up. He dialed 911 and was connected. The operator methodically asked a series of questions. Pascal interrupted her and screamed that this was an emergency. The operator calmly replied that yes, it was an emergency, since he had placed a 911 call. As he tried to explain that he had already called, the bars disappeared, and once again he was disconnected. He knew his efforts were fruitless. The operators were trained to follow a script and never deviate. They were calm, composed, unruffled collectors of information about violence, injury, and death.

As Pascal dialed 911 for the third time, he prayed the cell reception wouldn't break up. Once connected, he explained who he was, where he was, and what had happened. The operator assured him that she would notify the authorities but wanted him to remain on the line. He pleaded with the woman, insisting that he needed to return to the injured man. But she was adamant. She could not send help unless he remained on the line. Pascal said the cell service in the area was unpredictable, and they could be disconnected any minute. But the operator assured him she would know the difference between an intentional disconnect and service unavailability. Pascal could not believe this woman. Who the hell was she—God?

He gripped the phone tightly as he fantasized about how he would choke the operator to death. Then he heard the copter again and saw that it was headed directly down the road toward him. He figured it had to be Wegman, the surveillance guy who had chased Gillian and him out of Hagan earlier. He would have much preferred the medevac copter but knew that would take at least another half hour to arrive. At this point, anyone would be better than nothing.

He waved his hands in the air and yelled. Then he told the operator that a surveillance helicopter was approaching. He would still need medical assistance for the injured man—that is, if he wasn't dead. The operator assured him she had alerted the authorities including the University of New Mexico Trauma Center. Help would be on the way soon.

The chopper slowly lowered to the ground, smothering him in dirt and dust. Wegman jumped out and stood with legs splayed, hands on his hips.

"Where's your little lady friend?"

"Down there." Pascal motioned toward the canyon.

"The reservation? You guys seem to have made all the trespassing rounds today."

This guy, for the second time in eight hours, had infuriated Pascal. But he needed his help. "My friend's dog got away. We went after it, found the dog in the canyon. The dog led us to this guy tied to a twelve-foot cross."

Wegman laughed. "Twelve-foot cross?"

"The guy's unconscious." Pascal held up his phone. "911."

"Let's go," said Wegman.

"Wait a minute. I can't leave my friend down there."

"Get in. I'll put the chopper down as close as possible."

The last thing Pascal wanted to do was get in a helicopter with this cowboy, but he didn't see any other option.

As they descended into the canyon, Gillian looked up, shielding her eyes. Wegman turned out to be a skilled pilot and efficiently maneuvered the chopper through the canyon to land in the only available open space. The spot wasn't flat, but it would do.

Once on the ground, Wegman reached back and pulled out a fatigue-colored knapsack. "Let's go."

Pascal thought if he heard that phrase once more, he would strangle Wegman, but opened the door and followed.

Wegman stopped in front of the cross. "Jesus."

"Yeah, you got that right," said Pascal.

"Is he still alive?"

"Barely." Pascal nodded toward Gillian. "She climbed up and detected a faint heartbeat; breathing's shallow."

"We got to get him down, pronto."

"We already tried to move the cross. It weighs a ton. We considered untying him but didn't want to cause more injury."

"You were smart not to untie him. His leg looks a little wonky, probably broken or dislocated." Wegman studied the cross for a few minutes, then turned to Pascal and Gillian. "This is what we're going to do. The three of us will slowly and carefully pull the cross away from the canyon wall."

Pascal doubted, even with three people, they would be able to move the cross.

"The girl takes up the left front with you behind her and I'll be on the right. It's important, each time we pull, to get in touch with your inner strength." He looked over at Gillian. "Think like your baby has crawled up there and can't get down—she's terrified and crying. Mothers have been known to pick up cars to save their children."

Gillian thought, "Inner strength—bullshit." She was annoyed that this guy was such a sexist, but it did the trick. She was pissed. She took up her position and searched for her inner strength.

Pascal came up close behind her and whispered, "Your baby's up there."

Gillian whipped around and for a moment Pascal thought she was going to smack him.

Wegman took up the right side. "Pull when I say pull, stop when I say stop. Got it?" Gillian and Pascal nodded.

"Pull," Wegman shouted.

The three pulled and the cross started to move, but listed to the left. "Stop. Change sides."

As Gillian passed Wegman, he glared at her and said, "Honey, your baby's up there."

That did it. Now she was livid. This time when he instructed them to pull, the cross righted itself and miraculously inched down the wall. When it was halfway down, Wegman signaled for a break. Gillian couldn't believe that the man didn't seem tired in the least. She and Pascal were bent over, hands on their thighs as they gasped for breath. The sweat beaded on their foreheads and dripped down their cheeks.

"Positions," Wegman barked.

Gillian and Pascal took their places, and this time when he yelled, "pull," the cross slid the rest of the way down. Wegman grabbed his backpack and knelt down next to Bobby. "Untie his hands and set them at his sides, carefully."

"Let's wait for the EMTs?" said Pascal.

Wegman raised his head and shot Pascal a look of disdain. "Does this dude look like he can wait?"

Pascal looked down at Bobby Pilot and said nothing.

Wegman took out a pair of rubber gloves and pulled them on. Then he pried open Bobby's mouth to make sure nothing obstructed his airway. Next, he pulled a stethoscope from his backpack and began to move it around his chest. He reached up and lifted one of Bobby's eyelids. "Might be unconscious, but more likely he's in a coma." He next pulled out a plastic case, took out a needle and stuck it in the man's finger.

Gillian made a slight yelp and looked at Pascal with wide eyes.

The pinprick elicited a few drops of blood, but no response. Then he stuck the needle in Bobby's arm—again no response. Wegman took out a small flashlight, pulled Bobby's eyelid open, and flashed the light on and off several times. Nothing.

"Coma." He turned to Gillian and Pascal. "His pupils are dilated, no response to painful stimuli, no arousal signs to either movement or noise. Not sure of the cause. He's got dried blood on the back of his head, bruises and scrapes on his arms, so possibly trauma due to a fall. But we can't rule out drugs, especially with this outfit."

Wegman stood and stretched. "Let's get him off the cross."

Gillian didn't move. Her stomach gurgled as she looked at Bobby Pilot up close again. When Wegman stuck him with the needle, the bile had shot up in her throat.

Pascal had had enough of this guy. "This is a crime scene, and we've already disturbed it enough."

"The guy's alive and although unconscious, he can't be too comfortable." Wegman dug into his pack, pulled out two more pairs of rubber gloves, and handed them to Pascal and Gillian. "Don't want to mess up any prints."

Pascal and Gillian looked at each other but pulled on the gloves.

"We'll use his robe as a sling when we transfer him to the ground. We'll need the little lady's jacket for his head. Don't want his crown of thorns to fall off." Wegman chuckled.

Gillian glared at him. Not only did she dislike being called a "little lady" but she also wasn't thrilled about putting her mother's designer jacket under Bobby's dirt- and blood-soaked head. But her mother was dead and the jacket wasn't her style.

Wegman barked instructions. "Put the jacket under the man's head and hold on to the sleeves. When we start to move the body, raise his head and follow. Ruiz on the left, I'll be on the right."

Wegman and Pascal gathered up the robe material in their hands. Pascal was worried. He realized Wegman would have to lean over the cross to set Bobby down on the ground and somehow Gillian would have to keep in sync, trying not to break Bobby's neck or whack his head.

"You've probably seen this on TV." Pascal and Gillian stared at Wegman with blank faces. "You know—when they transfer the patient from the ambulance stretcher to the hospital bed. The important thing is do it fast but gently as possible. The slower the transfer, the more trauma." He motioned to them to get in position. "Let's go." Pascal gritted his teeth. It wasn't the smoothest transfer Wegman had done, but Bobby Pilot was now on the ground. Everyone was relieved.

But now Wegman could see that his leg hung out in the wrong direction below the knee.

"The knee's dislocated. Needs to go back in place. Better to do it while he's unconscious. It's extremely painful, but once you snap it back in place—poof—no more pain."

"I don't think that's advisable. You sure you know what you're doing?" Pascal said.

Wegman stared at Pascal with a blank face. When he'd come come back from Afghanistan, he was disoriented, adrift, as if the world didn't value him anymore. As an Air Force medic on the battlefield, he had been the one thing that stood between life and death. He knew he should tell this dick that he was a trained medic—it would make it easier. But it galled him, so he simply said, "Yes."

Pascal had his doubts about Wegman but didn't want to antagonize him. He didn't have much choice. He figured that if Wegman screwed up, Bobby wouldn't know the difference, at least until he regained consciousness.

Wegman crouched down and examined Bobby's leg. He was worried. It looked like it was broken somewhere below the knee, but he hoped it was only a hairline fracture. Without an x-ray, he couldn't tell for sure. But there weren't any signs of a more-severe break, like a bone poking out. The immediate problem was his knee. The patella had shifted completely outside its groove and needed to be returned to its normal position. Wegman had seen a knee on occasion spontaneously go back into place, but in most cases, the patella needed to be pushed back. He had performed the procedure numerous times on and off the battlefield. He would pop the knee back in place, then he could splint and stabilize the leg.

"I'm going to need an assistant."

Pascal got up from the ground and walked over.

"I need you to hold on to the thigh area. Not hard but I don't want it to move around. It's usually not an issue. What I'll do is take hold of his leg right below the knee and pull down gently toward me, then twist. The knee should pop right into place. Then we'll need to make a splint to stabilize his fractured leg."

Wegman looked over at Gillian, who held Birdie in her lap. "We need the little lady to stand by his head and let us know if there is any movement in the face area, especially the eyes."

Gillian again wasn't thrilled to be referred to as "little lady," but she set the dog down and took up her position at Bobby's head. She wondered what else she would be asked to do before this nightmare was over. She didn't want to look at Bobby Pilot. He didn't seem to have much life left in him. His skin had taken on an odd shade of ochre, and a few patches of dried, crusty scab had formed on his mouth. She wondered how he had gotten himself into this mess.

Wegman motioned to Pascal, who bent down next to Bobby and took hold of his thigh.

"Let's go." Wegman tugged the leg toward him and gave it a violent twist, which made Gillian yelp again. The knee snapped back into its socket.

"His eye lids fluttered," Gillian said excitedly.

"That's a good sign. He's still in there."

Pascal found a suitable piece of wood for a splint. Wegman pulled out an Ace bandage from his duffel bag. They secured Bobby's leg to the splint. Sirens could be heard in the distance, and a helicopter circled above. There wasn't room for the medevac to land in the canyon, so the pilot lowered the chopper on the ridge above them. Two EMTs jumped out and scrambled down the canyon wall.

"Hey, Wegman. Beat us again."

"Yeah, Martinez. Wasn't in my playbook but on my way back to Diamond Tail and this guy," he hooked his thumb toward Pascal, "was waving his arms, yelling like a banshee."

"What do we have?"

"As you can see, Jesus."

Martinez and Johnson, the other EMT, looked at Bobby Pilot. They had seen about everything in their job, so they weren't fazed.

"Signs of a coma, suspected leg fracture, dislocated knee but no worries, popped it back in while we waited for you yahoos," Wegman said.

"What happened?" Martinez asked.

"Your guess is as good as mine. Who's on the way?"

"San Felipe Tribal, Bernalillo County, state police. Maybe the FBI if looks like a kidnapping. Ought to be a real cluster fuck." Martinez turned toward Gillian. "Excuse my French, ma'am."

Gillian rolled her eyes. First "little lady," now "ma'am." She tried to subdue Birdie, who didn't like to be left out of the excitement. The dog struggled at her leash and lunged toward Johnson who was standing a few feet away.

"Yeah, you can add this Santa Fe dick."

Martinez and Johnson glanced at Pascal but got to work. "Get an IV going, Tony. I'll start the paperwork. He turned toward Wegman. "Brent, when we're ready to transfer this dude, you need to move your baby."

"Don't worry. Got to make Red Cloud before sundown."

Johnson scrambled down from the copter with portable IV equipment and began working on Pilot's arm. He had a hard time finding a vein but finally got the drip working.

Birdie let out a series of hysterical barks. Everyone turned and looked up at the opposite ridge. Four Tribal Police officers stared down; their faces revealed nothing. Pascal knew a few San Felipe officers but didn't recognize any of these. The four officers made their way down to the bottom of the canyon and stopped at the foot of the cross, then took in the man who lay next to it.

The San Felipe captain stepped forward. "Martinez?"

Nick Martinez looked up from his paperwork, walked over, and held out his hand. "Hey, Montano?"

"What's the story?" The captain asked.

Pascal walked over and joined the two men but didn't offer his hand. "Pascal Ruiz, Santa Fe Police Department."

"Santa Fe?" Montaño tilted his head as if he hadn't heard correctly, then waited for an explanation.

"It's complicated," Pascal said.

The captain pursed his lips. "Yeah, looks that way." He stared at Pascal, waiting for an explanation.

"Bobby Pilot." Pascal motioned toward the man on the ground. "He and his girlfriend were staying out at Diamond Tail Ranch. She had a part in a TV pilot filmed there. Bobby disappeared a few days ago. His girlfriend asked me to look into it as a friend—a favor."

"As a friend? A favor?" Montaño said.

Pascal decided it was best not to respond. "I talked to his girlfriend earlier today. She told me that Bobby left Tuesday morning to take some pictures out at Hagan. She hasn't seen him since. My friend and I drove over to the ghost town, looked around, but were asked to leave by this guy." Pascal lifted his chin toward Wegman.

The officers turned their heads toward Wegman.

"We drove back to the ranch and talked to Raymond Almond, who runs craft services for the film crew. He says he's a friend of Pilot but didn't have much information about his disappearance. After we left the ranch, we stopped on the county road to take some pictures." He jutted his chin toward Gillian, who was holding Birdie. "My friend's dog got loose. We went after her. Found the dog here. The cross was leaning up against the canyon wall, Bobby

Pilot on it, his arms and legs secured with twine. I went for help, flagged down Wegman's copter. The three of us pulled down the cross. Then the EMTs showed up."

The deputies looked down and exchanged glances, but their faces revealed nothing.

"What's his condition?" Montaño said.

"According to him"—Pascal raised his chin toward Wegman— "alive but in a coma."

Montaño turned back toward EMT. "Who else is on their way?"

"Bernalillo, State, maybe the Feds."

Montano mumbled under his breath, then turned and barked orders. "Candelaria, statements; Ortiz, evidence; Garcia, secure the area.

The three deputies scrambled up the ridge to the police cruiser and gathered their equipment.

Martinez turned toward the captain. "Sorry, but we've got to get this guy out of here, pronto."

The captain looked over at Wegman. "Move your chopper. Stick around. We'll need a statement."

Martinez scrambled up to the medevac—it was a much bigger copter. To move it into the canyon would be a tight squeeze.

~18~

THE DEPUTIES GATHERED THEIR EQUIPMENT, EASILY DESCENDED back down into the canyon, and began work on their assigned tasks. Candelaria asked Pascal to summarize the information given to the captain. He wrote down the main points, then asked a few more questions, and handed the statement to Pascal to sign. Meanwhile, Garcia sealed off the crime scene with yellow tape. Ortiz snapped several photos of the bare cross. He used a grid pattern to methodically move through the area, snapping photos and looking for evidence.

As Pascal handed the signed statement back to Candelaria, he saw Ortiz pick up something and examine it. The tribal police didn't take kindly to interference with their cases. Pascal respected that. It was their land, their case. But still, he wanted to know what the officer had picked up.

He motioned to Gillian and asked her to find out what the item was. She walked over to the deputy and reached in her pocket for a pottery shard she had found on the way to the canyon. As she held it out to the deputy, he had to transfer his object to his other hand. The officer examined the shard, handed it back, and told her she should return it to where she had found it.

Pascal didn't ask about the exchange when she returned. He was eager to leave before the Bernalillo Police showed up, or—God forbid—the Feds, who would want to know what he was doing on the reservation. He told her it was time to leave, and she gathered up Birdie for the long trek back to the SUV. As they exited the canyon, they saw the medevac make its way south toward University Hospital. They were silent, thinking of Bobby Pilot. Gillian mouthed a little prayer under her breath.

"What was the object?" Pascal said.

"The one I handed the officer?"

"No, the one he found."

"It looked like a film canister. You know pre-digital. It was black with a white label, but the label was torn. The only letters that were left were 'bayf.' "

Pascal didn't recognize the label, but it could be connected to whoever tied Bobby to the cross. That would be a task for Rupert Montoya. That is, if they were asked to help with the case.

"Okay, what did you hand him?"

"I'll never tell."

As they trudged along, Gillian took out the pottery shard and dropped it on the ground. Her thoughts turned to the prospect of a soak in a hot bath. The day's accumulation of dust and grime needed to be washed away. After that, she would search for some cheap plane tickets back to D.C. The stun gun attack on the violinist had been bad enough, but this crime spooked her. "Land of Enchantment," more like "Land of Entrapment." She plodded along behind Pascal and could kick herself. She had left her water bottle in the car. Her throat was parched, her lips on the verge of bleeding, and her eyes burned and watered. She tried to console herself; at least she wasn't hung on a cross left to ravens in an ancient pueblo.

Birdie was exhausted, but there was no way Gillian was going to carry the dog. She almost had to drag her. When they were back at the car, Gillian pulled the back door open, tossed Birdie in, and sank into the passenger seat before the terrier could jump to the front. Pascal got behind the wheel, leaned forward, and stared out the windshield. Gillian was about to ask him if he was all right when he said, "Let's make a quick stop at the Golden store."

Gillian groaned.

"Buy you a cool drink?"

Gillian closed her eyes and said nothing. She knew her behavior was unreasonable. The store was practically on their way home, and she would kill for a cool drink. She tried her best not to pout.

The mercantile parking lot was empty, and for a moment, Gillian hoped it was closed. Then she noticed a handmade "open" sign in the window. She wasn't about to be left in the parking lot, so she dug in her pocket for a dog cookie, gave it to Birdie, then quickly slammed the car door and followed Pascal into the store.

Gillian was surprised at the eclectic items on sale, a sundry offering of goods from snacks and soda to Indian pottery, jewelry, and even a collection of Southwest rugs. The building had thick adobe walls that kept the store cool and dark. Gillian had to admit the room soothed her after the dusty hike out of the canyon. She opened the cooler and leaned down as the icy air poured over her, then took her time rummaging around before finally pulling out two Dr Peppers. She handed them to Pascal, and he made his way to the back of the store.

A clerk sat on a stool behind the counter, chatting on his cell phone. As they approached, he ended the call and stuffed the phone in his shirt pocket.

Pascal set the two sodas on the counter.

"Three dollars," the clerk said.

Pascal reached in his pocket, pulled out his phone, and held it up to the man." Have you seen this man recently?"

The clerk leaned forward and studied the picture. "Is he in some kind of trouble?"

Pascal was annoyed that the clerk assumed or somehow knew he was a law officer. "No."

"Who wants to know?"

"I do." Pascal stared at the man with a blank expression.

"Yeah, he was in here Monday. Bought some water, candy. Never saw him before that, though."

"Do you know where he went when he left?"

The man hesitated. Pascal figured the clerk had the information, but whether he wanted to share it was another story. But Pascal sensed the man was the type who had trouble keeping things to himself. Basically a gossip.

"Was anyone else in the store that morning?"

The man sighed. "I don't want to get no one in trouble."

Pascal let the double negative slide. "I need to find this guy. His girlfriend's worried. They had a fight. Now he's missing. I wondered if you noticed which way he headed when he left the store."

The clerk stroked his scraggly beard and tried to look thoughtful. "Between you and me, right?"

"Sure." He figured this guy would probably rat out his grandmother for amusement.

"Marcos Alcazar was in here. He's a friend, a local. We were shooting the breeze back here when the kid came in. That boy acted a little suspicious, trying to eavesdrop on our conversation. But he paid for his stuff and left. About ten minutes later, I walked with Alcazar to the door. There was the kid in the parking lot near Alcazar's truck. I figured he wanted a lift. Not much traffic out this way. I watched through the window, and sure enough, the kid climbed into Alcazar's pickup."

"Do you know where Alcazar lives?"

"Half mile down the Hagan road. There's a small cluster of adobes on the north side, about where the road begins to straighten out—the only houses out there."

Pascal knew where he was talking about. It was supposedly a Penitente enclave. He paid for the sodas and thanked the man. Gillian was looking at the jewelry, but when Pascal motioned, she happily joined him.

Outside, Gillian said, "I wouldn't trust that guy."

"Yeah, bet he has quite the reputation around town. Before we go, I want to check the system, see if Alcazar pops up."

Gillian groaned, unable to suppress her exasperation. She grabbed her Dr Pepper and downed half the bottle.

"Five minutes?"

Gillian pursed her lips as she hugged her arms across her chest. "I don't know why you even bother to ask my permission. I'm your prisoner, your captive."

Pascal cocked his head, then turned on his dashboard computer.

Gillian thought, "Why can't I go home now—forget this day?"

The data bank gave Pascal an address for Marcos Alcazar but no phone number. Alcazar's record was clean, no arrests, not even a parking ticket. He wasn't in the system. Barely existed.

"Giddy-up, missy," Pascal said. He cranked the engine to life.

Gillian pursed her lips and squeezed her arms tighter around her chest.

~19~

THE HELICOPTER PILOT GENTLY LOWERED THE MEDEVAC ONTO the roof pad at University Hospital. The trauma team, ducking under the slowing blades, had seen almost everything over the years, but as they swung open the back door of the chopper, they stared at the patient's outfit. It wasn't just the loincloth, laced-up sandals, or even the crown of thorns on Bobby Pilot's head that gave them pause but the sparkly gold lamé designer jacket adorned with a leopard fur collar tucked around his neck. They merely raised their eyebrows as a doctor crossed himself in jest, but then they got to work. The team efficiently transferred the patient onto a gurney while Martinez briefed them on the injuries. Nobody bothered to ask what had happened—it wasn't relevant. Their business was to assess, treat, and fix bodies.

Martinez handed the written report to the trauma leader and made his apologizes. They needed to be on their way. There was an accident with injuries on the interstate west of Grants. The team maneuvered the gurney into the building as the copter's engines were cranked up.

They had tried to conceal the patient's outfit with a small sheet over his midsection, but as they wheeled Pilot through the ICU waiting room, the crown of thorns and sandal were conspicuous at either end of the gurney. The waiting room was packed with family members and friends who had probably hung around for days waiting for updates on someone's condition. They didn't bother to avert their eyes as Bobby Pilot was wheeled past on the gurney. Some gawked.

The team leader gave the nurse an overview of the man's condition, then wheeled him into a cubicle. An aide struggled to untangle the crown of thorns from Bobby's matted, blood-soaked hair, then took off his outfit and sandals, and bagged them for the police. Machines were connected, and Bobby's body cleaned up a bit. A neurologist and orthopedist were paged.

James Martin had left the maternity ward where his wife had undergone a C-section the night before. He had been up most the night. His wife and new baby slept peacefully nestled together while he sat in a chair tapping his foot on the floor, unable to relax. When he heard the copter land on the roof, he rushed upstairs to the ICU. He was desperate for a diversion, and hoped to find out about whoever they'd brought in. You never knew when some material could spice up your novel, get you unblocked. He had taken leave from teaching high school to write a novel, and had done almost two hundred pages when everything came to a halt. He knew where he wanted to go with the story but .... He blamed his writer's block on the impending birth of his new daughter, which would result in his going back to teaching.

Martin had caught a glimpse of a crown of thorns tangled in the man's hair as the medical team maneuvered the gurney through the waiting room. He had noticed the man's foot, clad in a sandal laced up his bare leg. Easter was right around the corner. He wondered what the story was but figured whatever it was had to be interesting.

The ICU waiting room was packed with relatives and friends of patients. Martin tried to blend in and appear that he had a legitimate reason for being there. He took a seat in the waiting room and opened his magazine, Writing News. As he leafed through the pages, an article caught his attention. It had a graphic of Sherlock Holmes, hand on hip as he leaned forward and looked through a magnifying glass. The article advised writers to think like detectives. Holmes, whom many consider the prince of deduction, relied on inference to solve cases. In other words, Holmes observed, then offered an explanation for the details.

Martin tossed around what he had observed—an unconscious man dressed like Jesus. Tomorrow was Good Friday; the man probably was on his way to an Easter reenactment and had had an accident.

Martin was intrigued. He needed to find out about the patient. He was about to head back to the maternity ward when Marion Sullivan, his daughter's third-grade math and science teacher, came out the restroom door. He had spoken to her briefly at a school open house. Martin figured it was a long shot but went over to where she was sitting and staring at a pamphlet in her lap.

"Ms. Sullivan?" Martin asked. He took in the dark circles around her eyes, and a pang of guilt hit him. Although he knew she must be in her 60s, she seemed to have aged years since he'd seen her last. Tight gray curls hugged her face and made him think of a rope mop.

She looked up with a puzzled expression.

"James Martin, Emily Martin's father."

"Oh, yes Mr. Martin. Sorry—I have trouble recognizing people out of context."

"Understandable in your job, with all those little ones." Embarrassed, Martin didn't know what to say next but took the empty seat on her right.

She tilted her head toward a cubicle across from the waiting room. "My father. A stroke."

Martin nodded, ashamed. The woman seemed genuinely forlorn. He had intruded on her time of grief, and for what reason?

"I'm sorry about your father. My wife had a C-section. I guess I should say she had a baby. All is well, but she has two more days in the hospital."

"Congratulations," the teacher said without much enthusiasm. "I guess a baby is one of the few happy things you visit a hospital for."

"Emily is excited to have a new sister. We had hoped they would be born closer together but. . . ."

"Yes. Things don't always end up how you plan. I probably won't still be a teacher when your new one is ready for the third grade." She gave Martin a weak smile. "But you never know."

He took in Ms. Sullivan's wan appearance and was certain she wouldn't be his new daughter's third-grade teacher. "I heard a helicopter land on the roof. I hope there wasn't a bad accident on the freeway."

"Oh dear, they brought in some poor young man," she said, hesitating and glancing around to see if anyone else could hear, then leaned in toward Martin. "Dressed weird, like Jesus, you know when the Lord was nailed to the cross. He even had a crown of thorns on his head."

"Dressed like Jesus? That is weird. Maybe he was in some kind of reenactment play. Easter's on Sunday. I wonder what was wrong with him?"

"One of the nurses was giving me an update on my father's condition when they brought him in. The doctor interrupted the nurse and told her about the man's condition. The nurse excused herself to tend to the man." She pointed toward a room with its curtain pulled closed.

Martin raised his eyebrows. "Gee—hope the guy's okay."

"I didn't understand all the medical jargon, but apparently, the young man suffered a head injury. He's in a coma. Also has a broken leg. My guess is it's an accident."

Martin thought he wasn't much better at deduction than a third-grade teacher. "Poor guy. Hope he didn't fall off his cross." As soon as the words slipped from his mouth, he knew his mistake. The conversation was over.

Ms. Sullivan, eyes bugged, shot him a horrified look.

"Sorry, sometimes when an accident happens, I get nervous and blurt out stupid things."

Several alarms went off, and nurses rushed to a cubicle. Ms. Sullivan looked over toward the commotion and hurried to her father's room. Martin noticed that most of the other occupants of the room stared down at their laps. They didn't want to witness someone else's sorrow. They probably would have their own to face soon enough.

Martin left the ICU. After that ridiculous blunder, he couldn't face poor Ms. Sullivan again—maybe ever. Emily would soon be in fourth grade, and he would be clear of the woman. She was bound to retire soon.

Martin searched the hospital directory for the administration office. It was on the seventh floor. He figured he could at least find out who was in charge of the case. That is, if it wasn't an accident but a crime. He pulled open the door of the administrative office just as a teenager in a volunteer outfit exited.

"Sorry," he said as he held open the door.

"No worries," the young girl said as she turned her head sideways and smiled at him.

"Hey, I noticed a helicopter brought in Jesus." He hoped the nurse's aide would think the comment was funny. Make him seem hip. He was relieved when she put her hand to her mouth and giggled.

"I dropped off his outfit." She turned and pointed to a bag sitting on an unmanned desk.

"Gee, what's the story?" He had blown it with Ms. Sullivan, but maybe he could get some information from the girl.

"Can't say." She glanced back nervously at the desk.

"Where did they find him?"

The girl leaned forward and whispered. "Out at some old pueblo."

"You're kidding?"

"Nope. The poor guy isn't awake yet."

Martin started to suspect it wasn't an accident. "Who's in charge of the case?"

"San Felipe Tribal, I think, since he was found on Indian land. But nobody's been here yet asking questions."

A stout woman dressed in a severe dark blue suit came in from a back room. She looked at the two of them and then frowned at the girl. "Yes?"

The girl pointed to the package on the desk. "That's the outfit from the guy they brought into the ICU. San Felipe Tribal is supposed to pick it up."

"And you?" she asked as she scowled at Martin, as if he had misbehaved during recess.

"My wife had a C-section. I wanted to check, make sure our insurance covers two more days in the hospital." Sometimes Martin was fast on his feet, other times . . ..

"Name?"

Martin could tell the woman wasn't convinced, but she sat down and typed in his name. Then she reassured him his wife and baby were covered for two more days. He thanked her and made his way to the elevator, hoping to catch up with the young girl.

He could almost taste a story. He knew it wouldn't help him finish his novel. But that wasn't going anywhere right now. If he could start writing again, putting words on paper, maybe use whatever happened to that guy in the ICU for a short story or an article—it could be just what he needed.

Now that his wife wanted to take a year's maternity leave from her job at Sandia Labs, he needed to support his family. They had a little savings left. He hadn't produced, and his time was up.

Martin had two more days at the hospital. If he could find out when San Felipe would pick up the costume, maybe he could get some information from the officer. For now, he would chat up the girl, buy her a coffee, and see what she knew. He saw the aide leaning against the wall by the elevator, staring at her phone.

~20~

ITWAS AFTER FIVE WHEN PASCAL DROPPED GILLIAN AND BIRDIE off at her house. She had been silent on the ride back to town. A few times, he had looked over, but her eyes were closed. He knew she must be exhausted, if not physically, then emotionally. The day hadn't gone how he had imagined it: a picnic in the country. He had wanted to spend some time with her, share something from his past, something personal. But instead, the events seemed to spiral out of control and ended up with Bobby Pilot unconscious tied to a cross.

He watched as she made her way to the front door. But as she turned, he couldn't read her expression. She gave him a slight wave before disappearing into the house. He reminded himself they were only friends. Although Gillian always seemed eager to do whatever he suggested when he called, once they were together, she didn't seem to be there. He wondered why he was so reluctant to make a move. Somewhere along the way, he had lost his courage. Maybe he was a little gun-shy after Madeline.

Pascal turned his car around and headed to the station. Although he wanted to go home and shower off the dust from Tonque, he was anxious to give a report to the captain, let him know he had found Bobby Pilot and probably the Jesus costume. As he entered the station, it was quiet and empty, and, as usual, dark. Susie, the receptionist, had turned down the lights so as not to exacerbate a migraine. She complained that the flickering fluorescents made her dizzy. "Where you been, gorgeous?" she asked, leaning over the front desk as she thumbed through a travel magazine.

"On an errand."

She raised her eyebrows as she handed him two small pieces of paper. "Ms. Aubusson, that opera lady, called for you. She's a grouch."

Pascal glanced at the two messages scribbled on torn scraps of paper. They were barely legible. "Has Office Max gone out of business?"

"Trying to do my part to save trees, detective." She tilted her head and smiled sweetly.

Pascal knew the truth: Susie had once again neglected to process the supply order for the station.

"The captain in?"

"Nope. The commissioner requested his honor at the Folk Art Festival down at the Plaza."

"Really?"

"Really. The captain has to say a few words at the opening cere-mony. You know how he loves making speeches? If that isn't bad enough, the commissioner asked for extra officers to mingle around, keep law and order. He wants a "strong visual presence" from the department. The captain has been grumbling all day about it. He looked like he swallowed a lemon when he left. He mumbled under his breath about missing evening Mass."

Pascal was disappointed. He would have to wait to give his report to the captain. He wanted to talk to him in person, and preferably not at the station, but definitely not at the festival. He knew he should go home and consider his "off-the-record" assignment com-pleted. It wasn't his jurisdiction, and he didn't have any business messing around with the investigation. But he suspected the Jesus costume Bobby wore was the one stolen from the opera, so he fig-ured it was sort of his jurisdiction. There couldn't be two crowns of thorns in New Mexico. He hoped the hospital would bag the cos-tume and save it as evidence. But with San Felipe Tribal in charge of the case, his involvement was complicated.

He decided to try tracking down the telephone number for Mar-cos Alcazar. Rupert was a computer genius and could find a needle in a haystack. He wished Rupert hadn't left for the day, but his desk was tidied up and his computer shut down.

Pascal scanned the cell phone database. No matches with the name Marcos Alcazar. Maybe the guy didn't have a phone. Who knows, maybe Penitentes, like the Amish, aren't allowed to own phones. Or maybe the phone is under someone else's name, a relative or girlfriend. Or maybe Marcos wasn't his real name. He searched the internet for Joe, José, or anything close to the name but didn't have any luck. He looked up the street addresses of the houses off Hagan Road near Golden. Then he did a reverse address check. Nothing came up with a match for Alcazar. Computer searches weren't Pascal's forte; they were his weak spot. He needed Rupert. Rupert was the expert.

He pulled out the messages Susie had handed him. Aubusson was demanding an update on the robbery. She wanted reassurance that everything that could be done was being done. The other message was from Wegman.

Pascal stared at the scrap of paper and considered tossing it in the trash, but out of curiosity, he punched in the number. He was annoyed when the call went immediately to voicemail. "Wegman, leave a message."

Pascal knew he was being childish, but this guy irritated him. He left Wegman a message: "Ruiz, call me."

Pascal was bushed, had enough for one day. As he headed back home, he passed a Lotaburger, did a U-turn, and pulled into the parking lot. After the holidays, he had sworn off junk food, but today's events warranted grease and calories. He ordered a green chile cheeseburger and large seasoned fries. When he got his order, he sat in his car, rolled down the windows, and ate. There was no way he would bring this food into his house. The smell would linger for a week and remind him of his digression.

When he finished his burger, he still hadn't heard back from Wegman. But before he pulled out of the parking lot, his phone rang.

"Ruiz," he said as he stuffed the last fry in his mouth.

"Wegman."

"Yeah?"

"I have information for you."

"Yeah?"

"Don't be a dick."

"Don't you," Pascal said, "Why would you want to give me information?"

"Hey, Ruiz, we're on the same team."

Pascal doubted that but was too weary to play any more games. "Okay, let's have it?"

"Not over the phone."

Pascal groaned under his breath. This guy was all cloak-and-dagger, too big for his britches. "Where?"

"Bernalillo."

This time, Pascal groaned loudly into the phone. "You got to be kidding."

"Nope. More later."

"I know it's a small town, but I need some directions."

"Call me when you get to 550."

The line went dead. Pascal held the phone to his ear for another minute. He couldn't believe the guy had hung up on him.

The last thing in the world Pascal wanted to do that night was drive to Bernalillo. Now that his stomach was full, he had looked forward to going home, having a beer, and watching a few episodes of Longmire. At least he had filled his cat's bowl that morning, so she wouldn't starve. But it might be her last meal for a while, the way things were headed. God knows what Wegman had up his sleeve.

Pascal turned down St. Frances Drive toward the freeway. While he waited at the light, he glanced down and spotted a CD on the floor. He picked it up. On the cover was a woman's profile painted in various stripes of color. The woman vaguely resembled Gillian, radiating that same unwavering expression. The album, Truckdriver Gladiator Mule, made him shake his head. He must be getting old, but he inserted the CD into the player and cranked up the volume. Something had to keep him awake. The eclectic collection of songs entertained him for most of the way south. One song would lull him into a trance, then the next would rock his bones. He had a new appreciation for Neko Case's music.

As the last song ended, Pascal had had enough of the freeway and turned off at the Algodones exit north of Bernalillo. He could wind his way south on the back road. Algodones barely totaled a thousand residents. He was amazed at the new home construction on both sides of the road. There wasn't much room to expand in this area, with the freeway to the east and Santa Ana Pueblo to the west. The area still had a rural vibe, but he could see the encroachment of Bernalillo on the south; now, the only way the expansion could go was north. The town was surrounded by several pueblos, not to mention the city of Rio Rancho, which had blossomed since the '70s.

Right before 550, Pascal pulled off into the Bernalillo High School parking lot and called Wegman. Again, the call went to voicemail. Pascal had to control himself not to throw the phone out the window. He had driven thirty miles. His eyes blurred with fatigue, and his right leg was numb from driving. He was beyond the ability to be civil. He left a cryptic message and fantasized about all the ways he would torture this man the next time he saw him. He decided to wait ten minutes max. After fifteen, he revved his engine and peeled out of the lot, screeching his tires like a teenager. His phone rang.

Pascal gritted his teeth as he almost spat in the phone. "Ruiz."

Pascal wasn't usually an impatient person, but this guy pushed all his buttons. He wanted to end the conversation before it got started, go home, and down a beer. He had had enough.

"Sorry. Needed to make sure no one could listen to our little chat," Wegman said.

"You mean tapping our conversation?"

"You can't prevent someone from tapping your phone because you usually don't know if they are. There aren't any sounds except an occasional click. I needed to put some measures in place in case someone's listening."

"That's reassuring?" Pascal was tired, and his head pounded. He wondered who in the hell would be listening but didn't have the energy to ask.

"Hey, no worries. Got a scrambler. It's a little cantankerous. Took a few minutes to get it activated. Sucks my battery like a hungry she-pup. I only turn it on when I need it."

"Need it?"

"Got to protect my source. It's not a perfect solution. It doesn't defeat the surveillance. The transcripts can be sent for analysis. The other problem is each phone you communicate with has to have a scrambler, and the phones have to be compatible. And I take it you don't have a scrambler."

"Yeah, you got that right. I am a member of the police force, re-member?"

"Yeah, I remember."

Pascal started to interject, but Wegman continued.

"So if my phone is tapped, what I say will be scrambled but your half of the conversation could be overheard and transcribed."

Pascal ran his hand through his hair. He had a bad feeling about this. All his instincts told him he should end the conversation, turn around, and drive back to Santa Fe. Again, he wondered why or who would tap his phone?

"My advice, say as little as possible. I'm only the messenger."

"Okay," Pascal snapped.

"It's not going to be easy. I'm sure you have a lot of questions, but for now, keep them to yourself. I'll try to address the pertinent ones." Wegman waited for Pascal to reply.

"Okay," Pascal snapped again.

"First off, I will tell you that I don't work for the ranch, the movie business, the Bernalillo Sherriff's Office, or tribal police."

"Okay." Pascal had to bite his lip to keep from asking Wegman who the hell he did work for.

"I will tell you that I was enlisted to monitor illegal traffic on Hagen Road. That's all I can say."

Pascal opened his mouth but before he could say anything, he was intercepted.

"Don't ask."

"Okay."

"San Felipe has their knickers in a twist. They suspect the Feds are behind my helicopter surveillance. They have made it clear they're not happy about it. But ...."

"But what?"

"But that's all the background I can share right now."

Pascal hoped he hadn't driven all the way to Bernalillo to hear about who Wegman didn't work for.

"I told you I have some info for you that may or may not be related to the Bobby Pilot incident out at Tonque."

"Incident." Pascal smelled FBI. When he got a chance, he would check with his source. Not that he cared who this guy worked for, but he just wanted to know.

"Over the weekend, I spotted a late model, premillennial, GMC van. You know one of those big '90s clunkers without windows. It was parked in the brush not far from Tonque off Hagan Road. It had some kind of faded signage on the side, but I couldn't read it from the air. Also, a New Mexico turquoise license plate, two letters and three numbers. Shouldn't be hard to track that down in your database if you have someone with a little technical knowhow."

"One sec. I'm putting you on speaker." Pascal pulled out his notepad and scribbled down the information on the van. "Okay."

"Unfortunately, before I could take a closer look, I was called off on another matter." Pascal started to ask more, but again, Wegman said, "Don't ask."

Pascal clenched his fists and imagined squeezing them around Wegman's neck but was intrigued enough to control himself.

"On Monday, when I started up the chopper, the check engine light flashed. The mechanic wasn't available until the next day. He had to order a part. It wasn't repaired until late afternoon Wednesday. I figured the van would be long gone but still planned to fly out that way on Thursday. But I got orders to focus my rounds on Hagan and the other ghost town. That's the day I spotted you and your little lady friend out there. After I asked you two to leave, I went to see if the van was still parked, but it was gone."

Pascal hoped Wegman had something more useful than the partial license plate of an old GMC van. He waited for him to continue.

"I ran into someone who might have some information for you, Elena Santiago. She's from San Felipe. Her husband and I were on a mission together in Afghanistan. When I returned, he asked me to check on his mother who lives in Bernalillo from time to time. He still has a few more months over there. I stop by at least once a week. Elena was there yesterday, told me she's training for the Golden Gate Marathon in Sausalito. She's a trail runner. Guess where her favorite place to run is?"

Pascal blurted out, "Hagan Road."

"My fault. I shouldn't ask a question if I don't want an answer. She runs from I-25 to Route 14 and back several times a week. Claims it's meditative, nothing to distract her out there—that is, usually."

"Okay."

"She went for a run on Sunday, planned to go through Tonque Canyon. But when she started down the arroyo, she heard voices, and went back up. Two men were dragging long pieces of wood into the canyon. She kept on the road until she hit Route 14."

Pascal sat up straight. It was a lead. But a risky one, especially since this woman was from San Felipe. That was a little too close for comfort.

"Did she . . .." Pascal blurted out.

"You'll have to ask her. But on Wednesday, she ran Hagan Road to 14 again. When she headed back, she saw two men load a bunch of stuff in a small car near Tonque Canyon."

"Okay."

"Elena trusts me. And even though her husband vouched for me, she wasn't keen to talk to you. I convinced her to tell you what she saw. She has a friend that has a yurt near the junior high on Camino Don Garcia. It's way back in the field behind the school. Her friend travels a lot, lets Elena use the yurt when she comes to town. Elena asks that you park at the school to avoid talk. Walk through the field toward the river. The yurt is nestled in a clump of cottonwoods. She'll be there for another half hour. You better get a move on."

"Okay."

Pascal hoped this wasn't a setup, but what would be the purpose? Unless San Felipe wanted to catch him meddling in its case. He punched in the address of the junior high on his GPS. It wasn't far.

When he pulled into the school parking lot, it was empty except for two pickups next to the gym. He wondered if one of them belonged to Elena or if she had run over from her mother-in-law's house. He parked next to a blue Ford truck and made his way to the field. He climbed over the sagging barbed wire fence and waded through knee-high weeds full of cheat grass that stuck to his pants. In the distance, he saw the yurt nestled under a patch of cottonwoods. Most trees in the bosque had suffered during the ongoing drought, but this group close to the Rio Grande looked healthy.

A dim light shone from the yurt's only window on the south side. Pascal knocked softly and waited. Elena opened the door a crack and peered out into the blackness.

"Pascal Ruiz." He considered showing her his badge but figured it would make her even more uncomfortable.

She opened the door barely wide enough for him to slip in sideways.

Elena was tall, close to six feet. Her body and demeanor were the epitome of a long-distance runner: strong, composed, and resolute. Her black hair, pulled tight into an efficient ponytail, hung halfway down her back. She was dressed in a light jacket and well-worn gray sweatpants, but her feet were clad in expensive running shoes.

She jutted her chin toward one of the two metal folding chairs near the door.

"This is a favor to Wegman. My husband speaks highly of him. He's been kind to my family. But . . ." she hesitated, looking down at her hands neatly folded in her lap. "I don't want to get involved. I don't want trouble. It's a distraction." She looked up at Pascal. "Everything has to be off the record."

Pascal nodded. "It would be awkward if I revealed the source of any information you share."

"Okay."

"Also, I also was asked to do a favor for someone. Bobby Pilot had disappeared, and his girlfriend was worried. They were staying out at Diamond Tail Ranch while she worked on a TV pilot. He left the ranch on Tuesday morning and hasn't been seen since."

Elena was quiet.

"Bobby Pilot was found out at Tonque Pueblo Thursday afternoon. He was alive but in a coma." Pascal paused, then added, "hung on a cross."

Elena's expression didn't change, but her eyes gave her away. He could tell the information disturbed her. She whispered, "Penitentes?"

"Maybe. Bobby was writing an article about the Easter procession to Chimayó. He had planned to walk in the procession on Good Friday."

Elena sat motionless. She didn't meet his eyes but stared out the window behind him. Pascal was amazed that someone who spent so much time running could be so still.

"Wegman said you ran Hagan Road on Sunday and Wednesday afternoon."

"Yes," Elena hesitated. Pascal figured she was deciding what or how much information she wanted to share. "I planned to do some hill work. Scale up and down the canyon ridges. Build up my stamina. But on Sunday as I got near Tonque, I saw two men drag some long boards into the canyon. I waited until they were out of sight, then went on my way."

"Did you get a look at them?"

"No." She shook her head. "But on Wednesday, I tried to add some hill work again. Before I went down the first incline, I heard some men near the canyon entrance. I scrambled back up to the road. Sometimes teenagers go out there to party, drink, take drugs. Although I've never had any encounters with anyone . . . . Elena looked down at her hands again. "I kept on toward Golden."

"Did you see anyone?"

"No, they were out of sight."

"Could you make out anything the men said?"

"No, but they were speaking English." She met Pascal's eyes with an impassive stare. "Not Keresan." The implication was clear.

"Why not Keresan?"

"Intonation."

Pascal started to say something but she added, "I'm a linguist."

"Did you keep running?" Pascal asked.

"Yes, when I got to Golden, I turned, started back down the road. When I was about halfway down that curvy stretch, past that cluster of houses on the north, I saw two men on the road near where you go into Tonque Canyon. They were loading stuff into a car."

"Had you seen the car on your way to Golden?"

"No. Might have been off in the brush or got there after I went by. When I run, I get in my zone, tend to block out my surroundings."

"Could you tell what kind of car it was?"

"Not really, looked old, small sedan, maybe Japanese."

"Could you describe the men?"

"I was far away but one was medium build, Anglo, with snow-white straight hair down to his shoulders; it glowed in the morning sun. The other was slim, taller, short dark-colored hair."

"How were they dressed?"

"Both had on sleeveless 'A' T-shirts like the gang boys wear. Miley Cyrus wore one in her 'Wrecking Ball' video." Elena suppressed a slight smirk.

Although Pascal wasn't a Miley Cyrus fan, he knew the type of T-shirt. In his line of work, he had come across plenty of wannabe gangsters who strutted around without sleeves.

"It was strange, those T-shirts, it was brisk that afternoon. The frost had melted, but there was still a cold breeze. I figured that to be dressed like that, those boys must have been high on something."

"What else did they wear?"

"Jeans, work boots."

"Could you tell what they loaded into the car?"

"Looked like some kind of equipment, boxes, lots of cords."

"What door did they get in, front, back?"

"The tall thin guy got in the front passenger seat and snow white the back."

Elena looked at Pascal, and a faint smile crossed her lips.

"So the driver already must have been in the car?"

Elena stared at him with a blank face. "You're the detective."

She did have a sense of humor, Pascal thought. "Did you see the driver?"

"No."

Pascal couldn't think of anything else to ask, so he gave her his card. "I appreciate you taking the time to talk to me. If you think of anything else, don't hesitate to call."

Elena stood and looked relieved that the interview was over. She walked Pascal to the door. As he made his way across the field, he looked back toward the yurt in time to see a tall figure sprint across the field and disappear into the night.

Pascal drove back to Santa Fe with more questions than answers. Too many loose ends swarmed around in his head. Wegman was a big question mark. Who the hell was he, and who did he work for? And why was he asked to keep an eye on Pascal?

Then there were the three men, the wood, the van, and their equipment. Not to mention the Penitente, Marcos Alcazar. So many loose ends that went in different directions. How could he sort them out? But truth be told, it wasn't his case.

He still hadn't talked to the captain. He needed to tell him about Bobby Pilot, Tonque, and San Felipe. But it was late, better to wait until morning.

~21~

GILLIAN STEPPED ONTO THE PORCH AND TURNED BACK TOWARD Pascal. She could barely lift her arm to wave goodbye. The exhaustion had seeped deep into the marrow of her bones and incapacitated her muscles. She had pulled open the front door with her last bit of strength. The relief of being home, even though it wasn't really her home, washed over her like a warm gentle wave. After the day's ordeal, she was grateful to be alone and not responsible for anyone but herself. A hot bath was in order, something to soak away all the dust but, more importantly, to erase the image of Bobby Pilot hung on that cross. She prayed she could wash away all the weirdness.

Her phone was dead, no chance to check her messages. The battery had run down after they left Diamond Tail Ranch. Pascal had a car charger but it wasn't compatible with her phone. Although she knew it was unreasonable, she blamed him nevertheless. It seemed to be indicative of their relationship—not that they actually had a relationship, although she guessed they were friends.

The last few months, she had worked her way, with Pascal's help, through her mother's extensive wine collection, not making a dent. But today, she needed something cold, refreshing, and loaded with calories and soothing alcohol. She hadn't remembered any beer in the kitchen, so she tried the pantry. When she opened the refrigerator door, it was packed with all sorts of refreshments, including two six packs of Santa Fe Pale Ale. She said a little prayer of gratitude to Zenaida, the housekeeper. The woman kept the pantry stocked and restocked. Miraculously, she appeared twice a week with bags of food and proceeded to make various dishes either ready to eat or packed in the freezer for later consumption. She somehow found time to clean, do laundry, and even listen to her sister Hallie's complaints, always available to distribute a reassuring hug. Gillian wondered how she would ever be able to return to her old life, the one where she was the caretaker.

When Gillian lived with her father, they rarely ate home-cooked meals. Her father, not the domestic type, never taught her to prepare meals. They survived on carry-out, frozen pizza, snacks, and a lot of peanut butter. They didn't have a housekeeper, so Gillian's sheets weren't changed often, and her clothes were only washed when she was down to her last pair of underwear.

She opened the beer and, not finding a pint glass, started drinking from the bottle. Zenaida had tried to compress a pile of mail into a neat stack on the kitchen counter. For weeks, letters had accumulated, unopened and untended. Gillian didn't want to deal with the sundry issues that had arisen from her mother's death. Before she tackled the financial situation, she needed time to process the death. Her stepfather, or ex-stepfather, Robert, had tried to walk her through the paperwork but had stepped back. He realized she needed time to grieve.

Birdie sprawled on the floor with her back legs stretched out behind like a squished lizard. She didn't even lift her head when Gillian opened her can of dog food. For the first time since Gillian had arrived in Santa Fe, Birdie didn't frenetically jump around and bark at feeding time. Gillian placed the bowl of food on the floor and nudged it in front of the dog's nose. Birdie lifted her head and stuck it in the bowl, not even bothering to stand.

Gillian upended her bottle of beer, grabbed another from the pantry, and headed down the hall to her mother's bathroom. The bathroom was enormous, at least twice the size of Gillian's bedroom at home. Next to the floor-to-ceiling windows sat a modern version of a claw foot tub. Although it was dusk, she could still make out the outline of the not-too-distant mountains. As she undressed, she shivered, not from the cold but from thoughts of the mountain range: Sangre de Cristo, Blood of Christ. Images of Bobby Pilot on the cross.

The tub filled while she examined her mother's scented bath salts. As she climbed in and sank down into the lavender infusion, water splashed over the edge of the tub. She held her breath and ducked her head under. The pressure hummed in her ears. Tranquility. Serenity. She wished she could stay under forever, oblivious. The sound waves traveled five times faster in water, eliminating the upper and lower notes. Sound in the air vibrates only the tiny ossicle bones in the middle ear. But sounds underwater are much louder; you feel them more. Visceral. She wondered what her violin would sound like under water.

Finally, not able to hold her breath any longer, she burst to the surface and gasped for air. The sensation was cleansing, expunging all the images of the day. As she soaked in the bath, she thought about her father. She hadn't talked to him since her mother's death, hadn't forgiven him. He had lied to her and she was still . . . what? She wondered. Although her father had recognized her musical talent early on, he had overlooked her flaw, her inability to commit to the violin, or maybe anything. Her father had doted on her in fear that she would quit, stop playing altogether. But his pathetic attempts had the opposite effect.

Then she thought of Pascal. Something had stirred inside her the first time she laid eyes on him. Even though the circumstances had been less than ideal, there was a connection, and she sensed it was mutual. But then her mother died, the case was solved, the violinist left on a tour. She was lost. She wanted to return home, but to what?

Her relationship with Pascal was stalled. Not moving forward, or in any direction except backward. She was to blame. She had told Pascal she hadn't planned to stay in Santa Fe and would return to Washington, D.C., after her sister finished the school year. But Gillian knew most men wouldn't let that stop them. They were hunters, after all. If a man had an interest, he usually pursued it.

Gillian felt stuck between a rock and a hard place. Although the D.C.-based Music & Arts Journal had published her article on the violinist, Mischa Zaremba, and it was well received, the publication had told her it couldn't keep her on staff unless she returned to the D.C. area.

But she had been appointed as the executor of her mother's estate and was stuck in Santa Fe for the time being. She looked over at her violin, concealed in its case, untouched, not played since she had disembarked from the plane in Albuquerque three months ago. Tears wet her eyes as the guilt and shame washed over her. Her commitment to the violin had always wavered. Sometimes she was obsessed, practicing new pieces for a month; then her interest waned, and she wouldn't pick up the instrument for weeks. She had a gift, and she let it rot.

~22~
Good Friday

IT WAS BARELY SIX IN THE MORNING WHEN PASCAL'S PHONE jarred him awake. Still half asleep, he cursed under his breath. Why hadn't he turned it off last night? There was nothing he hated more than the sound of the telephone jarring him out of sleep. To add to his annoyance, the phone wasn't within reach on his bedside table but somewhere across the room.

He staggered out of bed, rummaged through the mounting pile of clothes on the chair, and pulled the phone out of his jeans pocket. "Ruiz."

"What did you think I meant when I said to keep me informed?" the captain blasted.

When the phone started to ring, Pascal had been in midst of a dream. He was fleeing a helicopter on a donkey in the Grand Canyon. He couldn't make sense of what the captain was saying. He rubbed his forehead and tried to dismantle the cobwebs that clogged his thought process.

"Captain?"

"You got that right."

"Sorry, when I got back yesterday, you were down at the Plaza with the Folk Art Festival."

"Don't remind me, Ruiz. The bad taste is still in my mouth."

"Are you at the station?"

"No. I was woken up fifteen minutes ago by my niece. She was hysterical. Seems someone found her boyfriend, and he's in a coma at UNMH. Do you happen to know anything about that?"

Pascal could tell the captain was doing his best to control his anger, but as usual, the battle was quickly lost.

"I'm on my way, Sir."

"Dunkin' Donuts. Fifteen minutes. I need sugar and caffeine."

Pascal scrambled out of bed. He shooed his cat off the discarded heap of clothes. His sweater was covered in white hair. He tried to brush it off but knew it was useless. On his way out the door, he grabbed a role of duct tape. He would try the de-hairing at stoplights.

As he pulled into the Dunkin' Donuts parking lot, he spotted the captain's car. The captain had secured a table near the back. Two coffees and a dozen honey glazed donuts sat on the table. Pascal sat down and watched the captain stuff a third one in his mouth.

From past experience, Pascal knew that a wrong move could result in an explosion. He knew he was walking on eggshells. It took all of his fortitude not to pick up the cup of coffee and let the black liquid roll down his throat.

"I called Jessie last night, since I hadn't heard from you. She told me you brought your girlfriend yesterday."

"She's only a friend, Gillian Jasper. Remember? She helped out with the Stradivarius case?"

The captain nodded. "I know that you went to the ranch, talked to my niece, went to Hagan, were asked to leave by some surveillance guy, went back to the ranch, talked to Raymond. Let's begin there."

For some reason, even though the captain had asked him to look into Bobby Pilot's disappearance, Pascal worried that he was in trouble and had done something wrong. He had been caught trespassing on both posted land out at Hagan and on the San Felipe Reservation. But he had justified his improprieties since his assignment had been "off the record." Not to mention he was the one who had found Bobby Pilot. Maybe the captain would excuse a few transgressions.

"Bobby wasn't at the ranch, wasn't out at Hagan, and if he had been anywhere in between, the helicopter guy would have spotted him. If he was in that area, the only place we hadn't looked was Tonque."

"You and this Gillian girl took a little hike around Tonque and—bull's eye—you found Pilot?"

"Not exactly. As we made our way down into the canyon, Gillian tripped, and her dog got away. The dog found Bobby Pilot."

"The dog? Never a dull moment with you, Ruiz."

"When we found him, he was tied to a cross."

The captain automatically crossed himself and mumbled the sacrament under his breath.

"And he was dressed as Jesus."

The captain stared at Pascal. "As Jesus?"

"I'm sure the outfit was the one that was stolen from the opera. It fits the description. Pilot even wore a crown of thorns on his head. If it's the same costume, then the two cases are connected."

The captain was speechless for once.

"Pilot was alive but unconscious when we found him. Gillian and I tried to pull the cross down. The thing must have weighed three hundred pounds with Bobby's weight. Gillian stayed in the canyon with him, and I went for help."

"You left that girl out there all alone?"

"Didn't have a choice. There wasn't any reception in the canyon. She didn't know the way to the ranch. She had her dog. I gave her my knife."

"A dog? A knife?" The captain closed his eyes.

The story hadn't pleased the captain, but there was nothing Pascal could do about it now. "When I got to the road, I tried to call 911 but the reception was sporadic. Wegman, the surveillance guy, came along in his chopper. I flagged him down, and we flew back to the canyon. The three of us were able to pull the cross down. Wegman had some medical knowledge. He assessed Bobby's condition and administered some care until the medevac arrived."

"I guess some uniforms trailed the 911 call."

"San Felipe Tribal was first on the scene."

The captain squeezed his eyes shut, imagining the repercussions from this fiasco. As he opened them, he grabbed another donut and stuffed it in his mouth. Pascal worried that the captain, not the healthiest man, might go into a diabetic coma or have a heart attack before he could finish his report.

"Who else?"

"According to the EMTs, it was Bernalillo, State, and maybe the Feds. I gave a statement to San Felipe. Gillian and I left before anyone else showed up. The medevac took Pilot to UNMH. They probably bagged the costume for evidence."

"Is that it?

"I have some loose ends to tie up, some leads to follow."

"This is out of our jurisdiction, not your case, Ruiz."

"The costume?"

"You can call the hospital and check who has the costume. But I can't emphasize this enough: Tread lightly. Be respectful. Check to see if that Aubusson woman can identify the costume. If so, San Felipe might be willing to work with us, especially if we could be helpful but unobtrusive, stay on the sidelines."

Pascal knew he should leave it at that but wanted to mention one more thing. "When we left Tonque, we stopped at the mercantile in Golden to get a soda. I had a picture of Bobby Pilot on my phone that Jessie had sent me. I showed it to the store clerk, asked if he had seen him in the last couple of days. He said Pilot had been in the store on Monday. He had hung out in the parking lot and asked a customer for a ride. The customer lives down Hagan Road in one of the Penitente houses."

The captain raised his eyes toward the ceiling before he said, "That's it?"

"That's it." For now, Pascal thought.

~23~

I**T WAS SEVEN THIRTY WHEN** P**ASCAL LEFT** D**UNKIN'** D**ONUTS, NOT** enough time to go home and change. He pulled off another piece of duct tape and dabbed it across his sweater to remove the more-noticeable clumps of cat hair. He gave up—it was a losing battle.

As he entered the station, the lobby was dark as usual. He went over and flipped the master switch. The fluorescent lights were blinding. No one was at the front desk. He picked up his messages, then reached out and gave the bell on the counter a smack. He knew it was a silly thing to do. Susie, the receptionist, suffered from migraines, which were exacerbated by neon lights, not to mention noise. She poked her head around the corner.

"Easy does it with the bell."

"Sorry, Susie Q. Couldn't control myself."

"You have a mean streak, Ruiz."

He gave her a lopsided grin and went down the hall to his office. He groaned when he saw the pile of paperwork on his desk. It seemed to have doubled overnight, but he didn't have either the time or energy to tackle it today. And when was he going to get some help, when was his partner, Matt, ever coming back? Pascal needed to follow up on the leads before someone else beat him to it. But with this case, which wasn't even his, he needed to keep a low profile—at least until San Felipe let him in the door, although he doubted they would, even with the connection to the Jesus costume. Pascal was a visual person and liked to diagram the leads and the connections with color. But that wouldn't be possible with this case.

He decided to focus on the assignment from the captain—call Jessie and unruffle her feathers. It wouldn't hurt to have her on his side, especially if things blew up. Also, you never know where you're going to find useful information. It was still early, but since Jessie already had called her uncle that morning, she should be up. The phone rang several times, and Pascal was about to hang up when Jessie answered.

"Hello." Her voice sounded tired and hopeless, as if all was lost with the world. But she was an actress.

"This is Pascal Ruiz."

She exploded: "Why didn't you call me when you found Bobby?"

"I'm sorry about Bobby. I wanted to call when we found him out at Tonque, but San Felipe Tribal showed up and asked us to leave. It was their jurisdiction; they took over the case. Your uncle asked me to report to him first if I found anything out." Pascal knew this was stretching the truth if not a downright lie, but he needed her on his side. "It's terrible what they did to Bobby. I'm going to find out who did that to him. But I don't have a lot to go on, and it isn't my case."

"My uncle sort of told me that, but I'm still hurt."

Pascal thought it was nothing compared with the suffering her boyfriend had endured on the cross, but said nothing.

"I'm at the hospital with Bobby. He's in the ICU. They have an armed guard outside his door. It's scary. I'm so worried. They haven't let me see him yet."

"Do you know anything about his condition?"

"All they told me is he's in a coma but stabilized. Oh, and the nurse told me that if you hadn't found him, he'd probably be dead. I'm not a relative, so they won't tell me much. I made friends with Allen, the night nurse. He told me Bobby was probably given some kind of drug before they put him on the cross. They did blood work, but Allen went off duty this morning. The other nurses are tight-lipped, but I'm working on them."

"What about Bobby's family?"

"His mother's dead. His father lives in Santa Fe. A neighbor is bringing him to the hospital soon."

"Could you find out what happened to the costume Bobby was wearing?"

"Ugh, that costume. It's bad enough that they tied him to a cross, but I can't believe they put him in that silly outfit. It's ludicrous."

Pascal was sure Jessie could get whatever information she wanted. "A similar costume was stolen from the Santa Fe Opera warehouse last week. If it's the same one, we might have a lead on who did this to Bobby."

"Okay, I'll see what I can find out."

"Pretend it's a part in a movie. Or you could use your charm."

"Okay."

"Call me as soon as you find out anything."

Pascal braced himself for the next call. He dialed Catherine Aubusson, but the call went to voicemail. Nobody answers phones anymore. He left a brief message that a Jesus costume had been found, and wondered if she would be able to identify it as the one stolen from the opera. A few minutes later, Aubusson called back, sounding jubilant for the first time.

"You found the costume?"

"I'm sure. It's at UNMH in Albuquerque."

"The hospital?" she asked, bewildered.

"Yes, the man wearing it had been tied to a cross."

"Tied to a cross?" she sputtered.

"The man was transported to the hospital. He's in a coma." Pascal knew he shouldn't be sharing this information, but, as Susie said, he had a mean streak. "Probably the same pranksters that broke into the opera storage shed."

"Pranksters! I think you mean criminals," Aubusson said indignantly.

"Do you think you could identify the costume?"

"Of course," she snapped.

"Great, I'll be in touch." Pascal disconnected before Aubusson had a chance to respond. He mumbled, "touché, bitch!" and broke out in a smile. He did have a mean streak.

He hoped Jessie could locate the costume soon. That would be his ticket into the case. Without it, he would have to step back, let San Felipe Tribal and anyone else with a bargaining chip take the helm. In the meantime, he would operate under the radar.

~24~

WHEN MARTIN LEFT THE ADMINISTRATIVE OFFICE, HE WAS surprised to see the aide. She leaned against the wall next to elevator. As he approached, the girl looked up, raised her eyebrows, and whispered, "Sure could use a cup of coffee." Martin hesitated. He glanced around. It was one thing to inquire about a patient in the Intensive Care Unit when you were surrounded by people. But to walk down the hall with this young woman, not to mention sip coffee in the cafeteria with her, made him uneasy—especially since his wife was sequestered in the maternity ward with their newborn daughter.

Martin itched for a story, so he followed her into the crowded elevator. When they exited, he hung back and trailed behind. It unnerved him as he watched her long black braid swing hypnotically in front of him. She couldn't be more than sixteen, jailbait—but not that he would ever consider that. He hoped their encounter would not be misconstrued.

While she found a table, he ordered two cups of coffee and scanned the offerings for some decent pastries. The selection was limited—prepackaged donuts and cupcakes. Against his better judgment, he picked up a package of Ho Hos chocolate snack cakes filled with cream, which he had forbidden his daughter to eat.

As he set them on the table, the aide reached over and tore open the package. "I love these," she said as she stuffed one in her mouth.

"Tell all." He raised his eyebrows conspiratorially, knowing it was a silly gesture.

"Okay." She dabbed absently at the chocolate spread all over her mouth. "I clocked in, barely tied my apron when they wheeled in Jesus." She put her hand to mouth and stifled a giggle but then crossed herself self-consciously. "Ms. June, she's the head nurse, assigned me to the patient. Had to undress him, clean him up."

She stuffed another pastry into her mouth, and this time some of the filling squeezed out all over her hands. "I have to tell you," she glanced around before she continued. "He was bare naked under that loincloth." She grimaced and stuffed a third Ho Ho in her mouth. "I had a terrible time untangling his hair from that crown." Again, she absently crossed herself. "The poor guy, his skin was covered with dried scabs. No way would I be able to wash off all the dust." She closed her eyes and shuddered.

"Do you know the guy's name?"

"Sorry, not allowed to share patient's personal information. HIPAA regulations, you know?" She tilted her head back and raised her eyes to the ceiling. "They really stressed that. I don't want to lose my job. I'm gonna save for a new phone."

"I wouldn't ask you to jeopardize your job."

"Hey, I could blurt some words, you could put them together, like a puzzle. My friends and me sometimes do that when we want to share gossip about someone. It's a sin you know, to gossip."

Martin said, "Sure."

"The words would be random, you know?" The aide seemed pleased with her idea.

Martin was skeptical. He couldn't see how random words would be helpful, but he didn't want to jeopardize the girl's job. "Blurt away."

She looked around the cafeteria to make sure there wasn't anyone who could overhear. "Costume, pueblo, sandals, robe, cross, concussion, coma, broken leg, dehydrated, Percocet."

Martin already new most of the information, but the last word caught his attention: "Percocet?"

The aide said, "Mucho, mucho." She cocked her head toward a man who slowly had made his way across the room with a tray full of food. She leaned across the table toward Martin and mouthed in a stage whisper, "The father," then raised her eyebrows up and down like Groucho Marx, although Martin doubted she had seen any Marx Brothers movies.

The man, withered and much older than his years, seemed to take forever to find an empty table. Martin watched as he picked up each item off his tray, methodically arranging them on the table. His painstaking effort caused a pang of pity to wash over Martin. The man's pallid complexion and sagging shoulders presented a dismal appearance. His baggy pants were cinched tight around his waist with a too-long belt that hung down his side. Even from a distance, Martin could see a hole in the sleeve of his well-worn sweater.

Martin considered striking up a conversation with the man, but what would he say? He wasn't like his wife. She was the gregarious one, never hesitant to approach and chat up an utter stranger. His wife always came home from the grocery with a tale of some new person she had met while rummaging around for a ripe melon or a cut of beef. Martin, on the other hand, went to lengths to avoid running into anyone he knew, much less strangers. In the grocery, if he recognized someone, he would duck down the next aisle or sometimes dash out of the store, abandoning his half-full cart.

That's why he had chosen to be a writer, as the solitary activity of writing was a perfect fit for him: alone with his computer. Nothing calmed him more than to sit in his study with the muted light barely seeping in through the diaphanous curtains. His room was not much bigger than a closet, but it was his, and it had a calming effect, like a cocoon.

He decided to talk to Bobby Pilot's father later. The man would probably be at the hospital for most of the day. The officer would pick up the costume soon, and Martin needed to get back upstairs. He hoped he could work up the courage to talk to the officer.

Martin pushed himself out of his chair and thanked the aide for the information. She took out her cell phone, and he noticed it had a conspicuous crack that zigged and zagged across the screen. The aide smiled at him and then immediately became engrossed in her gadget. The younger generation! He shook his head with dismay. He'd better get busy and write something before print became obsolete.

The seventh floor was all business, rows of offices with closed doors. As he walked down the hall, he noticed there was nowhere to sit and wait. The last thing he needed was to run into the old bat from the administrative office again. She would be suspicious, might wonder why he was still there on the floor, maybe call security and have him removed from the hospital.

There was a small alcove at the end of the hall that housed soda and snack machines. He decided to wait there. He would be out of sight but able to monitor anyone who got off the elevator. He realized he didn't have a plan and wasn't sure what he would to do when he saw the officer. He would have to wing it. There was nowhere to sit in the tiny room, so he leaned against the wall opposite the machines. He took out his phone as a decoy. If anyone came into the alcove, he could hold the phone to his ear, pretending to talk to someone.

While Martin waited, he tossed around some ideas for a story. He always was able to entertain himself with imaginary characters and situations. He considered the bits of information he had discovered. The cross intrigued him. He wondered if the patient had been hung on a cross. And if he was, then how? Nails, ropes? Now that would be a story, especially with Good Friday tomorrow.

The annual Easter pilgrimage to Chimayó was under way. Hundreds of Christian devotees headed north and spilling onto the highways and back roads. Some even marched with huge wooden crosses on their backs. He had heard that Chimayó expected at least sixty thousand pilgrims during the Easter week.

Martin didn't know much about the Penitentes. There were rumors that some walked the Stations of the Cross and flogged themselves on their way to Chimayó. But those were only rumors. This story about the kid on the cross—if nothing else—might be the thing to get his writing unblocked.

For the past two years, on leave from his teaching job, he had worked on a dystopian novel. The story had stirred around in his head for several years, and the way the world was going, it was the perfect time for this book. The story was set in Washington, D.C., where society had become perilously estranged from nature. People were overly dependent on technology and the conveniences of contemporary life. His wife had teased that the story wasn't fiction but sounded like the current state of society. But he argued that the tale he wrote was much worse. The lights went out permanently, not a temporary blackout. People were left to cope without the basics like water, electricity, and food, and were forced to rely on themselves for survival.

Martin had been on a roll. He'd spent eighteen months cranking out two hundred pages, but then, inexplicably, two thirds of the way through the novel, progress came to a screeching halt. It wasn't that he didn't know where the story was headed, but he couldn't put any more words down on the page. He was frozen. He researched writer's block, even considered therapy. His wife recommended he put the manuscript aside and start something new, then come back to it later. But he didn't start something new. Nothing came, his head was empty—the page was blank.

Martin leaned against the alcove wall near the entrance and peered out each time the elevator dinged. The second time he heard the elevator door open, he looked out and saw two women deep in conversation walking down the hall in the opposite direction. He leaned back against the wall and checked his email for the tenth time. No new messages.

The elevator bell dinged again. This time, a man in a police uniform exited and walked toward the administration office. Martin was certain it was the officer from San Felipe. A slight burst of excitement, mixed with the familiar dread of an interaction with a stranger, made him wait. As he started to step out of the alcove, he heard the elevator door ding again. He peered out into the hall and noticed a man following behind the officer.

Martin was surprised. He recognized the man: a filmmaker whose avant-garde work he had seen in a preview at the university theater last fall. He had intended to review the film for the local paper, but the movie was really weird. After the show, the three filmmakers had come on stage for a question-and-answer session, which further muddled his understanding. He had struggled to write the review for several days but finally gave up. He tried to remember the man's name. It was German: Steg something. But there was no mistaking that snow-white hair and pale lifeless skin. It gave Martin the creeps to look into the man's colorless eyes. What was he doing here? Why had he followed the officer?

He watched as Steg walked past the administration office, hesitated, then moved toward the alcove. Martin quickly put his phone to his ear and pretended to talk. But before Steg reached the alcove, the door to the administrative office opened, and the officer walked out with a package in his hands. For some reason, instead of turning toward the elevators, he turned toward the alcove as Steg turned back around. The two men almost collided. They stood face to face for a few moments, then the officer turned back toward the elevator. Steg followed but got into the adjoining elevator which was going up. Martin found the incident bizarre. He still held his phone to his ear as he dashed to the elevator.

~25~

P ASCAL SANK INTO HIS OFFICE CHAIR AND GLANCED AT THE black clock hanging above the white board. It was identical to the one in his elementary school classroom. He suspected that the police station had acquired it as surplus when the school was renovated back in the 1990s. He looked at the scrap of paper where he had written a list of things to do. Susie hopefully would submit the supply order soon—if not, he would be taking notes on his arm. First on the list was Alcazar's phone number, which he hadn't been able to track down. The second item was the 1990s white GMC van with a blue New Mexico license plate, two letters, three numbers.

Computer searches were Pascal's nemesis. Not only did he dislike them but he also wasn't any good at it. Plowing through electronic files took finesse. Pascal had always found the process boring and tiresome. But if he didn't do something else, he would have to tackle the piles of paperwork on his desk. He logged into the DMV website and began a search for '90s vans. It amazed him how many there were. New Mexicans kept their cars forever, since the state didn't require any inspections for older vehicles. He narrowed his search to white GMCs, then tried blue license plates with two letters and three numbers, but nothing came up. He searched similar 1990s van models: Ford Econoline, GMC Ventura, Chevrolet's G series, and Astro and Dodge Ram, but there were no matches for a blue license plate with the right letter/number combination. He considered the possibility that the plate didn't belong to the van. It could have been stolen or borrowed from another vehicle. He was at a dead end.

He needed a break; maybe some caffeine would help. He went down to the break room and touched the coffee pot. It was hot, which was encouraging. As he poured his coffee, he watched Rupert rummaging around in the refrigerator.

"Hey, anything look good in there?" Pascal asked.

Rupert looked up. "Someone stole my lunch. There's a dirty cop among us."

"That's nasty. What did you have?"

"Hero sandwich, chips, chocolate cookie, Diet Coke."

The break room door swung open and one of the new desk clerks came in holding up a lunch sack. "Hey, Rupert, sorry. I grabbed your bag from the fridge, thought it was mine. Soon as I opened it, saw it wasn't."

"No problem," Rupert said, relieved.

The officer looked in the fridge and pulled out an identical sack. He looked inside and gave Rupert a thumbs-up, "Maybe we should put our names on the bags?" Rupert nodded as he inspected the bag.

"Boy, that was a close one," Pascal said.

"Yeah, I'll say. I'm going to go to Walmart tonight and buy a real lunch box, one that no one will mistake as theirs."

Pascal considered asking Rupert for help with the missing Jesus costume. That was his case.

"I'm working on a new case. Someone broke into a storage shed on the opera grounds, stole a costume, a Jesus outfit."

"Yeah, heard about that. The guys have been having a laugh, Easter and all."

"Well, it's no laughing matter. It's likely that it's connected to another, more-serious crime but not one in our jurisdiction."

Pascal could see he had perked Rupert's interest. Their cases in the last couple of months had been mundane, and Rupert was as bored as Pascal was. Rupert's past was well known around the force. Before he joined, he had been involved with a group called HACK-LAB. They touted themselves as a social collaborative with a mutual interest in technology, but in reality, they were vigilantes. They came onto the FBI's radar when they started helping people who had fallen victim to scams. Although they helped a lot of people, their assistance stretched the legal limits. The FBI's investigation ended with no arrests or prosecution. However, the group received an official letter warning it to cease and desist.

Rupert's participation had tarnished his reputation and made it difficult to get a job. When he applied to the force, the one thing in his favor was his run-in with the FBI. The captain, not a fan of the Feds, hired him to spite the bureau.

"I could use some help on the case—for starters, a list of possible suspects, most likely teenagers. The storage building reeked of pot. They probably took the costume as a joke."

"Sure, not much going on right now. What's the story about a more-serious crime?"

"Can't say right now. It's complicated. But if the lady from the opera can identify the costume as the one stolen, then that crime will fall in our jurisdiction."

"I need a copy of the case?"

"I'll have Susie make you one. Enjoy your lunch."

Pascal decided to try again to find a number for Alcazar. He did a general search for Marcos Alcazar. Again, nothing came up. He was frustrated. How is that possible? The man had to exist, had to be listed somewhere in the records. His phone rang.

"Ruiz."

"Hi, it's Jessie. I found out about the costume, but it already was picked up a few hours ago by a San Felipe officer."

"You don't happen to know the officer's name?"

"I'm nothing if not thorough, detective," she purred seductively.

"I appreciate your help," Pascal said. He figured she was the type of woman who needed to be stroked continually.

"His name's Ben Ortiz."

"He was one of the officers out at Tonque. He was in charge of evidence."

"Was that helpful, detective?"

"Yes. I hoped the costume would still be at the hospital. I'll get in touch with Ortiz. If San Felipe agrees, I have someone who is willing to look at the costume and tell if it's the same one stolen from the opera grounds last week. That would be a solid lead." Pascal knew that if there was a lead, it wasn't solid. It was a stretch. He had no idea who had burglarized the storage shed. He hoped somehow that Rupert could track down something useful.

"That's great," Jessie said.

"Any update on Bobby's condition?"

"No, but his father arrived a few hours ago. I get the feeling he blames me for what happened. The officer guarding Bobby's room allowed him in, but the nurses quickly shooed him out. He's waiting for the doctor to make his rounds. Maybe then we can get some information."

"Okay, hang in there. And thanks again for getting back to me about the costume. Appreciate it."

"Anytime, detective, ciao."

Pascal rolled his eyes and hung up. He wondered if Jessie knew he was half-Italian. Maybe she was flirting with him. He hoped not. That was all he needed—to become entangled with the captain's niece.

Pascal looked at his watch. Ortiz must have made it back to San Felipe by now. But when he called the station, the receptionist told him Ortiz was expected soon. Pascal left a message for the officer to call him as soon as he returned, then added that he had information on the Jesus costume. The receptionist paused and asked if there was anything else.

Pascal tried again to search for Alcazar. He did another reverse address search and even checked Facebook, Instagram, and LinkedIn. Although Alcazar didn't seem like the kind of guy who would have a social media presence, he might have kids or grandkids to keep track of, but nothing.

He thought about the clerk at the Golden Mercantile. He might have Alcazar's phone number, but when he called the store, nobody answered. That seemed strange, but then again, it was Easter weekend. Not a lot going on in Golden these days.

Pascal looked down at his bare wrist to check the time. It was the fourth time that day. His watch had stopped running, and he hadn't had time to buy a battery. Young people used their phones to check the time, but that seemed like too much trouble, your wrist was always there at the end of your arm.

He looked across the room at the black clock. It was almost three, and he hadn't heard back from San Felipe. Surely, the officer would follow up after Pascal left a message about the costume. He wondered if his message had been passed along. The captain wouldn't be pleased that he had called the Tribal Police, but he punched in the number. Again, he asked to speak with Ortiz. This time, the receptionist asked him to hold. He drummed his fingers on his desk as he waited. After four minutes, he started to hang up, but someone came on the line.

"Montaño."

"Ruiz. Santa Fe Police Department."

"I understand you wanted to speak to Officer Ortiz."

"Yes, I'm the one who found Bobby Pilot out at Tonque yesterday."

"What's your business with Ortiz?"

"I was told he went to UNMH to pick up the costume that Pilot wore out at Tonque."

"What's your business with the costume?"

"There was a break-in at the Santa Fe Opera storage building last week. Someone took a Jesus costume. It could be the same one Pilot was wearing."

There was a long silence. Again, Pascal waited. He figured that Montaño needed some time to figure out what to with the information. Pascal didn't want to rush him, but he would give him a little nudge.

"The woman in charge of the opera costumes might be able to determine if the costume Pilot was wearing is the same one stolen from the opera grounds."

"Well, that could be helpful. Do you know who stole the costume?"

"We're working on it."

"Yeah, Ortiz hasn't returned yet."

Pascal found that strange. Ortiz had left the hospital several hours ago. It shouldn't have taken more than an hour to get back to the pueblo. The back of Pascal's neck tingled.

"I thought Ortiz picked up the costume around one this afternoon. Had he planned to go anywhere else?"

"And how did you find out that information?"

"I talked to Jessie Archuleta, Pilot's girlfriend, this afternoon. She said she saw an officer at the hospital ask about the costume." Pascal could tell Montaño thought that was a crock. "Had Ortiz planned to stop somewhere?"

"We're working on that."

Touché, Pascal thought. This case was getting stranger by the minute. The stolen violin was a convoluted case, but the way this one was going, it might be a runner-up.

"Let me know if you want this woman to take a look at the costume. That is when and if Ortiz brings it back."

"We'll let you know when and if we need anything from you, Ruiz."

Montaño's remark didn't sound inviting, but Pascal was worried about Ortiz. His skin prickled. Something didn't seem right.

~26~

B EN ORTIZ WAS DOG-TIRED. HIS WIFE HAD GIVEN BIRTH TO their fourth child two weeks ago. Although the pregnancy hadn't been planned, they were looking forward to the new addition to the family. The Ortizes' three older children were excited—that is, until the baby was born. The new baby suffered from colic, making her finicky and irritable. She squirmed and twisted in her mother's arms and refused to latch on and nurse. She slept only in fits and bursts, so the family did too.

Ortiz had decided to apply for a leave of absence until they could get the baby settled and into a routine, but then they found that kid out at Tonque, the kid on a cross. Ortiz wondered who would do such a thing? Penitentes? That group had some strange practices, and although they were known for reenactments, their rituals were performed for themselves, within their communities. It didn't fit that they would dress up some Anglo boy, tie him up on a cross, and leave him out there. They had always respected the reservation.

When the emergency call came in that afternoon, the captain, short-staffed, had rustled up the only three officers at the station. Ortiz was caught in the sweep. Once they arrived at the crime scene out at Tonque, he had been assigned to gather evidence. Now he was stuck and wouldn't be able to apply for leave until the case was closed. There was little to go on, so it didn't seem likely the case would be wrapped up any time soon.

Last night, he'd volunteered to take care of the baby so his wife could get a few hours of sleep. She had squirmed and fussed as he walked back and forth in his attempt to soothe the girl. Most of the night, she was awake, unsettled—and so was he.

Ortiz was a desk officer. His job consisted of answering the phone and processing paperwork. He had been trained on the job, and had never been asked to work a real crime scene. He never watched crime shows on TV, finding them too violent. Most of the detectives were Anglo, and he couldn't relate. A few weeks ago, he saw an advertisement for a new show, "The Indian Detective," but when he tuned in, he was disappointed. The detective wasn't Native American but from India.

Ortiz found his new role intimidating. He was in charge of evidence, and there didn't seem to be any. He would have to take things one step at a time. Maybe watch some old detective shows like Columbo or Monk, see how they solved a case.

As he drove to the hospital, he thought about the new baby. They hadn't even named her yet. They were too exhausted. He tried to not think about it and focus on his job, turning his attention to the case. He was thankful that he had a task to accomplish: Pick up the costume and bring it back to the station. That seemed easy, but the freeway was crazy with traffic. Where was everyone going? Nobody seemed happy to be where they were anymore. He forced himself to relax, and took long slow breaths, but a car swerved into his lane, forcing him to brake hard. Adrenaline shot through his body.

He was relieved when he exited the freeway and made it to the hospital. He signed for the costume at the administrative office. But when he left the office, he decided to get a Coke and turned around, almost colliding with a ghost-like man. He had never seen anyone with such pale skin and colorless eyes. Hopefully, it wasn't an omen. Ortiz lowered his eyes, turned back around, and headed down to the parking garage. As he dug in his pocket for his keys, his fingers closed around an object: the film canister he had found out at Tonque. Growing up, he always had picked up stuff off the ground; rocks, shells, old coins, keys, shards. He made up stories about the objects, where they came from or who had dropped them.

Ortiz had forgotten about the canister. He remembered that the girl, the one with the Santa Fe detective, had come over when he picked up the canister. She held out her hand. In it was a small pottery shard with a few inches of slightly flared lip that indicated it had once been part of a jar-shaped bowl. It was mostly dark gray with a hint of orange matte glaze but still had a faint black line left of the original geometric motif. When Ortiz was a kid, he had found hundreds of pottery shards out at Tonque but always left them in place. Now there weren't many to be found. The Archeological Society had excavated the pueblo in the late '60s and preserved the larger shards. Trespassers had taken the smaller pieces.

For some reason, Ortiz had been compelled to explain that the shard was from a bowl used by the Tonque people. He had showed her how there was still a piece of lip that could be used to estimate the size of the container. When he handed it back to her, he suggested that she should put the shard back where she had found it.

When he looked up, the captain's face was frozen in a frown; he had barked orders to get busy. The girl had strained to see the canister as he stuffed it in his pocket, wondering whether it was important, something to do with the case, maybe evidence.

Ortiz decided that while he was in town, he would see if he could find out about the canister. He took out his phone and searched for photography stores. He chose one that wasn't far and had been in business a long time, one that claimed the staff was knowledgeable. Maybe they could identify the canister and might know who would use such film. He figured it was a lot of maybes, but what else did he have to go on?

As Ortiz made his way across town, he considered ways to approach the inquiry. He tossed around a few scenarios but finally decided to be direct. It was the way he had always done things, sometimes to his disadvantage.

The store was empty of customers. The man behind the counter was close to his father's age. Ortiz was relieved because he didn't want to have to talk to one of those young tech-type kids who always made him feel inept. The man wore an apron covered with stains from film processing liquids. On the upper left side of the apron was an embroidered nametag: John Stephens, Manager.

"Can I help you?"

Ortiz pulled out his badge, "Officer Ortiz, San Felipe Tribal."

The manager said, but not unkindly, "Yeah, I see the uniform."

Ortiz's face flushed; he realized his introduction had been over-kill, but it was too late. He pulled out the film canister and handed it to the manager. "We're working on a case—found this at the crime scene."

The manager put on the glasses hanging around his neck and examined the case. "Don't see many of these around."

"Yeah?" Ortiz perked up.

"It's made by Convestro. They produce and develop made-to-order films."

"Made-to-order?"

"Not your typical 35-millimeter camera film. The company specializes in polycarbonate, thermoplastic polyurethane, and specialty elastomer films."

Ortiz eyebrows wrinkled, and he pursed his lips.

"Sorry, a little too technical?"

"A little."

"This canister contained an experimental film made by Bayfol." The manager pointed to the torn label on its side. "You can still see the first four letters of the maker's name, Bayf. The film is a light-sensitive photopolymer. Convestro develops this type of film. It's used for industrial holography. You know—like your mobile phone's IT display. The film is based on diffractive optics. They also dabble in automotive virtual reality, like driverless cars."

"Who would use this type of film?"

"Not sure. We don't sell anything like it. Our lab isn't equipped to develop it. Maybe a photographer or filmmaker. Artists might use it to incorporate images into their work."

"Any names?"

"No." The manager shook his head. "Your best bet is to check out the art and film scene." The manager gave him back the canister.

"Thanks, appreciate your help." Ortiz gave the man his card. "If you think of anything else, don't hesitate to call."

Ortiz smiled as he left the building. He had always wanted to say that. He almost skipped as he crossed the parking lot. He had a lead. The canister held special light-sensitive film that could create holographic images. He wondered who had dropped it out at Tonque. It had to have something to do with that kid on the cross.

~27~

MARTIN MADE HIS WAY TO THE ELEVATOR AS THE DOORS closed behind Steg. The lighted numbers above the door increased. Steg had taken an elevator that was going up, not down. Maybe he didn't intend to follow the officer. Martin pushed the down button and watched the numbers continue to rise; ninth, tenth, eleventh, then start back down. When the elevator opened on the seventh floor, Martin got in and stood facing the doors. Steg was on his right, staring at the wall.

Martin felt his insides vibrate as adrenaline raced through his body. For the first time since his writer's block, he felt alive, his senses on alert. He pushed aside thoughts of his responsibilities—his wife and new baby, his young daughter at school. The suspense of the chase captivated him.

It now seemed plausible that Steg was following the officer, and had a connection to the patient in the ICU. As the elevator jarred to a halt on the first floor of the parking garage, Steg pushed his way through the crowd, knocking Martin off balance, and sprinted to his car, conveniently parked near the exit. Martin had parked one floor up, against the garage's back wall. He watched as Steg sped out of the building, barely missing an elderly man with a walker on his way to the elevators. As Martin sprinted toward the exit, he caught a glimpse of the Mini Cooper cruising through a traffic light that had turned red. Down the street, a couple of lights ahead was the officer's patrol car. At the next light, the officer turned right and Steg followed.

Martin called his sister, but even before he asked his favor, he heard the annoyance in her voice. She hated interruptions and disliked last-minute requests, but he made his plea anyway. Could she pick up his daughter from school? He heard banging pans and water running as she snapped that she was in the middle of preparing dinner. Then she huffed into the phone loudly. Martin chewed on his bottom lip, but then she acquiesced. She would bring his daughter to the hospital during visiting hours.

Martin tried to figure out his next move. He wondered if he should report what he had witnessed but didn't want to jump to conclusions. What if Steg's behavior and actions were a coincidence? And who should he report his suspicions to? He worried that the San Felipe officer could be in danger, although the police had firearms and were trained to defend themselves.

Martin thought about the patient in the ICU. He needed background information. Maybe he could talk to the guy's father, whom the aide had pointed out in the cafeteria that morning. But first, he would check on his wife and the baby.

When he exited the elevator on the floor of the maternity wing, he almost collided with a tiny gurney manned on either side by two nurses. He caught a glimpse of an infant hooked up with tubes. Two Native American women rushed behind the gurney, headed toward the neonatal intensive care unit. A sick feeling settled in Martin's stomach. He hurried to his wife's room.

Martin spent the rest of the afternoon with his wife. He helped her shower and change into fresh nightclothes. He walked along beside her down the hall as she tried to stand erect. With each step, the stitches in her abdomen sent pain streaking through her body. The first time, she had tried to walk after the surgery, dizziness caused her knees to buckle, and the nurse had to hold a small bottle of something under her nose. Now, she was steady on her feet, but when she walked, the pain from the incision made her stoop like an elderly woman.

Once they were back in the room, Martin sat on the bed and sang little songs to the baby and rocked her in his arms until she fell asleep. His sister had called and told him his daughter had come down with a cold at school. She had fed her some soup and tucked her into bed, and suggested that Martin stay and take care of his wife. His daughter could stay at her house until she was better. After his wife ate her super, she was ready for rest. When wife and baby were asleep, Martin crept out of the room and headed down to the cafeteria. He scanned the few occupied tables, but the patient's father wasn't there.

The smell of food from the kitchen made Martin's stomach growl. He realized he hadn't eaten since breakfast. He loaded food onto his tray and carried it across the room. He looked for an empty table and spotted the aide in the corner with another young woman.

"Hi," Martin smiled.

Both women looked up. The aide recognized him. "Hey, how's your wife and new baby?"

"Fine. They're resting. I wondered if you've seen the patient from the ICU's father this evening?

"No. Poor guy. He hung around the ICU waiting room most of the day, probably has gone home."

"How's the patient?"

"Still unconscious, his vitals improved."

"Well, thanks." Martin tried to hide his disappointment and turned to find a table.

"Hey," the aide said.

"Yeah?"

"See that girl over there against the wall? The one with the awesome canary yellow body suit with red peonies? No way could I pull off that outfit."

Martin, not sure what peonies looked like, followed the aide's outstretched arm. Even from across the room, he could tell the young woman was striking, the kind you see in TV commercials.

"She's the patient's girlfriend: an actress, Jessie Archuleta. She was in that soap, Here Today, Gone Tomorrow, played a school cheerleader who had an affair with the principal." The two girls looked at each other and giggled. "I got her autograph. She told me she finished a Western out at Diamond Tail Ranch."

"Thanks." Martin winked at the two girls, and they giggled again.

He made his way across the cafeteria. The young woman leaned her chair back against the wall, phone in hand, typing with both thumbs. She caught Martin in her peripheral vision, stopped typing, and lowered her chair. She stared up at him with an inquisitive look. He was immediately drawn in by her huge doe-like eyes that never blinked. For a few seconds, he stood mesmerized, unable to speak. Her translucent skin and the cascades of dark rich curls flowing down over her shoulders created a breathtaking image. He could imagine her face blown up on the screen, audiences captivated.

Finally, he swallowed hard and found his voice. "Sorry. Are you Jessie Archuleta, the actress?"

A coy smile emerged from her overly ripe crimson lips. "Yes, I am."

He knew it pleased her to be recognized but decided he'd better cut to the chase. He didn't want to get sucked into too many deceptions. "I'm sorry to hear about your boyfriend. I hope he's better."

Martin noticed a slight change in her demeanor. The topic had moved off her, and he sensed her disappointment. "Do you know Bobby?"

Martin was pleased. He had the patient's first name, but he needed her trust too.

"Not personally."

"Are you with the police?"

"No." He shook his head and smiled. "I heard about the abduction."

This seemed to satisfy her. "He's still unconscious. The whole situation . . .." She threw her arms up in the air. "Beyond horrible. The police are doing next to nothing."

"It must be terribly frustrating. Do you mind if I sit?"

She hesitated but then shrugged. "Go ahead, sit."

"I'm a writer. I'm interested in writing an article about Bobby."

He could see her mull this over, trying to think of a way it could be useful to her career.

"And you." He added.

"Well, that's funny, you being a writer and wanting to write about Bobby."

"Funny?"

"Bobby, all his life, had his heart set on being a writer. He was working on an article about the Easter procession to Chimayó and the Penitentes."

~28~

As Ben Ortiz pulled out of the camera store parking lot, his mind was full of thoughts about the canister, the special light-sensitive film, and holographic images. He glanced in his rearview mirror and was surprised to see a dark green Mini Cooper. Where had it come from? He had been the only customer in the camera shop, and the parking lot was empty when he left the store.

He noticed the car turn in the same direction as him. But when he checked his mirror a few streets later, it was gone. He shook his head and chuckled to himself. This case was making him paranoid.

The clock on his dash read 3:15. The freeway would already be slowed with rush-hour traffic. Nobody worked nine to five anymore—that is, if they worked at all. He realized he was behind schedule but figured that the back roads, although they would take longer, would get him to the pueblo without stress.

Ortiz's stomach growled as he made his way across town to Second Street and headed north. He hadn't eaten since breakfast, and realized that he was famished. When he'd pulled out his sack lunch earlier in the day, the captain asked him to collect the costume from UNMH. He figured he could get to the hospital and back in less than two hours, but now, he was sorry he had left it behind.

Eating in the car was one of Ortiz's pet peeves. It was a distraction. And driving, especially in Albuquerque, you didn't need any distractions. There should be a law against eating while driving, as there is for texting or talking on your phone. Hands free should mean hands free. He had been in a car with officers who did all three, sometimes at once—not paying attention to the road.

Near the end of Second Street, a weathered sign advertised Murphy's Mule Barn. The cafe had a reputation for good old-fashioned food. Ortiz's stomach grumbled again, and he pulled off the road. He would have loved to order the chicken fried steak, the Mule Barn's specialty, but thoughts of his wife at home alone tending to a fussy baby made him settle for a burger and fries. He sat outside at the stone table and chairs. The sun wasn't much use this time of day, but the brisk air made him less tired. Once he popped the last fry into his mouth, he decided to keep to the back roads and digest his lunch before getting on the freeway at Bernalillo.

As he passed Sandia Pueblo, a pang of guilt hit him like a thump. He wished he had time to stop and check on his great auntie. She suffered from gout and had difficulty getting around. With the new baby, he hadn't seen her for several weeks. But he was already late. He made a promise that the entire family would visit on the weekend and bring some green chile stew and fry bread, her favorite.

His phone buzzed, and he was thankful he had remembered to hook up the Bluetooth speaker. He reached over and pushed the button.

"Ortiz, where are you?" the captain asked.

"On my way, sir, past Shady Lakes, almost to Bernalillo."

"Taking the scenic route?"

Ortiz decided it was best not to answer. It would only make matters worse.

"Did you pick up the costume at the hospital?"

"Yes, but I have something else that may help with the case. That's why I'm late."

The captain cut him off. "The detective from Santa Fe called, the one that was out at Tonque with the girl. Said a Jesus costume was stolen from the opera grounds last week. Thinks it could be the same one the kid was wearing. Has someone that might be able to identify it."

Ortiz sat up a little straighter. This morning, the case seemed hopeless—nothing to go on. But now, things were looking up. Two pieces of evidence and a lead on the costume.

"That's great."

The captain paused. "We'll see. Not sure I want Santa Fe messing around in our territory. Could get complicated."

Ortiz was aware of the pueblo's constant struggle to be autonomous. Over the years, San Felipe had had several cases that involved jurisdiction issues with other entities: the Bernalillo Sheriff's Office, State Police, even the FBI. Now maybe the Santa Fe Police Department. Everybody always wanted a piece of the pie, always nudging in on them.

"Yeah." But Ortiz would keep an open mind. They didn't have much to go on with this case. And if the costume turned out to be stolen from the opera, that gave Santa Fe an open door.

"See me as soon as you get back."

Ortiz started to say something, but the line went dead.

He leaned back in his seat, took a deep breath, and gradually let out the air. Ortiz wasn't one to rush. He had always found that you get there when you get there. Life had no shortcuts.

It had been a dry winter. The barren fields spanned both sides of the road. Ortiz knew they would soon be planted in alfalfa, and hoped the monsoons would come early this summer. He loved the open space, and didn't mind the nothingness. In the high desert, you went with the seasons. What was brown would soon be green, thanks to the irrigation ditches. But lack of snow in the mountains meant there would be less water in the river, less water for the fields.

As Ortiz drove along, he tried to forget about the case, the costume, and the film canister, and think about his wife. She had been left alone with the baby all day while he was at work and the kids were in school. Once they got home, they would pitch in and help their mother.

As he came into Bernalillo, he slowed down, mindful of the 25-MPH speed limit. The town was growing. It seemed that new traffic lights had sprouted up like the late winter daffodils. He was forced to stop at every red light in town, and it took forever to reach the main intersection.

Ortiz decided to bypass the freeway and continue up the back road. When he was about a mile from Algodones, he heard a loud pop, and his car swerved to the right. He took hold of the steering wheel, turned into the skid, and gently applied the brakes. The car wobbled as it came to a crawl. Damn. He had a flat tire. A few yards away, he spotted a driveway. But as he came closer, he found it wasn't much more than an overgrown path. It looked as if no one had driven on it in a while. Ortiz didn't dare drive much farther for fear of damaging the wheel. He pulled off the road and turned down the drive. There was no house on the property, only an abandoned barn that leaned precariously to the east. The roof had a few pieces of tin still nailed down but otherwise was open to the sky.

At least he was off the road. He knew how dangerous it was to change a tire on a narrow road at night. People with broken down cars were often hit or killed while on the side of the road, especially these days, with young people preoccupied with texts and tweets while they drove. They looked at their phones, eyes off the road, and you were history.

The driveway was gutted with deep grooves of dried and hardened caliche. On either side someone had years ago planted rows of Chinese elms. The trees were now massive and looked healthy.

Because it was difficult to find a level patch in the uneven driveway, Ortiz finally gave up, shut off the cruiser, and set the emergency brake. Once he was out of the car, he realized it was going to be difficult to change the tire on the uneven surface, and considered moving up next to the barn. But first he wanted to assess the damage. The sun was still up, but the trees, even with only the few leaves that had hung on over the winter, blocked out most of the light. Ortiz took out his flashlight and knelt down to inspect the tire. He took in a breath. Couldn't believe it. The tire was shot—literally. Someone had shot his tire.

Ortiz starred at the tire, unable to fathom what he saw. As he poked at the bullet, he heard a faint sound like the crackling of dried leaves. His heart thumped in his chest as he realized he wasn't alone. Someone was making his way up the drive. He hugged close to the tire and stayed as still as possible while he reached in his pocket for his keys and clicked the car doors locked. The sound seemed to reverberate in his ears, and he hoped whoever was out there hadn't heard it. He had left his phone and gun in the car—planning to change his tire, not defend himself. He held his breath and listened again. The sound was clearer now, coming closer up the drive.

Ortiz was glad he had inherited good knees, not like his uncle Hector, whose legs bowed out like those of a seasoned cowboy. His years working in the alfalfa fields had left him in good physical condition. He remained in a crouched position, slowly inching toward the stand of elms on the north side of the drive. Although they wouldn't provide much cover, it was all he had. Most of the property was flat, with nothing but scrub and brush.

Once he reached the trees, he rested and considered his next move: lie down flat or run. As for many natives, the ability to run came second nature. He had been a track star in high school and still ran regularly to keep both his mind and body in shape. Another thing in his favor was familiarity with uneven terrain. Although he knew he could outrun anyone who chased him, the thought of the bullet in his tire made him hesitate. He chose to keep low and move away as quietly as possible. But first he wanted to get a look at whoever was pursuing him.

Ortiz waited, taking shallow breaths. Out in the open, sound tended to carry, and there wasn't anything to muffle even the faintest noise. The outline of a man came into focus. Although the sun had sunk near the horizon, casting the area in darkness as the man turned his head, a shaft of dim sunlight caught the long strands of white hair. Ortiz had seen this man at the hospital today.

The man's hand gripped a large rifle hanging down by his side, the gun that must have been used to shoot out his tire. Even from a distance, Ortiz could tell it wasn't your typical hunting rifle. He was glad he hadn't decided to make a run for it.

There wasn't enough light to make out the man's face, but Ortiz shivered as he remembered the man's colorless ghost eyes. His shoulder-length white hair continued to pick up the last remnants of light from the sun. Ortiz concentrated on the man's details: average height, slight build, dark nondescript clothes.

The man leaned over, cupped his hands on either side of his face, and pressed them against the car's passenger window. Ortiz knew what he was looking for: the Jesus costume. Then the man drew back the butt of his rifle and smashed it into the window. Ortiz startled and almost let out a yelp but then realized this was his chance. He pushed back from the tree and made his way down the drive toward the main road. He moved from one tree to the next. He could hear the thud of the rifle against the window and counted three blows before the glass finally shattered.

When Ortiz looked back, the man had the package and was heading toward the elm trees. Ortiz figured that if he was crouching, the last cutting of alfalfa would provide cover while he crossed the property. The rifle had changed his plan to flag down a car on the road. It would be safer to make his way back to the station on foot.

He reached in his pocket and caressed the film canister. It was his talisman. He hoped it would bring him good luck. The costume was lost, but he still had one piece of evidence. And he had a description of the suspect. There couldn't be too many ghost men with white hair and colorless eyes in New Mexico. He hoped the man wouldn't think to remove the bullet from the tire. Ballistics would be able to match it to the rifle—another piece of evidence.

As he made his way across the property, crouching as low as he could, he stopped periodically to listen for sounds, but heard nothing. Maybe the man thought he had opted for the road. As he continued, the case was shaping up. Two pieces of evidence: a description of the perp, and possibly a bullet. He was starting to like being a detective. It was better than sitting at a desk all day.

~29~

S TEG COULD KICK HIMSELF. HE HAD BLOWN HIS CHANCE TO GET hold of the costume at the hospital. He had seen the officer in the underground garage, but too many people were around. A large crowd had gathered in front of the elevator. Steg held back, and right before the doors closed, he ducked in. Luckily, the officer resting against the back wall never looked up, keeping his eyes on the floor. When the elevator stopped on the seventh floor, the officer pushed his way to the front and exited. Steg waited. When the doors started to close, he stuck out his hand and slipped out.

When the officer came out of an office with the costume, Steg started to follow, but then the Indian turned around and they came face to face. The man had stared at him while Steg mumbled that he was sorry. He knew his looks were an anomaly, especially in New Mexico. Most people stared. His whiter-than-white shoulder length hair, pale ivory skin, and colorless eyes usually earned him at least a sideways glance. He decided to play it safe and take another elevator to the parking garage. That was his second mistake.

The elevator door opened; it was crowded, but he pushed his way in. As the doors closed, he looked up, but it was too late—the car was going up, not down. By the time he reached the basement, the officer had pulled out of the garage. Luckily, Steg's car was nearby, and he easily caught up with the officer. But at the next intersection, he almost lost him again. Thankfully, the officer was a cautious driver. When the next light turned yellow, he slowed and dutifully stopped. Steg decided to follow close, maybe one car behind. His innocuous green Mini Cooper wouldn't raise suspicion, not like a black sedan with tinted windows— the ones used for tailing in the movies.

Steg followed the officer through the streets of Albuquerque and was surprised when he pulled into a camera store north of Broadway. He wondered what the Indian was doing there. Nobody used real film anymore, everything was digital. And even if you did want to develop film, there were cheaper services available at the drugstore. Who would use a camera store? Unless you were a professional. But the officer didn't strike Steg as a professional photographer.

Since Steg's cover was blown at the hospital, he would have to wait in the parking lot for the officer. He pulled the Mini around to the side of the building. When the officer left the store, Steg hoped he wouldn't take the freeway. He needed him on the back roads. Then he would have a chance.

Steg heard the chime on the store's door and briefly considered accosting the officer in the parking lot, but although it was empty, it was too open. He couldn't risk any witnesses. He realized too late that he should have broken into the officer's car while he was in the store. The crimes portrayed in movies seemed easy, like spreading butter on warm toast, although the perp often was apprehended in the end.

While Steg tailed the officer through the North Valley, he sulked. He was blamed for whatever went wrong. Coriz made fun of him. He nicknamed him Goldjunge, (the golden boy) and somehow pronounced it with a perfect German accent, always with a grin on his usually expressionless face. But in Coriz's eyes, Thomas, who barely had scraped his way through a state university and relied on the reputation of his uncle (some second-rate Hollywood producer nobody had never heard of) could do no wrong. He wasn't given a nickname, and was always Thomas, never Tom or Tommy. Steg clenched his jaw as he considered the inequity. He was the one with the stellar resumé and amazing talent, not to mention money. He had bankrolled their film project, Der Geist Jesu (The Ghost of Jesus), insisting that they use the German translation for the title. Coriz and Thomas had rolled their eyes, but Steg persisted. Coriz conceded. Still, Steg remained the underdog.

The production was fraught with problems. Coriz had brought some mushrooms to Tonque, which turned out to be amazing but not conducive to filmmaking. He and Thomas had been so stoned they could barely stand. Then they found that stupid kid, Bobby Pilot, who had fallen off a boulder. He kept whining about needing medical attention and Coriz left, promising to send someone to pick them up that afternoon.

Before Coriz left, he gave the kid a bottle of Percocet. Coriz had a torn ACL, an old basketball injury that had never healed. It flared up from time to time, and he would complain to his doctor, who shelled out pills under the counter.

Steg was incensed that Coriz would leave the kid with them, not because he worried about Pilot's condition but because they had work to do. He begged Coriz to drop him off on the highway, call 911. He and Thomas needed to finish this project, not babysit some hurt guy. But Coriz flashed Steg one of his blank expressions, turned, and left without a word.

Steg and Thomas tried to set up the final scene, but the effect of the mushrooms seemed to get in their way. Steg looked over at the kid and saw that he was slumped over on his side, passed out. Steg wondered how many pills he had taken. When Thomas went over to check on Pilot, he noticed a half-eaten mushroom next to him. That's when they had the idea for the last scene.

Coriz's nephew, Benny, didn't show up that afternoon. The van had suffered a flat tire going down La Bajada hill. Benny had left it on the side of the road and hitched a ride to his friend's house south of Santa Fe. But his friend didn't get home until late, and there was no way he would drive to an abandoned pueblo in the middle of the night. He borrowed his friend's Nissan sedan the next day, but the car barely had room for the three of them and their equipment. There was no room for Bobby Pilot. They would have to change the tire on the van, come back, and then pick Bobby up.

When they inspected the van's tire, they saw that it wasn't only flat. Benny must have driven on it long enough to bend the rim. They couldn't get the tire off, much less put on the spare. Steg pulled out his AAA card and called for a tow truck. They waited almost two hours.

Thomas tried to convince Benny to go back for Bobby Pilot while they waited, saying that they would pay him. But he refused. How could he carry him out of the canyon? The tow truck took the van to Tire Mart in Santa Fe. The clerk said it wouldn't be ready until tomorrow. Benny drove them to the warehouse and unloaded the equipment in the driveway.

Thomas insisted they restock the equipment in his usual OCD way, cataloging each item from the shoot. Thomas pushed the last box toward Steg and asked, "Where's the Bayfol canister?"

Steg shrugged, then bent down and picked up a cord that had fallen. He remembered loading the film in the camera but that was it, no memory of what he had done with the canister. When Thomas looked away, Steg searched his coat pockets. Nothing.

He knew that Thomas couldn't wait to tell Coriz about the missing canister. The faggot always ratted him out. Once the equipment was unloaded, they considered flipping a coin to see who would go back to Tonque but knew it would take two of them to get Bobby off the cross. They weren't sure he would fit in the Mini either, but they didn't want to wait until tomorrow for the van to be ready.

The Mini, not made for back roads, was Steg's baby. There was no way he would take it from Golden down Hagan Road with all its ruts and potholes. If they could get around the roadblock San Felipe had put up off the interstate, it would be faster and easier. As Steg pulled off the highway at San Felipe Casino, the parking lot overflowed with cars, campers, and trucks. The Easter holidays must bring out the gamblers. He pulled next to a Coke machine at the gas station and hopped out to buy a soda, not bothering to ask Thomas if he wanted one. It was a passive-aggressive move, although Steg knew that Thomas was a health freak and would never put anything that wasn't organic in his body. He got back in the car, but as he started to pull out of the parking lot, two San Felipe police cars, lights flashing, sped out of the underpass and headed east, sending clouds of dust in every direction. Someone had found Bobby Pilot.

Later, Steg found out that Thomas had squealed on him about the lost canister. When Coriz confronted him, Steg told him everything:

the final shoot, Bobby Pilot left out at Tonque, the San Felipe police. Steg figured that if he was going down, Thomas would join him.

Coriz was furious. He couldn't believe they had left Pilot out there. He was worried not only about their involvement but also about Pilot. He had always liked the guy. Coriz had called the hospital, claiming to be Pilot's uncle. The nurse gave him a brief report on Pilot's status: stable but still unconscious, in a coma. He inquired about Pilot's belongings, and the nurse hesitated before she confessed in a hushed tone that he had worn a Jesus outfit when brought in. She reassured Coriz that San Felipe Tribal was investigating the incident, and told him an officer was on his way to pick up the costume.

Coriz was worried. If police got hold of the costume, they might link it to the opera burglary. Although Coriz wasn't involved—that had been Steg's ridiculous prank—the robbery could implicate the film company. He ordered Steg to get the costume before the police arrived.

The interstate, clogged with traffic, was down to one lane because of construction and delayed Steg's getting to the hospital. When the officer left with the costume, Steg followed him through the back streets of Albuquerque. He couldn't believe this guy. He must not be on the clock, or maybe he was paid hourly. It was taking him forever to make his way back to San Felipe. They were barely out of the city limits when the officer pulled over at Murphy's Mule Barn. Steg turned into the lot the next door, a former appliance repair shop which looked as if it had been closed a long time. He cursed as his car bumped and scraped along the broken concrete driveway. When the officer emerged from the cafe and settled down at an outdoor table to eat, Steg mused that if he was this guy's boss, the officer would be history.

Finally, the officer was finished and got back in his car. Steg hoped he would stick to the back road and not turn east to the interstate. Traffic was light, so Steg would have to hang back to avoid being noticed. As the officer turned off Second Street onto Route 313, Steg breathed a sigh of relief. Finally—a bit of luck. There weren't any cross streets on Route 313, no chance of the officer pulling off. Steg could follow at a safe distance. It was a clear shot to Bernalillo, and once the officer was on the other side of town, Steg would have his chance. He knew not to go back empty-handed.

~30~

BEN ORTIZ BIT HIS LIP. HIS PHONE AND GUN WERE IN THE PA-
trol car. He seldom needed to carry a weapon. When he left
the tribal office, he usually locked his firearm in the glove compartment.

Still crouching, Ortiz crab-walked down the line of trees until he
was no longer within sight of the patrol car. The neighboring field
had been planted with alfalfa last summer, but nobody bothered to
harvest it. Barely two feet tall, the dried stalks didn't provide much
cover, but it was better than the scraggly weeds and rabbit brush that
surrounded him. He easily scrambled through a place in the sagging
barbed wire, stepping on the bottom strand and pulling up on the
top, careful not to snag his clothes. He could do it blindfolded, having done it so many times over the years.

As soon as he made his way into the field, he heard a car coming
up the road. For a second, he considered flagging it down, but hesitated. The driver flew past, skidded to a stop in front a neighboring
house, and laid on the horn. The vibration reverberated through the
air as the house door swung open and two young people stumbled
out. They piled into the back seat, and before they had even closed
the door, the driver took off. Ortiz again considered flagging the vehicle down, but it sped away, swerving erratically. He was afraid the
driver might not see him in time, or if he did, might get spooked and
crash. The people in the car would wonder why a stranger was wandering around in their field after dark. They wouldn't be likely to stop.

He heard the tires squeal on the asphalt as the car turned onto
the main road and headed south. Dust lingered in the air momentarily, then drifted back down to the ground. Ortiz resumed his
crouched position. His legs burned as if on fire as he started across

the field in a zigzag pattern he had learned in the Reserves, glad he didn't have far to go. He had decided that if nothing happened by the time he reached the driveway, it would be safe to stand and somehow make his way back to the pueblo. He looked forward to being able to stretch his cramped legs.

Although Ortiz experienced pain like most people, his heritage enabled him to mentally block it out. In the Reserves, he had attended a seminar on pain and the abuse of drugs. The widespread misuse of opioids and the realization that they were highly addictive had become apparent. Soldiers were warned that pain could rewire their brain and send signals that the body was in pain even after the pain had abated, resulting in the need to take more and more opioids. Ortiz could block out pain with meditation, like the Buddhists. He had acquired the ability to separate his body from his mind.

While he made his way across the field, his mind was filled with images of his new baby, the girl without a name. She would be his focus. She would be his salvation, and he would be hers. He would help her settle into her new life outside the womb. As he moved back and forth through the field, his only thoughts were of the baby. She had inherited her delicate features from her mother, and her black almond-shaped eyes from him. Her tenacious spirit she had inherited from her tribe. He sang her the little song, the one he had sung to each of his children when they were unhappy or hurt.

When he finally made his way to the edge of the driveway, the pain and cramping in his legs had disappeared. Although he knew he could have continued, he was relieved to be able to stand and stretch at last. He turned and looked back toward where he had come and strained to see any sign of movement. The sun was long gone, but it was too early for the moon, and a layer of low thin clouds effectively blocked any light from the stars.

When he started to turn back, he sensed a disturbance, the movement of air, and the back of his neck tingled with anticipation. An explosion reverberated across the field and resonated in his ears. His leg buckled as an object slammed into it. He looked down and lost his balance. Something was wrong. He fell forward, reaching out at the last minute to break his fall.

As he lay splayed on the ground, he tried to make his mind work. A queasiness had settled in his stomach and caused involuntary shudders throughout his body. He forced himself to take long slow breaths, and tried to calm his panic. Finally, he looked down at his leg. Dark liquid oozed from his pants above the knee. Someone had shot him, just like his tire had been shot. Someone was after him— wanted him dead.

His only hope was to keep low and move. There was no way he could stand up, and even if he could, it would be foolish. He turned on his side and slithered out of his jacket. His hands shook badly as he tried to unbutton his shirt. He ripped it open, sending buttons flying around him. It had been chilly when he dressed this morning, and now he was glad he had put on a long-sleeve T-shirt. As he lay on his side, he reached down and tugged at his pants leg. If he could pull it up above the knee, he could look at the wound. The effort exhausted him. He gave up, then wrapped the T-shirt over his pants leg and used the sleeves as a tourniquet.

Whoever had shot him would want to make sure he was dead or would need to finish the job. Ortiz knew he had wasted too much time bandaging his leg and needed to get moving. There was no way he would be able to crouch; his only option was to crawl on hands and knees. As he moved his knee forward and set it down on the hard-packed earth, a pain shot through his body and caused another wave of nausea. The strain clogged his mind with fog. He moved on automatic pilot. In order to survive, he had to be unpredictable.

Although the temperature had dropped considerably since the sun went down, the effort caused sweat to soak his hair and run down his back. His temperature fluctuated. Flashes of heat closed his throat until he gasped for breath. Icy chills made him shiver violently and caused his teeth to rattle so hard in his mouth he was sure they would fall out.

He crawled about twenty yards along the drive, then decided to turn back toward the fence, hoping whoever was chasing him wouldn't consider his moving in that direction. He shook his head, worried he would pass out, and forced in long, slow breaths. He needed to focus. He started to sing the little song again under his breath, the one he had sung to his children and would sing to his new baby.

Ortiz made his way to the barbed wire fence and crawled back to the original property. Then he continued toward the road. He looked down and saw that when his injured knee hit the ground, spurts of blood shot out. The shirt he had tied as a bandage was soaked and no longer gave enough pressure to contain the wound. Waves of pain shook through his body. He started to go in and out of consciousness. He needed to find somewhere to hide.

As he neared the main road, he spotted an ancient cottonwood leaning precariously to the east. The tree stirred a childhood memory of a fall afternoon out in the pasture playing hide and seek. When his turn had come to hide, he'd found the perfect place—a large hole in a tree—climbed in, curled up, and waited to be found. But nobody came. After a while, the air took on a chill, and he knew the sun was setting. When he crawled out of the hole and stretched his cramped legs, he was all alone. Everyone had gone home and left him behind.

This cottonwood, as some trees do when they age, had partially lifted out of the ground, creating a hollowed-out cavity. It wasn't a perfect hiding place, but it gave him some cover and a place to rest. As he started to wedge himself into the hole, a pair of headlights flashed on the road. The car slowed to a crawl, turned into the property, and went up the drive where he had left his cruiser.

Ortiz scratched around for some twigs and brush to cover the entrance. Once he nestled into the tree's cavity, he was safe at last. In the dark, at least from a distance, it would be almost impossible to spot his hideaway. Relief spread through his body. Although he was off his knee, blood continued to gush, but his leg was numb. As he curled his body into a fetal position, his head spun. He tried to steady his breath, singing his little comfort song, but everything went black.

CAPTAIN MONTAÑO PACED BACK AND FORTH IN HIS OFFICE. He was concerned. Ortiz hadn't made it back to the station yet. His stomach stirred uncomfortably, and a familiar ache worked its way around his intestines. The sensation usually meant something wasn't right.

It had been over an hour since he had talked with Ortiz. Even if the officer dawdled, that was plenty of time to make it to the station. He knew that Ortiz had been distracted lately. Whispered talk had floated around the station the last couple of weeks about the new baby, adjustment troubles to "life outside the womb." Well, join the club. He was old school. Women took care of babies. Men did their jobs. No whining, no excuses.

Although Montaño would turn seventy in August, he had no intention of hanging up his badge. He couldn't imagine how he would fill his days without work. His parents had tended their alfalfa fields until they couldn't get out of bed. They had raised eight children who never complained, helped out, didn't cause waves. These days, Montaño thought, parents spoiled and indulged their children.

The captain knew that Ortiz was a good worker, dedicated and competent within his capacity. But he was a desk officer, not a crime detective. He didn't have the training to work a crime scene.

When the 911 call had come in, the captain rounded up the only three officers available that afternoon. The station had been short-staffed for three months, and Montaño made clear that every officer needed to pitch in and do whatever was asked.

The officers had followed the captain out of the station, glad for a chance to leave their desks and paperwork behind, perhaps see some real action out in the field. They headed toward San Felipe

Casino and continued east. About a mile down the old Hagan Road, they came to a roadblock pueblo elders had asked the tribal office to construct. Montaño knew it was an official county road, but what of it? Nobody, not the county nor the state, bothered to grade it regularly. After the rains, it became impassable. The tribal office received numerous calls about cars stuck or left stranded. It had been pueblo land for hundreds of years, way before New Mexico became a state and counties were created. When the roadblock was installed, the situation escalated from protests to a lawsuit, but the issue remained at a stalemate.

The captain barked orders for the officers to remove the blockade. Afterward, they continued in silence. Once they were near the canyon, Montaño pulled off the road. The captain motioned for the men to follow. They scrambled to the top of the canyon and looked down at the scene below. It was a mess. Montaño recognized the EMTs, Martinez and Johnson, and also the helicopter pilot who was always buzzing around the area. He didn't know who the other two were but soon found out they were a Santa Fe police detective, Pascal Ruiz, and his girlfriend. The detective had given him some lame story about their dog running away, chasing the dog, and finding this kid tied to a cross—the same kid they had been looking for "as a favor."

The whole thing threw him off balance. He couldn't believe it. Five people traipsing all over a crime scene, mucking it up, contaminating any possible evidence. The EMTs had already removed the boy from the cross. Martinez and Johnson were preparing to load the kid into the copter and leave his team with nothing but dust and dirt to investigate.

The three officers rustled up from the station were not detectives, or even field officers—they were desk clerks. But they were available. After the EMTs debriefed him, he had randomly assigned each officer to a task. Now he had doubts. Ortiz, the least experienced, had been assigned evidence-gathering.

Montaño needed this case wrapped up and off the books as soon as possible. If the newspapers got hold of a story about some white boy dressed as Jesus and hung on a cross on pueblo land, they would have a heyday—especially with Easter in a few days, not to mention the procession to Chimayó. The Hermanos would be enacting their rituals, marching the Stations of the Cross, chanting and whipping themselves with yucca branches.

When Montaño last talked to Ortiz, he was about five miles south of Bernalillo. He must be somewhere between there and San Felipe. It was possible he had car trouble, but if so, he would have called in. That was standard procedure, known even to desk officers, who were the ones who took the distress calls. The captain had tried numerous times to call Ortiz, but each attempt went directly to voicemail.

Montaño tried to reassure himself that nothing had happened and he was blowing the situation out of proportion. He needed to slow down, be patient. Ortiz would probably walk into the station any minute with some story about why he was late. He remembered that Ortiz had mentioned finding something from the crime scene. That was why he was delayed. Now, Montaño was sorry he hadn't asked him about it.

Standard procedure was to alert officers out in the field to be on the lookout for Ortiz. But for some reason, Montaño hesitated. The case was already messy; he definitely didn't want to contact his superiors about Ortiz's disappearance—unless things had really gone south.

He briefly considered calling the Santa Fe detective—maybe let it slip that Ortiz hadn't shown up yet. He was sure Ruiz would jump at the chance to try tracking down Ortiz—stick his nose in the case, then ask for favors. He hoped he wouldn't have to stoop that low. He would give Ortiz another hour.

The phone rang, and he grabbed it in the hope it was Ortiz. But it was his secretary. She said Ortiz's wife had called. There was something wrong with the baby, and her sister had taken them to the hospital.

Montaño never cursed, as swear words meant nothing to him, providing little if any satisfaction. Instead, he pounded his fist on the desk several times until his knuckles bled. Then he called Ruiz.

"Ruiz."

"Captain Montaño." For a split-second, the captain almost hung up. "Is Ortiz back?"

"No."

Ruiz was speechless. Why would Montaño call him? He held the phone to his ear and waited. Silence. For a moment, he wondered if Montaño had hung up.

"Wanted to give you an update. Ortiz's still not back. Don't know where he is. I talked to him almost two hours ago. He was heading north on 313, past Shady Lakes. I've called his cell, no answer, goes to voicemail."

Pascal's muscles twitched. Something was wrong. Ortiz should be back by now.

"Who's been alerted?"

Although Montaño knew it was a normal question, it irritated him. "No one, yet."

Pascal had the impression Montaño was trying to deliver some kind of coded message, something he couldn't come right out and say. It would not only mean losing face but also was against protocol. Pascal decided to play dumb. If nothing else, he knew it would frustrate Montaño. "Thanks for getting back to me. Let me know when Ortiz shows up."

Montaño glared across the room and bit his tongue not to blurt out something he would probably regret. He slammed the phone down, not sure Ruiz had the brains to decipher his message. But if he did, he was the cocky sort who would need only a nudge. When they were out at Tonque, Montaño could tell the detective itched to stick his nose in the case. Montaño was familiar with that type, always stretching the envelope, never content to only do his job.

~32~

STEG COULDN'T BELIEVE HOW TOUGH IT WAS TO BREAK THE PATROL car window. The crime shows he watched always made it look easy: whack, and the glass breaks. It had taken three blows, each one mercilessly jarring his body and rattling his teeth. By the third hit, he had created a hole big enough to grab the costume through the window. But as he reached in, he realized too late that the prudent move would have been to unlock the car door. The broken glass caught his shirt, and as he tried to tear free, he gashed his arm.

Steg had always been squeamish about blood. Once when his dog snagged his hip on barbed wire, Steg had looked down at the bloody leg and passed out. His friends found him on the ground and figured he had fallen and knocked himself out.

The flow of blood oozing out of his arm made him nauseous and dizzy. He had to close his eyes, and tried to steady his breath. As he reached up to rub his sore shoulder, he winced. It still throbbed from the rifle kickback when he had shot out the cruiser's tire. When he pulled the trigger, he wasn't prepared, and the butt of the rifle jammed into him with such force that he let out a yelp. It had taken all his strength to steady the gun, and he was amazed when he saw the cruiser swerve. He had hit the tire.

Although Steg had played endless video games involving gunplay, he never had fired a real gun. Throughout his childhood, he had coveted his father's collection of antique firearms but never was allowed to touch them, much less fire one. His father, not the sharing type, kept them locked in a cabinet in his study. Steg wasn't even allowed in the room. But once when he was ten, the housekeeper had sent him to fetch his father for lunch. The study door was slightly ajar. Steg stood riveted in the hallway as he watched his father lock the gun cabinet, pull back one of the curtains, and hang the key on a hook. Steg had tiptoed back down the hall, waited for a minute, then called his father to lunch.

He tore open the bag to make sure it contained the costume, and sighed with relief. At least something had been accomplished. Now maybe Coriz would get off his case. But his jubilant state faded as his attention turned to the officer. Where was he? Steg was worried that the man might have seen him in the driveway or watched him break out the car window. If he got a look at Steg, he would remember their encounter at the hospital. The officer had stared a second too long, although people always stared at him. His appearance was an anomaly, especially in New Mexico. His white hair and skin, not to mention his almost-colorless eyes, stood out like a sore thumb. People often assumed he was an albino. As a youngster, he had been teased relentlessly. His father had insisted he be tested for the genetic mutation that causes albinism, but the results were negative even though the pigmentation of Steg's skin, eyes, and hair was minimal. He was a freak of nature.

Steg was concerned. If the officer identified him, he would link him to Coriz and Eubank. Then they would all go down. It would be worse than the police finding the Jesus costume, although the costume could implicate him in the opera break-in. What was he supposed to do now?

Questions popped up in Steg's mind and caused him to sweat, even though the temperature was dropping. He wondered if maybe the officer had gone for help. But why hadn't they crossed paths? Why would the officer need help? Couldn't he change his own tire? But what if he saw the bullet in the tire? Maybe he would think it was teenagers. Steg remembered as a youngster throwing eggs at cars driven by tourists who wanted to catch a glimpse of Los Alamos, the home of the atomic bomb.

As Steg scanned the property, he realized there weren't many places to hide. There was an old barn and a stand of bushes over on the north side of the property. He hurried over, peered in the barn, and illuminated the interior with his phone's flashlight. Nothing.

Then he made his way through the knee-high brush to the clump of bushes, careful where he stepped. He used his rifle to move the branches apart. But as he pushed his way farther into the cluster, his toe sank into something damp. "Ugh." Nausea churned in his stomach again. He couldn't imagine what it was but didn't want to find out. He backed out of the bushes, satisfied nobody was in there.

There was nowhere else to hide. Steg presumed that the officer had seen the bullet and made a run for it. A barbed wire fence snaked along the property line from the main road almost to the interstate. In places, the fence sagged on decayed posts, releasing the wire almost to the ground. Steg made his way down the fence line with his eyes to the ground, worried he would step in a hole, on a snake, or in something disgusting. He had never been the outdoor type. His light skin burned easily, so he stayed out of the sun.

Those days they filmed out at Tonque had been the worst experience of his life. Even worse than the summer his father had sent him to Outward Bound on Lake Michigan for three weeks. For ten days, he had been forced to carry a huge backpack that shifted continually on his skinny frame and created a huge sore on his hip. The next ten days, sea kayaking exposed the sore to the water, further exacerbating it. He could barely walk when the three weeks were over.

Coriz had brought mushrooms he supposedly had gathered up on Mount Taylor. He insisted they all try them, saying it would be a cathartic experience. Steg wasn't sure he wanted his emotions purged but wasn't about to admit that to Coriz, much less Eubank.

At first, the mushrooms made him nauseous. But after he vomited, he started to hallucinate, and things got weird. Right at the height of their trip, they came out of the canyon, and there was Pilot against a boulder. Coriz knew him from high school, said Pilot was cool. Maybe he could help with the last scene. But as they started to walk back into the canyon, Coriz got a text, an emergency. Something had to be taken care of at the pueblo. Steg thought it was strange, because cell service had been sketchy down in the canyon.

Coriz took the van and left them to wrap up the project. He assured them someone would be back in a few hours to pick them up.

But nobody showed until the next morning. His nephew, Benny, arrived with this Datsun sedan that barely had room for the equipment. Apparently, the van had a flat tire. Thomas reassured Pilot, who kept nodding off, that they would be back shortly after they changed the van's tire. There wasn't any way they could fit him in the car. He was so out of it, having taken too many Percocets and maybe even eaten a mushroom. They tried to take him down from the cross, but he kicked and waved his arms in the air, and they figured he would be safer off the ground anyway.

Once the car was loaded, Thomas jumped in and claimed the front seat. Steg had to squeeze into the back. He was forced to sit sideways with his feet on a huge box of cameras and a tangle of cords balanced on his lap.

The sound of a car engine startled Steg back to the present. He instinctively fell to the ground. When he looked up, he saw a set of headlights making their way toward the house on the next property. The car seemed to be going much too fast. In front of the house, the driver slammed on the brakes and sent a plume of dust in the air. He blasted the horn three times, then the front door of the house swung open and a young couple stumbled out clinging to each other and laughing. After they climbed into the car, the driver stepped on the gas and swerved back and forth all the way down the drive. Steg could hear the occupants squeal with glee. He looked at the house, which was dark now; they hadn't even bothered to turn on the porch light. Steg shook his head in disgust. He had little patience for frivolity.

Steg continued down the fence line, searching both sides for any sign of movement. He was about a hundred yards from the main road when he spotted the officer across the adjacent field, figuring that he must have climbed over the barbed wire. Periodically, the top of the officer's head popped up above the alfalfa. He moved erratically back and forth, as if he couldn't decide which way to go.

The sun had gone down behind the mesa, leaving the field in dark shadows. Steg could barely detect the officer's outline. He had been surprised when he shot out the cruiser's tire, as he had doubted he would be able to hit a moving target that far away. But the car traveled in a straight line and gave him time to adjust his sights. Although he was within range of the officer, it would be difficult to hit a target that moved unpredictably.

Steg let the costume fall to the ground, raised the rifle, and set the butt against his shoulder. He lined up the officer in his sights and tried to anticipate his movement. Then he steadied his breathing, ready to take a shot, but the officer stood up and turned toward Steg. For a few seconds, Steg froze, then took in a deep breath, held it, and squeezed the trigger. The gun slammed into his shoulder and threw him backward to the ground. He got up and looked across the field. It was empty. The officer was gone.

He wondered if he had imagined the entire scene; maybe it was a flashback from the mushrooms. It spooked him. He looked down at his hands, which were shaking uncontrollably. The temperature had dropped considerably, but sweat ran down his brow, stung his eyes, and blurred his vision. He wanted to wipe them with his sleeve but worried about shards of glass stuck in his jacket from the cruiser window. He bent down and picked up the costume. His legs wobbled as he continued down the fence line searching for an opening. He came to a place where the wire drooped almost to the ground and easily stepped over it, careful not to catch his pants.

Steg was worried. If the bullet hadn't hit the officer, he would be in big trouble. And if the bullet had hit the officer and he couldn't find him, he would be in bigger trouble. The crimes against him seemed to be mounting. When he and Eubank had put the kid on the cross, that was one thing, a prank, but now, he had shot out a police cruiser's tire, broken the cruiser's window, stolen evidence, and maybe wounded or killed an officer. It astounded him that only a few days ago, he had been an ordinary person, an artist, a filmmaker, but now he was a violent felon. He wondered if other felons found themselves in similar situations—waking up one day and discovering they were criminals by circumstance.

Steg tramped back and forth through the field. He became more and more exasperated as he tried to find the officer. He was almost positive his shot had hit its mark. The man had to be somewhere in the field. He saw a clump of crushed weeds a few yards away. As he bent down to get a closer look, he saw buttons scattered around and specks of blood in the dirt. His spirits rose; at least the man was wounded. But where was he? Steg stood and scanned the field. Nothing. The air was static, not even the slightest breeze.

Steg looked back toward the barbed wire fence where he had crossed into the property. Nothing. At the end of the drive, the silhouette of the house, left dark by its occupants, disappeared into the horizon. Nothing. The grass and weeds stood rigid and motionless. Nothing. It was if all the air had been sucked out. The officer had vanished.

As Steg continued down the drive, a set of headlights strobed through the trees along the main road. Instinctively, he ducked as the car passed. But then it slowed and turned down the drive where the police cruiser sat. His heart pounded in his chest as he dashed toward the road, then crossed to the other side and backtracked to where he had left the Mini Cooper in a turnoff a few hundred yards south. Whoever went down the drive would see the cruiser, notice the broken window, and call the authorities. Cops would be all over the place soon.

Although he had the costume, it wouldn't be of any use now. He carelessly gunned the car, spit gravel, and made too much noise. He needed to get rid of the gun, cringing at the thought of disposing of it in the Rio Grande—his father would never forgive him. But then again, his father would never forgive him for any of this. There was no turning back now. He had crossed the line.

He would drop off the costume at the warehouse, then leave the country. His dual citizenship with Germany would let him travel seamlessly throughout the European Union. No passport inspections. He could slip in and out of countries without notice. A college friend, Kuba, had invited Steg many times to visit him in the Czech Republic, where Kuba helped his family tend its vineyards along the Vltava River. It would be the perfect place. No one would think to look for him there. He would be safe. His only regret was the film, his film—but YinYangYazzie was over. Finished.

~33~

PASCAL HAD GOTTEN THE MESSAGE LOUD AND CLEAR. HE WAS sure Montaño had passed along the information about the missing officer to tempt Pascal. But he couldn't figure out Montaño's angle—unless he wanted to save face and not have to report the officer missing on his watch.

It was strange that Ortiz hadn't returned to the pueblo. Something wasn't right. An officer in a police vehicle couldn't disappear into thin air. But a drive to Bernalillo again was the last thing he wanted to do this afternoon. He couldn't remember the last time he had to go to Bernalillo, but now he might be headed there for the second time in two days.

Sandia Pueblo bordered the highway from Shady Lakes all the way to Bernalillo. The captain had mentioned that the last contact with Ortiz had been around that area. Pascal figured that if someone had stopped the officer, it would be between Bernalillo and Algodones, as that stretch was more desolate, only a few privately owned farms and small ranches dotting both sides of the road. Pascal was reluctant but didn't want to jump to conclusions. He always tried to check himself—keep from going off half-cocked. Maybe the man had stopped for a burger.

Pascal starred at the clock hanging on the wall above the white board. It still ran slow just as it had in his school days. No matter how many times Pascal reset the clock, it continued to lose time. It was half past three, a few hours away from calling it a day.

He turned back to his desk. As he rummaged through the pile of paperwork, being someplace other than the station started to become more appealing. He racked his brain for a plausible excuse to leave early, but nothing came to mind. Susie raised her eyebrows as he smiled and walked toward the door. He had learned it was best to say nothing. Making up excuses only digs you in deeper.

The rush hour traffic had already started to build. Nobody seemed to live where they worked. Pascal was thankful that he didn't have much of a commute. As much as he liked to get out of the office, spending hours in the car was the last thing he wanted to do on a daily basis. The traffic slowed to a crawl as he merged onto the freeway and joined the commuters on their way back to Albuquerque after a day at the Roundhouse.

The cars picked up speed, settling into their lanes. Pascal's head started to clear, as it always did when he was on the move. The fog that settled in his brain after sitting for hours at his desk dissipated. For the first time since Tonque, he thought about Bobby Pilot. Pascal realized that he had slipped into the typical trap lured by the scent of a perpetrator. The victim who was whisked away and forgotten becomes a mere piece of evidence to explore at some later date. Criminal investigations focus on the scene, not the victim. The attention is directed toward the criminal, as if the crime happened in a vacuum. He was familiar with tunnel vision, the loss of the periphery. Relevant information and important clues attached to victim are often overlooked and lost.

Pascal had been offered the detective job partly as a favor to his uncle and partly because the department needed a warm body. His employment was provisional. He realized he would be replaced as soon as someone qualified was found for the position, not that Pascal didn't have some assets for the job. He could think critically and solve problems, and also had excellent written and oral communication skills. After all, he had attended the Sorbonne in Paris.

But he quickly realized that he was a fish out of water. If he was going to be successful, he needed to understand criminals and their motives. Pascal had immersed himself in forensic literature. He watched crime and detective shows, from CSI to Murder, She Wrote. He read detective novels. He studied techniques for gathering facts for investigations and honed his skills for interviewing witnesses. He explored modes of gathering and examining physical evidence and methods for observing and interrogating suspects and understanding motives. Pascal became fascinated with forensic psychologists who work with law enforcement officials to integrate psychological science into criminal profiling. David Webb's book, Criminal Profiling: An Introductory Guide became his bible. It was clear and concise.

Pascal thought about, as Webb would term it, the perpetrators' modus operandi. Why had they dressed Bobby in the Jesus costume? Crucified him on a cross? Was it symbolic? Retaliatory? Vengeful? Happenstance? A prank? Who were they? Each question made him feel like he was sinking deeper and deeper in muddy water and didn't know how to swim. Not to mention that this wasn't his case.

~34~

MARCOS ALCAZAR OPENED THE FRONT DOOR OF HIS SMALL adobe. He drank in the sparse surroundings and welcomed the emptiness. People's obsession with nonessential items or fascination with embellishments had always been a mystery to him. He couldn't be comfortable around too many things.

When he married Mary, she had been a busy student, and once she graduated, she had been a busy nurse. She didn't have time to accumulate things, and in order to keep their house in order, they agreed to keep it sparse. But after they lost the second baby, Mary Theresa began to fill all the spaces and eliminate the emptiness. This smothered her husband. The once-naked windows offering bucolic views were now cloaked in thick, floor-to-ceiling drapes that shut out the light. His wife filled the rooms, already too full of furniture, with overstuffed chairs, bookcases, and tables.

One day, she had an ornate antique armoire delivered that took up an entire wall of the living room. Any flat surface became piled with knickknacks and detritus. Sometimes he found it a challenge to make his way through the living room without hitting his shin or knocking something over.

Magazines that rarely saw their way to the recycle bin came in the mail daily. Mary Theresa balked at the idea of throwing away an issue, claiming there was still an article she hadn't read yet. The magazines were left stacked in piles on the floor. He wondered now if it had been all the clutter, or Mary Theresa, that caused his throat to close, his breath to wheeze, and his heart to race with panic. He was suffocating.

Alcazar felt uncomfortable about the kid, Bobby Pilot. He had agreed to meet him at the house on Tuesday. But he quickly brushed away his pang of guilt. After all, the kid had practically stalked him, climbed into his truck, then went on and on about the Good Friday procession to Chimayó. Alcazar hadn't any intention of walking to Chimayó. He wasn't going anywhere.

He sank into his recliner, tilted the chair back, and closed his eyes. He had spent three exhausting days in Albuquerque advising the Brotherhood. His move north had been mostly prompted by the breakup of the marriage, but it also allowed him to extricate himself from the Brotherhood. He was relieved to disentangle himself from the group's mounting problems, or at least put some miles between them.

Alcazar, the eldest son of a Penitente father, had been initiated into the Brotherhood automatically at the age of eighteen. Although he never had questioned his right to participate, he sometimes lamented his effortless entry into the sect. He wasn't required to apply or undergo initiation like others. Because his background was known, his faith was accepted, and there was never any doubt about his conviction.

Aspirants were only allowed to apply for admission to the Brotherhood after mature thought and religious promise. New candidates' lives and motives were investigated before they could even receive instruction in the Brotherhood's regulations and rituals. And before the rite of initiation, they had to pass an examination and obtain a sponsor.

There never was a doubt that Alcazar would join the Brotherhood, and over the years, he had willingly participated in it to honor and obey his parents. He was thankful that his membership had come at a time of reconciliation between the Brotherhood and the Catholic Church.

In the latter part of the nineteenth century, a movement to Americanize the church in New Mexico had led to attempts to suppress the Brotherhood. The suppression drove the membership underground, which fostered rumors of strange behavior and claims that the Penitentes were a "secret society." During this period, the Brotherhood continued to perform a modified form of religious rituals and pursued its commitment to acts of community charity.

Alcazar, drained after listening to endless bickering among the members, realized that his move up north had helped him be more objective when considering the issues. He advised them about how best to address the situation with the church and approach the up-coming lawsuit. But he wondered how the members were ever going to come to a consensus and achieve what they wanted.

Although in the past, the group had weathered the Catholic Church's attempts to suppress it, there were new issues. Recently, a growing swell of women, who were not considered members but an-cillary personnel, had demanded equal representation and partici-pation in the ceremonial practices. A few practitioners were open to the inclusion of women, but no one was willing to champion their request. A growing contingent of the Brotherhood adamantly pro-tested the participation of women. Alcazar had grown weary of the ongoing controversy, which disturbed his new serenity.

But when the Brotherhood called about another matter, he didn't hesitate. Three members had been arrested and charged with tres-passing on the San Jose church property that had served the Broth-erhood for a number of years.

The land where the chapel sat was part of a seventeenth-century land grant handed down to Spanish settlers by King Charles II of Spain. The system had been intended to expand the Spanish empire in the Southwest. Prominent individuals in communities could request large parcels of land to create settlements and increase eco-nomic development. The descendants of the original Atrisco land grant recipients still held title to the land.

The controversy began when the descendants of the land grant decided to sell their shares to a development company that would manage the land and create a heritage foundation. The foundation took charge of the chapel and intended to repurpose it as a commu-nity center.

The Brotherhood contended that the church functioned as a vital service for the community and provided residents with regular reli-gious services. It insisted that the chapel remain a place of worship, as it had been for a number of years.

The dispute over the ownership of the chapel had reached the Archbishop of Santa Fe, who supported the Penitentes' assertion that it had been a Catholic place of worship for many years. Unfortunately, since the land grant owned the property where the chapel sat, the Church conceded that it had no legal claim.

The foundation, with plans to reopen the chapel as a venue for public events, hadn't lost any time. It put a fence around the property and locked the gate, then removed all the contents of the chapel, including the church bell, pews, life-sized santos carved from cottonwood, and even the wood-burning stove.

The men of the Brotherhood had taken Alcazar to see the seized property. He didn't blame his brothers, who had torn down the gate to pray in the chapel. They were incensed that they were barred from the church they had called their own and had attended for years.

Alcazar arranged bail for the jailed men and advised the group to take a different path. The only option would be through legal channels if they were to regain control of the church. The group pleaded with him to represent it, but he insisted there would be a conflict of interest. The Brotherhood spent hours in deliberation but finally voted to obtain an outside attorney to sue the foundation. It was going to challenge the nonprofit's legal right to bar the Penitente brothers from the Morada de San José. Alcazar wished them luck.

~36~

As Pascal pulled off the freeway at the Algodones exit, his phone rang. He maneuvered his car over to the side of the road, turned off his engine, and glanced at the caller ID: Rupert.

"Ruiz."

"Hey boss, found something on Alcazar. I located his wife, Mary Theresa. They're separated. She's an E.R. nurse at Presbyterian. She didn't have his phone number, wasn't even sure he had a phone. When she last talked to him a few months ago, it was in person. But she gave me his sister's number, Anna Lucero. She lives in Socorro."

Pascal wrote down both numbers. "Thanks, Rupert. Appreciate it."

"Hey." Rupert hesitated. "What's this all about?"

"It's not our case officially, but it's connected to the stolen costume from the opera grounds."

Silence on the other end of the line. Pascal sighed. "Look, Rupert. I'm wrapping up something that the captain asked me to check into."

"Well, tread lightly, boss. Just saying."

"Yeah, I know, Rupert. I need to talk to Alcazar, then I'm done."

Pascal knew that wasn't exactly true, and didn't like being dishonest, especially with Rupert. He knew he shouldn't involve him in this business. Rupert, a good cop, worked hard and was always helpful. He didn't want to endanger their relationship. But Pascal hadn't seen any other way. He needed to locate Alcazar. He would call the guy's sister later and see if she had a number for him. If not, that would be the end of it.

This trip to Bernalillo only dug him deeper in a case that he didn't have any business messing around with. The right thing to do would be turn over the information on Alcazar to Montaño and let him work it. Pascal hung on to the idea that if he found Ortiz, it might give him an opening to the case. But he knew that wasn't likely. He knew the way things worked. It wasn't his territory. But he couldn't help himself.

He pulled back on the road and drove south toward Bernalillo. Although the sun hadn't totally sunk below the horizon, the road seemed muted in darkness. There were no street lights, and the cottonwoods and elms, even without leaves, blocked most of the light left in the sky and created an eerie haze. He drove slower than the limit, looking for pulloffs or driveways. There were no designated cross-streets. The land was locked in by the freeway on the east and the river on the west. The properties on each side of the road were long and narrow. Pascal figured that if Ortiz had pulled over somewhere between here and Bernalillo, he had to be down someone's driveway. He wondered why? If he'd had car trouble, it seems that he would have notified the station.

Pascal circled through the empty parking lot of the new elementary school, then continued south until he came to the first cutoff on the west. He was surprised to find an improved road, graded with crusher fines, and wide enough for two cars to pass easily. The drive crossed over the ditch, then curved to the right and headed north along the west side of the ditch. A few hundred yards up, the drive curved to the left and went over the railroad tracks. He figured it must have cost a fortune to grade and surface. Finally, the drive straightened out, and he had a clear view of the property.

It wasn't your typical Algodones venue. Instead, it was an elaborate equestrian facility that looked as if it had been transported from the Virginia hunt country. Pristine white wooden fences corralled small herds of horses that grazed on what he imagined to be Kentucky bluegrass. An enormous barn was flanked by two riding arenas: an outdoor ring set up with an array of jumps and the other covered to provide an escape from the relentless New Mexican sun.

Pascal pulled up to the first of three houses staggered along the north end of the property. There was no sign of Ortiz's patrol car, but it wouldn't hurt to ask. As he started to get out of the car, the front door of the house burst open. An enormous Irish wolfhound covered with wiry gray hair stood on the porch, alert but silent. Pascal recognized the breed. Santa Fe had a notorious wolfhound owned by a pugnacious woman who insisted that the dog go wherever she did. She hadn't even bothered to get one of those therapy dog certificates. The dog snarled and snapped at anyone within reach—not to mention the fact that it suffered from an accumulation of gas in the alimentary canal and was famously known for clearing out a room in twenty seconds. The station had been inundated with complaints about the animal.

The wolfhound bounded down the steps toward Pascal. He was relieved to see a woman appear at the door. She was dressed in full English equestrian attire. White riding pants hugged her tall, slim body, and black shiny boots stretched up her calves. Her sky-blue show coat was trimmed with red piping and accessorized with rhinestones on the front pockets that glittered in the fading sunlight. Pascal was thankful the woman didn't carry a whip, because she looked ready to put one to use. Her jet-black hair, constrained in a tight bun, set off her smooth ivory skin. The expression on her face was one he had seen many times: defiant and belligerent.

At the bottom of the steps, the woman called the dog, which immediately turned and hugged her left side. Pascal pulled himself out of the car and flashed his ID. The dog's tail wagged, and his huge body wiggled with excitement. Maybe the dog was friendly, but maybe he was anticipating his next meal.

"Sorry to bother you. I'm looking for a missing officer."

"Well, he doesn't seem to be here." The woman said as she fanned her hand in the air around the property.

"He's with the San Felipe Police, in a patrol car. We think he might have had car trouble and pulled off somewhere between here and Bernalillo."

The woman stared at Pascal without expression. He wondered how she kept her skin so creamy in the New Mexico sun.

"Has anyone been down your drive this afternoon?"

The woman pursed her lips. "No."

Pascal found it difficult to believe. With an establishment like this, there had to have been a dozen or so people coming and going daily. But the drive ended at the third house, and there didn't seem to be any sign of life anywhere. Unless Ortiz was hiding in the barn, he wasn't here. Pascal considered asking if he could take a look but decided against it, at least for now.

"Thanks for your time." Pascal started to leave but turned back. "Are there any abandoned properties between here and Bernalillo?"

The woman let out a humorless laugh. "God, yes!"

Pascal waited. He was good at waiting. It usually unsettled people. Most people didn't like silence; they eventually gave up and answered.

The woman sighed. "There's a property, been vacant for years—has only a barn, or what's left of one. It's down the road about a mile; the drive is on the east side. There's an old faded blue mailbox barely standing, with the name Salazar."

"Thanks. Appreciate it, ma'am." Pascal for the umpteenth time wished he wore a cowboy hat so he could tip it to the little lady. Next time he visited Albuquerque, he would stop at the Man's Hat Shop and check out the cowboy hats.

Pascal, careful not to kick up too much dust, drove slowly. Before he approached the first bend, he glanced in his rearview mirror. The woman still stood in the middle of the drive, the dog's collar in hand. Once he turned the corner, he picked up speed and headed back toward the main road.

He turned south, clocked three-quarters of a mile and started looking for a blue mailbox on the left. But he still almost missed it. The mailbox rested against a bush, the pole mostly rotted. The driveway wasn't much more than an overgrown rutted path. As he turned up the drive, a canopy of elm trees choked out the light even more. His headlights picked up Ortiz's police cruiser halfway up the drive.

He pulled up behind it and stared out his windshield. As the woman had said, the only structure on the property was a dilapidated barn. Even from a distance, the barn looked as if it would collapse any minute. It sagged to the right against a massive cottonwood tree, the roof almost nonexistent except for a few rafters.

As Pascal got out of the car, he took in the stillness. The only sound came from a slight hum that occasionally drifted over from the freeway when the wind changed direction. As he came up to the side of the cruiser, he saw the broken glass. The passenger window had been smashed out. Nothing seemed damaged as he shined his flashlight into the car. He reached in his back pocket for his handkerchief, reached in and opened the door, careful not to smudge any prints, although he doubted there would be any. Ortiz's phone rested between the seats still attached to its Bluetooth cord. He looked around the floor and under the seats but there found nothing but broken glass. No Jesus costume. As he closed the door, he looked down and noticed the flat tire. He knelt to take a better look and couldn't believe it: A bullet was wedged in the tire.

"Jesus Christ," he said under his breath.

A sound, a slight crackle of a leaf startled him. A familiar tingle crept up the back of his neck and made a buzzing sound in his head. He held his breath as he scanned left and right. Nothing. He turned back to the tire and took out his penknife to remove the bullet but stopped. What was he thinking? Not his case. If he tampered with evidence, they'd throw the book at him. He knew he should call Montaño right now. But first he wanted to look around. Once San Felipe arrived, it would be over for him. Even though he had found Bobby Pilot, even though he had found Ortiz's car, he wouldn't be invited to join the party.

As he walked over to the barn, he kept his eyes on the ground, checking for any signs that someone had been there. Although it hadn't rained in two weeks, there wouldn't be any tracks in the hard-packed caliche, but maybe some scuffed dirt or crushed leaves. He stopped and listened every few feet. Nothing.

Up close, the barn looked even more unstable. He wasn't about to even stick his head inside. Someone would have to be crazy to use it as their hiding place. The front door hung open, held in place by only one hinge. He shined his torch through the opening. The barn had a dirt floor, and except for piles of dead leaves and mouse droppings, it was empty.

He scanned the rest of the property. It was about ten acres with a typical New Mexico layout, long and narrow, the width a couple of hundred feet but the length extending almost to the freeway. There weren't any outbuildings, only weeds and brush. Strands of drooping barbed wire fence barely contained the property. Pascal walked halfway down the length of the field but could tell that the bare land left nowhere to hide, not even a bush.

He went back to his car and called Montaño, debating whether he should stay until San Felipe arrived. The costume, his connection to the case, was either with Ortiz or gone.

The captain answered on the first ring.

"Ruiz."

"Yeah?"

"Found Ortiz's cruiser."

"Where?"

"Near Algodones. Mile and a half south from the freeway exit, down an abandoned driveway. There's a blue mailbox, barely standing, with the name Salazar."

"Ortiz?"

"He's not here."

"And?"

"Looks like he had a flat tire, pulled off the road to change it."

"Ortiz is the cautious type. What else?" Montaño was irritated. He could tell Ruiz held back information and let each piece of news settle in before he offered the next. Typical police strategy.

"His tire has been shot out."

"Shot out? Like with a gun?"

"Looks that way. The bullet's still in the tire."

"And?" Montaño said gritting his teeth.

"Someone smashed the cruiser's passenger window." Pascal felt Montaño's anger pulse through the phone.

"Anything damaged?"

"Don't think so. His phone is still plugged in. But no Ortiz, no costume."

"Stay put. On my way."

Montaño disconnected before Pascal could say anything. He didn't want to be mixed up in Ortiz's disappearance. He wondered how he would he explain what he was doing out here. His standard answer for being somewhere he wasn't supposed to be would have to suffice: pulled off to take a leak.

~36~

Pascal leaned against his car and waited for Montaño. This was one of those moments when he wished he still smoked. It would give him something to do, take his mind off the hole he seemed to be digging himself deeper and deeper into. Although the captain had asked him to look into Bobby Pilot's disappearance, once San Felipe took over the case, his involvement should have ended. The captain would have a fit if he found out Pascal had driven to Algodones to look for a San Felipe officer, not to mention that he had found the patrol car and then hung around for San Felipe Tribal to show up.

Pascal knew he should spend his time on the only case he actually had, the break-in at the opera storage shed, but he had gotten sucked into this mess. The Jesus costume was the link. The one Pilot had worn out at Tonque had to be the same one taken from the storage shed. But now it had gone missing. What did he have? Nothing. Unless San Felipe let him ride on its shirttails, he was out of luck.

While he waited for Montaño, Pascal decided to make use of his time following up some loose ends. He figured he had at least fifteen minutes to check something off his list.

He hadn't talked to Jessie since he'd left the ranch. He punched in her number. It rang five times before she answered, identifying herself in a monotone: "Jessie Archuleta."

"Hey, Detective Ruiz."

There was a silence on the line. Pascal waited. He wanted to give her time to collect herself, decide how to respond.

"What can I do for you, detective?" she asked coldly.

Pascal stared at the ground. Once again, he realized his ineptness in dealing with women. He couldn't understand Jessie's abrupt change in attitude. She had been flirtatious out at Diamond Tail Ranch, but now, her coquettish behavior had evaporated, and in its place was wrath.

"I wanted to check in with you, see how things are going."

"Oh?" she said with mock surprise.

Pascal always found it was best to say what was on his mind, not that it always went well.

"Hey, what's going on?"

"What's going on?"

"Yes, what's going on?" Pascal repeated calmly.

"Well, I'll tell you. My boyfriend is in a coma. The nurse told me today he has a brain bleed. You never called and told me you found Bobby. I haven't heard one iota from anyone. Nobody is doing anything about what happened to Bobby."

"I'm so sorry. I know how frustrated you must be. San Felipe took over of the case since Bobby was found on the reservation. It's their jurisdiction. I've tried to find out as much as possible, but I have to fly under the radar."

Jessie softened a little. "I'm grateful you found Bobby, I really am. The doctors said he probably wouldn't have survived out there much longer."

"What else do you know about his condition?"

"He's still in a coma. He can't feel, speak, hear, or move. Jesus— you can stick a pin in him and he doesn't respond, can't feel it."

"What's the prognosis?"

"They say he'll come out of it when he comes out."

"I'm sorry."

"One of the nurses told me that a coma sometimes is good, a protective response to injury, gives the body time to heal before the person wakes up. I guess that's supposed to give me hope."

Pascal considered apologizing but said nothing.

"They've done a million tests on him. They think the coma was caused by a combination of hitting his head when he fell and the physical and mental stress of being left out there on the cross—not to mention the amount of Percocet they found in his bloodstream."

"Percocet?"

"Yes, someone must have given him a bottle because they found one tucked in his loin cloth." Jessie giggled. "Sorry, I know it's not funny but it's really bizarre."

"Was there a name on the prescription bottle?"

"No, the label had been rubbed off. Only part of the pharmacy name was there. They think it was from Walgreens, but there are a hundred of those around. It would take forever to track down all the Percocet prescriptions. The police haven't even inquired about his condition. Can you believe it?"

Jessie had a right to be incensed. Ortiz should have inquired about Bobby's condition when he picked up the costume. And now with Ortiz missing, the victim would have to wait.

"What about this brain bleed?"

"The bleed is from the fall, but they can't operate until he comes out of the coma. Oh, God—it's so horrible."

"If there's anything I can do, Jessie, let me know."

"Please find out who did this to Bobby, please."

"I'm on it."

He heard a siren and saw the multicolored flashing lights of the San Felipe police, and he ended the call. The lead car overshot the driveway, slammed on the brakes, and swerved to make the turn. Both cars immediately stopped as they hit the deep grooves in the drive. Then they slowly maneuvered up behind Pascal's car. Montaño jumped out, then the front doors of the second car swung open and two officers climbed out. Pascal recognized them from Tonque: Tommy Candelaria and Ralph Garcia. They stared at Pascal with blank expressions, but he could tell they wondered what the hell he was doing there. They waited for their orders.

Montaño walked over to Ortiz's cruiser and inspected the smashed-in window. He shook his head, then looked down at the tire, turned to the two officers, and barked orders: "Candelaria: Prints. Garcia: Secure the area, check for evidence." Then he raised his chin toward Ruiz. "I'll deal with him."

The two officers quickly got to work. Montaño turned to Pascal with a slight grin on his face and asked, "What brings you out here, detective?"

"Was on my way to Bernalillo, pulled off to take a leak, saw the cruiser, called it in."

Montano pursed his lips. "Yeah, sounds plausible, but with your history being always where you aren't supposed to be," Montano shook his head, "nobody's going to fall for that."

Pascal shrugged.

"What do you figure happened?" Montaño added. "Off the record."

"Off the record?"

Montaño shrugged. Pascal was starting to like this guy.

"Someone shot out Ortiz's tire. Looks like they used a rifle. It would be difficult to hit a tire with a handgun. Maybe kids, or someone with a grudge against the police. My money's on whoever dressed Bobby Pilot in that costume and tied him to that cross out at Tonque. I'm sure whoever did this was after the costume—it's incriminating evidence."

"Ortiz?"

"He either left on foot, or whoever shot his tire got hold of him."

"And the window?" Montaño jotted his chin toward the cruiser.

"Ortiz had a blowout, pulled off the road, inspected the tire, saw the bullet, heard someone coming, locked the cruiser, and took off on foot. The guy saw the costume in the cruiser, broke the window."

"Sounds plausible."

"Yeah, but could have gone down another way."

"Yeah?"

"After the guy gets the costume, he looks for Ortiz and either kidnaps or kills him."

Montaño shot Ruiz a cold stare. "Not likely. Ortiz is an Indian. He could easily slip away, disappear, make his way back to the pueblo on foot."

"I hope you're right."

Candelaria came over and held out his hand with the bullet from Ortiz's tire. Montaño picked it up and inspected it. Then to Pascal's surprise, he handed it to him. Pascal had seen enough bullets to recognize that it wasn't from your typical hunting rifle. He had no idea what kind of firearm would shoot this bullet, but took notice of the etching on it: Patrone 88.

"Not your everyday hunting rifle; that's for sure. It's a Patrone 88, but I'm not familiar with the cartridge." Pascal handed the bullet back to Montaño.

"We need to find out who owns a rifle that would use this type of bullet as soon as possible," Montaño said as he gave the bullet back to Candelaria. "Anything else?"

"I dusted for prints, doors and inside. Nothing out of order." He nodded toward the cruiser. "Except for the broken window."

The other officer, Garcia, had been inspecting a clump of bushes near the fence. He walked over and joined the group.

"What did you find?" Montaño asked.

"No sign of another vehicle. Maybe they were on foot. No trace of Ortiz either, but there is from someone else, maybe whoever was after him."

Pascal looked over at Candelaria, curious. He hadn't found or seen anything indicating someone had been there other than the broken cruiser window.

"What did you find?" Montaño asked.

"A print of a shoe—mostly the toe. I'm going to make a cast. It was in the clump of brush over there." Garcia pointed with his chin toward the small cluster of bushes that Pascal had ignored. "Some animal, maybe a raccoon or stray dog, must have taken a leak there recently. It was still damp enough to make a faint impression when someone stepped into the bushes. Probably seeing if anyone was hiding in there. Nowhere else to hide around here besides the barn. His toe sunk in some damp pee." Garcia grinned.

"Okay. After you make a cast of the foot, you two go back to the station. Find out what kind of rifle fired that bullet. Follow up on the prints. Maybe there are some that aren't Ortiz's. Have Margaret call a tow truck for the cruiser and arrange to have the window replaced." Montaño sighed as he looked back at the car. "Let's keep this under the radar for now."

The two San Felipe officers exchanged sideways glances, then moved toward their cruiser. Pascal figured they weren't happy keeping Ortiz's absence to themselves. Pascal had to agree. It was time to call in Search and Rescue, or at least alert Bernalillo for some backup. If Ortiz was out there, injured or worse, they would need to find him before someone else did.

Montaño's phone rang, and Pascal turned to leave.

~37~

PASCAL DROVE BACK TO THE STATION. IT WAS GOOD FRIDAY, but he wondered what was so good about it. The costume was gone. Now it was back in the hands of whoever took it and put Bobby Pilot on the cross out at Tonque. Although Montaño had initially seemed appreciative that Pascal found Ortiz's cruiser, he hadn't welcomed him with open arms. Pascal hoped Montaño was right and that Ortiz would make his way back to the station. Then he could identify the man who had shot out his tire. But unless he showed up soon, it was a moot point.

Back at the office, Pascal slumped in his chair and again tried to ignore the stack of unfinished paperwork. His phone screen flashed a number. He had put the phone on mute after talking to Jessie. He had two voicemails.

One was from the captain and the other from Gillian. He debated which to listen to first. Hands down, he wanted to hear whatever Gillian had to say, but he suspected the captain was already pissed that Pascal hadn't answered his phone. The captain had certain expectations. The primary one was to answer the phone when he called. He listened to the captain's message. It was brief: "Call me." He assumed the call involved complaints either from Aubusson about the break-in at the opera grounds, or from Jessie about the lack of attention to Bobby Pilot's case. He didn't want to hear either.

He needed to update the captain on the costume and missing San Felipe officer, but his mind was elsewhere, wrapped around the bullet in Ortiz's tire. If San Felipe turned the bullet over to forensics, it could be days before they would get a report. The bullet was an unusual one, and if it was fired by the same person who broke into the storage building at the opera, it could lead to whoever did the break-in. He was tempted to ask Rupert to research the bullet but couldn't figure out an angle that would explain where the bullet came from, much less how it was connected to the opera case. Rupert already was suspicious about the request for Alcazar's phone number. Pascal knew he was digging himself in deeper, and that most likely, it would result in his downfall.

He dialed the captain. "Returning your call, sir."

"Where have you been?" The captain snapped but thankfully didn't wait for an answer. "This Aubusson woman is crawling up my back. Today again, she whined to the commissioner, who in turn chewed me out this afternoon. Oh, you are going to love this. Turns out that the outfit, the Jesus one, is some rare antique costume. It never was supposed to end up in the annual sale. After the Christmas show last year, it was supposed to be returned to the collector, Robert Hainsworth. Mr. Hainsworth had planned to donate it to the Creation Museum in Kentucky. Hainsworth's estate has contacted the opera, and they want the costume back. Now."

"His estate?"

"Yeah. This case is a dozy. Shortly after the production ended, Mr. Hainsworth suffered a brain hemorrhage and died a few days later in the hospital. Nobody inquired about the costume because his estate has been tied up in probate for the past eighteen months. Hainsworth's will was contested by his daughter, Melinda Mistleton—born out of wedlock, no less." The captain paused. Pascal heard him mutter under his breath: Mary, mother of Jesus. "Apparently, Mistleton was Hainsworth's only living blood relative and was supposed to inherit a sizable portion of the estate. Ms. Mistleton's attorney claims that Hainsworth's current will, which was drawn up three years ago, is invalid. The daughter insists her father suffered from dementia and was unduly influenced by Hainsworth's "partner." Again, the captain paused, and Pascal imagined he was crossing himself. "The new will gives control of the entire estate to the partner and doesn't mention the daughter. It's a royal soap opera, and it's giving me a headache."

"Je . . ." Pascal stopped himself before uttering the Lord's name in vain. "What's the status of the probate?"

"It was settled out of court yesterday to everyone's satisfaction. Now the estate needs all the assets, including the costume, in order to distribute them according to the new settlement. I want this off my plate. Please tell me you have something?"

"I talked with Barbara Novak, the guidance counselor at the high school, told her about the break-in and theft of the costume. She couldn't think of anyone who fit the bill. The pot-smoking juveniles she works with wouldn't be caught dead on the opera grounds. If they were stoned and wanted to have some fun, they were more likely to break into a pizza parlor or candy store. Dressing up in costumes isn't exactly their M.O."

"I want those dope-smoking idiots that took the costume found and strung up. Anything else?"

"I have some good news and bad news."

"I don't have all night for the good, bad, and ugly, and my ear is going numb."

"I talked to Captain Montaño at San Felipe Tribal, told him I had someone who might be able to identify the Jesus costume. An officer was on his way to pick up the costume at the UNMH. He was open to having Ms. Aubusson take a look at it. If she could verify the costume was the same one taken from the opera, that would give us a connection to their case."

"It's stepping over the line a bit. But I guess it's all we got. What's the bad news?"

Pascal realized too late that he never should have prefaced the information that way. It was only going to irritate the captain. He wasn't one to play games. "Well, the officer picked up the costume at the hospital but he's disappeared, hasn't made it back to the station." Pascal didn't want to elaborate and mention the bullet in the tire. The captain would wonder how he'd found out about it.

"Oh Lord. If these two cases become intertwined, it's going to take forever to unravel. San Felipe moves at the pace of out-of-season rain. Speaking of which, Jessie is upset. She thinks nothing's being done to find out who put Bobby on that cross. Now with the costume gone and this officer missing, they won't have much to go on. Do they suspect foul play?"

"I'm afraid it looks that way. But let's hope Ortiz stopped off somewhere for a burger and shows up soon with the costume in hand."

"Yeah, when hell freezes over." The captain disconnected.

Pascal sat at his desk and stared at the flickering computer screen. Then he brought up the web browser and typed in "Patrone 88 cartridge." He clicked on his standby, Wikipedia. Sure enough, it wasn't an ordinary hunting rifle. The cartridge had a history. In the late 1800s, the German empire used the Patrone 88, a rimless bottleneck, as its service cartridge. Apparently, the bullet was responsible for starting a military rifle ammunition revolution when it was touted as a new smokeless propellant. The bullet's fast twist let the rifle fire long, heavy bullets with remarkable penetrating ability.

A rifle that fired that kind of bullet could easily shoot out a tire. Pascal wondered who in New Mexico owned such a firearm. Not your local deer hunter. Probably someone who collected antique arms. It should be registered somewhere unless it had been obtained illegally. To track down the owner, he would need Rupert's skills. But he couldn't ask him until they were officially involved in the case.

This case was beginning to exasperate Pascal. He was itching to be involved but knew he needed to step back and let San Felipe do its job. He printed the Wikipedia information and shut his computer.

Then he clicked on Gillian's voicemail. She was inviting him for dinner around 6:30. Gillian had been helpful with his previous case involving the stolen violin. Maybe she could provide a fresh look at the evidence. At this point, anything would help.

~38~

PASCAL GATHERED SOME SUPPLIES TO TAKE OVER TO GILLIAN'S. Although he usually balked at a whiteboard because of its impermanence, he couldn't see taping pieces of newsprint to the immaculately painted walls of Gillian's mother's house. He relied on Gillian to provide some input on the case—another perspective, another viewpoint. There was no one else to ask, since the case wasn't in his jurisdiction.

As Pascal turned down the driveway, Gillian's front door swung open. He was surprised to see Joseph Santiago step out. Pascal knew Santiago had been her mother's gardener. But he also knew her mother had fired him because of his involvement in Hallie's disappearance. Pascal wondered why Santiago was at the house. He tried to ignore the slight pang of jealousy tightening in his chest.

Pascal had a history of troubled relationships. Women always seemed to be in control, and used that to their advantage. His few prior relationships had ended with his heart broken and his ego damaged.

He had been in love in Paris, but the relationship ended shortly after graduation. It was his fault. He had become disillusioned with the city and complained about it endlessly. Gone were the days when writers and artists gathered in cafes and exchanged intellectual conversations. Paris had become just another busy metropolis full of obnoxious tourists and disgruntled residents. Pascal had become sullen and uncommunicative until his girlfriend suggested they take a break. He returned to New Mexico.

In New Mexico, a friend had introduced him to Madeline Cody, an abstract painter who was wild and spontaneous, the opposite of Pascal; he instantly became infatuated. The relationship had its challenges. Madeline lived thirty miles north of Santa Fe and made clear that she had no intention of ever moving to Santa Fe, much less visiting it. If Pascal wanted to see her, he had to do the traveling.

One weekend, there was no answer when he called. He left a voicemail and continued to call several times over the next couple days. Finally, Pascal became worried that an accident had happened. He bought several items Madeline loved at Whole Foods, ones she couldn't find in Truchas: olives, cheeses, hard-cured salami, a loaf of fresh rustic bread. He splurged on a $20 bottle of red wine and her favorite flowers, anemones. As he headed north, he imagined her delight as she opened the package of goodies. But when he stopped at the end of her drive, a massive twin-cab pickup truck blocked his access. As he walked to the door, he tried to convince himself it belonged to a friend, a relative, a plumber.

When Madeline opened the door in only a ripped T-shirt that barely came to the top of her legs, he knew immediately the owner of the truck wasn't the plumber or a relative. His heart was in his throat as he shoved the bouquet toward her, dropped the package on the stoop, and walked away. Madeline called his name but he didn't stop; he didn't want her to see him cry.

Most women in his age group were either in a relationship, married, or gay. He had lost hope of a serious relationship. Then he met Gillian. The first time he laid eyes on her, the circumstances were not what you would call idyllic. She was shivering in the Lensic Theater parking lot; at her feet lay a Czech violinist, unconscious. Pascal had the urge to wrap his arms around her.

A lot had happened in the last three months, but it hadn't been a romantic relationship. Although he and Gillian remained friends, the relationship had stalled. Tonight, he planned on changing that. Even if she decided to return to D.C. in the summer, he would make his move. What did he have to lose?

Pascal got out of the car at the porch. Gillian stuck her head out the door and a warm smile spread across her face while she gave him a princess-like wave. Santiago reached out and shook Gillian's hand, then walked off the porch. As he passed by, he gave Pascal a curt nod, which unsettled him.

Gillian was shivering on the porch and Pascal had to resist the urge to sink his hands into the soft wool of her cashmere sweater. He leaned forward and kissed her on the cheek and hoped Santiago was watching. Gillian hugged her arms tightly across her chest while hopping back and forth on the cold bricks.

Pascal looked down at her feet. "Not even socks?"

"Radiant heat. I love the warmth of the Saltillo tiles on my bare feet."

He shook his head as he handed her a paper sack. They had worked their way through her mother's extensive collection but had barely made a dent, so he knew better than to bring a bottle of wine.

Eyes wide in expectation, Gillian peered inside the sack.

"I drove past Clafoutis and couldn't resist— best French bakery this side of the Rockies. Hope you like choux à la crème."

Gillian stuck her hand in the bag and scooped up a finger full of cream. She closed her eyes and savored the flavor. "Céleste." Then she gave him a little peck on the cheek. "Dinner's almost ready, but there's still time for a few bottles of wine."

"Only a few?"

Pascal followed Gillian into the living room, where she had set a low table and cushions in front of the fireplace. A bottle of Bordeaux was open next to two crystal wine glasses. A plate of paté sat alongside a baguette that emitted a fresh-baked aroma.

Gillian filled their glasses, held up the bottle, and read the description on the label. It had become a ritual to honor her mother, who insisted on the performance each time they opened a new bottle. "Chateau Simard Saint-Émilion. This vintage shows the classical characteristics of Saint-Émilion, with plum, cherry, bramble fruit, and tobacco. Medium bodied, the soft textured tannins are still present in good measure and well balanced with the acidity that brings a persistent finish." She set the bottle down, picked up her glass. "A votre santé."

"A votre santé et à votre mere." Pascal clicked her glass and took a sip. "Ah, an exquisite depth of hazelnut and blueberries, not to mention the bramble fruit and tobacco. It transports me back to Bordeaux."

"As long as it doesn't take you back to Paris," Gillian said before she could stop herself.

Pascal stared at her with a quizzical expression.

Gillian tore off a piece of the baguette, slathered it with paté, and stuffed it in her mouth.

"What did Santiago want?" Pascal said as he chewed his lower lip.

"Me."

Pascal stared at her, not sure if she was serious.

"Don't tell me you're jealous?" Gillian said.

"Only curious."

"I called him. Asked if he was available to do some work in the garden this spring. He's busy now but could give me a few days a month." Gillian tore off another piece of baguette.

Pascal decided to change the subject. "I hoped you could help me sort out some of the information on the case—give me your perspective. I've reached a stalemate."

"Sure. The beef bourguignon is in the slow cooker, so we can eat anytime."

"Beef bourguignon?"

"Although I'm no Julia Child, I can follow a recipe. If you want, we can talk about the case now—give us time to digest the paté."

Pascal leaned the white board against the wall, pulled out his markers, and tried to organize the information on it. On one side, he wrote "Opera" and the other side "Tonque." Between the two columns, he placed the Jesus costume. "These two crimes are connected with the costume—it's the link."

He set down his marker and turned to Gillian. "I'll bring you up to date."

Gillian prayed that nothing else bizarre had occurred. The image of Bobby Pilot hung on the cross was etched in her mind and still made her stomach flutter. Pascal told her about Wegman's call, Elena Santiago's sighting men near Tonque, and Ortiz's disappearance.

"Wow." Gillian had to laugh. "Never a dull moment with you."

"I went to look for Ortiz, checked the back roads around Algodones, found his squad car. His tire had been shot out. Someone smashed out his window and took the costume he had picked up at the hospital."

"Did you find Ortiz?"

"No, still missing."

"If the costume is the connection, what's the motive? Why did someone steal it in the first place? If it was a prank, why did they steal it back?"

"I can't come up with a motive. Or a suspect."

"You said the vandals broke into the storage shed, smoked a lot of pot, rummaged around, set up the props and costumes. If they only were interested in the Jesus costume, they would've taken the costume and skedaddled."

"Skedaddled."

Gillian pursed her lips and squinted. "Whoever took the costume from the opera must have brought it to Tonque and probably brought the cross as well. Remember Raymond told us he gave Bobby a map of the Tonque Pueblo? Bobby hiked to the pueblo and stumbled on some people out there. You mentioned that Bobby had a high dose of Percocet and some mushrooms in his bloodstream. So they get stoned, dress him up, and put him on the cross."

"But what were they doing with the costume and cross?" Pascal said.

"Maybe a reenactment. Easter's this weekend. Maybe they wanted to take some pictures of the costume, the cross."

Pascal was amazed. It sounded probable, or at least possible. "I still haven't been able to reach Marcos Alcazar, the Penitente guy. Bobby Pilot hitched a ride with him on Monday, the day before he disappeared. Maybe the Penitentes were involved in some kind of crucifixion reenactment out there."

"If the Penitentes want to repent for their sins or wrongdoings, it doesn't fit they would put someone on a cross, someone who isn't part of the Brotherhood."

"You're right. Maybe I should pass along the information on Alcazar to San Felipe, let them follow that lead."

"Yeah," Gillian said, nodding her head.

"It's that . . . ."

"You want control. But it's not your case. And you're interfering with the progress of the people who are in charge."

Pascal knew she was right, but he hated to admit it.

"Hey, remember that film canister that Ortiz picked up out at Tonque?" Gillian said.

"Yeah, forgot about it."

"Maybe someone was shooting a movie out there. Along comes Bobby and they decide to cast him as the star."

"As crazy as that sounds, you could be onto something."

"The costume must implicate whoever took it from the opera grounds. Obviously, they were desperate to get it back, since they shot out a police officer's tire and smashed the window of his cruiser."

Pascal stared at Gillian. He had begun to suspect a similar scenario but was impressed with how she had come up with it out of the blue.

"I think you need to hand over the information to San Felipe, the sooner the better. It's to your advantage."

"How?"

"If the costume is the one from the opera, you'll have to be involved eventually."

Pascal chuckled. He didn't need any lectures tonight. Something gnawed away at his memory, something about the film canister.

"Let's eat." Gillian grabbed the half-empty bottle of wine and headed toward the kitchen.

After dinner, they sat on cushions in front of the fire, stuffed after devouring two bowls of the rich stew. Pascal for once declined dessert. Gillian started to open another bottle of wine, but Pascal shook his head. The crackling of the blue-orange flames was the only sound. He reached over and pulled Gillian toward him in an embrace. She was so startled that she froze, not able to return the kiss.

Pascal fumbled and started to apologize, but Gillian leaned forward and kissed him. They stretched out toward the fire and set their glasses on the adobe ledge. Pascal, no longer reluctant, took her in his arms. Gillian for once let all her defenses down and gave in to the waves of pleasure that rushed over her body.

~39~

S TEG FINALLY MADE HIS WAY TO THE FILM COMPANY'S WARE-
house in Santa Fe. When he hadn't found the officer, he realized
he needed to dispose of the weapon. Gangsters and criminals in the
movies often tossed their guns in nearby rivers, but the Rio Grande
was low after a mild winter with little runoff from the mountains.
The only deep body of water in the state was the Blue Hole, a cir-
cular, bell-shaped artesian well east of Santa Rosa. But the Blue
Hole was a hundred thirty miles away. He didn't have the time or
energy for that.

His father would be furious that he had taken his gun and disposed
of it, not to mention shot a police officer, not to mention what had
happened at Tonque. Then he remembered his cousin, who had told
him that the best place to hide something was in plain sight. Nobody
expects it. Steg decided to put the rifle back where he had gotten it,
in his father's gun cabinet. At least that would be one less sin to live
with. But first he needed to leave the costume at the warehouse.

The windows, covered in dust and grime, were dark, indicating
that the building was empty. The last thing Steg needed was a con-
frontation with Coriz or, worse, Eubank. After all that happened
today, especially shooting the officer, there wouldn't be any suitable
explanation. He was drained, and all he wanted to do was drop off
the costume and be on his way.

The warehouse was a bastion, practically impenetrable. The
building not only stored the filmmaker's photography and equipment but also housed an impressive collection of archival photographs that Coriz had amassed over the last several years.

Before they leased the warehouse, Coriz had researched security
systems and chosen the most effective one on the market. The sys-

tem provided cellular monitoring, crash and smash protection, re-
mote access, video control, and phone, email, and text alerts. In addition, the only entrance was protected by a massive steel door
secured with three locks. A decorative plaque ingeniously camou-
flaged the surveillance camera hanging high out of reach.

As Steg stepped out of the car, the last bit of adrenaline drained
from his body, and his knees wobbled unsteadily. He leaned against
the door for support as he reached into his satchel for a key ring.
Coriz had bought the most effective locks for the door. Steg took
one of the keys and inserted it in the Schlage deadbolt. Next, he unlocked the mortise lock, chosen for its uncompromised strength and
durability. The third lock was a keyless pad that required a series of
ten numbers. After all the locks were disengaged, he pushed the
door open, disarmed the alarm system, and turned on the lights.

He stood rooted in place scanning the cavernous room. Over the
last three years, thanks to Steg, they had amassed all a film company
needed. After they signed the lease, Eubank, a zealous organizer,
spent weeks methodically arranging the space. Each item, no matter
how insignificant, had been labeled and stored in a specific location.
Boxes of shot footage arranged in chronological order lined the
north wall. Locked metal cabinets on the east and west walls stored
an assortment of film and photo equipment. In the middle of the
room sat an incongruous French Oakley Style tallboy, intricately
carved, with a cabinet underneath instead of a chest of drawers.
Coriz had come across it at the Santa Fe flea market and picked it
up for a song. The tallboy held various lenses and adapters. Another
section of the room stored tripods, lighting equipment, and micro-
phones and audio equipment, mixers and video mics, a variety of
stands, and even a drone. Thomas had hung on each cabinet or case
a clipboard describing the equipment, its condition, and when and
where it had been used. He also had transferred all the information
onto Excel spreadsheets that provided a digital record.

Although Steg wouldn't miss Eubank or even Coriz, he would
miss planning and shooting movies. But it was too late; too much
had happened. He walked to the back of the warehouse and set the

costume down on a large table, then looked for a piece of paper to write a message. Thomas kept the building spotless and uncluttered. There wasn't a thing out of place. Even the trashcan was empty. He tore off a sheet from a clipboard, folded it in half, and wrote in large block letters, "ADIOS!" It was childish, but he didn't care.

He took one more look around the warehouse, and for a second considered taking some of the equipment. After all, he had financed most of their projects. But what would be the point? His entry into the building would be recorded with date and time. He didn't need any more trouble. He glanced at the film canisters lined up near the back wall, the projects they had finished. Again, a pang of regret swept over him. He had to leave what he considered some of his best work. Time was running out, and he needed to take the rifle back to Los Alamos and get out of town.

As he drove north, the weariness smothered him and made it difficult to concentrate on the road. Thankfully, it was late and there was hardly any traffic. He pulled into the driveway and clicked open the garage door. He maneuvered his Mini Cooper next to his father's Mercedes. The house was dark. But Steg noticed a dim light in his father's office, the place he needed to return the rifle.

For some reason, he thought of his mother, wondering whether things would have been different if she had stayed. On his fourth birthday, his father had told him his mother had died, but later he found out the truth. He was raised by a series of housekeepers who never stayed long.

He picked up the rifle, went to his room, and shoved it under the bed, then made his way down the hall to his father's office. The door was ajar, his father slumped in a dark green wingback chair, one leg planted on the ottoman and the other stretched out on the floor. On the table next to the chair sat a bottle of brandy and an overturned glass. Steg stared at his father. For years, burdened by his mother's absence, he had been plagued by insecurity and frustration.

Steg gently nudged his father's shoulder. Throughout the years, Steg had performed this ritual many times. It was his burden, the price he had to pay, born without pigment. His father opened his glassy eyes and tried to focus. Steg reached down, pulled the old man to his feet, and helped him to his bedroom. Steg didn't take the time to undress him, just pulled the covers up around his neck.

"Sorry, papa." Steg bent down, kissed his father's forehead, and left. He took the rifle to his father's office, locked it in the gun cabinet, and hung the key on the hook behind the curtain.

It was already after two in the morning. Steg had to hurry if he hoped to make the six o'clock flight to Chicago. Once there, he would decide where to go next—maybe Germany, eventually Prague. He was sure the police weren't after him yet, but better play it safe, book one flight at a time. He remembered a movie in which Brad Pitt was on the run. He zigzagged around the country and confused the police, until finally he slipped across the Mexican border undetected. Steg didn't want to think about the end, in which the police found Pitt and deported him from Mexico.

He went back to his bedroom, realizing how sterile it was, furnished with only a bed and dresser. The walls, once an intense shade of azure plastered with travel posters, were now painted a callow institutional green that made Steg shiver.

When he left for college, Steg's father had the housekeeper wipe his room clean, his boyhood erased. He rarely came home, but on a visit after graduation, Steg discovered that his father's mental health had declined to the point of depression. He often drank himself into a stupor. Although Steg never forgave him for the loss of his childhood, the ill old man was his father, and duty compelled him to help. He returned home and lived in his old room but left it as it was, a clean slate.

Steg pulled open the drawer of his childhood desk. Empty, not even a scrap of paper. Where was his German passport? He rummaged through his practically empty closet and checked the pockets of the two ski parkas which for some reason his father hadn't discarded. He pushed his way to the back of the closet and found a coat crumpled on the floor. It was a London Fog raincoat his father had given him as a high school graduation present. Steg had complained that the coat was too bourgeois, something he wouldn't be caught dead in, especially in New Mexico. His father had become enraged. Steg worried that he would be beaten, but instead his father began to list the raincoat's qualities. It provided protection from the elements, and the fur lining would keep him warm. At the mention of elements, Steg had started to shiver involuntarily.

He had worn the coat only once. His father had taken him to Dusseldorf, supposedly to visit his mother's grave. But they didn't go to the cemetery, because his mother wasn't dead. His father drove him to a small village and parked in front of a charming cottage covered in ivy, the windows decked out with flower boxes, the stoop washed clean.

His father's face was taut, and his eyes were like bits of coal. Steg knew not to speak. As they walked toward the house, the front door swung open. A petite woman in a flowered dress and canary cardigan stood with a tentative smile. Her gray-streaked hair was pulled back in an immaculate chignon, and although she wore little makeup, she was beautiful. Her eyes, the lightest blue, were glassy with tears, and her lips trembled. His father gave him a shove, turned, and left. The woman reached out and cupped his hands in hers. He knew who she was: his mother. So many emotions cascaded over him as he stood on that porch in Germany, then a pain radiated through his body and settled. But what persisted over the years were feelings of resentment and indignation over having been lied to.

As his fingers closed on the passport in the raincoat's inside pocket, he exhaled a sigh of relief. The Dusseldorf trip was the last time he'd used his German passport. After that, he chose to be an American. Being German still conveyed a stigma, which perplexed Steg.

He flipped the passport open and was surprised to see how young he looked. His white hair cut short made him appear bald. The photo resembled one of a cancer patient on a billboard. At least his eyes looked dark, as the photo had somehow overlooked their lack of pigment. He stared at the name printed on the passport, Albrecht Stegmann Engle. God, how he hated that name! The first day of kindergarten, the students were asked to stand and introduce themselves. When it was his turn, he defiantly blurted out, "Steg Engle." Thankfully, his classmates preferred Steg to Albrecht, and soon the teachers followed suit.

He stuffed the passport into his backpack and grabbed his carry-on. He would travel light, not checking any bags. Before he turned off the light, he took one last look around the room and realized there was nothing left of him. The hollowness in his chest resonated through his body.

~40~
Holy Saturday

IT WAS CLOSE TO FOUR IN THE MORNING WHEN STEG MADE IT TO Rio Rancho, north of Albuquerque. The city was originally part of the Alameda Land Grant founded by Spanish settlers in 1710. But by the early twentith century, much of the grant had been sold to investment companies. The Amrep Corporation bought fifty-five thousand acres in the early 1960s, built reasonably priced houses, and advertised all over the East Coast. It since had developed into a sprawling suburban city that boasted over ninety thousand residents.

Steg's GPS directed him through the tangle of streets lined with one-story nondescript ranch houses. Isabelle Rodriguez's house sat deep in the heart of the city. It was identical to the others on the block except for each being turned in a slightly different direction. As he opened his car door, Isabelle came out of the house and raised her finger to her lips.

When YinYangYazzie had staged its film premiere at the university's SUB theater a few months ago, Isabelle, a photography major, became totally smitten with both the film and Steg. She had hung around after the show and approached him outside as he left campus. As she leaned toward him, she murmured, "Miraculous, Marvelous, Mind-blowing, mmm." Steg's ear tickled with her hot breath. Something moved inside him that he hadn't felt for a long time.

After that night, they had mostly talked on the phone until a few weeks ago when he had picked her up at her dorm and taken her to dinner. They had nowhere to go afterward. The Mini was too cramped to complete a decent sexual act, so they kissed and fondled each other until the cold sent them on their way.

When Steg called and asked Isabelle for a ride to the airport, she had hesitated, then confessed that she didn't own a car. But since she was visiting her parents for Easter weekend, she could borrow their car. He said he would leave her his Mini but that it was low on gas. In reality, he didn't want his car to be seen at the airport. Steg loaded his carry-on into Isabelle's parents' late model station wagon parked in the driveway. He opened the passenger door and started to get in.

"Could you help me push the car out of the driveway?" she whispered.

That's all Steg needed—car problems. He would miss his flight for sure.

"I don't want to wake my parents," Isabelle said.

She released the emergency brake and put the car in neutral. Luckily, it was a standard and the driveway was sloped. Without much effort, the station wagon rolled back onto the street. Isabelle jumped in and turned the wheel.

"Could you give me a little push?"

Steg's patience evaporated. He wanted to scream, "no!" but noticed that the street sloped down in the direction they were going, and instead got behind the car and pushed. The car slowly moved fifty feet and came to a stop. That seemed to appease Isabelle. When Steg jumped in, she turned the key and the engine came to life. She crept down the street and didn't dare switch on the headlights until she had turned the corner.

The airport was still forty-five minutes away. He had cut it close to make his flight. He looked at his watch for the third time. He was glad the Albuquerque Sunport wasn't a large airport. It had only two corridors and twenty gates, but if there was a long line at security, he might not make it.

"Where are you off to?" Isabelle said.

"Off to see the wizard."

Isabelle turned toward him, narrowed her eyes, and pressed her lips together. Steg knew she deserved more. He shouldn't be flippant. "Don't bite the hand that feeds you," his father always warned.

"Sorry, it's been a long night. I'm really exhausted."

She turned her head slightly and waited for him to continue.

Throughout his life, Steg's father had pontificated about the sin of lying, but lately, Steg had found it was not only necessary but also had become easier. "I'm scouting a site for our next film project."

"What's the project?"

"Something less abstract. A narrative, perhaps. An experiment. About redemption and recovery."

Isabelle seemed to mull this over but then changed the subject.

"Why haven't you called me since that dinner at Two Fools?"

Steg leaned back and closed his eyes. He wasn't sure he could bear the ride.

When Isabelle pulled up at the airport, she hopped out, embraced him, and gave him a long kiss. Steg tried to force his lips when she pulled back, but he didn't have the energy to return her smile.

His hair was tucked under a stocking cap, and his colorless eyes were concealed behind an old pair of his father's sunglasses.

It was the weekend. There were only a few early flights, and the crowds were thin. Steg was relieved to see that the security lines were short. They moved along efficiently until the woman in front of him stopped and rummaged through an enormous bag that continually slipped down her shoulder. Two toddlers were tangled around her feet, and a fussy infant strapped to her front kicked and fussed. Finally, her bag slipped onto the floor and Steg saw his chance. He moved around the woman as one of her toddlers pulled away from his mother. Steg knocked into the boy, sending him to the floor. The child screamed hysterically as he rolled around. Steg didn't have time for this. His plane left in fifteen minutes. The TSA agent looked up alarmed as Steg shoved his passport across the desk. He apologized in German, "Es tut uns leid." The woman, furious, screamed in protest as she tried to drag her brood up to the desk.

The agent, in a panic, picked up Steg's passport, scanned it, and waved him through. Steg ran to the gate. The last passenger had made it to the end of the entryway and entered the plane. The flight attendant took hold of the door and started to pull it closed. Steg pushed his way into the plane and ignored her scowl. He was on his way.

~41~

PASCAL WOKE UP AND FOUND HIMSELF IN AN UNFAMILIAR BED, disoriented. Sunlight poured in through the floor-to-ceiling windows. As his mind cleared, memories of the previous evening started to form. He remembered eating a delicious meal, drinking an enormous amount of red wine, holding Gillian in his arms, and falling asleep in front of the fire. He also remembered waking at one point to find a dog licking his face.

He disentangled himself from the sheets and found his clothes in a heap across the room on an antique settee. He pulled them on and followed the smell of coffee to the kitchen. Gillian had set out some croissants and fruit on the counter. When she turned around, he noticed the slightest blush appear across her cheeks, "Morning, sleepy-head." She tilted her head and smiled.

Pascal looked at his watch and groaned. It was 9:15. He was late. He pulled out his phone and turned it on. He had six missed calls and three messages. He apologized as he started to check the messages. The first was from the captain, the next from Montaño, and third from an unknown caller. He slipped the phone back in his pocket, figuring that they had waited this long and could wait until he had a cup of coffee. He came up behind Gillian, pulled back her unruly tangles, and kissed her neck.

She smiled, pushed him away, and carried two plates to the table. He poured a cup of coffee and joined her.

Pascal started to say something, but his phone rang and he moaned. He looked at the screen: San Felipe Tribal.

"Ruiz."

"Do you ever answer your phone?" Montaño snapped.

"Sorry, I. . . ."

"We decided it was best not to wait. Ortiz could have been in-jured and may still be somewhere out in those fields."

Pascal thought that was a no-brainer but kept quiet.

"We brought in the search-and-rescue dogs. They found Ortiz hidden in the crotch of a tree. If it wasn't for the dogs . . .."

"How is he?" Pascal said.

"He's still alive, conscious but in bad shape. Someone shot him in the leg. Same type of bullet that was in his tire."

"Have you been able to talk to him?"

"Not yet. He was incoherent when the S&R team found him. Hummed a little song under his breath. They waited until morning before they put him under. The doctor wanted his temperature down and infection under control. He's in surgery now." Montano hesitated.

"Thanks for the update," Pascal said.

"I know it's against protocol, but since you already skirted the line when you took a leak and came across Ortiz's car, maybe we should collaborate, not compete."

"Okay," Pascal said guardedly.

"We've identified the bullet and rifle, tried to track down the owner. Our resources are limited. It's difficult to search outside the pueblo unless we bring in the Feds. You can imagine how much I want to do that."

"Been there. I'll have to check with my captain, but I think we can work together, get this case off our books. I still believe the Jesus costume was the one stolen from the opera. The cases are connected, which gives our collaboration precedent."

"Whatever it takes. We need to find out who owns the gun that shot Ortiz."

Pascal stifled his delight. He couldn't believe Montaño had asked him to help with the case. He knew he should have passed on some of the information to the tribal police, but now they could put two and two together and solve both cases.

He called the station and asked for the captain. Susie told him it was Good Friday, and that the captain was at Mass. He wouldn't be back before noon. Pascal finished his coffee and made his apologies to Gillian before heading to the station. He scanned through his missed calls while he was at traffic lights. Besides the captain, he had missed the call from Montaño, three unknown numbers who didn't leave messages, and one message from an unidentified number. He had already talked to Montaño and didn't have time to check the other message now. Bigger fish to fry.

As soon as the captain returned from Mass, Pascal rushed in and proposed the idea of collaborating with San Felipe. He explained that it was Montaño's suggestion. Pascal emphasized that they could kill two birds with one stone. If they found the shooter, they would find the Jesus costume. They could return the costume to the estate and get the commissioner off his back. Pascal wanted permission to have Rupert search for the owner of the rifle.

The captain wasn't happy about the arrangement. He thought it was suspicious that San Felipe wanted their involvement. "It's not right," he grumbled, but finally gave his okay.

Pascal pulled together the information he had found on the bullet and gun. Rupert would need reassurance that it was a legit request with the captain's blessing. He would tell Rupert as little as possible.

Rupert pounded away at his keyboard as Pascal came over to his desk. "Morning."

"What's up? Anything new on the opera break-in?"

"You read my mind." Pascal handed him a printout on the rifle and bullet. "The rifle is most likely part of an antique gun collection. You'll have to focus your search in that direction. We need to find out the identity of the owner."

"Case?" Rupert raised his eyebrows.

"The weapon is connected, circumstantially, to the burglary on the opera grounds." Pascal swallowed, but his mouth was dry. He knew he was stretching the truth. He had a lot of respect for Rupert Montoya, and always tried to be up front with him. But time was running out. "The captain has been apprised."

Rupert saluted Pascal, turned back to his computer, and clicked away at the keyboard.

"Let me know as soon as you find something."

Rupert knew that most gun laws differed drastically from state to state. He had amassed a comprehensive knowledge of New Mexico gun laws over the years working for the police department. These were some of the least restrictive. Gun owners can legally openly carry their weapons even without a permit. But he had always found it strange that the owners need a permit to conceal their weapons.

During a search a few years ago involving an antique gun, he had found that the statutes are the same for all firearms. The one thing that amazed Rupert was that you could legally possess a machine gun as long as it was registered and complied with federal laws and regulations. He didn't want to think about what someone could do with a machine gun.

Rupert spent a few hours perusing the New Mexico firearms databases. Then he widened his search to other states. By early afternoon, he had looked everywhere in the country for gun registrations. Nothing.

~42~

CAPTAIN MONTAÑO GOT TO THE HOSPITAL A LITTLE AFTER NINE in the morning. He made his way to Ortiz's room, gave the door a quick knock, and pushed it open. Rita, Ortiz's wife, sat in a chair by the window. She jumped up, wrapped her arms around Montaño, and squeezed him tight.

Ortiz lay on the bed, holding his baby tight against his chest. She cooed as he sang to her.

"Hey, boss, what do you say? Name her Angel?" He held the baby out toward Montaño.

Montano smiled and nodded his approval.

"Diagnosed her with a milk allergy. Hogwash! Who ever heard of a baby allergic to milk?"

He continued to rock his daughter gently back and forth, but Montaño could see that Ortiz's arms had started to shake with fatigue.

"Once they put Angel on goat's milk, all her symptoms disappeared. Rita's not too happy about not being able to nurse the baby—not natural." He lowered the baby onto his chest. Beads of sweat dappled his forehead, and his breath came out in labored puffs.

His wife rose and gathered the baby in her arms. "See you at home." She kissed Ortiz on the forehead.

Montaño saw the effort it took him to hide the pain in his eyes. Once Rita closed the door, Ortiz let his body relax and sank back onto the pillow. He grimaced as he aligned his leg, the one that had been shot, alongside the other one.

"Waiting for the doctor. To get a release."

Montaño was skeptical. He knew that Ortiz wanted out, and probably would rest better at home without the interruption of constant routine checks of vital signs. "Want to go over what you remember about yesterday, last night."

Montaño pulled a chair over to the side of Ortiz's bed. "Remember anything about who shot you?"

"I looked at the tire, saw it had been shot out, figured either it was a bunch of kids or some nut. Thought the latter, sensed it."

Montaño knew about intuition; you couldn't explain it. He had experienced it once during a manhunt.

"While I inspected the tire, I heard the snap of a twig, crush of a leaf. Not much cover out there. Hid behind a tree. Waited." Ortiz winced as he tried to adjust his pillow. "A man came up the drive. The cruiser was locked." Ortiz shot Montaño a weak smile. "Protocol. The man broke out the window with his rifle butt."

"Did you get a look at him?"

"It was overcast, getting dark, but when he raised his rifle, the clouds cleared, and the sun hit his hair. I had seen him at the hospital."

"The hospital?"

Ortiz nodded. "When I picked up the costume. I wanted a Coke for the ride back, and he turned around, came face to face."

Montaño sat up and leaned forward. "You recognized him?"

"No, but I could definitely ID him. No mistake about that white hair and those ghost eyes."

Montaño got a tingle in the back of his neck, but he said nothing. He needed all the details Ortiz could remember.

"Then?"

"He busted out the window. I headed toward the property on the north, climbed through the barbed wire, crouched down and started to zig-zag my way through the field, like they taught us in the Army. Nobody had bothered to cut the alfalfa in the fall, so it was high enough to give me cover. By the time I got to the dirt drive, my legs were on fire, and I needed to stand and stretch. Thought I was far enough away. But when I stood, bam, something hit my leg. It had to be the same guy, the albino."

Montaño was pleased. Another piece of the puzzle. Then he remembered the canister.

"When I called yesterday, you said you had found something out at Tonque, another piece of evidence."

"Yeah. Almost stepped on it. When I picked it up, that girl, the one with the detective, came over. I could tell she wanted to see what I found. She tried to distract me, but I stuffed the canister in my pocket." Ortiz pursed his lips. "Should have bagged it. Forgot about it. At the hospital, I reached in my pocket for some change for a Coke, and there it was. I stopped at a camera store in Albuquerque. That's why I was late. The manager told me it was for a special light-sensitive film, creates holographic images, makes them look 3-D."

"Did he say who would use that kind of film?"

"Maybe an artist, filmmaker. No one in New Mexico sells or develops the film. He gave me the name of a Midwest company where you can order it."

It was a piece of the puzzle. Montaño wasn't sure where it fit. Engle was a filmmaker. That would connect.

Ortiz jutted his chin toward the closet on the other side of the room. "The canister is in my jacket pocket."

Montaño retrieved it and the note with the company's name. "I'll put Garcia on it. See if anyone in New Mexico has ordered the film recently."

Ortiz was exhausted. Retelling the experience had drained him. His eyes closed as Montaño slipped out of the room.

~43~

I T WAS SATURDAY; TOMORROW WAS EASTER. BESIDES A SKELETON crew, the station would be deserted. Pascal knew the captain had no intention of setting foot in the station until after the holiday weekend. He was reluctant to disturb him again. He had forgotten to ask last night for approval to bring in Coriz and Eubank for questioning. He needed some backup, but Matt was still on sick leave and wouldn't be back in the station until Monday at the earliest. Monday would be too late.

There were things he needed to take care of now. Montaño had hesitated when Pascal broached the idea of questioning Coriz and Eubank. Although there was circumstantial evidence leaning toward their being out at Tonque, there wasn't any proof they were involved in his case, the opera burglary.

Pascal's patience had waned. He needed to do something, question the filmmakers, check their alibis for Sunday night. Suspects sequestered in an interview room sometimes became rattled, leading to slip-ups and incriminations.

He switched on his desktop computer and leaned back in his chair. While he waited for the outdated machine to come to life, he thought about Wegman. The guy was so full of himself. All cloaks and daggers. It irked him, and he wanted to know who this guy was and what he was doing out there. He put in a call to his old friend, Ollie West, down in Florida.

"Yeah, Ruiz?"

"Hey, old buddy. How you doing?"

"I'm trying to play golf."

Pascal chuckled, "Trying is right."

"What do you want, Ruiz?"

"Information on helicopter pilot Brent Wegman. He's doing surveillance in a rural area north of Albuquerque.

There was a long silence. "Leave it alone."

"Come on, Ollie, you owe me."

"Jesus, Ruiz." West cursed under his breath. "You didn't hear this from me. The DEA has been working on a multi-agency project investigating a New Mexico-based poly-drug trafficking organization. They allegedly are operating between Albuquerque, N.M., and Las Vegas, N.M. They contracted Wegman to monitor that area. I don't know all the details, but rumor has it they're close to moving in and taking down the big guns. I'm sure they don't want you sticking your nose where it doesn't belong. Now can I tee off? There are six geezers breathing down my neck, got their nickers in a twist, which isn't a pretty sight."

"Thanks, Ollie, now I owe you one."

"Yeah, like you got something for me."

Pascal hung up but wondered why DEA would want Wegman to keep an eye on him. Maybe that was just a ruse. Or like Ollie said, they didn't want anyone scaring away the smugglers. Still, something didn't add up. But he needed to let it go and get back to the case.

He'd hoped Rupert could find the owner of the rifle but hadn't heard back from him. It was the weekend, and he didn't want to ruin his weekend too, but he needed some help. Pascal thought about the white van that Wegman had seen out near Tonque. If it was linked to the filmmakers, he could place them at the scene. He left Rupert a message apologizing for asking him to work on his day off but saying that he needed help. He wanted to find out who owned the white GMC that had been seen out near Tonque. He also needed Leonardo Coriz's home address and the address of the YinYangYazzie warehouse.

He stared at the flickering monitor. The few pieces of evidence that had been found were linked to Tonque and Bobby Pilot. Nothing pointed to the burglary at the Opera Grounds— except the Jesus costume. If he could get his hands on the costume, Aubusson might be able to identify it.

He rocked back and forth in his chair, thinking about the motivation for dressing Bobby in the costume and putting him on the cross. Maybe a scene for a movie. An Easter movie? The YinYangYazzie were avant garde filmmakers, abstract, weird. But maybe they'd shot some footage out at Tonque. If Pascal could find it, that would put them at the scene. He wondered why they had left Bobby out there. He thought about Elena Santiago. She'd said the men got in a small sedan. Maybe there was no room for Bobby in the car. Maybe they were going to come back and get him.

For once, he wished it wasn't the weekend. Burglary, not a time-sensitive crime, was never a high priority on the force. It didn't rate overtime, especially on a holiday weekend. The burglary was the only crime on the docket. The station was a virtual graveyard.

Pascal decided to give Alcazar's ex-wife a call. She didn't answer, and he didn't bother leaving a voicemail. He called the sister. She answered on the first ring, but when he identified himself, there was silence on the line. Pascal didn't want to make her any more suspicious then she already was.

"Your brother isn't in any kind of trouble. I'm talking to people who live near Golden who might have seen a man in the last few days who has disappeared. The Golden Mercantile manager said that Alcazar was in the store when the man came in. I wanted to find out if your brother might have talked to him or given him a ride somewhere." Even as Pascal rambled on, he realized his explanation sounded phony.

"What dates are you concerned about?"

"The young man disappeared on Tuesday, or at least didn't return to Diamond Tail Ranch that night. Hasn't been seen since."

"My brother's an attorney. He got a call late Monday night. Some fellow parishioners were detained in Albuquerque. He stayed in town all week on legal religious business. He didn't return to Golden until yesterday afternoon."

"Does your brother have a telephone?"

The woman hesitated a moment. "Yes . . . a cell phone."

She was reluctant to give Pascal her brother's number, but he reassured her he only wanted to ask him a few questions.

Pascal called Alcazar's number, but there was no answer. He hadn't set up his voicemail either. Pascal chewed on the end of his pen as he leaned back in his chair. For the first time, he was relieved that the case wasn't all his responsibility. He was getting nowhere fast. Alcazar had a tight alibi that could easily be corroborated. For now, he wasn't a suspect.

Pascal needed to find where in town the filmmakers stored their equipment and footage. He might be able to get a search warrant. Maybe the costume was there, or some footage from Tonque.

An uneasiness came over him when he realized he should have called Gillian sooner, especially after last night. He wondered why he was dragging his feet. He would call her later and invite her to lunch.

He turned back to his computer and searched through the Santa Fe database for information on Leonardo Coriz and Thomas Eubank. There was no listing for Coriz. Maybe he lived outside the city or shared a place with a friend or relative. Eubank had a loft in the new Railyard Flats on Camino de la Familia. Pascal wasn't familiar with the complex but knew the area had experienced a building boom. The Rail Runner, the local train service from Belen, south of Albuquerque, terminated at the Railyard.

He decided to check out Eubank's apartment later in the afternoon. First, he needed to call Gillian. He hoped she could meet him for lunch at the Plaza. He had left the house without breakfast. Images of green chile stew, tamales, and enchiladas drifted through his mind as her phone rang. Pascal's stomach rumbled as pictures from the restaurant's extensive menu flashed before his eyes.

"Hello," Gillian said.

"Hey. How are you?"

"Fine."

"How about a late breakfast, early lunch? The Plaza Cafe?"

There was a pause. "Okay."

Pascal noticed a hesitation in her voice. "Or we could eat somewhere else."

"No . . . no, that's fine. See you in twenty."

The Santa Fe Plaza was packed with Easter weekend visitors. A strolling mariachi band entertained tourists as they circled through the Plaza. Native American artists and craftspeople were lined along the covered walkway on the north side across from the Plaza. Their wares were set out and arranged on colorful woven blankets. On the other side of the Plaza, pounding Indian drums reverberated. Pascal pushed his way through the crowd to the restaurant, wanting to secure a table—his table—before Gillian arrived.

Santa Fe overflowed with eating establishments, most of them noteworthy. Pascal realized he should diversify, find another restaurant, branch out. But he loved the Plaza Cafe. It was like home, and only a few blocks from the station. Convenience trumps all.

The restaurant was packed. Pascal was disappointed that an elderly couple had already nabbed what he considered "his table." The only one available was in the back near the kitchen. When Gillian came in, she hesitated as she looked toward the window where they had sat the last time. He stood up and waved his arms like a cheerleader. Gillian grimaced as she made her way across the room, dodging chairs and tables overflowing with customers. He could feel her irritation.

"Morning, sunshine," Pascal chirped.

"Morning."

Pascal shook his head. He tried to pull out her chair but she yanked it away, slumped down, wiggled out of her parka, and unwound her scarf. Pascal hoped her crankiness was due to being overheated. Gillian's outfit was more appropriate for the ski slopes than a sunny spring day in town. Although the weather couldn't be considered warm, there were some signs that winter was over.

Gillian buried her face in the menu.

"Is something wrong?" Pascal said.

"Oh, wrong?"

Pascal struggled with interpreting sarcasm, but he knew there definitely was something wrong. Again, he had a slight twinge of queasiness. Maybe it was hunger, but he doubted it. He had felt it when Madeline had come into the station with her attorney. Women always set him off balance. They were a different species. He had no choice but to use the straightforward approach. "Yes, wrong?"

Gillian pressed her lips together. As she started to say something, the waitress, the same one who had served them the last time, the one who winked, appeared out of nowhere.

"Ready?" the waitress asked, poised with her pencil floating expectantly above her pad.

Pascal looked across the table at Gillian, but before he could say anything, she snapped, "Huevos rancheros, eggs over medium with Christmas, tortilla, no butter."

"Anything to drink?"

"Water, no ice."

The waitress turned to Pascal, took in a deep breath, and opened her eyes wide.

"Same," he said.

"Okie dokie, detective." The waitress gave him a wink.

As soon as she was out of earshot, Gillian said, "Ugh, I hate that woman."

"Why?"

"Don't know." She rubbed her temples as if her head ached.

"Gillian, I'm sorry I didn't call. When I got back from Albuquerque, it was after midnight."

Gillian stared at the table and tried to decide what she wanted to say. She didn't like being one of those women who were always pissed off about something. "I thought . . . oh never mind, let's let it go."

Pascal was relieved and happy to let it go but could tell there was still something rubbing Gillian the wrong way. Right now, he was too tired and hungry to figure it out. Whatever it was would have to wait.

The waitress reappeared and set down their plates. "Plates are hot," she cautioned. "Anything else?"

"That's it," Pascal said, trying to suppress his smile because he knew it would irritate Gillian.

The waitress raised her chin, turned, and left.

Gillian took a drink of water. "What's new with the crimes and misdemeanors business?"

"Martin, the man who called yesterday morning, had some useful info. He saw this guy follow Ortiz out of the hospital. And he recognized him, Steg Engle."

"The filmmaker?"

Pascal was taken aback. "Yeah. Do you know him?"

"No, I read an article the other day in the Alibi about the YinYangYazzie film company. They've been nominated for an award."

"Well, looks like Engle might be the person who shot Ben Ortiz."

"Really?" Gillian said, surprised.

"And the filmmakers might be responsible for putting Bobby Pilot on the cross. The Jesus outfit Pilot wore could be the same one stolen from the opera grounds."

"Good thing the police don't have anything similar to HIPAA. You'd be in violation."

Pascal squinted and tried to sound menacing. "I hope you'll keep this information to yourself, young lady."

"Who would I tell? I don't know anyone."

"Oh, they found Ortiz last night in a tree. He'd been shot in the leg. He's at UNMH."

"A tree?"

"He had crawled in a hole near the bottom of a cottonwood. A team of search-and-rescue dogs found him."

"Everyone who is anyone seems to end up at that hospital. It must be getting crowded."

As they left the restaurant, Pascal took Gillian's arm. With his eyes he tried imploring her for forgiveness, but he knew how guarded she had become. It was as if a veil had come between them and made their relationship ambiguous. He would see her tonight for dinner; he needed to make amends. Flowers?

~44~

THE CROWDS AROUND THE PLAZA HAD INCREASED SO IT WAS almost impossible to make his way through the mass of people. He circumvented them and finally was forced to step into the street, glad when he made it to his car. Halfway through lunch, he had decided to go down to the Railyard and talk to Thomas Eubank, even without the captain's blessing. He would ask a few questions, see where Eubank had been Sunday night.

The Railyard wasn't far, but it took longer to drive there than he had planned. It was Saturday and the day before Easter. People were all over the city, enjoying the warmth of mid-afternoon before the temperature started to drop at sunset.

The Railyard Flats was the antithesis of the classic Santa Fe structure: a contemporary building with sharp edges and an overabundance of glass. Although it conformed to the city's height restriction, three stories, each floor rose to twelve feet. The Flats' exterior was nondescript. The only ornamentation was the address in large black block numbers. The first floor had been reserved for commercial use, although most of it appeared vacant.

Eubank's third-floor apartment faced east. Pascal imagined that it gave him an amazing view of the Sangre de Cristo Mountains. As he pushed the doorbell, his skin prickled and his heart thumped with a rush of adrenalin racing through his body. He was flying by the seat of his pants. There wasn't anything solid to put on Eubank. If things fell apart, this would make it worse.

The door opened halfway. Eubank was taller, lankier, and younger than Pascal. He looked like a model out of a Sundance catalog. His outfit screamed casual expensive, and although his Frye boots could use a polish, Pascal figured that was intentional.

His jeans bore a sharp crease down the front that suggested dry cleaning.

"Are you from the magazine?" he asked as he started to open the door wider.

"No." Pascal fumbled in his pocket for his badge. "Are you Thomas Eubank?"

"Yes. Is this about the bike?" Eubank asked as he stared at the badge.

"Uh, no—it isn't. I wanted to ask you a few questions."

"About what?"

Pascal had hoped Eubank would invite him in. Standing in the doorway made him uncomfortable, and it gave Eubank the advantage.

"We're following up on a break-in out at the opera grounds last Sunday."

"I'm not sure I understand, detective. What does this have to do with me?" Eubank said as he folded his arms across his chest.

Pascal felt the interview slip away even before it started. This guy was either a great actor, or he hadn't been involved in the burglary.

"I need to know where you were last Sunday night?"

"Hey, man, is it within the law to come to my door and ask random questions? Do you have reason to believe I was involved in this robbery? Maybe I should retain a lawyer."

The ground seemed to shift under Pascal's feet. He needed to back up, slow down, soothe Eubank. "We're only checking some leads right now—preliminary. Need to see if you know anything, maybe saw something out there?"

"What would I be doing out there?"

"Well . . .."

"I think it's time for you to either lay your cards on the table or get the hell out of my doorway."

"Sorry—maybe I barked up the wrong tree."

Eubank glared at Pascal.

Pascal took out a card and held it out to Eubank. "If you think of anything that might be helpful, give me a call."

Eubank didn't even look at the card in Pascal's hand as he slammed the door shut.

Pascal couldn't believe it. He had screwed up. Good God—what had he imagined? Knock on someone's door and they offer a confession? He had messed this up royally, his one lead. It was worse than when he had interrogated his old girlfriend Madeline about the stolen violin. He had driven to her house in Tesuque and never bothered to ask about an alibi. His skills as a detective were nil.

He should have dragged Eubank into the station, cloistered him in one of the worst interview rooms, the one in the basement reeking of vomit and piss, and let him stew. But without the captain's blessing, he couldn't have gone that far. But the captain hadn't sanctioned knocking on Eubank's door either. Lawsuits and headlines flashed in front of him. He suspected that Eubank might be gay. Straight guys never dress that nicely. Profiling and intimidation: another case of the police harassing a citizen. The LBGTQ community would be up in arms.

As he left the Railyard Flats, Pascal tried not to think about what had happened—block it out, forget it. He was shaken. The mishap had rattled him. Hopefully, he hadn't screwed up San Felipe's case.

As he drove back to the station, he focused on where to take Gillian to dinner. Definitely not the Plaza, maybe La Boca. It was stylish with white tablecloths but low key—the perfect venue, with a selection of Mediterranean and South American wines. He and Gillian could share small plates and linger over delicious wines. He called and made a reservation for seven thirty. Then he called Gillian. He was about to tell her he would pick her up at seven when a call came in from Jessie. Maybe Bobby Pilot was awake.

"Hey, can I call you right back?"

There was silence on the line, then it went dead. This wasn't his day. He seemed to piss off everyone. He answered Jessie's call.

"Ruiz."

"Hey, stranger. Have you found out anything yet?"

"I'm working on it. How's our man doing? Woken up yet?"

Jessie paused, then said, "No. But the doctor is encouraged. This morning he got Bobby to respond. The doctor touched him with this pen-like thing and Bobby pulled away.

"That seems hopeful. Let me know when he's awake. I'd like to hear his side of the story."

"Sure."

"Promise, I'll let you know as soon as I find out something."

"Yeah. Whatever."

~45~

PASCAL REMEMBERED A VOICEMAIL FROM AN UNIDENTIFIED number. He decided to check it out and clicked on the message.

"This is James Martin. I have some information. It might be helpful for the Bobby Pilot case. Call me back as soon as possible."

Pascal could kick himself. The one time he turns off his phone, he misses an important call. Not that he regretted a minute of last night. But maybe in the future he should turn his phone to vibrate. Maybe not—the phone could squash romance.

He punched "call back" on Martin's message.

"Where have you been, detective?" Martin demanded.

Pascal, taken aback almost sputtered. "I . . . who are you?"

There was silence on the line. "Where does this guy get off?" Pascal thought.

"I've worked on this case—which, I need to elucidate, isn't my case—non-stop since the disappearance of Bobby Pilot," Pascal said.

"That's not what Jessie Archuleta told me."

Pascal groaned. That's all he needed, some pawn of Jessie's. She probably worked her charm on this guy and asked him to give Pascal a hard time. "And what does Jessie say?"

"She told me you found Bobby Pilot out at an old pueblo near Diamond Tail Ranch. He was tied to a cross dressed as Jesus. So if it wasn't your case, what were you doing out there?"

"Who are you?"

"James Martin. My wife had a baby three days ago, C-section. She's still in the maternity ward."

"Congratulations. Now if you would explain your role in this case, I would appreciate it."

"Well, like you, I don't have an official role."

"Are you a police officer?"

"No," Martin chuckled. "I'm a writer."

"Reporter?"

Martin laughed. "No. Fiction, dystopian, sci-fi."

That's all Pascal needed. Some half-baked writer obsessed with an imagined world.

Martin continued. "I'm sequestered at the hospital right now but have information that might illuminate some aspects of this case."

"Illuminate?"

"Yes. I would be glad to share the information but need to do it in person."

Pascal groaned out loud. The last thing he wanted to do was get back in his car and drive to Albuquerque.

"Detective?"

"Okay. I need to check on someone anyway. I'll call when I get there."

Martin was surprised. He didn't think the detective would agree to meet him. He was giddy and couldn't resist blurting out. "Over and out."

"Roger," Pascal said glumly.

He straightened a pile of paperwork that he had almost knocked off his desk with an elbow. He stopped in the station lobby, but the front desk was unmanned. He hit the bell on the counter harder than intended. Susie popped up with a pen in her hand and an annoyed look on her face.

Pascal apologized and told her he was off to UNMH to interview a source. He assured her his phone was on, but she pursed her lips and glared at him.

He headed south on the interstate. Although driving often exhausted him, he admitted it was better than sitting at his desk. As he drove toward Albuquerque, descending two thousand feet, he took in the landscape's subtle changes. The scenery became drier and vegetation scarce.

It was Good Friday, and a few pilgrims were scattered along the highway, making their way to Chimayó. They still had a grueling trek ahead, as La Bajada awaited—the notorious hill known for its steep incline. A group of young people futilely tugged at a shaggy donkey that was not interested in continuing up the hill, instead lunging at the scraps of weeds that had popped up after the last rain. These stragglers had better get a move on, Pascal thought. They still had a way to go and would be lucky if they made it to Chimayó by Easter.

Portable neon signs on the east side of the highway warned drivers to watch for pedestrians. Most cars gave the pilgrims a wide berth and switched to the left lane. But occasionally, adolescents would stay put and blast their horns at the walkers.

As Pascal approached the Big I in Albuquerque, he was thankful the interchange remodel was complete and traffic was scarce. For years, it had been a mess, with two major interstates meeting smack in the middle of the city. The interchange still wasn't perfect, but it was a little less precarious.

The University of New Mexico Hospital served as the state's trauma and emergency medical center, as well as the primary teaching hospital for the school of medicine. Pascal wound his way through the garage until he found a parking space on the fifth floor. As he got out of his car and stretched, he hoped this trip wasn't for naught. He wondered who this James Martin was and how he had obtained this "illuminating" information? How had he found out about Pilot, Jessie, and Ortiz in such a short time?

Pascal took the elevator to the first floor and headed for the information desk. He flashed his badge at an elderly woman there who didn't bother looking at it. Her eyes were glazed over, and she was half asleep. When he asked for Officer Ortiz's room, she turned toward the computer monitor and typed in Ortiz's name. She recited the information in a monotone: "ICU, Elevator B, second floor, turn left."

Pascal called Martin as he made his way to the elevator and said he would meet him in the cafeteria after he got an update on Ortiz's condition. The ICU waiting room was quiet. He saw Jessie by the nurses' station, resting her arms on the counter as she talked to a male nurse who nodded a few times while he sorted papers. Pascal sighed. Even being a nurse involved paperwork. The nurse, probably the one Jessie had pumped for information, leaned toward her and whispered something in her ear. Jessie broke into giggles as she shook her finger at him. Then she caught sight of Pascal and flashed the nurse a coy smile. Pascal knew it was all pretense. Shyness or modesty wasn't part of Jessie's persona.

She marched over, stopped a little too close, and put her hands on her hips. "Detective, it's about time you made an appearance."

"Hi, Jessie. How's our patient doing?"

"Our patient?" She said as she cocked her head. "Well, he's conscious but disoriented, confused and befuddled. Shall I go on?"

Pascal couldn't tell if Jessie was being descriptive or sarcastic. He figured the latter. "Conscious is good."

"Yeah, I suppose. I've been waiting forever for his doctor to make his rounds." She looked back at the nurse, who had arranged the paperwork into neat piles. "Nobody will tell you anything. Don't get me wrong; the nurses are super, and caring, but they aren't allowed to give out information on patients."

"It's related to HIPAA regulations."

"Please don't talk to me about HIPAA," Jessie grimaced. "Bobby's father left a few minutes ago. The poor man has been here around the clock. He's totally bushed. I finally talked him into going home, promised I'd wait for the doctor and call him right away."

"That was decent of you."

"Yes, I suppose it was," she said smugly, "especially since he blamed me for what happened to Bobby. I don't know why he thought it was my fault. By the way, what's the story with the case?"

"As I said before, not my case."

"Yeah—but you're here?"

"I got a call that a San Felipe officer who had been out at Tonque was admitted last night. I wanted to find out about what's happening with the case."

A disheveled doctor rushed into the ICU and shifted his clipboard from hand to hand as he tried to pull on his white gown. Frustrated, he approached the nurses' station. The nurse reached over and took his clipboard. The doctor slipped his arm into his coat, and the nurse clipped a pile of paper onto the board and handed it back.

"Got to go, detective." Jessie gave him a wink as she followed the doctor toward Bobby's room.

Pascal went over to the nurse and pulled out his badge. He stared at the badge, then up at Pascal with a blank face.

"I need an update on Officer Ortiz," Pascal said.

"Are you a relative?"

"No."

"We aren't allowed to divulge information on patients except to relatives. HIPAA."

"Ortiz and I were working on a case together."

The nurse gave him a sympathetic look. "Unless you get permission from the hospital authorities, I can't help you. Sorry."

"I understand. Thanks anyway." Pascal started to leave.

"The officer is resting comfortably after surgery. Still sedated. They moved him this morning to the Acute Unit on the third floor."

"Thanks. Appreciate it."

It seemed that both Pilot and Ortiz were out of commission for a while. He might as well go find out what this Martin guy had to say. Pascal hoped it was something—anything.

The day was late, and there weren't many people in the cafeteria. He spotted a man sitting alone near the window and figured it must be Martin.

"Martin?"

"Detective?"

"What's the scoop?" Pascal said as he slid into a chair across the table

"I've been here since my wife gave birth three days ago. And as you can imagine, there isn't a lot to do. When I heard that the mede-vacs had brought in some guy wearing a Jesus costume, my interest was piqued. As a writer, I'm always on the lookout for new material. With Easter around the corner, there has to be a story."

"How were you able to find out information on the patient?"

"Sorry, can't reveal my sources."

"You already did. You told me you talked to Jessie Archuleta."

"Yes, but she said I could talk to you because you two are friends."

"Friends?" Pascal couldn't figure this guy out, and wasn't sure he wanted to. "Why don't you tell me what you know about the officer who was brought in with a gunshot wound."

"Wow, didn't know he was shot."

Pascal closed his eyes. He could kick himself. "Go ahead."

"Yesterday afternoon, I waited for the San Felipe officer to pick up the Jesus outfit."

"How'd you know he was picking up the costume?"

"Sorry, can't reveal my sources."

It didn't take much to get Pascal irritated, and this guy seemed to know how to push all his buttons. He glared at Martin.

"I went up to the seventh floor and waited in an alcove where I could see when the officer got off the elevator."

"What did you plan to do?"

"You know, now that I think about it, it was a silly idea. I didn't have a plan. No clue."

"Continue."

"When the officer got off the elevator, a man followed him. He hung around and waited for Ortiz to come out of the office with the costume." Martin took a sip of coffee.

Pascal wondered if Martin had let his imagination run away with him. UNMH was a big hospital, full of people lost and on the wrong floor or in the wrong wing. "What happened next?"

"The officer came out of the office and headed for the elevator, but for some reason stopped, turned around and almost ran smack into the guy who was following him. They stared at each other for a few seconds, then the officer turned back and got in the elevator. The other guy went to the elevator but didn't get in and went up instead of down."

"Probably figured he was on the wrong floor."

"No. I punched the elevator down button. When it stopped, the man was in there. I got in, but when we reached the parking garage, he pushed his way out, almost knocked me over, jumped in his car, and took off. I ran and looked down the street and sure enough— he was tailing the police cruiser."

Pascal considered Martin's story. It was plausible. The vandals needed to get hold of the costume; it was evidence. Maybe this guy followed Ortiz from the hospital, shot out his tire, broke into the cruiser, took the costume, and shot Ortiz. "Can you describe this man?"

"Better than that: I know who he is."

Pascal was speechless. He clenched his teeth as he took in the information. Martin knew the identity of the man but hadn't told him over the phone, making him drive to Albuquerque. They could have put out an APB an hour ago.

"I think he's German, Steg something, looks like an albino. Can't mistake him; that's for sure. He's a filmmaker with that weird group, YinYangYazzie films."

Pascal hadn't heard of the filmmakers. He took out his phone and searched for them. A page popped up with three men standing in front of an iconic image of an atomic bomb explosion. Coriz, who looked to be way over six feet tall, was standing in the middle with a bare hairless chest and a long black ponytail. He dwarfed the two men at his sides: Steg Engle with his ghostly pale skin, and Thomas Eubank's immaculate appearance. Pascal held his phone out to Martin, who confirmed Engle's identity. Pascal couldn't make his fingers work fast enough to call Montaño. As much as he wanted to have all the glory for this case, he knew it wasn't possible.

~46~

Montaño walked to his car in the hospital's underground parking garage. His phone buzzed in his pocket. He sighed, thinking the day would never end. He had been up for over twenty-four hours. For the first time, Montaño considered that he might be too old for the job. He couldn't stifle an audible groan as Pascal asked to meet him in the cafeteria.

A middle-aged Anglo was sitting at a corner table with Pascal. Montaño took his time walking over, partly because he was tired and partly because he wanted to size up the Anglo. Pascal stood and reached out his hand. Montaño shook it and pulled out a chair but didn't acknowledge Martin.

Pascal raised his chin toward Martin: "James Martin."

Montaño stared at Martin and gave a curt nod. Pascal could tell that Montaño was spent; his entire body sagged.

"Martin witnessed a man follow Ortiz out of the hospital yesterday. Could be the one who shot Ortiz's tire, took the costume, and wounded Ortiz."

Montaño forced himself to sit up a little straighter but waited for Pascal to continue.

"Martin was on the seventh floor when Ortiz picked up the costume yesterday. A man followed Ortiz off the elevator and waited outside the administration office. When Ortiz left, the man followed him to the parking garage."

"Can he describe the man?" Montano asked, not looking at Martin.

"Martin recognized him: Steg Engle."

Finally, Montaño turned toward Martin. He squinted in an effort to assess the man's credibility, then turned back to Pascal. "Can we connect the rifle to Engle?"

"Not at this point, but I have an officer on it. The rifle is an antique; there wasn't a registration for that model, but it's not required. We're looking into owners of antique firearms, also clubs and shows. I hope we'll have some news soon, but it's the weekend, not to mention a holiday."

"Can we place Engle out at Tonque this week?"

"I have a source who saw a man in the area on Wednesday who fits Engle's description: pale skin and white hair. He was with another man, taller, slim with dark hair."

"Who's your source?"

"Sorry, can't reveal it."

Montaño stared at Pascal with an annoyed expression.

"Didn't Ortiz pick up a film canister out at Tonque?"

Montaño bit his bottom lip. Ortiz hadn't mentioned a canister, but Montaño wondered if that was what had detained him in Albuquerque. He remembered that Ortiz was excited and said he had found another piece of evidence. "If he did, it wasn't recorded as evidence when he left Tonque. But I'll ask him about it in the morning after he's rested."

"I suggest you bring in Engle, question him right away," Pascal blurted out before he could stop himself. He knew it was a mistake. Such an obvious suggestion would irritate Montaño, but .... "Maybe he had a legitimate reason for being at the hospital yesterday. See if he has an alibi for when the tire was shot out."

"What else do you know about Engle?" Montaño asked.

Martin interrupted. "Engle's father's a German physicist at the Lab. Steg grew up in Los Alamos, studied cinema at Yale, and spent a year abroad in the Czech Republic. He met Coriz and Eubank at the Sundance Film Festival a few years ago. They formed the YinYangYazzie film company."

Both Pascal and Montaño stared at Martin.

"Googled him," Martin said.

Montaño closed his eyes and sighed. "The Lab—that's all I need. They're not easy to deal with; they have some federal protections. We have to tread lightly and not ruffle their feathers. I'd like to talk to Engle. I'll put an APB out. For now, he's only a "person of interest." Hopefully, someone will drag him into the station soon."

"FYI, he drives a dark green Mini Cooper," Martin said.

Pascal and Montaño again looked over at the man.

"You might want to notify public transportation, airport, train, bus—in case Engle decides to take a trip," Pascal said.

Pascal noticed Montaño brisling. Again, he didn't appreciate the suggestion, even though it was an obvious one.

"I'd like to bring in Engle's buddies, Coriz and Eubank. See what they have to say," Pascal said.

Montaño pursed his lips and looked uneasy.

"I'd focus on the opera grounds break-in, nothing about Tonque. See if they have alibis for last Sunday. Since they're filmmakers, they might have needed a costume for a movie they're filming."

"Have you seen their movies?" Martin laughed.

Pascal was annoyed at him for another interruption. He turned back to Montaño. "The way I see it, the filmmakers found out about the costumes stored on the opera grounds. They broke in, smoked a lot of pot—the place reeked of it—then took the Jesus outfit. The place looked like they got a little carried away, tried on some of the costumes, even arranged a few scenes with the furniture and props. Probably shot some footage. Not sure why they wanted to keep the Jesus outfit. But it has to be the same costume that Pilot wore out at Tonque. There can't be two identical Jesus outfits floating around New Mexico."

"Maybe," Montaño said.

"The thing that worries me is why they needed to get the costume back, go to such lengths. Unless the costume implicates them, links them to the storage shed break-in and ties them to what went down out at Tonque."

Montaño didn't agree.

Martin said, "You never know what goes through a person's mind. Sometimes a minor incident spirals out of control. Things get blown out of proportion, then before you know it, something terrible happens."

Pascal stared at Martin but continued. "The burglary at the opera grounds would be a second-degree offense. Although they took a costume, they could argue it was a prank. They didn't damage anything, although Ms. Aubusson might beg to differ. With a good lawyer, they could easily get off with some community service. But the fact that they left Bobby Pilot tied to the cross out at the pueblo might be a different matter."

Montaño's shoulders drooped. He looked as if he could barely hold up his head. "Keep in touch, Ruiz." He leaned heavily on the table to push himself up.

"Will do." Pascal was about to say, "You too," but for once held his tongue.

Montaño gave Martin a cursory nod, turned, and left the cafeteria.

Pascal looked over at Martin. "Appreciate your help. The information on Engle will be really helpful."

"I'd hoped to be involved in the case, maybe use it for a short story. Could you at least keep me in the loop?"

"I'll try. San Felipe might need you as a witness. Right now, I have to get back to Santa Fe and get some sleep. Tomorrow's going to be a busy day."

As Pascal made his way to the parking garage, he called the captain. He knew it would not go down well, especially on Easter weekend. But Pascal also knew the captain would be furious if he waited until morning to give him an update on the case.

The captain's phone rang five or six times, and Pascal started to formulate a voicemail message, but the captain answered, his voice sounding groggy and with a nasty edge. Pascal blurted out that a possible suspect had been identified and gave a brief update on Ortiz.

There was a definite change in the captain's demeanor. He sounded almost amenable, but then he ranted on about precautions and how to proceed: Don't jump the gun, let them take the lead, have them make the mistakes, don't give them an opportunity to complain. It's their ball game for now. He added that Montaño was right about the Los Alamos Lab. We all need to be careful. The Lab thinks it's invincible. The captain was content with San Felipe taking the first plunge.

Steg's flight to Berlin wasn't scheduled to leave Chicago until 6:30 p.m. Although he had eight hours to kill, he wasn't about to venture out into the Windy City. As they approached Chicago, the pilot announced that an Alberta Clipper had brought the temperature with wind chill to eight degrees below zero. Steg didn't know what an Alberta Clipper was but wasn't about to find out. He hated cold weather. The toasty airport had the mind-numbing ambiance and decor of most large terminals. It comforted him, and he didn't mind the wait.

But he needed coffee. He passed a Starbucks but was reluctant to give the chain his business. The company was full of itself, like Apple and Amazon. It had driven most of the small coffee shops out of business, but there didn't seem to be an option, so he resigned himself and stood in a line snaking out into the terminal. He stared at the board on the wall: all those different names for drinks and silly sizes of cups. He found it tedious. When he finally made it to the counter and placed his order for a double espresso, the server had asked for his name, and he wanted to yell "Hitler" but instead said "Joe."

Shouldered by the other caffeine-depleted customers, Steg waited for his order. Weariness cascaded down from his head to his feet and caused his shoulders to sag. His neck wobbled, barely able to support his head. He wanted nothing more than to close his eyes, forget everything, and disappear—poof.

The barista called out "Joe," and for a minute, Steg forgot that was the name he had given. He pushed his way through the crowd to the counter, desperate to empty the thick black contents into his body. He grabbed the cup, but as he turned around, two men standing side by side blocked his way. There was no mistaking who they were: close-cropped hair, not a strand out of place, black wool coats snug against their formidable bodies. Federal agents. Who else wore crisp white button-down shirts with skinny black ties? Steg wanted to turn and run but forced himself to carefully step around them. The taller of the two, the one with steel blue eyes, reached out. "Steg Engle." It wasn't a question.

Steg knew this was the end of the line. Maybe because all the adrenaline had seeped out of his body or simply because he suffered from sleep deprivation, he lost his viability, as if he wasn't even there. Nothing could touch him. He stared at the agents, shook his head, and stepped away. He caught a glimpse of the shorter agent and detected a slight upward curve of his lips, almost a smile. This was a game, and he needed to hold his cards tight, keep control.

"Passport."

Steg stared at the agent.

"You can either play nice or we can cuff and drag you out of here—your choice, Buddy. Passport."

Customers jockeyed for position as they waited for their orders. The agents and Steg blocked the access to the counter. The barista had an expression on his face like he had stepped in dog shit. Some customers became agitated; others, who had overheard the agents, were nervous. They probably assumed Steg was a criminal, a bomber, a madman wanted by the authorities. For some reason, Steg felt important, and this lifted his spirits. He was someone at last, even if that "someone" was a criminal.

~48~

PASCAL CHECKED HIS MAILBOX AND SAW A CRUMPLED SHEET OF paper crammed in the back. It was a note from Aubusson. At the top of the message, Susie had written "PISSED" in all caps. The note was short but not sweet. "An update, please?" He crumpled it up and with an overhand throw tossed it neatly in the trashcan. Although he had his suspicions about the burglary, right now, he had nothing concrete to share with the woman.

He turned to the paperwork on his desk. It was strange how the pile seemed to grow even though nothing much had happened in the last couple of weeks. He resigned himself to sorting through it, and worked diligently until four, when he gave up and left the station.

Des Fleurs Pour Vous had been his mother's favorite florist. She had said that Madame Bisset seemed to know what you needed, if not wanted, when you walked in the door. His mother had sworn the woman was clairvoyant.

The shop was nestled up against the foothills at the end of a narrow lane. A variety of perennials which would be covered in blooms in another month dotted the property. A groomed gravel path led the way to the door, lined with a variety of daffodils, all in full bloom. In the stark surroundings of early spring, the range of shapes and color was conspicuous. Some displayed multiple flowers per stem, while one variety shot up almost two feet tall, with orange trumpets encased in golden petals. Other daffodils flaunted delicate white petals with bushy muted centers. Pascal remembered his mother forcing paper whites for Thanksgiving. They had filled the house with an intoxicating aroma that competed with the turkey.

Double French doors painted in canary yellow were partly propped open. As Pascal approached, the overwhelming fragrance of fresh flowers drifted out into the garden. He drew in a deep breath, his body relaxed, and he ignored the vibrating phone in his pocket. It could wait.

Madame Bisset looked up from the counter, came around, and blew two kisses toward Pascal's cheeks.

"Comment vas-tu, mon ami?"

"Bien. Et tu?"

"Comme-ci comme-ça. Des fleurs?" She waved her arm slowly around the shop and its bouquets arranged in urns.

"Oui. J'ai besoin de fleurs pour . . . mon amie."

"Ah, une amie," Madame Bisset said with a sly smile.

Pascal laughed. One could not fool Madame Bisset. She excused herself and ducked behind the cascading silk periwinkle curtains delicately embroidered with flowers along the edge. Pascal knew the curtains concealed her special stash. The florist parted the drapes and held a bouquet of stunning calla lilies. The flowers' delicate fluted shapes were in various hues of plum and pink, blushing pale, and bold, dark almost red.

"Si belle."

"Merci, mon ami."

"Je tu souhaites bonne chance."

Madame Bisset blew him a kiss as he left.

Pascal wedged the flowers between the front seats to protect them and checked his phone. Jessie Archuleta had left a message: Bobby Pilot was awake.

When Pascal returned Jessie's call, she sounded exhausted, her usual flirty banter gone. But she agreed to wait for him at the hospital.

Once he dropped the flowers off at his house, Pascal figured he had time to get to the hospital and back before he had to pick up Gillian. If he didn't, he didn't want to think about the consequences.

Thankfully, traffic was light on the freeway. Everyone must be home preparing for the Easter holiday. He remembered that when he was a child, his mother had made an egg tree for the holiday. His father thought the idea was silly and would grumble, Whoever heard of a tree with eggs? But he dutifully accompanied his wife, found the perfect branch, and painted it silver or gold. Then Pascal and his mother would blow the eggs, decorate them with homemade dye, and hang them on the branches with thread.

Pascal parked and made his way to the ICU. When he pulled back the curtain on Bobby's cubicle, he was amazed at the tangle of cords and tubes running from various machines that beeped and whined. Bobby's eyes, although muddled and cloudy, were open. Jessie sat in a chair by his bed, stroking his arm. Pascal couldn't hear what she was saying, but Bobby nodded intermittently.

Jessie turned and saw Pascal in the doorway: "Hey." Then she turned back to Bobby. "This is the detective I told you about, the one my uncle asked to look for you. The one that found you out at Tonque."

Bobby turned his head, blinked several times, and gave a slight nod.

"Is it okay if he asks you a few questions, Sweetie?"

Pascal was amazed at how tender and compassionate Jessie sounded. Gone was her flirty, coquettish tease. Bobby hesitated, but Pascal couldn't tell whether it was because he couldn't process the information or didn't want to answer questions. The detective's knowledge of comas was limited, but he figured once someone came out of one, there had to be an adjustment time.

The curtain on the door was yanked back as Pascal started to ask his first question. Montaño was standing with his hands on his hips, his entire body radiating annoyance.

"Ruiz—outside!" he barked.

Pascal left the room. "Hey, what's up?"

"What are you doing here?" Montaño asked.

"Stopped by to see Jessie."

Montaño's eyes narrowed. He knew that although Pascal's explanation was plausible, it wasn't the whole truth.

Montaño was sick of this case and tired of Ruiz always showing up one step ahead of him—always dangling a bit of information like some gnarly bone that turned out to be nothing significant. Tomorrow was Easter, and he needed the case off his plate. He was still concerned there would be a leak to the press about some guy tied to a cross on the reservation. There would be hell to pay.

"How's Ortiz doing?" Pascal asked.

"I'd love to stand around and chit-chat with you, but I have an interview to do before the Feds show up."

"Feds?"

"Yeah, seems Engle is a clever one. The airport had been notified to apprehend him, but he caused a disruption at security and was able to slip through undetected and board his flight."

"How did he manage that?"

"Not sure it was intentional. A woman with three kids was in front of him. She couldn't find her tickets and held up the line. When she tried to disentangle her twins, who were wrapped around her legs, Engle lost his patience, shoved the woman out of his way and rushed up to the agent, knocked down one of the kids on the way. The agent tried to tell Engle it wasn't his turn, but he babbled away in German and flashed his German passport, playing the innocent tourist. The woman had a major tantrum."

Pascal shook his head and chuckled. "What a fiasco."

"Before a supervisor could intervene, the TSA agent, first day on the job, waved Engle through. Several officers came over to assist, but Engle was gone."

Pascal shook his head. He couldn't believe TSA had let Engle slip through.

"By the way, the name on Engle's German passport was Albrecht Stegmann Engle. Guess that was enough to throw TSA off the scent," Montaño said with disgust.

"Where was he headed?"

"Chicago. He booked a ticket to O'Hare. But once he landed, he bought a ticket for Frankfurt, scheduled to leave this evening. Now, if you'll excuse me."

"How did you know he went to the airport?"

"He loaned his girlfriend his Mini Cooper. She was on her way to the Range Cafe in Bernalillo this morning when a state trooper spotted the car. She told him she had dropped Engle off at the airport around 5:30 this morning but didn't know where he was going. The Feds were notified since he had crossed state lines. They picked him up buying a cappuccino at the Chicago airport a few hours ago. They're supposed to escort him back to New Mexico. Besides you, now I'll have them breathing down my neck."

Pascal decided to hang around the ICU, hoping Montaño would share whatever information Bobby gave him. If not, maybe he could get something out of Jessie. Now that Bobby was conscious, he should be able to provide whatever was needed to wrap up the case, maybe even before the Feds arrived with Engle.

Jessie pulled back the curtain on Bobby's door. "Montaño asked me to leave. He wanted to talk to Bobby alone."

"Did Bobby tell you what happened out at Tonque?"

"Some. He was supposed to meet this guy, Alcazar, that morning. But when he got to his house, no one was home. He decided to hike over to Tonque and check out the ruins on his way back to the ranch. When he came to the canyon, he heard voices, tried to climb up on a boulder to get a look. That's when he slipped and fell. Coriz and the other two guys found him. He recognized Coriz, knew him from high school. But Coriz had to leave, some kind of an emergency. He gave Bobby some Percocets for the pain, told the other guys to finish the shoot, and said someone would pick them up that afternoon. Bobby said the guys were stoned on mushrooms, mostly stumbling around giggling."

"Did Bobby say anything about the cross?"

"Yeah." Jessie looked uncomfortable. "He talked about being out there. Wondered what it would feel like to be hung on a cross, crucified, persecuted by the people you loved. But I think he was delusional at that point. He doesn't remember much after that. I think between the concussion, the Percocet, and the mushrooms, he was out of it."

Pascal glanced at his watch. It was five thirty-five. If he waited any longer, he wouldn't have time to get back to Santa Fe, change, and pick up Gillian. His phone buzzed. He thanked Jessie and turned away to take the call.

"Hey, Rupert."

"Got some bad news. Couldn't find Coriz. This guy is elusive, doesn't exist on paper. Also, the GMC van is a no-go. I searched

'60s to '90s GMCs, but nothing matched the partial plate. But the good news is that I found the address of the film company's warehouse in Santa Fe. It's off Airport Road on South Polo Drive across from HIPICO, the old horse park. It's the only building on the south side."

"Thanks, appreciate it. I owe you one. Call me if you find out about the gun."

It was the weekend. Tomorrow was Easter. Pascal knew there was no way he would get the captain to agree to a search warrant until Monday. By then, the place would be crawling with Feds. He was reluctant even to broach the subject. The captain would be pissed to have his sacred holiday interrupted and would demand concrete evidence connecting the warehouse to the opera burglary. Pascal didn't have anything. It was all supposition.

Since Montaño figured that Engle had been out at Tonque with Pilot, maybe he would be able to get a search warrant. If the Jesus costume was in the warehouse, and it was the same as the one stolen from the opera, then Pascal had a right to pursue the case.

As he headed back to Santa Fe, his phone buzzed in his pocket. He fished it out, pulled off the highway, and answered the call. It was Rupert.

"What did you find out?"

"Not any luck with the state gun registration. Left a message yesterday with New Mexico Gun Collectors Association. The head, Robert Plank, called back this afternoon, gave me a spiel about the association's focus on the preservation of weaponry. But I picked up on the underlying message: "An armed militia is necessary to secure a free state." These guys are adamant about the protection of people's right to keep and bear arms. He shared his member list, but it only has contact information, nothing about who owns which weapons."

"Did you ask about the bullet found in Ortiz's tire?"

"Yeah, I asked if he knew what kind of rifle would be able to fire that bullet. Most of the members owned more traditional weaponry, but he was familiar with the ammunition and the rifle. He either wasn't sure who owned that particular rifle or didn't want to say, but he gave me the names of three people in the state that have extensive collections of antique firearms."

"Well, that's a start."

"I emailed you the contact information. Two of them are from southern New Mexico and one's from Los Alamos."

"Thanks, I'll check it out when I get back to Santa Fe. Appreciate it."

"Anytime, boss. See you Monday."

"Happy Easter."

"Don't remind me," Rupert sighed. "First, I got to take my mother to Mass at the crack of dawn. Then the entire family has a reservation in Chimayó for lunch. It'll be packed, take forever to get served. Don't know how those pilgrims who trekked for miles to the chapel are going to find a place to eat."

Pascal chuckled but then thought of poor Bobby Pilot stuck in the hospital. He had wanted to participate in the procession, find redemption, write an article, and become a journalist.

Rupert's information was another lead that led nowhere, at least not to the opera burglary. He should pass it along to Montaño. The only thing he needed was the costume. Then he could have Aubusson identify it, and that would tie it to Engle.

As he pulled into his driveway, he checked the time. He had thirty minutes—tops—to take a shower, get dressed, and pick Gillian up. When his phone rang, he groaned. It was Captain Vargas.

"Ruiz."

"I don't need this, I don't. Tomorrow is Easter for Christ's sake. That ... that woman called, said that the estate contacted the commissioner. They want the costume back now. Their attorney sent a letter threatening to sue. A Fed Ex delivery guy pounded on the commissioner's door at six this morning. The heathens don't have any respect for the Lord Jesus Christ." The captain broke into a coughing fit.

"I've located the costume," Pascal blurted out.

It took the captain a minute to suppress his cough. "Where?"

Pascal knew he was out on a limb, one that might easily send him crashing to the ground. He prayed that he was right, "It's at a warehouse near the horse park. Some filmmakers lease the building to store their equipment"

"And you know this how?"

"It's complicated."

"Always is with you."

"If we could get a search warrant for the warehouse, we could get the costume, have Aubusson identify it, and arrest the filmmakers for the theft."

"And what do we tell the judge to justify a search warrant? It's complicated?"

Pascal took in a deep breath and let it out slowly. He didn't have time to explain, and if he did, he would be in big trouble. "It's mostly circumstantial."

"Circumstantial. You want me to ask a judge, the day before Easter for a search warrant on circumstantial evidence?"

Pascal glanced at his watch, now he only had twenty minutes to get ready for his date. He put the phone on speaker and muted the background noise, a trick he had learned from his ex-girlfriend, Madeline. A sponge bath would have to suffice.

"San Felipe discovered evidence that connects the filmmakers to Bobby Pilot and Tonque," he said. There was silence on the line, and Pascal figured the captain was mulling over his story.

"Maybe I should turn over what I have. Let San Felipe get the search warrant. Once they get hold of the costume, it's theirs until the case is settled. Could take a long time."

Pascal could hear Vargas wheeze into the receiver. "If you can come up with something, I'll move forward. But it's got to be plausible. When you get it, call me, and it better be tonight, not Easter Sunday for God's sake." The phone went dead.

~49~

PASCAL RACKED HIS BRAIN FOR SOMETHING THAT WOULD SATISFY the captain, something credible. He needed that costume. Everything so far had fallen into San Felipe's lap, some of it thanks to him. He wasn't about to give away the only piece of evidence that was tied to his case, handing over all his hard work. He needed to come up with plausible circumstances that would convince a judge to issue a search warrant for the warehouse.

As he maneuvered his car up Canyon Road, Pascal was careful to avoid the tourists who never bothered to look as they wandered across the street. An oversized van had stopped in the middle of the road to let people climb aboard. As he pulled into Gillian's driveway, he realized he had forgotten the flowers in his kitchen, the perfect bouquet Madame Bisset had selected especially for him to give her.

The house was dark, not even a porch light on. He rang the bell and waited, then rang it several more times. He pounded as loudly as he could on the massive oak door. Finally it swung open. Gillian stood there, hair tangled, eyes crusted with sleep, and a ripped sweatshirt in need of a wash hanging off her shoulder. Pascal was dumbfounded. Thoughts zinged through his head. Was it the wrong night? Was he late? Was she sick?

Gillian wrinkled her forehead. "What time is it?"

"Almost seven."

"Oh, my God, sorry. I lay down on the couch to read and must have dozed off."

Pascal was relieved. For once, he wasn't the one who had messed up. But then he was annoyed and almost was glad he had forgotten the flowers. "Do you think you can pull yourself together? We have reservations in five minutes."

Gillian pressed her lips together. "Sure." She turned away and left him in the doorway.

Pascal made his way to the living room and noticed an open bottle of wine on the coffee table. That explained why she had fallen asleep. He poured himself a glass and wondered if he should be worried about her drinking—or his.

Miraculously, Gillian reappeared ten minutes later dressed in a short maroon slinky dress with black sparkly stockings. Her hair was pulled back in a tasteful chignon. He lifted his glass. "A votre santé."

She shot him a satisfied smile but said nothing.

When they arrived at the restaurant, a host stood bent over the desk, ignoring them as he stared at the seating chart. Pascal cleared his throat, but the man took his time before he raised his eyes, a flash of irritation on his face.

"Ruiz, party of two." Pascal hated service people who took themselves too seriously. The man studied the list of reservations, then looked at his watch and sighed. He glanced around the room before telling them there would be a wait.

Gillian leaned forward, peering at the seating diagram and scanning the room for an empty table. "We take that one, hey, darling?" she said haughtily in an Eastern European accent as she stretched out her arm and pointed toward a premium table nestled next to the fireplace.

The host, taken aback, sucked in his breath and stared at the chart, then looked over to the fireplace and at Gillian.

"Oh, well, not sure."

"Yah, darling. Let's sit."

Although she didn't snap her fingers, she threw her scarf over her shoulder and strutted over to the table. Gillian's dress shimmered in the low light. Pascal followed, noting the appreciative glances from several men. The host scurried over to a waiter and whispered in his ear.

Pascal sank into the chair next to Gillian. "Bravo, countess."

They shared several dishes and a bottle of wonderful Spanish wine. After they had ordered dessert and coffee, Pascal told Gillian about the warehouse and his conversation with the captain.

"I need to come up with something substantial for a search warrant. Got any ideas?"

Gillian took another sip of wine. "From what you've told me, you've got nada nooda."

"Nada nooda?"

Gillian stuck out her tongue.

"That's not lady-like, countess."

"I have an idea. But it isn't exactly above-board," Gillian said. Pascal knew it had to be something outrageous or illegal. "What?"

"What if there was an attempted break-in at the warehouse? Then the police—that would be you—would be notified. When you arrive at the scene, you check it out, make sure nothing's missing. Then you happen to see the costume, recognize it's the one that was stolen from the opera grounds. And Voila!"

Pascal laughed, but the more he thought about it, the more ingenious the idea seemed. He could break a window, set off the alarm, then be the first on the scene.

"You know, you're amazing, Gillian! There's a naughty side of you that I'm beginning to appreciate and love."

Gillian smiled sweetly and stuck out her tongue again.

"I want this case to be over, have your full attention at last," she said.

"Moi aussi. How are you at B&E?"

"B&E?"

"Breaking and entering?"

"I would need to change into something a little less sparkly."

"Good idea."

"You know I was kidding?"

"This is the only way. You don't have to be involved."

"Promise I won't go to jail?"

"Promise."

They stopped at Gillian's and Pascal's to change clothes, then drove across town toward the airport. The warehouse was set back from the road and a little west of the horse park. The area was mostly dry scrub—nowhere to pull the cruiser off where it wouldn't be noticed. Pascal considered parking at the hippodrome, but then spotted a small outbuilding several hundred feet past the warehouse. He drove up to its far side. The windows were boarded over, and on the front door, a "Keep Out" sign hung sideways from a nail. He turned the car around and tucked it up close to the building but facing out to the street.

Gillian opened her door but shined her phone light around on the ground before stepping out. She wasn't about to step on a snake or whatever else lived out there.

On the way to the warehouse, they had discussed several scenarios for the caper, as Gillian called it. Now that they were there, Pascal had doubts. He tried to convince Gillian to wait in the car while he checked out the place, knowing there would be a surveillance camera and not wanting her to be captured on video before he set off the alarm. There was no way he was going to leave her alone out there, she said. She would take her chances.

They both pulled on black stocking caps and tugged them as far down as possible while still being able to see, then wrapped dark scarves around their necks and over their noses. That would have to do. They cut across a field, following Gillian's phone light on the ground. Pascal reassured her that it was too cold for snakes, but the mention of the reptiles caused her to shiver.

As Pascal got closer to the building, he realized they had their work cut out for them. The warehouse was an impenetrable fortress. Someone had gone to a lot of trouble to keep people out. A surveillance camera and alarm system were set high above the only entrance, a massive steel door. The windows were secured with bars, and the thick glass was lined with wires attached to an alarm system. It would be easy to set off the alarm, but Pascal realized he needed to get inside. It had to appear as if someone had gained entry into the building. Then he would have a reason to check for intruders, make sure nothing was missing, and find the costume.

"What do you think, mastermind?" Pascal said, turning to Gillian.

"Unless you're superman, there's no way you'll be able to get through that door. Maybe a window?"

"I think I have something for the window in the car. Are you okay out here a few minutes?"

Gillian looked around nervously. "Sure."

"Keep away from the camera above the door."

Pascal jogged across the field and rummaged around in the back of the car. When Matt, his partner, was diagnosed with appendicitis and placed on medical leave, he had asked Pascal to store the stash of tools from his police vehicle. He didn't want anyone messing with the collection he had amassed over the years. Pascal rummaged through the tools until he found the dynamite. Matt had intended using the explosives on his property in Pecos. His plan was to dig a tank on the south side of a small stream and use the explosives to divert water into it. In the spring, he had planned to stock it with perch. But he had never gotten around to it. Pascal stuffed a few mini-flares in his pockets, and put the dynamite, a crowbar, and Matt's famous loppers that could disarm any padlock in a duffel bag. Fully loaded, he made his way back across the field.

"What's the plan, Stan?" Gillian said.

Pascal set down the tools. "Once the alarm goes off, we won't have long before the alarm company sends someone." He hesitated, and for a few seconds, he doubted his sanity, but he brushed away his hesitation. "Take the car over to the horse park. When you hear the alarm, wait two minutes, drive up to the building, then get in the passenger seat."

"What if someone asks what we were doing out here?"

"I wanted to show you the horse park. You wanted to take riding lessons."

"Riding lessons?" Gillian said, wrinkling her forehead. She looked at the warehouse. "How are you going to break into the building?"

"Not exactly sure. The windows are barred. I think I might have better luck with the door. I can send up some flares, block the camera, then try to dismantle the locks. It's a long shot. Not a perfect plan. If I'm caught, my goose will be cooked."

"Yummy."

"I'll wait until you get to the horse park. When you hear the alarm, don't wait more than a few minutes. I don't want to be caught with these tools."

"I'll visit you in prison—promise." Gillian gave him a kiss on the cheek. "After all, it was my idea."

Pascal pulled up Gillian's stocking cap, looked into her eyes, and placed a kiss on her forehead.

Even from a distance, Pascal could tell that the door was secured with several imposing locks. He watched as Gillian drove the car past the warehouse, made a U-turn in front of the horse park, and parked. Then he tugged his ski hat down so it covered his eyes and took a slow deep breath to calm the panic that made its way through his body and caused his limbs to freeze. He took another long, slow breath. As he moved toward the door, he lowered his head, set down the equipment, lit a flare, and flung it up toward the camera. It veered to the right and missed the target. He lit another and threw it. This time, it hit the camera, which immediately became engulfed in smoke. He heard the snap of the sparks as they hit the electrical wires, but no alarm. He prayed it wasn't a silent one.

The door's combination lock could easily be snapped with Matt's loppers but the other two locks would be difficult to pick, even if he knew how. Pascal had already decided to use the dynamite as a last resort, but he hadn't told Gillian. For a moment, he wondered once again if he had lost his mind. He remembered what Martin had said about things sometimes getting out of hand. He guessed this was one of those times. His hand shook as he reached into the duffel bag for the dynamite.

He wasn't sure the dynamite had enough power to blow the door open. This could be the end of his short career as a detective—or as a free man. He closed his eyes and took in three breaths, inhaled to five, and exhaled to seven. As the last of the air was forced out of his lungs at the end of the third exhale, he held his breath, stepped forward, wedged the explosive up next to the door, lit the fuse, turned, and ran toward the road. The detonation was deafening, interspersed with the shrill earsplitting cry of the alarm. Gillian screamed and gunned the car. Pascal stopped in the middle of the road, hands on his thighs, and tried to force air into his lungs.

"Jesus Christ. What was that?" Gillian screamed as she jumped out of the car.

Pascal, his ears ringing from the blast, shook his head. He straightened and looked toward the door. Most of it was gone. His stomach flopped and soured as the acrid smell from the explosion wafted toward them.

Gillian was frantic, flapping her arms in the air as she stared at the building. "Jesus! What's the plan? Oh my God. Jesus!"

In the distance, they heard sirens. The police would be here any minute. But Pascal couldn't move.

Gillian tugged at his sleeve. "Jesus, come on. Get the equipment in the car."

Pascal turned to her and mumbled in a monotone. "Get in the passenger seat. Say as little as possible. I'll take care of everything. Act like you're in shock."

"That won't be hard."

Pascal drove up to the building and parked. He stuffed the loppers, crowbar, and unused explosives under the spare tire. Then he got back in the car and reported the explosion. They stared mesmerized at the door, or at least what had been the door a few minutes ago.

The first to arrive at the scene were a pair of off-duty cops, Harold Butler and Louise Sanchez. They had finished their shift and were on the way back to the station when the call came in from the dispatcher. Louise had already worked a double shift, volunteering to fill in for Harold's partner who had come down with the flu. She was exhausted, and wanted to go home, soak in a tub, and sip a cold beer.

The last thing Harold and Louise wanted to do tonight was process a burglary—and, worse, an explosion. The Feds would have to be alerted. The paperwork would be insurmountable.

They efficiently took charge of the scene. Harold put in a call to forensics. The premises needed to be combed for physical evidence that could be analyzed in the lab. The forensics clerk who took the call sounded bored and distracted until Harold asked for an explosives expert. Harold could imagine the clerk's eyes bugging out. They would need the place fingerprinted.

Louise pulled out a roll of yellow crime scene tape. Pascal volunteered to help her put it up. They tried to be careful not to disturb anything, but already, there were footprints in the dirt all over the place; it was unavoidable.

As they approached the building, Pascal was pleased to see that the locks were no longer secure. Louise took her nightstick and gave what was left of the door a push. It swung open a few feet. Pascal knew he didn't have much time. The alarm company would be here any minute, probably with Coriz or Eubank in tow. He needed to get in the building before anyone else.

He turned to Louise. "How about we take a look inside? Make sure nobody's in there."

She starred at Pascal suspiciously. "You think someone's in there?"

Pascal shrugged.

Louise squeezed through the opening, and Pascal followed. Once inside, they were unable to see anything at all. The room was pitch black. Pascal ran his hands up and down the wall on either side of the door but found no switch. Louise unbelted her enormous flashlight and flashed it around the walls. It landed on a switch ten feet to the right of the door.

Pascal flipped the switch several times. Nothing. The explosion must have disconnected the electricity. He turned on his phone's flashlight. It was ineffective, illuminating only a tiny circle of light, but it was all he had. Louise looked over at him and warned, "Don't touch anything. We've already messed up the crime scene."

"But we're the police."

She stared at Pascal with a look he couldn't or didn't want to interpret. Then she started to flash her light around the room. Pascal desperately searched for the costume. The room was orderly, meticulous, nothing out of place. He worried that the costume might be packed away in a cabinet. As he made his way toward the back of the room, he was ready to give up when he spotted something on a table near the back of the room. As he came closer, he noticed a sheet of paper taped to a bag. Someone had scribbled, "ADIOS." He lifted up the paper and saw the UNMH logo on the bag.

~50~

THOMAS EUBANK HAD PULLED THE HARASSMENT CARD, AND maybe he had rattled the detective. But now he fretted as he paced back and forth in his condo. Although the detective didn't accuse him of anything, he had insinuated his involvement. Thomas knew his deflection was temporary and that the detective would be back. He wondered where the hell Steg was. He was supposed to pick up the costume at the hospital and take it to the warehouse.

Coriz had come up with the idea after he attended the opera's costume sale last year. He had found out from one of the volunteers that the costumes were stored in a shed on the opera grounds during the off-season. He wanted to take some stills of the costumes and props and incorporate them into their film projects.

Since their current film was Steg's baby, he had been assigned to the task. He had hired a couple of homeboys from Española to help. The guys had been happy to hang out and smoke pot while Steg rummaged through the costumes, pairing them with the props. Once the home boys were stoned, Steg had them dress up and pose, and took some amusing stills.

When Steg came across the Jesus costume, he decided he had to have it for the final scene. He tried to straighten up the storeroom, but it was a mess, with costumes thrown all over the place. He was tired and wanted to go home. The Española boys offered to put everything back in order for another $50. But they were laughing, and Steg wasn't sure he should leave them in the shed.

Then when they were out at Tonque working on the last scene, this dude showed up. He had fallen off a boulder and injured his leg. Coriz gave him some Percocet but then had to leave on some kind of an emergency. The kid rambled on about penitence—even pleading with them to be put on the cross. Steg had said, "Why not make the kid happy?" When Coriz's nephew picked them up in his small car, they had to leave the kid out there. When they came back, the police already had found him. Thomas knew they were complicit.

He punched Steg's number in again. They needed to be on the same page—get their stories straight. But the little prick didn't answer. Coriz was still sequestered out at Santo Domingo, which was closed.

Thomas paced around the loft, cursing under his breath. Finally, he slammed his fist into the wall, knocking down his favorite print and sending shattered glass across the floor.

His phone rang, and he grabbed it. It was the alarm company. Someone had broken into the warehouse. The man on the phone explained that they were unable to reach Mr. Coriz and asked if Mr. Eubank could meet Mr. Abbot at the building. He assured Thomas that the police were already on the scene, but someone needed to make sure nothing was missing or damaged. An uneasy feeling came over Thomas. The warehouse was a secure stronghold. How could anyone break in?

As he drove there, although the temperature had dropped below freezing, his moist hands slipped on the steering wheel as cold sweat beaded on his forehead. He tried consciously to slow down his heart, which thumped so loud in his chest he worried it would burst. He needed to get control. Be a man. But he dreaded dealing with the police—they could be pricks. They had a way of making him feel shriveled and insignificant, always had.

As he turned down Airport Road, he saw several vehicles parked in front of the warehouse. He pulled up as close as possible and was stunned to see the door of the building, or what had been the door, almost blown away, left vulnerable. The metal was ripped and torn as if a blowtorch had scorched open a cavity. Someone had blown up Coriz's impenetrable door.

Abbot, the alarm company representative, rushed over to Thomas and held out his hand. Thomas stood paralyzed, barely able to lift his arm. The agent reached down and encased Thomas's limp hand in both of his. He shook it several times.

Thomas remembered him from the initial alarm company presentation. Abbot, or was it Asshole, had assured them that the company's system, High Sierra, was impenetrable, the best in the business. "Impenetrable," Thomas mumbled under his breath.

"I can assure you, Mr. Eubank, all appears to be in order," he said, finally releasing Thomas's hand and turning toward the building. "Well, except for the door. But we have someone on their way to secure it."

Thomas nodded. It took all his effort not to wipe the sweat from the man's hand on his jacket.

"Two officers are in the building. I asked them to wait, but they wanted to make sure no one was inside. You know—safety concerns."

Thomas's mind was blank. He couldn't think what to say.

"Well, shall we?" Abbot said as he swept his hand toward the building.

Thomas trailed behind Abbot. Each step took an enormous effort. When he reached the door, he paused and stared in disbelief at the ripped metal. As he entered, he instinctively ducked his head, and as he straightened up, he almost ran into Abbot's back. It was pitch black inside. He couldn't see anything. Then a flash of light hit him, and he raised an arm to shield his eyes.

Abbot turned toward Louise. "Mr. Eubank, one of the leasers of the building, is here to inspect the premises."

Louise moved toward the two men. She was exasperated. This was a crime scene. "Don't touch anything," she snapped. "Take a cursory look, but that's it. Let me know if you notice anything out of place, missing." Louise led them down the east side of the cavernous room. Thomas's head whirled as the officer sporadically moved her flashlight left and right. His stomach tightened, and the nausea made its way up his throat.

Pascal was on the other side of the building. When he looked up, he saw Thomas Eubank and the alarm guy trailing behind Louise. A sense of dread spread down the back of his throat and made it difficult to swallow. Time was up. He had a sudden impulse to grab the costume and run. What did it matter? He already was in so much trouble that one more indiscretion wouldn't matter. As he stretched out his arm toward the package, Louise flashed her light in his eyes. Pascal was temporarily blinded. He raised his arm defensively to block out the light.

When he lowered his arm, Louise stared with her mouth open.

"What the hell, Ruiz?" He was sure if she had been within reach, she would have slapped his hand like a naughty boy. A queasiness swirled in his stomach, and for a moment, his knees started to buckle.

Eubank recognized Ruiz, the officer who had come to his loft and interrogated him about the opera burglary. What was he doing here? Questions swarmed around in his head. What had the detective reached for? A package—the costume?

Louise marched over to the desk and flashed her light on the package, then turned to Eubank and snapped, "What's this?"

Thomas was speechless. He stared at the bag with the hospital logo. Then he looked at the scrap of paper where Steg had scribbled "ADIOS." Anger quickly replaced his fear, but when he opened his mouth, nothing came out. Everyone stared at him and waited.

Louise was out of patience. "Mr. Eubank?"

Thomas shook his head. He was afraid to say anything. Once he did, he knew it wouldn't go well.

She turned to Pascal. "Ruiz?"

"I think the package contains a Jesus costume that was stolen from the Santa Fe Opera storage shed last week." He hoped to leave it at that, but he knew Louise wouldn't. Around the station, she had the reputation of being a pit bull. Once she got hold of something, she wouldn't let go.

Louise raised her eyebrows. "And how do you know this?"

Pascal cleared his throat and wondered how much he should divulge. He was exhausted. The wine buzz from dinner had worn off and left him empty. He didn't have the stamina to let her drag the information out bit by bit but wasn't about to hand it over on silver platter either. "A man found on the San Felipe Reservation dressed in a Jesus costume was taken to University Hospital. I am certain the costume had to be the same one stolen from the opera grounds. San Felipe Tribal, now in charge of the case, agreed that Santa Fe could inspect the costume. But the officer who picked up the costume at the hospital was shot. The costume went missing."

"San Felipe Tribal?"

"Yes."

"I guess this is the kid that was tied to a cross out at Tonque?"

"Yes."

"And what's your connection, Ruiz?"

Pascal could tell that even though Louise, who only a few minutes ago had been beyond weary, now was intrigued. "The opera burglary is my case. I figured—how many Jesus outfits could there be?"

"Well, with Easter tomorrow, who knows?" Then Louise turned to Eubank. "Do you have any idea what this package is doing in your warehouse?"

Thomas opened his eyes wide, shook his head, and tried to look surprised. But he knew exactly what the costume was doing there. Steg had brought it to the warehouse and wrote that stupid note. What a prick.

"Okie dokie, boys. I think this little party needs to reconvene down at the station. We can sort this out in the comfort of an interrogation room. Louise picked up the package and the note and headed toward the door. The three men followed behind her like naughty schoolboys.

~51~

As they walked to their cars, Pascal told Louise he would drop Gillian off at her house, then meet her at the station. Louise shot him a look he couldn't interpret. She said she was sorry, but Pascal could tell she wasn't sorry—Gillian would have to go to the station and give a statement.

Harold stayed behind at the scene. His shoulders sagged as realized that an already-long night would be even longer. Tomorrow was Easter. His wife would insist on early Mass no matter what time he dragged himself into the house. He wished he had a cup of coffee, and maybe a donut.

Abbot stayed behind. He had called for someone to secure the warehouse door, but Louise insisted they would have to wait until the technicians and explosive experts finished their job.

Louise opened the back door of the cruiser and reached out to put her hand on Eubank's head. He looked at her alarmed. She assured him it was policy; he couldn't ride up front with her. She shot Pascal a stern look and told him to follow her to the station.

As soon as Pascal closed the cruiser door, Gillian blurted out. "What the hell am I supposed to say to that woman?"

"Tell her the truth."

"Jesus!" Gillian exploded. "You've got to get me out of this! I don't want to go to prison."

"We can either tell the truth or not—or somewhere in between." Pascal sounded strange, like he was somewhere else.

Gillian turned away and glared out the windshield. She could kick herself. Although the break-in was her idea, she had been kidding, hadn't she? Then she thought of her sister, Hallie. If Gillian went to jail, who would take care of her? She was supposed to be the responsible one. How had her life become so out of control? She was sorry she had ever agreed to come to New Mexico.

"Okay," Pascal sighed. "This is what's going to happen. Say we went to dinner. Afterward, I wanted to show you the horse park. You were interested in riding lessons. When we pulled up to the hippodrome, I saw something suspicious at the warehouse. I asked you to wait in the car across the street while I went to check it out."

"What did you see?"

"Movement, a flash of light." Pascal shrugged. "As I started to cross the street, there was an explosion."

"Is that what you're going to say?"

"Don't worry about me. You weren't involved in the explosion. You were in the car across the street. Keep it simple."

The station on most nights was tomb-like, dark, empty, and cold. Someone had turned down the heat. It was Easter morning. The night officer at the front desk had on his coat. He giggled as he stared down at his iPad. Pascal hoped he was watching some stand-up comic, not porn. The officer looked up as they opened the door and quickly turned off his iPad.

Louise frowned. "Danny, we need two interrogation rooms set up."

"Yes ma'am." Danny almost knocked over his stool as he jumped up. "Ruiz, take Ms. . . . ah?"

"Gillian Jasper," Gillian offered.

Louise turned back to Pascal. "Take Ms. Jasper to Interrogation Room 1. I'll put Mr. Eubank in 2."

Pascal was about to say something, but the look on Louise's face made him stop. At least she'd assigned Gillian to the nicer room.

He took Gillian's arm and could feel her resist. He squeezed it and guided her down the hall. Once they were in the room with the door closed, Pascal said, "Remember: I saw something near the warehouse. You waited in the car. I went to check it out, but as I reached the street, there was an explosion."

Before Danny opened the interrogation room door, he gave it a cursory rap. His arms were loaded with recording equipment. As he set up and tested the equipment, he didn't look at either Pascal or Gillian.

When Louise came in the room, Gillian noticed she was carrying one of the tiny notebooks that officers use at crime scenes. "Ruiz." She pressed her lips together, then let out a long slow sigh. "Although this might involve your case, the situation seems a little convoluted. These multiple layers need to be sorted out. The situation requires a fresh eye, someone not involved. With San Felipe Tribal and all. . . ." She slapped her notebook down on the table. "I'll do the interviews."

Pascal started to protest, but again, Louise gave him that look—she was a ball-buster.

"You can wait in the observation room, listen in. Might learn something."

Pascal had to fight the urge to hang his head like a whipped puppy. He knew that all hell would break loose soon. The Feds would show up with Engle. Bobby Pilot would identify who was with him out at Tonque and explain what went on. If Louise thought the case was convoluted now, she had no idea. It soon would be a total debacle. Pascal knew he had crossed too many lines. His days as a detective were numbered, but he couldn't decide whether he was sad or relieved.

~52~

LOUISE WAS A PATROL OFFICER, AND SHE PREFERRED THAT JOB, but everyone knew she was a master at interrogation. She knew how to make a suspect comfortable and unguarded, defenses down. She had an arsenal of inane anecdotes for any occasion. Her questions were "sleight of hand," slipped into a circuitous tale.

Gillian slumped in a chair and yawned, not bothering to cover her mouth. The night had been long, and she was fading fast. A pang of regret came over Pascal as he watched from the observation room. He worried that Gillian wouldn't be able to keep up the charade, but he didn't need to worry. She never wavered from their fabrication.

Louise wrapped up the interview. She figured there wasn't much she would get out of the woman, and she wanted to save her strength for Eubank. She accompanied Gillian out to the front desk and told Danny to type up her statement and have her sign it. Then Louise flashed Gillian a stern look. "Don't leave town anytime soon." Then she chuckled. "Always wanted to say that."

Eubank, who had been in the interrogation room for over an hour, still sat with impeccable posture, butt to the back and shoulders erect, but his demeanor was sulky. His arms were wrapped protectively around his chest.

Louise slid into the chair on the other side of the table, leaned forward, and rested her arms on the faded, chipped surface. Over the years, the table had been scarred by detained criminals left too long in the room. She waved her hand in the air like an orchestra conductor, then touched the play button on the recorder. "Thomas Eubank."

"Yes?"

"It's late. I'm beyond tired. Already worked two plus shifts. I suspect you're tired too. Let's cut to the chase. Okay?"

Eubank was apprehensive but nodded.

"Let the record show that Mr. Eubank nodded his acquiescence."

Eubank narrowed his eyes and glared over at Louise.

"Where were you the night the opera storage shed was burglarized?" She looked down at her tiny notebook. "That would have been last Sunday."

"Home."

"Can anyone substantiate that?"

"No."

"What was the Jesus costume doing in your warehouse?"

"No idea."

"Who wrote the 'adios' note that was taped to the costume?"

Eubank shrugged.

"Let the record show that Mr. Eubank shrugged."

Again, Thomas glared at Louise. He was at the end of his patience. This was all Steg's fault. He couldn't wait to get his hands on the little weasel. And Coriz—what the hell. He never was around, always off on some pueblo business.

"Mr. Eubank, where were you last Tuesday and Wednesday? And again, can anyone substantiate that?"

Eubank had had enough. This woman was never going to stop. Once Pilot was conscious, he would tell them the whole story. It would be over. There was no way out of this mess.

"I'd like an attorney."

Louise looked up at him, surprised. "An attorney? From what you've told me, you're not involved."

Thomas couldn't believe it. What was with this bitch? He knew she knew he was guilty. Although he hadn't been with Steg the night he took the costume, they had taken it to Tonque. Then Steg had left it at the warehouse. And who knows what else she might suspect he was involved in? "What am I doing here? Why am I being interrogated?"

"Well, those are legitimate questions, Mr. Eubank. Primarily, you

are here because we found a stolen piece of property, a Jesus costume, in the warehouse your film company leases."

He was beside himself. First, the bitch says he's not guilty, then
she says he is.

"I'd like to see an attorney. It's my right."

"Yes, you have a right to an attorney. But maybe we can talk, dis-
cuss your options first."

Thomas's mind raced. Work something out? Make a deal?
Maybe there was a way out of this. He would have no problem
throwing that asshole Steg under the bus.

"What are you alluding to, ma'am?"

"You tell us the truth, and we go easy on you."

Thomas had watched his share of cop shows and knew how
things worked. He needed some assurance: an attorney to look after
his best interest, plead his case, seal the deal.

"I would like an attorney to negotiate my best interests."

"Your best interests? How about saving your ass from going to
prison?" Louise chuckled.

Again, Thomas tried to flash a brave face, but Louise noticed his
arms clutching his chest tighter. He was worried.

"Okay. I'll notify the public defender—that is, unless you have
your own attorney on retainer."

"Public defender is fine."

"Unfortunately, Mr. Eubank, it's well past two in the morning,
not to mention it's Easter, for Christ's sake." Louise chuckled at
her little joke. "It might take some time before I am able to drag
the P.D. down to the station, not to mention find the district attorney. But I'll be back shortly and let you know how long it's going
to take me."

When Louise came back into the interrogation room, she found
Eubank leaning forward, his elbows on the table, his hands covering
his face. When he looked up, for the first time, Louise detected fear
in the man's eyes.

She apologized for the long wait. Then she said in a monotone.
"You have the right to remain silent. Anything you say can be used

against you in a court of law. You have the right to an attorney. If you cannot afford an attorney, or don't have one, there is one available who can represent you."

It wasn't the first time she had seen a perp's mouth drop open.

*   *   *

It wasn't until late Sunday morning that Michelle Wyeth, the assistant public defender, strolled into the station with a big Starbuck's coffee in one hand and a half-eaten croissant in the other. Although most people wouldn't consider her overweight, she seemed to take up more space then another woman her size. A mass of black curls framed her freckled face. Her gray trench coat hung open and revealed a conservative navy-blue striped suit that fell below her knees and met a pair of swanky leather boots.

"Hey, Michelle, my belle," Susie beamed as she leaned over the counter. "Missed you last night at Versace's. They were playing your song."

"Yeah? Jailhouse Blues?" Both women chuckled. "How come Ruiz isn't working this case?"

"Long story, not a happy one."

Wyeth raised her eyebrows, "Where's Ms. Louise and my perp?"

As Susie paged Louise, Wyeth looked down the hall and spotted Ruiz coming toward her. She tilted her head. "Hey, Ruiz, what's the story, my man?"

"You don't want to know, but I might need your services soon."

"Sounds a little risqué. But please don't tell me you got your little fingers or worse caught in the cookie jar again?"

Pascal knew Wyeth had a sense of humor, but he never could tell if she was joking."

Louise came down the hall.

Pascal said, "You two are welcome to use my office to go over the case."

Wyeth closed her eyes, took in an exasperated breath, and let it out. "Jesus, Pascal, please tell me you're not dirty."

Susie lowered her eyes and busied herself with the paperwork on the counter.

Louise took Wyeth down to Pascal's office. She gave an overview of the incident at the warehouse and told her about Eubank. She included the information Pascal had shared about Bobby Pilot and San Felipe Tribal's involvement.

"And you got this guy under lock and key already?" Wyeth shot Louise a wicked smile. "You didn't ask him any questions before you read him his rights?"

"A couple preliminaries. You know, warm him up for you. Give him something to think about while he waited in that dingy, airless interrogation room."

"Jesus, my luck. Whenever Ruiz brings in a big fish, Reggie is out of commission. This time, he supposedly is walking the Easter Procession to Chimayó —which is a crock. He can barely make it around the block with his wonky knees."

She reached down, took out her reading glasses, and positioned them almost to the end her nose.

"Okay, let's see what my guy got himself into, then I'll have a little chat with him."

Louise handed her Eubank's arrest report and notes from the interview with him. Wyeth shook her head as she looked them over. Santa Fe was still down one judge because of a recent retirement, which had left the other judges with packed caseloads. She figured the D.A. would be happy to get this one off his plate, and might drop the charge in exchange for a guilty plea and Eubank's testimony against Steg Engle. With so many agencies involved, she figured, he'd want to wrap up the case as soon as possible and move on before any shit hit the fan.

"I'll send it over to Barnard for review, see if he wants to play nice," Wyeth said as she stuffed the papers in her briefcase.

~53~

L OUISE FOUND PASCAL IN THE LOBBY TALKING TO SUSIE. SHE motioned with her head for him to join her. "We need to have a little chit-chat. Wyeth is in your office waiting for the D.A. Let's take a little stroll over to the interrogation room. More official that way."

Pascal followed Louise down the hall. With each step, his heart beat a little faster. Once they were in the room, he hesitated, but Louise guided him to the other side of the table. As he took a seat, a twinge in his chest caused him to feel light-headed. He wondered if it was nerves or possibly the start of cardiac arrest. The latter would solve a lot of problems.

This side of the table provided a different perspective. Although he had been in the room many times, tonight it seemed foreign. He glanced over at the window that disguised the observation room with a two-way mirror. Thankfully, the blinds were closed. Dingy white blotches of plaster were splattered here and there on the gray-green walls. No one had bothered to repaint after the repairs. He never had noticed the hole below the light switch that some perp must have punched on his way to lockup.

A recorder was set up in the middle of the table. Louise tilted her head, pressed her lips together, and sighed. She flashed Pascal a sympathetic look, then reached for the Record button. Pascal reached out to stop her, but Louise grabbed his hand. Her grip was firm as she shook her head, the sympathy gone.

"What happened between the time you and Ms. Jasper arrived at the horse park and the warehouse explosion?"

Pascal had decided to stick to his story and match it to Gillian's. Now wasn't the time to confess all, although he knew that time would come.

"Gillian asked me about riding lessons. After dinner, we drove to the horse park. She's only been in Santa Fe for a few months, doesn't know her way around yet. When we pulled up to the park, I saw some movement, then a flash of light over by the warehouse. I told Gillian to stay in the car and went to check it out. As I crossed the road, there was an explosion. I went back to the patrol car and called it in."

Louise realized she should have had ballistics check Ruiz's hands for explosive residue. She wrote a reminder in her notebook to call ballistics as soon as the interview was over.

"Then what happened?"

"That's it."

"I need to review the alarm company tapes, check if the camera caught anything before the alarm was disabled. And . . . I need to have ballistics check you for explosive residue. Sit tight."

He couldn't believe she was going to leave him in the room like a common criminal, although basically he was. He had crossed the line too many times in his short tenure as a detective. He wondered if he would be charged, convicted, and sentenced to prison. At least he would have plenty of free time to get back to his novel. He wondered if Gillian would wait for him, or even want to have anything to do with him.

He had called Aubusson about the costume, and she was on her way to the station. At least there would be some resolution in this fiasco. He tried to focus on what he had accomplished. He had found Bobby Pilot and the Jesus costume. He hoped that would amount to something in his favor—make up for his trespasses. Blowing up a building! Thank God it was Easter and the captain was sequestered in church. He hoped it would be a long service.

~54~

Tommy Candelaria gave a cursory knock on Captain Montaño's office door before he pushed it open. Montaño paced back and forth behind his desk like a trapped animal.

"Tell me you got something," Montaño said.

Candelaria flashed a satisfied grin. "The film company called back. Those filmmakers were regular customers. The woman told me they ordered the 3-D film on a regular basis and had it developed at their labs."

Montaño was pleased. "Good work, Tommy." The cards were stacked against this Engle guy. And it looked like the other filmmakers were involved also. Montaño needed to bring in Coriz and Eubank. He hated to admit it, but Ruiz had been right about checking their alibis. Maybe he should have done it sooner, but he hated going off half-cocked. It never served him well. He looked up at Candelaria, who stood waiting for instructions. "Put out an APB on Coriz and Eubank. We need to bring them in, have a little chat."

Montaño's phone rang. It was the Feds—they had picked up Engle at O'Hare. But since he had crossed state lines, there were certain procedures that needed to be followed before they could escort him back to New Mexico. The soonest they could deliver him would be tomorrow afternoon.

Sure, Montaño thought. They wanted to take over the case, get all the glory. He controlled himself from slamming his desk phone back in its cradle.

There was another knock on the door. Montaño looked up and glared as Candelaria opened the door.

"We located Thomas Eubank."

"Good, bring him in."

"He's in jail in Santa Fe."

Montaño was beside himself. He almost tore the receiver off the phone as he yanked it up and punched in Ruiz's number.

"Ruiz."

"What the hell? You got Eubank in lockup?"

"Good morning, Montaño."

There was silence on the line.

"Hey, he's not the only one. I'm holed up in an interrogation room, waiting for ballistics to check me for explosives."

"Not funny."

"Not kidding. It's a long story, but not my case anymore. I found the Jesus costume at the film company's warehouse. That's why Eubank was brought in and locked up. I heard a rumor he's ready to plead."

Montano could tell Ruiz sounded defeated, but he couldn't bring himself to pity the man. "The Feds picked Engle up at O'Hare this morning. They're dragging their feet, but he should be back in the Land of Enchantment by tomorrow afternoon."

"Well, at least you got your man."

"I still need to track down Coriz. Bobby Pilot said he was out at Tonque, at least when he fell off the boulder."

"Yeah, should have brought those guys in."

Montaño let the comment slide. "We tracked down the film canister. YinYangYazzie is a regular customer."

"Looks like you'll be able to wrap this package up soon." Pascal looked up and saw Louise in the doorway. She motioned for Pascal to follow. "Thanks for the update, appreciate it. Gotta go—my carriage awaits."

Pascal followed Louise down to his office, where the man from forensics had set up the equipment to test for explosive residue. Pascal hadn't thought about gloves when he decided to use the dynamite. But then, he hadn't thought about much of anything. He had washed his hands since, but he knew that probably wouldn't erase all traces.

The technician had him take a seat next to the equipment. He swiped Pascal's hands with a sampling probe that resembled a plastic spoon covered in terry cloth, them inserted the spoon in the machine. Nothing. Pascal controlled a sigh of relief. Then he took another probe and swiped Pascal's shirt. Nothing. Finally, he took Pascal's coat, which was draped over the arm of his chair, and wiped over the front and sleeves. The machine flashed and chirped.

The technician looked over at Louise, who stood and looked out the window, lost in thought. He cleared his throat.

Pascal wasn't ready to give up. "Excuse me, couldn't the residue result from proximity to the explosion?"

The technician was unsure if he should answer the question. He looked over at Louise for guidance. She nodded.

He turned to Pascal. "No, that residue would have a different re-action; it would be recorded as a passive substance."

Pascal knew his goose was cooked. The technician packed up the equipment and left the room.

"How did you get yourself in this mess? And don't tell me it's a long story." Louise looked at Pascal with tired eyes.

"Well, it is a long story and some of it is censored," he said.

"I paid a visit to the alarm company this morning, looked over the surveillance tape. It showed someone throwing up a flare, prob-ably with the intent to disarm the camera and alarm system. The guy disguised himself with a stocking hat and scarf. But when the first flare missed, the guy looked up. He looked a lot like you, Ruiz."

Pascal raised his arms in surrender. "I plead the Fifth. I think you better contact Wyeth."

"I'm sorry Ruiz—not only for you but for me. Hadn't planned on this case Easter weekend."

Pascal gave her a weak smile.

"You're like that little girl in the nursery rhyme, the one with the curl in the middle of her forehead. When you are good, you're very, very good, but when you are bad, you are horrid."

"Please, no nursery rhymes."

"We, as officers of the law, have to stay within the line. It's our duty. Otherwise, we're no different from criminals. Minor indiscretions are one thing—but this?" She shook her head and sighed so heavily Pascal worried she might collapse.

Pascal was sorry he had caused Louise trouble, but what was done was done. His pulse slowed, and there was a hollowness in his chest that made him feel empty. He was wasted, drained, not in the mood for a lecture. "Now what?"

"Since Wyeth is tied up with Eubank, I'll release you on your own recognizance." Louise took in a deep breath and let it out. "It doesn't seem like you have the energy to leave town anytime soon. I'll submit the paperwork for administrative leave. The captain will be back tomorrow. We'll sort it out then."

~55~
Easter Sunday

PASCAL WALKED OUT OF THE STATION IN A FOG. HE STOOD AT the top of the steps and tried to collect himself. His head spun. He looked up at the few waning stars left in the predawn sky. He was free—at least for the time being. He closed his eyes, took in a long, slow breath, and let it out. The brisk air chilled his lungs and caused his throat to constrict. Once his coughing subsided, euphoria spread through his body. He had a sudden urge to run through the streets, wave his arms, and laugh hysterically. But instead, he carefully made his way down the steps to his car. As he drove toward his house, something tugged at him, at his heart: Gillian. He swerved to the right, made an illegal U-turn, and headed toward Canyon Road.

It was Easter morning. The road, usually glutted with tourists, was deserted. Nothing was open, no need for anyone to be out and about. People were home with their families. Soon, there would be eggs to hunt, ham dinners to prepare, Mass to attend, and family gatherings to endure.

Easter marked the end of Lent. For some, this had been six weeks of solemn religious observance. The true believers paid penance through prayer and renunciation. As Pascal drove through the deserted streets, he thought about Holy Week, the death, burial, and resurrection of Jesus Christ after his crucifixion. Although Pascal wasn't raised Catholic, he had many friends who were. During Lent, they fasted, gave up luxuries, or made solemn promises to replicate the sacrifice of Jesus's journey into the desert for forty days.

Pascal thought of Bobby Pilot and his obsession with penitence. Pascal hoped his ordeal had brought him some solace. The Penitentes had a devotional commemoration to Christ: walking the Stations of the Cross, repenting their sins, almsgiving, self-denying, and some even mortifying their flesh. He wondered how satisfied they were on Easter morning. And he wondered whether if he allowed God to take him under his wing and guide him through life, he would experience everlasting salvation. But no matter how Pascal wanted to believe, he knew he would never be a true believer.

As he pulled into the driveway, he saw that Gillian's house was cloaked in darkness. The muted stillness made him momentarily doubt his intentions. But he couldn't stop now. Pascal banged on the door and rang the bell over and over. He had made a mess of everything. This was his last chance. He had to see her, hold her in his arms.

Lights started to come on one by one throughout the house. Birdie barked ferociously. Finally, the door swung open. Gillian stood there, woozy, her hair in a tangle of disarray, her nightshirt as usual hanging off one shoulder. She looked as if she had spent the night wrestling with a demon. "Pascal?"

He grinned, wilted, his feet floating on a gelatinous mass. Where had the earth gone? His knees wobbled. He wanted to melt into her arms. But as he leaned forward, he realized too late that she wasn't strong enough to hold him. He crumpled into an untidy pile on her front porch. Everything went black.

Somehow, Gillian dragged him into the house. She pulled a blanket off the couch and lay on the floor next to him, one arm tight around his waist, murmuring comforting words that tickled his ear. She closed her eyes and listened to the sound of his rasping breath. It was soothing, and soon she drifted off.

Pascal was awakened from his deep sleep as a wet tongue lapped his face. As he pried his eyes open, a set of black beady eyes stared at him: Birdie. He pushed the dog away and tried to untangle the blanket wound around his legs. The smell of coffee drifted into the room and spurred him upright and toward the kitchen. Gillian turned from the stove with a spatula in her hand, asking, "Pancakes?"

Pascal had a sudden urge to rush over, throw his arms around her, and declare his undying love. But instead he croaked, "Coffee?" He had no business loving her. He was a criminal.

~56~
The Monday after Easter

FROM FRENCH DOORS IN GILLIAN'S BEDROOM, PASCAL HAD AN unhindered view of his beloved mountains, the Sangre de Cristos, the Blood of Christ. The blood Christ had shed when nailed to the cross on Good Friday, the blood He shed for sinners. The mountains had been named by a Spanish explorer in the early 1700s. The explorer, enthralled by the red-tinted, snowy peaks at sunrise had uttered an impassioned "Sangre de Cristo." But in the late afternoon light, the mountains turned a glorious emerald black that stretched skyward. Only the slightest dusting of winter snow remained near the crest.

Today was Matt Padilla's first day back at the station in two weeks, and it had been torturous for him. Pascal had received a call from Matt after Louise briefed him about the case. He had sounded cranky and petulant but maybe still in pain from his surgery. Probably, it was because of the mess Pascal had created. Matt, usually an easygoing amiable guy, had practically sputtered as he recited all Pascal's indiscretions, including the finale when he blew up the warehouse door with dynamite, not to mention the fact that it was Matt's dynamite. He had always given Pascal some leeway, but this was over the top. There was no way to appease him. Pascal knew Matt needed to run down, finish his rant, and get it out of his system. When he finally fell silent, Pascal asked for an update on the case.

Matt told him Aubusson had shown up at the station Sunday afternoon, identified the costume, then proceeded to have a hissy fit when she was told that it was evidence and she couldn't take it until the case was closed. She stormed out of the station threatening to call the commissioner. Pascal thought his administrative leave had one positive note: He didn't have to interact with that woman again.

Pascal asked Matt about Eubank. Apparently, the district attorney had an agreement. If the judge went along, Eubank wouldn't get much more than a slap on the wrist for his involvement. The deal required his testimony against Steg Engle. Pascal wondered if Wyeth knew about Eubank's involvement out at Tonque, but that wasn't his problem anymore.

Although Louise had given Matt an update on the case, Matt wanted to hear it from the "horse's mouth," or the "horse's ass." Pascal told him the highlights of his Holy Week. If Pascal hadn't been in so much trouble, Matt would have laughed. In retrospect, it all seemed preposterous.

Pascal could imagine Matt shaking his head in disbelief at the series of events: the stolen Jesus costume, Bobby Pilot's disappearance, Bobby found tied to a cross, Ortiz shot in the leg and found hiding in a tree trunk, Steg Engle's escape and capture by the FBI. He didn't elaborate on why he had gone to Diamond Tail or how he had found Bobby out at Tonque. And he didn't explain why he had blown up the warehouse door. It was a moot point, and he was sure Louise had filled in all the sordid details.

Pascal passed along the contact information for the captain at San Felipe Tribal. He told Matt that the Jesus costume was involved in both cases. Somehow, the two agencies, not to mention the FBI, would have to work together to sort things out. He heard Matt curse under his breath. Pascal also would forward the information that Rupert had found on the antique rifle. It was probably the one Engle had used to shoot Ortiz. That information also needed to be sent to San Felipe.

Matt said his head, stomach, and feet hurt. He was going home. But before he hung up, he asked about his stuff. Pascal remembered too late that Matt's tools had been left in his cruiser, under the spare. Pascal's car had been confiscated, taken to forensics, and impounded. Matt's tools would have been found and seized. There was silence on the line, then nothing.

Pascal sank back into the comforter as Gillian walked into the room. "Bad news?"

"Lost a friend." He turned away and stared at the mountains, still dusted in snow near the top. He couldn't look her in the eye.

Gillian lay down next to him as she had the night before. "You better call Wyeth, see if she can get you a deal."

"Don't have the strength."

It was Monday. Thank God, Holy Week was over.

"Got to pick up Hallie at the high school at eight tonight. If we want some alone time, it's now or never." Gillian brushed his ear with a kiss.

He turned over and faced her. Pascal imagined he was the luckiest man alive. Who wants to be a detective anyway?

THE END